D0980055

MAR   2012

Plunder

Books by Mary Anna Evans

Plunder

A Faye Longchamp Mystery

Mary Anna Evans

Poisoned Pen Press

Poisoned Pen Press
6962 E. First Ave., Ste. 103
Scottsdale, AZ 85251
www.poisonedpenpress.com
info@poisonedpenpress.com

Printed in the United States of America

To little Andrew and Avery

Acknowledgments

I'd like to thank everyone who reviewed *Plunder* in manuscript form: Rachel Broughten, Erin Garmon, Michael Garmon, Mary Anna Hovey, Leonard Beeghley, Kelly Bergdoll, and Bruce Bergdoll.

I'd also like to thank these folks for their expertise on fishing, boating, local color, and Louisiana legal issues, as well as for their helpfulness and hospitality: Cheryl Landry, Kenny Tamm, Janice Buras, Cynthia LeBreton, Jane Scheuermann, and Karen Jahn.

These people helped immeasurably in making *Plunder* as accurate as possible. Any errors, obfuscations, or mild blurrings of reality are completely mine.

Episode 1 of "The Podcast I Never Intend to Broadcast", Part 1

by Amande Marie Landreneau

How long have I been stealing my grandmother's stories? I've been doing it longer than I've been telling my own stories, that's for sure, and I've been doing that for most of my sixteen years.

I don't remember falling in love with books. I just remember the boat rocking beneath my bed as Grandmère read me fairy tales. And I don't remember learning to read. It was a gradual thing, as if the letters on the pages of my picture books slowly came into focus, day by day, materializing out of the fog as my grandmother spoke.

Some days, my naptime came and went without a book in sight, because Grandmère knew more stories than the Brothers Grimm. Her people—our people— have always lived here in the deep delta country, way below New Orleans in the between-land where the Mississippi pours itself into the Gulf. If there's a story floating around about ship captains or long-lost lovers or endangered children or voodoo priestesses, and if my grandmother didn't tell it to me, then it isn't true. Or, at least, it didn't happen anywhere near here.

Young children like their worlds to be just so—it's less scary that way—so it bothered me that some of the stories she told me came out of thin air. All stories should be captured in books, or so it seemed to me.

To fix that problem, I wrote my first story in the margins of a coloring book, one word on each page: Ship. Gold. Thief. Kidnap. *(Quite a word for a pre-schooler, don't you think?)* Run. Home.

All my stories end safe at home, just like that one. My social worker thinks this is significant. Well, duh. My mother ran away when I was six months old, and I've always lived on a houseboat that could've theo-retically floated away some school day while I was learning things and playing kickball on the playground.

After I wrote that immortal coloring-book tale, Grandmère bought me a spiral-bound notebook. The blank pages made me happy, since I didn't like writ-ing books with pictures that didn't match my story. Actually, I was tired of picture books in general. The drawings never matched what I saw in my head, and they took up space that could've been used for more words.

I love words. They mean what they say, and they never change. You can trust them. (I'm not even going to bother you with my social worker's interpretation of those last two sentences. You know what she thinks they mean.)

Sally the Social Worker says that recent events may put me in foster care a while. Frankly, I'd rather just get started taking care of myself. I think I'd be pretty good at it, and I'm not sure I trust anyone else to do the job. Still, there are days when I feel like a little girl whose home floated away in the last hurricane.

When I need something to hold onto, I've always reached for the two silver coins I found buried in mud, back when I was a little kid messing around the islands in my boat. I would hold them, one in each hand, and think, "These must be worth something. If the houseboat and everything else goes back to the bank, I can sell these. With a silver coin in each hand, I'll never starve."

Those coins are gone now, stolen. I really need to go looking for more silver coins.

Until then, I'll sit here, alone with my cheap digital recorder, and I'll tell it my grandmother's stories. Nothing else makes me feel quite so safe.

Chapter One

The Gulf of Mexico lapped at Faye Longchamp's toes, as flaw-lessly blue as the water that wrapped around her home on Joyeuse Island. The waves splashed on her bare feet, blood-warm, just as they did on her own beach. The scent of salt water was as familiar as the soap smell on her husband's neck.

Strictly speaking, she wasn't really looking at the Gulf of Mexico. Faye wasn't sure how to name this water. In south Louisiana, the land just drifts to sea. The water at Faye's feet was connected to a bunch of canals and island-dotted estuaries and grassy coves that extended south and west until they eventually connected to Barataria Bay, and *it* was connected to the Gulf of Mexico. Regardless of its name, this water smelled like the gulf breezes that blew in her bedroom window every morning.

Faye had never traveled much. There had simply been no money. Starting her own archaeological consulting firm had held the promise of frequent business trips, paid for by someone else. What could be better than seeing the world and being paid to do it?

This first out-of-state consulting trip had brought her here to south Louisiana, five hundred miles from her front door… to a place that looked and felt pretty much like home. Maybe someday she'd land a client who wanted to send her someplace exotic, but not this time.

This client had just called with a change in assignment, and Faye was still trying to wrap her brain around it. Everything had changed in the days since the *Deepwater Horizon* rig exploded and sank, though none of those changes were visible to the naked eye. Yet.

The water at her feet was still just as clear. The sky was as blue. Pelicans flew overhead without a care in the world.

Actually, one ripple from the offshore disaster *had* already reached shore—fear. It showed on the faces of boaters at this marina, where a rented cabin served Faye as project headquarters. It showed in the reluctance of shoppers to part with money at the marina's tiny convenience store. It showed in the concern on the face of the marina's manager, Manny, as he stood at the cash register and surveyed an empty restaurant.

It showed the most at the waterfront. Every time someone walked to the shore and stood there looking, as Faye was doing now, the fear showed.

Joe appeared at her side. It was a comfort to remember how many times they'd stood on their own island and looked out to sea in just this way. He leaned down to speak in her ear, so that she could hear him over the wind that whipped off the water hard enough to stir even Joe's heavy black ponytail.

The expected endearment didn't come. Instead, he said, "We're out of bottled water to mix Michael's formula. I'll get some at the marina store."

Ah, romance.

Faye snaked an arm around his waist and rubbed her hand over the muscles of his flat belly, just to remind him that she was a girl. "Grab some of that turkey he likes while you're there."

He put his lips next to her ear again, then headed for her neck. "If I get sweet potatoes, too, he'll sleep better…and longer."

Seduction between parents moves at lightning speed. It has to. There's no time.

Faye whispered, "If you get some of that microwave rice to go with it, he'll sleep till sunup," and Joe was gone, making tracks to the convenience store so that they could carb-load their baby. Faye was left to watch the setting sun bleed into the sea.

Somewhere out there in the Gulf of Mexico floated actual blood and crumpled wreckage and a whole lot of oil. Before many days had passed, the oil would come here. Faye's job had become a race against time.

◇◇◇

Steve Daigle's wife was hardly cold in the ground. Actually, she was neither cold nor in the ground. He'd cremated the body, since it was the cheapest way to get rid of her, and that had just happened yesterday. He doubted she'd really had time to cool off before he dumped the ashes into the stagnant, lukewarm bayou behind their duplex.

Justine was gone. He did not miss the hospice workers trooping in and out of the house, taking her vital signs and recharging the morphine in her IV. Why in hell couldn't somebody hook *him* up to a morphine pump?

He did not miss the months when she was on chemo, retching and vomiting on schedule, three weeks on and one week off.

Did he miss Justine herself, before the cancer erupted from her breasts and consumed the rest of her? Steve wasn't sure his memory reached back that far. He remembered the breasts. They'd been on the small side, but soft. She'd trembled when he touched them. Yes, he missed those. And he missed her firm little ass.

Had he loved her? Was that why he stuck around to watch her shrivel and die?

No.

Maybe he'd loved her and maybe he hadn't, but Steve Daigle was not the kind of man who stayed around for the hard times. Justine's diagnosis of terminal cancer would ordinarily have sent him out the door and on his way to the next parish, but not in this case. He had an inheritance to consider. Justine had owned a piece of her late father's houseboat, not to mention a piece of a nice little pile of stock in the oil company where he'd worked.

After he'd found out about that inheritance, it had taken him a while to understand why Justine couldn't just go back to her hometown and kick her stepmother off that houseboat. Finally, he'd called a cousin who'd almost finished paralegal school, and she'd walked him through Louisiana's twisty inheritance laws.

She'd repeated herself until her words sank into his brain, but that didn't mean he liked those words.

She'd said, "Like Justine told you, her father died without a will, so all the property he'd owned before he married didn't go to his wife. It went to his natural children. This means his wife Miranda didn't inherit the houseboat she's living on, nor the stock that provides the income that pays her bills. The kids own it."

This was the part Steve liked. Unfortunately, there was more to the story.

"When there's no will, the state of Louisiana gives the surviving spouse a 'usufruct' on the property. This means that Justine's stepmother, Miranda, has the use of the houseboat and the income from the stock for as long as she lives. But the children, the actual owners—they don't receive their property until she dies. Her estate will owe the children, or their heirs, all the money she collected in dividends for all these years, but Miranda's got no money. There won't be anything in the estate to repay those dividends, so his children are screwed in that regard. They'll eventually get the boat and stock, but that's all, and it won't happen till Miranda dies and that could be a lot of years."

The cousin delivered the final bad news with a colloquial definition she'd learned from a classmate. "It's easy to remember the word 'usufruct.' The person holding the *us*ufruct has the *use* of the property. And the actual owners are 'fruct.'"

Steve didn't see himself as stupid, though he may in fact have been. His immediate reaction to this news had been to ask his cousin to help him draw up a will for Justine.

Thanks to the terms of that will, there would be no usufructs for Steve. When Miranda croaked, Steve would own all of Justine's worldly goods outright.

Now that Justine was gone, paying Miranda a visit seemed like the obvious thing to do. He could tell her about Justine's death, pay his respects to the grieving stepmother. He could also get some idea of just how old Miranda really was, because he really needed her to die soon so he could move onto that boat. The rent on this duplex was killing him.

Justine had described her stepmother as physically frail and mentally tough. Mental toughness was all well and good, but it didn't keep a person alive.

If God was good, Steve would arrive just in time to see Miranda succumb to sudden cardiac arrest. It could happen. He threw some clothes and a razor into a duffle bag, hooked his boat to the back of his truck, and hit the road.

◇◇◇

Faye's client, a humongous environmental firm, had originally sent her to survey archaeological sites along the Mississippi south of New Orleans as part of a run-of-the-mill environmental assessment. The *Deepwater Horizon* disaster had exploded her routine project into a job so huge that it just might swamp her little company.

She'd hung up the phone after accepting the new work and wandered to the waterfront, hoping the water on her bare feet would tell her what to do. Faye's client had not grown to be humongous by hiring foolish people. The managers knew that their firm would be well positioned to land the Mother of All Environmental Impact Statements if it could provide a good assessment of the land as it was now, before it got messed up. Faye was now officially contracted to race with the oil.

Others would be hurrying to assess the other aspects of the area—the plants, the animals, the towns, the roads, the economy, the air quality, the water quality—but Faye just needed to focus on its archaeology: the physical remnants of human history near the mouth of the Mississippi. Humans had lived here and fought over this land ever since they figured out that boats made it easy to go places and move stuff.

Most of this vast area was accessible only by a boat captained by somebody smart enough to navigate water that was way shallower than your average bathtub. There was no way around it. Faye's new project was gargantuan, and it just might be impossible. The only point in her favor was the fact that she and Joe had been piddling around in little-bitty boats for a combined half-century. She'd upgraded their rental boat when the new scope-of-work came in, and the new one didn't count as "little-bitty."

Manny, the marina's manager, had grinned from ear to handsome ear when Faye told him she needed something bigger. Then he'd reached up a mahogany hand and brushed one long dreadlock back over a broad shoulder, revealing three hoop earrings and a diamond stud. "Let me show you the boat I rent to the rich Yankee fishermen. A beautiful business owner like you, ma'am, should ride in style."

Faye didn't like to think that she could be swayed in her financial decisions merely by being called beautiful, but she was now in temporary possession of a watercraft that was way nicer than any boat she or Joe had ever owned. It was more than twenty feet long and luxuriously outfitted, yet designed to navigate waters less than two feet deep. It was good that the thing was comfortable, because she and Joe would be coming to know it intimately. They would be doing a lot of this work themselves, since they were working with a skeleton crew.

Oh, who was she kidding? She was working with Joe and a part-time technician. Even the term "skeleton crew" was a bit much.

The original job had been a perfect fit for her startup company—an initial survey, heavy on library research and site walkovers, without the need for excavation that would have required a big crew. The best part about the job had been that they could even bring little Michael.

And the worst part about the job had been that they could even bring little Michael.

Joe was much better than Faye at handling the distractions of having a nearly-one-year-old underfoot. He also was much better at dealing with the natural behavior of a tiny child, which can only be described as suicidal. Faye knew she was capable of laser-sharp focus on her work, which meant that she was capable of forgetting to watch a toddler every split second. Michael had his father's strength and coordination, so he'd learned to walk before he was nine months old. And he was fast. Her nightmares were now haunted by speeding cars and sharp objects and the still bodies of water that are so seductive to children who can't swim.

Faye's inspired solution to the problem of Michael had been to hire Dauphine, a technician who had done fabulous work for her at the Chalmette battlefield near New Orleans. No less significant was the fact that Dauphine had also saved her life.

Most of the time, Dauphine was Michael's babysitter, but when he was napping or otherwise occupied, she reverted to being a crackerjack technician. Even better, when she was being a technician, she was billable to the client. This warmed the deepest depths of Faye's businesswoman heart.

Dauphine was a stout woman who dressed like the part-time voodoo mambo that she was, covered in mismatched, candy-colored scarves and turbans and flowing skirts. Her personal style was not a problem in this part of the world, where voodoo mambos in full ceremonial regalia didn't attract one whit of attention. Michael had adored Dauphine from the moment he laid eyes on her. Faye was pretty sure he just liked to watch his mambo babysitter float by in a sea of multicolored gauze.

Whatever worked.

Chapter Two

Hebert Demeray missed his old hangouts, the ones that had washed away during Hurricane Katrina. He missed the way beer bottles stuck to the tops of their bars, grimy with old shellac and spilled bourbon. Nostalgia gripped him when he remembered worn floorboards so uneven that the bathroom doors scraped and squeaked and sometimes didn't close all the way. He even missed the stench of old urinals, served by plumbing that had rebelled after years of carrying an overload of beer piss and vomit.

It had only been a few years since the storm. The replacement drinking establishments didn't have enough age on them to make Hebert feel at home, and maybe they never would. The government had made the barkeeps rebuild on stilts. By the time folks got to the top of all those stairs, they'd stomped the mud off their feet. How on earth was a bar's floor to get dirty enough to make a dirty man feel comfortable?

And the cheapest thing to put on top of those stilts was a premanufactured building. How on earth was a man supposed to drink enough to blot out the world when he was sitting in a double-wide? And when that man was drinking early in the afternoon, like now…well, the sunlight shining through the clean new windows onto the shiny new bar made the atmosphere almost too perky for total drunkenness. Almost.

The only things in sight that were seedy enough to suit Hebert were his fellow drinkers. He recognized all but one of them. He'd been in brawls with at least half of them. Three of them had pulled knives on him while brawling, which Hebert frankly considered cheating, but he was a big man with more than a little extra flesh. On those few occasions that a blade had made contact with his body, it had buried itself in a roll of fat. Hebert had suffered nothing more than the loss of a little blood and a sharp stab of pain that was quickly blunted by booze. The knife wielders had suffered a lot more, and Hebert had delivered that suffering with his bare fists.

Hebert thought of his mother, as Cajun men will do when under the influence of booze and nostalgia. He hadn't spoken to her in years, not since the last time she cursed him and cast him out. Miranda Landreneau was well able to curse a man, so he'd never had the guts to go back and ask her forgiveness, though in all that time he'd never lived more than ten miles from her shabby little houseboat. He'd spent those years staggering from one rented room to another. And from one rented woman to another.

The stranger raised his beer bottle in his direction, beckoning for Hebert to join him. This was unusual behavior in the bars where Hebert liked to drink. People didn't go there to look for new friends, unless you counted the ones who were looking for one-night friends. Most of the drinkers here weren't even looking for sex. They sat alone, or they sat silent next to the friends who came out drinking with them, and they raised one glass after another until the world looked like a place they could possibly tolerate. Or until they passed out, whichever came first.

But Hebert was a friendly sort, and he was inclined to like a man who was drinking heavily while the sun was still high overhead. He was perfectly willing to go keep the stranger company, especially because the stranger might decide to buy his new friend a drink, if Hebert could manage to be charming enough.

◇◇◇

Faye slipped on her flip-flops and shuffled back to the marina, finding Joe burdened down with grocery bags. The neck of a wine bottle stuck seductively out of one of those bags, and Faye started calculating just how quickly she could get Michael settled in his portable crib. She thought two bedtime stories would do it. Three, tops.

"This little man has been talking all the day long," Dauphine said, gathering Michael up, giving him a noisy kiss on the cheek, and thrusting him into Faye's arms. "What he was saying, I cannot tell you. But any fool could tell it was very important." She leaned in for another kiss. "Tell your *maman* the things you told me."

Michael did not intend to chat on cue. He pursed his little lips, which made him look exactly like Joe. Well, he always looked a lot like his father, but the stoic pout made him look like Joe when Faye had done something dire...like, for instance, forgetting to tell him about a contract so big that it could sink their fledgling company.

Oops. She decided to tell him about the new job after he'd had one glass of wine, but before he'd had two.

Laughing, Faye held Michael up so Joe could see his little twin. Something made her look over her husband's shoulder and focus on a houseboat so nondescript that it should have been invisible among the shiny pleasure crafts and well-maintained working boats. It was moored well away from the transient boats that constantly moved in and out of the marina, and it was accessed by a floating dock that wrapped around two sides. It looked like it had sat in that spot since it was shiny and new. Nothing stood between the houseboat and open water, so the shabby craft had a million-dollar view. For that reason, Faye thought it might be a more inviting place to live than it looked.

Faye would never have noticed the boat at all, but for the girl standing on its deck. It was as if somebody had whispered in her ear: "Look. Your baby may look like his father made over, but here is a mirror for you."

Faye was nothing if not rational, and it took only a split second for her to catalog the ways this girl was *not* her mirror. She was tall and broad-shouldered and well-muscled, and Faye was a hundred-pound wisp. Her shoulder-length hair was a dark mass of brunette curls, which could hardly be less like Faye's cropped and straight black locks.

On the other hand, her creamed coffee skin tone and sharply defined features were very like Faye's, and their golden-brown eyes were more alike than not. But these were not the things that caught Faye's eye. Faye was riveted by the girl's confidence as she grabbed a flashlight and leaned close to one of the boat's windows to inspect the caulk that she'd just applied.

An old woman emerged onto the boat's deck, scolding the girl in French. The girl answered her in French, hugged her, then mischievously untied the woman's apron strings.

Dauphine had stopped tickling Michael when she heard French being spoken. Faye raised an eyebrow in her direction.

Dauphine answered the unspoken question. "The woman is the girl's grandmére. She is convinced that her granddaughter is rendering herself unmarriageable by doing something so unladylike in broad daylight. The girl said that she could hardly be expected to caulk in the dark, and that she was sure her grandmother liked the water to stay *outside* their home."

At this girl's age, Faye had already spent a lot of time on the roof of her own aging home, trying to keep the water out. Unlike this girl, she'd had the advantage of a grandmother who had crawled onto Joyeuse's roof with her, because Faye's grandmother had wanted her to know how to keep the leaks stanched when the house passed to her.

It was probably a good thing that Faye already had more work on her plate than she could possibly do. Otherwise, she'd have hopped onto the houseboat and helped the girl make it shipshape. Faye's grandmother had taught her boat maintenance, too. How else could Faye be expected to live on an island when Joyeuse was hers?

Instead of volunteering to help a stranger lay down a bead of caulk, Faye turned to the child in her arms. Reflexively catching the sippy cup that he kept tossing to the ground, she noticed Dauphine's face. Pensive and watchful, the mambo watched until the old woman disappeared into the houseboat. Her hand strayed toward a pocket in the side seam of her voluminous orange pants.

Faye knew that Dauphine kept a protective talisman in that pocket at all times. The mambo's hand slid out of sight and returned to view, clenched around something Faye couldn't see.

Didi Landreneau Channing hadn't seen her husband Stan in a good long while. This was not the first time he'd bolted.

Or maybe he hadn't bolted. Stan worked out in the oil field, seven days on and seven days off, and sometimes he picked up an extra shift that kept him offshore for three weeks at a stretch. Didi loved it when that happened. She didn't miss his sorry ass, and seven extra days of work brought in a pile of extra money in terms of both straight salary and overtime. Or it would have, if he didn't head straight for the New Orleans casinos as soon as his paycheck arrived.

She'd almost convinced herself that Stan had told her he was taking some temporary contract work between his regular weeklong shifts, so that he could pick up a little extra money. She was almost sure she remembered him saying that he'd be working on the rig they called *Deepwater Horizon.* The newspaper was saying that eleven people had died. But did they really know? Amid the flames and confusion, was anyone really sure who was out there?

Maybe twelve people had died, and Stan was one of them. Maybe Didi was entitled to some cash compensation. And even if she wasn't, maybe she could fake her way through a bunch of paperwork and get some anyway. She'd heard that a lot of people faked their way into a lot of money after Katrina. Besides, since she really didn't know where Stan was, collecting a check for his death couldn't actually be called fraud, could it?

Didi knew she would be much more convincing as a helpless widow if she looked as needy as possible. Maybe it was time for her to go sleep on a houseboat again. Maybe it was time to run home to Mother.

Chapter Three

Faye picked her way through the muck, moving quickly and trying her best to keep up with long-legged Joe. They'd already spent a full morning on this task, and they just might lose their afternoon to it, as well. It would be really nice to have something, anything, to show for their trouble.

The marina was in sight to their west, but they were alone here. Not even tourists were foolish enough to walk through this marshy wasteland. The black goo sucked at her feet, but she fought back. If she lost a work boot, Joe would laugh at her forever.

He had elected to shed his moccasins and go barefoot. This would probably work out just fine for him, since there were no rocks to stub his calloused toes, but the marsh grasses were hard on Faye's dainty feet. Besides, if they found what they were looking for, Faye knew she could find herself bashing her feet on rocks or cutting them on nails or skewering them on splinters of old wood preserved by being submerged for decades. Joe might be willing to take this risk, but she wasn't. Or perhaps his bare feet proved just how much he doubted their ability to find a rotten old dock in the middle of this swamp. This thought made Faye even more determined to find it. Today.

Historic maps said that there had been a wooden dock here, back in the days of steamboats. It was probably long-gone, blown away in a hurricane or sunken beneath the muck. Joe's bare feet said that he wasn't too worried about the dock and its splinters. Nevertheless, it was Faye's job to look for it.

Further from the water, Michael was running rampant on dry land. Dauphine stood, one fist on her cocked hip, and watched him frolic. And Faye, pausing in her work more frequently than she should, watched them both.

"Why'd you hire somebody to watch the baby if you ain't gonna let her watch the baby?"

Joe's shy smile got wider and cockier when he knew he was right.

Faye snatched up a clump of oozy mud and threw it at him. It hit his bare thigh and oozed downward. "He's your son. It'll take more than one person to keep him from doing something dangerous."

Then she looked over her shoulder again to make sure that Michael was okay.

In the distance, she saw the golden-skinned girl from the houseboat, walking slowly through knee-deep grass, wearing headphones and waving a metal detector in front of her. The sun, almost directly overhead, cast a shadow at her feet, as black as the muck under Faye's own boots. She wore an oversized Hawaiian shirt, untucked, with khaki shorts, red deck shoes, and a red baseball cap. She would have stood out in any crowd, based on her unusual height and shoulder-length curls, but the colorful clothing made double-sure that she caught the eye.

Faye was several years away from intimate knowledge of school schedules, but she could think of no good reason for a teenaged girl to be out of school this early in the afternoon on a weekday. It was too late for spring break and too early for summer vacation. Faye could think of no school holidays in April. The girl shouldn't be sweating under a bright sun or breathing in fresh gulf breezes. She should be crouched over a school desk, getting ready for her final exams. Faye wondered if she should speak with her grandmother.

Belly laughter erupted behind her, and Faye looked back to see Michael smearing mud on a pair of cocoa-brown shins.

"Why you do such things to your Dauphine?" The babysitter turned the toddler around to pick him up, so that the filthy hands waved in the air but did no harm. She hauled him to a not-too-muddy puddle for rinsing, still laughing.

In the distance, the girl stooped and picked something up, studying it with a deliberation that Faye recognized, because it was very like her own. After a moment, she hurled it, overhand, and it landed in the open water with a plop. It occurred to Faye that this young woman might know whether a ruined steamboat dock was lurking nearby.

Making her way to more solid ground, she said, "I want to ask that girl if she's seen what we're looking for."

Joe mumbled something that sounded like, "Go ahead," so she did.

◇◇◇

When other mothers cursed their wayward children, they merely shouted four-letter words. When Miranda Landreneau was the one doing the cursing, her target was actually damned, in the original sense of the word. Hebert's mother was gifted in the dark arts. He believed this with all his heart. He was indeed damned. The sorry state of his life proved that.

Sometimes when Hebert was really drunk, like right now, he staggered down to the waterfront. There was a secluded dock where he could see his mother's houseboat, without much chance that anyone could see him. Although his mother probably had ways of knowing he was there...

He was squatted on the dock, dabbling his hands in the water and wishing that Miranda would lift her curse, when the knife fell between his shoulder blades. It was a big knife, wielded with power, so it was more than sufficient to penetrate Hebert's skin and the copious layer of fat beneath it. Severing a number of important nerves, the first blow embedded itself deeply into Hebert's right lung. He went to the ground hard, on his chest, and somebody's foot held him down, getting leverage to pull the blade out of his back. The second blow sliced through his spinal cord and nicked his aorta. The third blow pierced his heart, but by this point that hardly mattered.

The foot struck Hebert's side hard and repeatedly, shoving him toward the dock's edge. As he dropped into the water, a weak breath and a few words passed his lips. These last words were a curse, one that his mother had taught him.

◇◇◇

The girl's response to Faye's offered handshake was impressively confident for a teenager. "You're an archaeologist? That is just so cool. I'm Amande Landreneau, and you would not believe some of the stuff I've dug up around here. Here. Look…"

She fumbled in her pocket and pulled out a quarter. "This is from 1968. That's more than forty years ago!"

Having been born in 1968, Faye knew exactly how long ago the coin had been minted. She had to take Amande's word for the date, though, because she couldn't make out the numbers on the quarter without her reading glasses.

"If it were just a few years older, it would've been silver and I could've sold it. I could sure use that money."

"I hear you," said Faye, who had sold more artifacts than she cared to think about, back before she scraped up enough money to finish her PhD and reinvent herself as a legitimate archaeologist. "We're looking for an old dock that's supposed to be around here somewhere. It goes all the way back to steamboat days. You know where it is?"

"Sure I do. But you're in the wrong place." She pointed out across the marsh grass, cut with ditches and canals. "It's out there in open water, maybe fifty feet from here."

Faye followed the pointing finger. The water line was hardly twenty feet away…now. Who knew where it would be when the tide was low, nor where it had been when boats ran on steam?

In the years since then, people had strangled the river and sent its silt out into the Gulf. At times like this, Faye got a good hard look at something that was hard to imagine—solid and useable land simply sinking into the swamp. If the shoreline had retreated this far, she wondered how long it would be before the marina buildings and their surrounding cabins were claimed by open water. Maybe Amande and her grandmother were smart to live on a houseboat.

"I cut my toe on one of the dock's timbers when I was a kid, and Grandmère told me she remembered when it used to poke out of the water at low tide. I'll wade out there with you. I bet we can find it."

She buffed the old quarter on her shirt and held it out for Faye to see again, with the friendly enthusiasm of someone who has never before met anyone else interested in old dirty things and broken rocks.

A tiny feminine form approached, wrapped in shawls despite the heat. Amande's voice dropped, as if there were things she must say before her grandmother got close enough to hear.

"I know some islands where we can find arrowheads and stuff, too. Want me to show you? I haven't been out there since my grandmother sold my boat. God, I miss that boat."

Faye lowered her own voice. "You should've known my grandmother. She would've yelled at me or grounded me or maybe even spanked me if I broke one of her rules, but she'd never have taken away my skiff." Faye grinned, as she always did when she remembered Grammy. "When she got old and sick, I used to push her wheelchair to the end of the pier and help her into the boat. Once I got her settled at the tiller, she wasn't frail and sickly anymore. She was back in charge. But she wouldn't have wanted to go looking for arrowheads. Grammy only ever wanted to fish. If she couldn't eat it, she didn't want to waste her time on it."

Amande's grandmother was moving slowly in their direction, looking intently at Amande as if to say, "Don't you dare move before I get there."

Out of the corner of her eye, Faye saw a tiny boy clad in shorts but no shirt, toddling fast on his muscular legs and sturdy feet. Michael caught up with Amande's grandmother from behind, flinging his wet arms around one of her legs and bleating "Pick me up!" noises.

The old woman staggered but didn't fall. She glared down at Michael, who fell back onto his diapered bottom and burst into tears.

Faye was at her son's side in seconds, scooping him onto her hip.

Dauphine was two steps behind her. "Oh, excuse me, ma'am, I tried to stop him," she said as she reached out a hand to steady the older woman. Dauphine was panting, and Faye could see that her scarf was damp where it crossed her forehead.

Amande's grandmother's angry face did not soften.

"Grandmère," Amande said as she leaned down to kiss the weatherbeaten cheek, "I think he thought you were *his* grandmother. You're wearing the same color scarf." She tucked the fuchsia chiffon behind the old lady's ear. "Faye, this is my grandmother, Miranda Landreneau."

Faye didn't even bother to butt in and say, "No, Dauphine isn't his grandmother. She's his babysitter." She was too busy watching Amande charm a crabby old woman.

She was pretty sure that the girl was right. Both Miranda and Dauphine dressed like they'd fallen into a gypsy's washbasket. Michael only knew one woman whose clothes flowed behind her like a wet watercolor painting, and he associated that woman with cookies and kisses and unconditional love. Looking up to find Miranda's timeworn scowl, instead of Dauphine's soft smile, must have turned his tiny world upside down.

Faye nuzzled the back of Michael's neck, trying to get him to stop squalling. No dice. Then Miranda reached out an arthritic hand and touched the child on his shoulder. Her touch was neither loving nor violent, but it silenced the child. Instantly.

Faye stifled the urge to draw her son to her breast and take two steps back. She could tell by Dauphine's reaction that the babysitter was not amused, but she *was* intimidated. Faye herself was hard to intimidate, but she found herself wanting to leave Miranda's presence. Immediately.

"It's very nice to meet you. You have a lovely granddaughter. If it's okay with you, I'd like to—"

Amande, standing behind her grandmother, had embarked on violent headshaking. She was also mouthing the word "No," repeatedly. It did not take a genius to see that she didn't want her grandmother to know about their plans to go arrowhead hunting. Faye had no intention of taking the girl anywhere without her grandmother's permission, but she followed Amande's lead.

"—um…I'd like to talk to her about archaeological sites in the area. Actually, I think both of you may be able to help us."

Joe had joined them, and she could tell he was wondering just how these two people could be any help to them at all. She raised an eyebrow in his direction that signaled, *I'll tell you later.* Then she nodded at Miranda and Amande and said, "Right now, though, we should really get back to our cabin. You two have a good—"

Amande interrupted Faye, and the girl's bad manners caused Miranda's disapproving black eyes to swivel in her direction.

"But I wanted to show you my silver coins. And all those arrowheads. Can you come now…please?"

Chapter Four

Faye counted heads. Miranda, Amande, Michael, Joe, Dauphine…counting Faye, there were six people crowded into the houseboat's tiny dining room. The dinette table was built to seat two.

Michael sat on Joe's lap. Amande was perched on a stool in the corner, blowing into a cup to cool her tea. The others crowded around as Miranda handed teacups out. Faye felt the need to watch the old woman's every move, though she couldn't have said why.

Perhaps it was because she'd had experience of her own with Dauphine's voodoo chants and potions and powders, but some primitive part of her believed Miranda could slip something into her tea that would silence Faye as effectively as Miranda's withered hand on Michael's shoulder had silenced him. She noticed that Dauphine was watching their hostess just as intently.

Then Miranda pulled a (thankfully) clean dishrag out of a kitchen drawer and laid it on the counter beside a bowl of sugar and the bottle of rum. "I shall make the boy a sugar tit. He'll be happy, and we can talk."

Her shriveled but competent hands twisted the dishrag into a point. Dipping it first into her tea cup and then into the sugar bowl, Miranda was already poised to drizzle rum over the twisted rag and pop it into Michael's mouth before Faye could act.

Hastily grabbing a teething ring out of Michael's diaper bag, Faye said, "Oh, don't go to any trouble. He just loves this thing." Then she stuck it into his mouth so that there would be no room for a rum-spiked sugar tit.

He accepted the toy happily and she was absurdly grateful. They would need to leave when he got fussy, because sometime in the twentieth century it had stopped being okay to quiet a crying child with a dose of liquor. But not in Miranda's world.

"You are a mambo, yes?" Miranda's black eyes raked Dauphine from head to toe

Faye hadn't heard Dauphine say so, but maybe voodoo practitioners had their ways of recognizing each other. Dauphine's quirky clothing could be a clue, but anybody could wrap a robin's-egg-blue shawl around her hips. Maybe there was a secret handshake or a sign…sort of like the Masons or the Shriners. Or maybe voodoo ladies could *feel* each other, the way that Darth Vader could sense a disturbance in The Force whenever Luke Skywalker was around.

Dauphine said only, "Yes," but Faye noticed that she cradled her cup close to her chest, with her free hand draped over it. Did she think that Miranda could magically fling a hexing powder into her tea?

"Faye, did you find anything really old yet? When are you going to start digging? Can I help? What's the oldest and coolest thing you ever found?"

Amande showed no sign that she noticed the voodoo duel happening at the table, probably because teenagers routinely ignored their parents and grandparents. Amande surely found Miranda's in-your-face eccentricity profoundly boring.

Faye shook her head. "We just got started so, no, we haven't found anything exciting yet. And there won't be any digging. The client only wants preliminary work."

Amande's disappointed face said that she was expecting Hollywood-style archaeology with armies of workers carrying shovels. And a pith helmet for Faye.

Faye felt compelled to deliver some really exciting archaeology, but she was having trouble competing with Indiana Jones.

"Hmmm…I've found some Paleolithic points near my house, underwater. They're thousands and thousands of years old."

Amande was still looking expectant. Faye had been enjoying the girl's hero worship more than she realized. She looked to Joe for help. He held up the hand that wasn't tickling Michael's belly. Opening it wide, he slowly squeezed his long and slender fingers shut, as if he were gripping a baseball.

"Oh, yeah! The PPOs. Poverty Point Objects. We've found a lot of those." She leaned closer to Amande and said, "The PPOs we found are maybe three thousand five hundred years old, so they're not nearly as old as the Paleolithic stuff, but they're just so cool. The Poverty Point people cooked by heating clay balls, then throwing the hot balls into the food they wanted to cook. They did that every time they cooked a meal, so when you're at a Poverty Point site they're just…everywhere."

Faye flung her hands as wide as the close quarters allowed, trying to convey acres and acres of land, peppered with ancient wads of clay. "To make them, people reached down, scooped up some clay, squeezed, and threw the balls in the fire." Her own fist clenched and opened. "The really cool part comes when you can still see the shape of somebody's fingers in the fired clay, and you know that the person has been dead for *thirty-five hundred years*. I wish you could see one."

Amande gave a geeky little sigh that made both Joe and Faye grin. "Me, too."

Miranda snorted, wordlessly communicating that Faye's pointless stories about ancient trash would now stop, in favor of something interesting.

"Fetch a doll," Miranda said, flinging out an open hand as if she expected the doll to drop right into it.

Amande seemed accustomed to receiving abrupt orders, because she disappeared into the next room and came back with a naked doll, woven out of basket straw. It was too large to rest on Miranda's palm, but Amande laid it across the old lady's lap, with its head rested in the outstretched hand. The doll's face was blank, with no features adorning the smooth straw. Its bald head wasn't simply round. It was carefully modeled to the oval shape of a human head. The body, pear-shaped, sprouted unnaturally tubular arms and legs that were much less lifelike but, when dressed, this life-sized doll would look a great deal like a young toddler.

"My family has always made these. They are not toys, no, they are guardians. Parents, godparents, aunts, uncles—people buy them for little children in their care. This one will get a face when I sell it. I make them to look like the children they will guard. See?"

She slapped her other hand on the table, and Amande laid a second doll in that spot so quickly that Faye hardly realized she'd left the room. The second doll had strong cheekbones crafted of straw and its embroidered eyes were a warm brown. Its head was covered with corkscrew curls twisted from raffia dyed cocoa-dark. This was obviously Amande's guardian.

The guardian dolls creeped Faye out, yet she found herself able to admire their craftsmanship. Dauphine, on the other hand, had noisily pushed her chair back from the table as soon as the first doll entered the room. The room was too small for Dauphine to put much distance between herself and Miranda's craftsmanship, but she had instinctively moved as far away from the dolls as she could manage. Even Joe, whose calm manner was so ever-present that Faye sometimes suspected him of being anesthetized, had wrapped a bronze, sinewy arm around Michael's middle so tightly that it was making him squirm. Joe's green eyes never left Miranda's hands.

"They're beautiful, Miranda," Faye said, since she seemed to be the only guest capable of speech. And they were. Creepy, but beautiful.

"My granddaughter thinks they don't make me enough money. Maybe I might make more by doing things her way. Maybe I might not. But I don't understand why I need a 'site'... everwhat that may be."

"It's a website, Grandmère. They tell people about your work. Artists need them. You'll see, once I get it up and running."

Miranda fondled the dark curls on Amande's guardian doll. "People come to me. I make their dolls. My *maman* did it that way. Her *maman* did it that way. You will do it that way. Everybody around here knows I make dolls, and they come. What do I need with any website?"

Faye saw Amande flinch at the suggestion that she would take over the family doll-making business.

"You'll see, Grandmère. When you get your first order from someplace like…um…New Zealand, you'll be glad I built you a website."

"If I get too many of them New Zealand orders? You gonna spend more time helping me then, yes? And less time doing calculus? Everwhat calculus is. Sure as hell ain't useful."

Amande rolled her eyes and Miranda was silent for a moment, sizing Michael up as if designing a guardian doll for him. Faye wondered how she could possibly refuse such a gift if it were offered, but even her oversized plantation house wasn't big enough for her and one of those spooky dolls. She wouldn't sleep a wink until she threw it into the Gulf or, even better, burned it.

Taking advantage of the silence, Amande beckoned to Faye and Joe. "Come see what I've found."

They followed her out of the room, with Michael in Joe's arms, and Faye felt more than a little guilty about leaving Dauphine alone with Miranda, eyeball to eyeball, mambo to mambo.

The houseboat wasn't new and it wasn't fancy, but it wasn't all that small, either. Amande led them through a compartment that must have been Miranda's bedroom. A small berth in the corner was made up with a clean, worn patchwork quilt. Faye recognized the altar in the corner, because it was so like Dauphine's. It was a small table, spread with fine silk fabric and adorned with pictures of spirits with frightening faces, including one she recognized from Dauphine's altar—*La Sirene*, the lady of the sea. What better voodoo *loa* to guard a houseboat? Candles and a jigger of amber liquor were carefully arranged across the altar.

Doll heads hung from the ceiling all around Miranda's bedroom, waiting for faces and bodies and legs. Faye had to push two of them aside to enter the room. They swayed with the boat's gentle motion.

Built into the wall was a compact workbench. A well-worn set of tools was arrayed neatly atop the bench. A basket of straw, ready for weaving, sat nearby.

Faye was glad when she'd passed between two more dangling straw heads and entered Amande's room, where another hand-made quilt adorned another narrow berth. An ancient computer sat atop a built-in desk that was just barely big enough to hold it, and it occurred to Faye that, for a girl Amande's age, this was its own kind of altar.

A wicker basket beside the table overflowed with dirty clothes. Other than that sloppy spot, the room was painfully neat for a teenager, although maybe not so neat for a person who had lived all her life in very close quarters.

A rack full of baseball caps in every shade of the rainbow hung on one wall, over a bank of wood-fronted drawers. Any ordinary teenager would have stuffed those drawers with clothes. Amande opened one, revealing that she had stuffed most of hers with trinkets and chipped stone and a few treasured pieces of silver.

"It's a good thing my aunt grew up and moved out. I was running out of room for my stuff," she said.

Faye noticed the second berth folded into the wall above Amande's bed. From Faye's perspective as the owner of a plantation house that was old and bedraggled but huge, this room would have been utterly claustrophobic with two young girls in it.

Joe set Michael on the bed and reached for the shallow box Amande was holding out. It was lined with cotton and filled with a neat array of stone tools. "It's been a long time since I saw anything like these. I need to look them up to be sure, but I'd say most of them were made before the Europeans got here." He reached into the leather bag that he always wore at his waist, and pulled out a few chunks of stone. "I'm still working on these. See the way I shaped the cutting edge on this one? This one of yours looks a lot like it. Yours still has a nice edge on it, after all these years."

He gently picked up one of Amande's treasures, a palm-sized stone blade, and held it up to the light, then he handed her his own half-finished work.

"You made this?"

Faye hoped Joe heard the awe in the girl's voice.

While Amande took Joe on a guided tour of her arrowhead collection, Faye looked through the drawer that held the girl's European artifacts. There were the expected bits of broken china and several metal buttons, but Faye was particularly taken with a bent piece of brass that she was pretty sure had been part of a sextant, once used for navigating. A sextant found so near the mouth of the Mississippi could have been used to guide a ship to the far corners of the earth, before it ended its life here at one of the shipping crossroads of the world.

"I've thought about trying to reconstruct that sextant. This is the important piece, it seems to me, but it's really warped. Maybe I could make the missing pieces out of wood or something," Amande said, rubbing a finger over the numerical scale etched into its weathered brass. "I like navigating. It's like solving a puzzle, only you use maps and stars. I'm pretty good at finding my way around in a boat, because I know the islands and landmarks around here. In open water…not so much. I'd love to learn to navigate out there, and it would be fun to do it with something this old. Grandmère would feed me to the sharks before she'd let me go out that far, though."

She turned her attention back to the drawerful of European artifacts in Faye's lap. "I don't find so much stuff any more. I mostly stick with surface collecting now, since I started reading online about how digging can mess up an important site if you don't know what you're doing. But sometimes my metal detector starts beeping and I can't stand it, so I cheat a little."

Amande pulled a glass jar full of change out of the drawer. "These coins are new and they're pretty beat up. With my metal detector, I find coins all the time. These are only worth their face value, but I don't spend them. I want to spend my found coins on something special, but I don't know what that'll be, so I just throw them in here for later."

"Because the things you find are like treasure, and you don't want to waste them on candy bars or movie tickets." Faye stated this as if it were fact and not a question. It was the way she would have felt in Amande's shoes.

Amande didn't contradict her. She just nodded once and groped further back in the drawer.

"*This* is where I keep the good stuff…" She opened a protective folder and showed them dozens of coins minted during the first half of the twentieth century. "They're beat up and not worth much now. But they're all silver. I figure they're only going to be worth more and more. I'm thinking I can sell them to buy my books when I go to college.

Reaching so far back into the drawer that Faye heard her hand bump its back, Amande drew out a small wooden box and opened it. Inside, cradled in yet more snowy cotton, rested two very old chunks of silver. And "chunk" was the right word. The objects were vaguely disk-shaped, at best. Faye only recognized what they were because she'd seen very old coins before.

The irregular shapes of the blackened and corroded silver chunks were typical of coinage from the early days of Spain's invasion of the Americas. Silver had been formed into cylindrical rods, then sliced into rounds. The image always made Faye think of slice-and-bake cookies.

The images stamped into the front and back of these disks had often been equally crude. With a magnifier and some cleaning solution, Faye would have had a fighting chance to pinpoint the age of Amande's coins, but she didn't offer. She had the feeling that Amande would prefer to do it herself, even if it took her a lot of time and effort to learn how.

"I found these when I was a little girl," Amande said. She held up one of the coins. "I found this one underwater near an island beach, just after the tide went out. This one—" She held up the other one. "I found it buried nearby."

Faye was impressed that the girl could tell the two coins apart. They'd look like identical twins to most amateurs. Amande had picked up on the subtle differences in size and weight, possibly without even thinking about it.

"I remember the day I found them. Grandmère had taken me on a picnic to a little island somewhere out in Barataria Bay. She says she doesn't remember which one. I wish she did, but it only makes sense that she wouldn't remember one picnic from a hundred others. I guess. It was years ago, and for a long time I didn't realize what I had."

"The sextant came from right where we were walking today. It was just a couple of years ago, so I knew enough by then to understand what a cool thing I was looking at," she said, holding it up to the light. "When I saw what I had, it set me on fire to find more. Ever since then, I've walked the shoreline around here every day, and I've found all this silver money," she gestured toward the folder, "but I've never seen anything like the sextant or like either of these." She held the oldest coins out. "Do you think they're worth anything? I need college money."

Faye took them, handing one to Joe. He had the sharpest vision of anyone she knew. If there was an identifying mark on either coin that was visible without magnification, he would be able to see it. Several minutes spent holding them up to the light and squinting convinced both Faye and Joe that there was nothing to see. Amande spent all those minutes detailing her plan for finishing her education.

"I left school last year, when I found out that the online school would let me take more advanced placement classes than my brick-and-mortar school would allow." She waved her hands at Faye and Joe like she was trying to catch their attention. They were listening while they worked, but they must not have looked like it to Amande.

"Those AP classes are important! Every one I take earns me college credit. No tuition. No dormitory bill, because I'm living right here. Free books, even. Look."

She grasped Faye by the elbow and dragged her over to her desk, where a basket of old potsherds held down a stack of papers and photos. Pulling a piece of notebook paper covered in handwriting from the pile, she laid it on her desk beside the computer and smoothed a hand across all those words.

"This is my schedule for the rest of high school, including summer classes. I've signed up for every AP course that the online school will let me take, even the ones that sound really boring. I actually signed up for AP Accounting." She said "accounting" as if the word tasted bad. "It won't be much use to me as a historian or archaeologist, but it'll give me credit toward my bachelor's degree. I figure I can get almost halfway there by taking AP courses. To get the rest of my degree, I'll just have to figure something out. I can get a job. I ought to qualify for some grants, and maybe I can borrow some money. Or sell a kidney."

"Keep your kidneys. You're smart enough to find a better way to pay for your education than *that*." Faye took the paper. "You'll be glad you took accounting if you wind up being a consultant like me. Our business has to file taxes and make payroll and bid jobs all the time, and I never learned any of that stuff."

"She made me take accounting so I could do it for her," Joe said, still fingering the old stone tools.

Faye didn't even look up. "Somebody had to take it. Might as well be you."

"You won't like it when I cut your salary."

Faye punched him on the arm, but she still didn't look up from Amande's planned school schedule. She read it. She thought about it a minute. Then she read it again, before asking, "Are you sure you want to do this? When do you plan to sleep?"

For the first time, Faye saw teenaged rebellion on the girl's face. "Maybe you've always had the money to do the things that were important to you, but…"

"No. I haven't. I was thirty-five before I had the money to finish my bachelor's degree. I wish I'd had this kind of opportunity, and my hat's off to you for going after it."

Faye resisted the urge to add, "Just don't forget to enjoy being sixteen," because she figured Amande wouldn't listen. She didn't seem to be the kind of girl who got wrapped up in proms and cheerleading squads, anyway.

Amande took the paper. The rebellious expression was gone. "It took you that long to finish your first degree, and you still went for your PhD? Was it worth it?"

Faye nodded silently, then she went back to studying Amande's ambitious plan for her own schooling, trying to decide whether it was merely ill-conceived or whether it was actually suicidal.

Chapter Five

Miranda pulled a bottle of rum out of the sideboard behind her. Faye heard the seal break as the old woman twisted off the bottle's cap, a good indicator that the rum was less likely to be doctored with voodoo boneyard dust than, say, this cup of tea she was sipping. This did not make her feel any better about drinking anything in Miranda's creepy presence that could cloud her judgment.

The old woman had interrupted Joe and Faye and Amande as they rifled through the girl's treasures, sticking her head through the door and saying simply, "Come." And they'd come, without questioning her and without dragging their feet.

Why? Amande was accustomed to obeying Miranda's curt orders, but Joe and Faye were of legal age, and then some. They didn't have to do what they were told, but people like Miranda got their way because they understood that most people avoided confrontations whenever possible.

Everyone crowded once more around the little table, which was now spread with a pretty tablecloth and lit with candles. Miranda sloshed some rum in her tea, then did the same to Dauphine's, without asking her permission. Next, she offered the bottle around the table and Joe poured a splash in his cup.

Faye got the sense that he was more than ready for a little stress relief, but she put her hand over her own cup. "Somebody's gotta be sober if Michael wakes up in the middle of the night."

An ounce of rum wasn't going to render Faye unfit for mother-hood, but Faye didn't like being impaired, even a little, when Miranda was around.

"You come here to learn about the history of this place?" Miranda looked around like a woman who was thrilled to have a captive audience who had never heard her old stories. "Well, know that the ground is never firm beneath you in this here wet land. But there is power at Head of Passes, where the Mississippi breaks up and flows willy-nilly to the sea. Power flows down the river and empties the heart of the land. Power and riches. Why else would the pirates call this place home?"

She cocked her head and paused, as if she were preaching to converts who were expected to sing a chorus of "Amen." Faye, Joe, Dauphine, and Amande disappointed her, but Michael took his pacifier out of his mouth and burbled softly. Miranda seemed to think this was good enough.

"Jean Lafitte his own self built his lair nearby, on Grand Terre, at the mouth of Barataria Bay. And other pirates. And murderers and thieves and slaves, yes. Let me tell you about the pirate Gola George, stolen from Africa by slavers. It took ten men, no… twelve men…to get George on that slave ship, and you'd best believe that George hurt those men, every one."

She held out the rum bottle, intending to top off Joe's teacup, but he took it from her hand and poured himself a polite drizzle. Faye found that she had unconsciously assumed Dauphine's pose, legs crossed tight and teacup hugged to her chest, with one hand draped over the cup's rim.

"By the time the slave ship was two days at sea, Gola George had made friends with the sailor who fed the Africans stored below decks. This sailor, with the name of Henry, was young, but he was as smart as George was strong. He owed the ship's captain nothing—hated him, in truth—because the captain had ordered him kidnapped from the docks where he worked. He'd told his men to steal Henry, specially, because he knew the boy could read and write and add, and he needed someone to help him manage the ship's affairs. Someplace in England it was, though I never knew exactly where Henry come from. Henry never saw the place or his people again, not in his long life. It weren't hard for Gola George and his whisperings to sway Henry into mutiny."

Michael was standing beneath the table, clamped between Joe's legs, but he wanted to be wandering loose around the room. His rebellious bleat interrupted Miranda's story. Amande reached over and clasped Michael around the chest, wordlessly asking Joe if it was okay to take him. Joe nodded and handed the baby over.

The world-weary set of Amande's shoulders and the angle of her head said, just as clearly as if she'd said it out loud, "I've heard all your stories ten thousand times."

She took Michael out on deck and, as she went, a cool breeze drifted in, carrying Amande's words. "Let's go out and look at the moon! Would you like that, little boy? Here, give me that pacifier. You don't need it…"

And the door closed, cutting off Amande's baby-pleasing monologue.

How long had they been cooped up on this little boat? It must be nearly sundown. Maybe Amande and Michael *could* see the moon out there. Faye wished she could think of a graceful way to join them.

Miranda never faltered when Amande left. The woman hardly drew a breath as the old tale tumbled out of her, uncontrolled. Faye was impressed, in spite of herself. She'd heard many people tell stories, but not so many of them were true storytellers. Miranda had that gift, and it showed in the changing timbre of her voice and in the melodic shape of her sentences. She knew when to pause and wait for her audience to lean forward, wanting more. And she knew when to make them stop waiting. Like any artist, she knew when to deliver the goods.

"When the open ocean was behind them and America wasn't nothing but a dark line across the water in front of them, they struck. Henry, the scrawny little sailor in charge of keeping the slaves alive, held power over the whole ship, 'cause he held the keys. He unlocked the shackles of the biggest prisoners, knowing full well that they planned to kill the men he'd worked beside for years. George, who spoke the men's language, told the other prisoners to wait for his word. One short hour after he give it, the blood of every white man aboard except young Henry flowed across that ship's deck."

Faye was intrigued by Miranda's story in spite of herself, but she had no idea how long the woman was planning to talk. She didn't intend to spend the whole night listening to stories and fending off offerings of rum. She decided to pretend that she thought Henry's mutiny was the end of Miranda's story, when she knew full well that the old woman wanted to tell them every last thing that happened to Henry and Gola George, for the rest of their lives.

Making eye contact with Joe and Dauphine, she rose and signaled to Joe that it was time to make their escape. When the scream came, she was just beginning the ritual words of parting drummed into her by her mother and grandmother.

"Thank you so much for inviting us. The tea was just lovely. We—"

Amande's scream pierced the houseboat's seaworthy walls. It rattled Faye's heart in her chest. This was no adolescent silliness.

Picturing a baby gone overboard, Faye was out the door in a breath, leaving a broken teacup on the floor behind her. Joe moved just as quickly.

They arrived on deck to find a happy Michael, his chubby fingers tightly laced through Amande's curls. Amande, on the other hand, was stooped over the boat's gunwale, staring down at the water.

The upturned face of a corpse stared back.

Miranda shrieked at the sight of it, and her masterful presence evaporated in the face of death.

"My son! My son…my Hebert…" She put one foot on the lower railing that encircled the houseboat, as if to scale it like a ladder. Her heavy shoe clanked on the metal rail, and the sound reverberated. "He needs me. Look! Look how bad he needs his *maman*."

Joe caught her around the waist, keeping her from throwing herself into the water with her son's corpse. In the same motion, he gently pushed Amande and Michael back, away from the railing. "You can't help him, ma'am. Look. Faye's calling 911. Help will come. You just stay where you are."

The old woman struggled, but she was no match for Joe, who kept murmuring, "You can't help him. He's not in any pain. You need to stay with Amande. She needs you."

Miranda never stopped trying to throw herself into the water, but there was no way for her to overcome Joe. She just kept flailing at him with her old lady hands, and he just kept taking her slaps and punches, quietly repeating, "You can't help him, but Amande needs you."

Faye parted the curtains of their rented cabin's kitchen window and used her binoculars to look outside. It wasn't the first time she'd watched as a murder investigation was launched.

She had stayed at the scene long enough to be interviewed by the deputy so, while everyone had been asked to stay well away, she'd still seen more of the retrieval of Hebert's body than she would have liked. She saw the terrible wounds on the big man's back, so she knew that he hadn't drowned. And those wounds didn't look like they'd been gnawed on by fish, so she knew that he hadn't been dead long. But she'd known that already.

Faye had seen a body fished out of the Matanzas River after days in the water. Hebert's face had still looked…human. He'd been strangely pale for a burly man who had likely spent big chunks of time with no roof over his head, but the grievous wounds on his back explained that his pallor was due to blood loss. Hebert's corpse had belonged to a big burly man whose life had bled out of him, but it didn't belong to a man who had bobbed in the water, dead, long enough for the flesh to lose its turgor and begin to decay.

Her interview had passed quickly. There were plenty of witnesses to account for her whereabouts all day. The deputy had asked her a few simple questions.

What did she remember about the minutes surrounding the actual discovery of Hebert's body?

How did the people around her behave when the body was first discovered? Miranda, Amande, Dauphine, Joe…was there anything odd about their behavior?

Did she remember seeing anyone else? Maybe a fisherman had been sitting on a nearby boat or some drunks had emerged from the marina store with a fresh case of beer? No?

Once she'd satisfied the investigator that she'd seen nothing important and that she'd never met the dead man and that she'd had no idea he even existed until he floated into view, she was free to go. She'd given Amande a good-bye hug, gathered Michael and his diaper bag, and retreated to the cabin. A murder scene was no place for a baby. It was also no place for a young girl, but she wasn't responsible for the girl.

For the first half hour, she'd thought Joe and Dauphine would come walking in the door at any time, but she'd thought wrong. Surely their testimony was no different from hers. Why should their interrogation take longer?

As she sat alone in a tiny and flimsily built cabin, listening to the quiet night, she came to realize why her interview had been so perfunctory. Hebert had stood a foot taller than five-foot-nothing Faye, and he had weighed nearly three times as much as her hundred pounds. It was physically impossible for Faye to be the killer, or at least it was physically unreasonable. Joe, on the other hand, was more than big enough to have done Hebert harm. Dauphine's two hundred pounds of mambo concealed enough muscle to take on Hebert, though her odds would have been better if she'd caught him by surprise. Faye couldn't imagine that they were serious suspects, but she understood why they rated more careful investigation than she did. It was just too bad that she couldn't force her imagination to stop right there.

As the sound of Michael's soft and rhythmic breaths filled the cabin, Faye found herself imagining the kind of person who was capable of knifing a big streetwise man to death. Since she knew that this person was neither Joe nor Dauphine, she was left to spend her evening hours with an imaginary killer.

That killer was somewhere near. The good condition of Hebert's body made this clear. He...She?...could be creeping stealthily through the marsh behind her cabin, looking for a safe and dry place to hide. As Faye waited for Joe and Dauphine to come invade her aloneness, she listened for the sploosh of a fleeing foot in the mud or the telltale scratching of a pick attacking her door's lock.

By the time Joe's key turned in that lock, Faye had spent far more time alone with her imagination than was strictly healthy.

Episode 1 of "The Podcast I Never Intend to Broadcast," Part 2

by Amande Marie Landreneau

Sally the Social Worker thinks that all the deaths in my family must be affecting me, but this makes no sense. For example, I never met my Uncle Hebert.

He wasn't even my blood uncle. He was Grand-mère's son from her first marriage, and my mother was my grandfather's daughter from his first marriage, so they were stepbrother and stepsister.

Did you follow that? I didn't think so.

How's this? When my mother and Uncle Hebert were little kids, her dad married his mom.

This means that I'm not actually any blood-kin to Grandmère at all. When you think about it, it was pretty awesome of her to take responsibility for me when my mom walked out. I wasn't even potty-trained. That's a pretty huge thing for a woman to take on when most of her kids are already grown and gone.

So I'm not kin to Uncle Hebert and I never met him. That means my only personal connection with him is that awful moment when I looked down and saw his dead face in the water.

If there are things in my family that haunt my psyche, Sally probably doesn't need to look any *further than the stories my grandmother weaned me on. Let's take Gola George and his friend Henry the Mutineer, who Grandmère says we're supposed to be related to, somehow. Was it right for my supposedly distant cousin-by-marriage Henry to help Gola George slaughter every sailor on that slave ship?*

Well, maybe. Slave ships were floating buckets of evil, and that mutiny might have saved the lives of hundreds of people who were about to be sold into slavery. But maybe Henry wasn't the only innocent sailor on that ship who was kidnapped and forced to steal slaves.

And is that really innocent, anyway? Maybe Henry should have just let the captain kill him on the very day he was captured, instead of taking charge of the keys and calmly locking up hundreds of men, women, and...oh, God...little children. Lots of human beings died in those shackles.

Henry the Mutineer worked on that slave ship for years before he helped Gola George take it over. He knew what he was doing. He knew that he was part of something monstrous.

So, yeah, it's entirely possible that I'm haunted by deaths in my family, but I don't think Uncle Hebert's is one of them.

Chapter Six

Dane Sechrist never wanted to see another rock again.

Dane had been diving for weeks now, and he was doing it alone, which wasn't precisely safe. He was also spending dollar after dollar on fuel for his boat and air for his scuba tanks. These were dollars that weren't precisely his to spend. Sooner or later, the Mastercard people were going to want those dollars back.

Granted, he hadn't had to pay for the sonar or the magnetometry. Who knew that a crappy summer job doing scut work on an archaeology boat would pay off so well? Or, rather, that it would pay off so well on the day—hopefully soon—when he stopped finding rocks and started finding Spanish gold?

Though Dane was pushing six feet and carried plenty of lean muscle, he wasn't heavily built, so he'd learned early to stand back and watch larger men jockey for position. When he was in high school, the jocks would strut and threaten and insult each other, vying for the coveted spot of alpha male. Eventually, the posturing would end in a fight behind the gym, complete with broken noses, black eyes, a bloodthirsty crowd, and weeping girlfriends. After a coach or two arrived to break up the fight, the sweaty and bleeding would-be alpha males didn't look nearly so good to their weeping girlfriends. Dane, who had spent the fight wiping those girlfriends' tears with his gentle hands, looked like a hero by comparison. He'd earned quite a few girlfriends of his own with those gentle hands.

Dane's finely honed beta-male skills had served him well while he worked aboard the archaeology boat, when the principal investigator had squared off against his most talented graduate student, time and again, over the remote sensing results. Dane had simply taken a step back and looked over their shoulders to see what all the fuss was about.

It had been interesting to see that, despite a boatload of expensive equipment and overeducated people, underwater archaeology was still more of an art than a science. And even when the hearts of the artists were pure, money still swamped everything.

The artists/scientists could argue for hours about the things detected by their fancy machines.

The future-alpha-male graduate student would bark, "Look at the shape of that anomaly. It has to be a wreck."

And the tenured professor would shoot him down. "Too small."

Fueled by excess testosterone, the grad student would make the unwise decision to argue. "It could have started out bigger. Who knows what happened to it over the past four hundred years?"

A PhD and tenure would bolster the professor's denial. "Nope. Too small. Not worth the money to check it out."

The young man's surging testosterone would urge him to try again. "What about this one, then?"

But the older man still had enough circulating male hormones to deny him. "That? That's nothing. Just background noise."

Without enough life experience to tell him he could never win, the student would persist. "Couldn't it be a debris field?"

Again, the student would be shot down.

"Noise. But I like the looks of this thing over here…"

And so it went. The opinion of the principal investigator trumped anything anybody else said, and money trumped everything.

Dane watched and learned, and he made notes on the locations of the anomalies that *he* thought were worth checking out. Later, when his employers published their work, he had access to their data and their (possibly wrong) interpretations. He'd been diving on the anomalies they'd ignored ever since, focusing on the ones in shallowish water, because he wasn't idiot enough to go after the deep ones alone. Dane enjoyed breathing.

At first, these exploratory dives had been a harmless thing to do on Saturdays. Now that he'd actually found something, they were an obsession. If only he could find something besides rocks.

He'd checked the Internet, and he knew these weren't ordinary rocks. They looked like the ballast stones carried deep in the bellies of old sailing ships, and here they sat under Barataria Bay, stacked in a ship-shaped pile. Dane was no artist and he was no scientist, but he was romantic enough to appreciate that the rocks making him so miserable had been plucked off the shores of faraway seas.

It didn't take an archaeologist to appreciate the romance in the stones Dane had discovered. And it didn't take an archaeologist to think up the notion that a ship had foundered here long ago. Somewhere in the vicinity of those rocks lay the broken and rotting pieces of the ship. More importantly, somewhere in the vicinity of those rocks lay everything that had been aboard that ship. Dane believed to the core of his soul that it had been loaded with treasure bound for the court of some European monarch or other. The next shapeless lump that he lifted out of the sandy muck could be made of gold. He knew this, because it had already happened three times...well, only one of those times had he uncovered gold. The other two times, he'd uncovered silver, but silver was treasure enough for Dane.

Lots of ships had been lost near the mouth of the Mississippi. The shifting shoals built by the river itself had seen to that. Combine these treacherous waters and their hurricanes with the constant flow of ships sent from the Old World to plunder the New, and there was no numbering the lost ships waiting to be found. There was also no limit to the amount of treasure that might be waiting with them.

Dane had found one of those treasure ships. He knew it to his very core. So how come this wreck hadn't yielded anything but stone and a few nails and a couple of hinges and three lone coins?

◇◇◇

If Faye had been a pirate, she was pretty sure that she could have found a better place for a pirate lair than this godforsaken swamp.

Maybe it wasn't a swamp in the eighteenth century when the pirates were doing their pirating?

Nah. She was pretty sure that it was. Most all the land south of New Orleans was of the gelatinous variety—glistening with organic material and barely able to support the weight of a full-grown man. It was a good thing Joe's feet were huge. Even a lean man like Joe carried more than a little weight at six foot six. Joe's feet seemed to hold him above the muck like water skis, or even surfboards.

Faye's small, narrow feet functioned more like the blades of a pair of ice skates. She was certain that, if she ever stopped her forward motion, she would sink up to her knees and never get free.

They'd driven several miles down Plaquemines Highway, the road that served as the backbone of civilization here. Faye's map had told her to leave the highway and drive out onto a patch of land protruding into the waterways on the Gulf side, but Faye really didn't trust the map's assertion that the land under this dirt road could support her fully loaded car. She pulled onto the highway shoulder to think about whether she really wanted to do this.

Joe had read her mind, saying only, "The map says you can drive on this road. So does our client."

"Our client's project manager wants us to finish this job yesterday. And he wants us to do it cheap. Do you trust him?"

"*I* think you can drive on this road."

With a sigh, Faye put the car in drive and pulled out onto the squishy-looking dirt roadway. When dealing with a situation that required book smarts or potsherd identification skills or child discipline, Faye was the go-to woman in their family. But when it came to woodcraft and accounting and lithics and an instinctive knowledge of the natural world, Joe was in the driver's seat. If Joe said the car wouldn't sink, then she would bet the car on it.

The squishy road had wound deep into the marsh, sometimes comfortably bounded by solid ground and sometimes running along a causeway, one car wide, that only rose above water at high tide because somebody had piled up a lane of dirt. This lane of dirt was necessary because, unbelievably, people lived on top of all this squishiness.

Taking a hard right onto a barely marked side road and following it to its end, they reached their destination—a mound built by Native Americans before Columbus arrived, surrounded on three sides by water. Oral history said that pirates had used it as a meeting place, centuries later, where they gathered to trade contraband, and also to drink more rum than was strictly good for them.

Faye and Joe were only contracted to locate known sites and document their condition, not to excavate but, oh, how badly Faye wanted to get out her trowel and start to dig. She could just see the pirates perched on the side of this mound, drinking and carousing.

She grinned at Dauphine. "Reckon Gola George and Henry the Mutineer ever came here?"

Dauphine grunted, as if to say that she didn't want to be reminded of anything Miranda had said. She was wearing a charm around her neck that Faye had never seen before, a silver vial with a red wax stopper.

"What's in that thing?" Joe had asked.

"Boar bristles, if you must know." Then, anticipating his next words, she'd barked, "Don't ask," and turned her attention to a fretting Michael, to no avail. The child had been whining all day, and Dauphine could work none of her usual magic on him.

It worried Faye to see Dauphine standing atop the old mound, looking out at the water with Michael in her arms. The wind riffled his hair. It had always been straight and black, but lately it had begun to lose the downy look of baby hair. Soon, too soon, it would be time for haircuts and combs.

Faye didn't like Dauphine's stiff silence. Her mambo friend was ordinarily in constant motion, a trait that was enhanced by the gauzy clothes that trailed behind her like a pursuing ghost. Dauphine was light on her feet for a woman her size, and it always made Faye smile to watch her flit constantly around Michael. Standing still made her look heavy...flat-footed...old.

Dauphine saw Faye looking at her. She disengaged a hand from Michael's tiny leg and gestured out at the water. "It's coming," she said. "The oil, I mean. I feel it, like a thundercloud rolling in."

Faye walked up the side of the mound toward Dauphine. "I know. I don't feel it, but I know it in my head. It's huge, and it's coming, and there's nothing we can do about it. Nothing except do our jobs. We can tell people what this mound is like now, before the oil gets here and spoils it forever."

Dauphine nodded, but she made no move. It was as if the strength had gone out of her during the hours she spent with Miranda. Faye knew that mambos considered contact with corpses to be powerfully bad magic. Discovering Amande's Uncle Hebert floating dead in the water had weirded Faye out, and it could only have affected Dauphine more. Faye's mambo friend was suffering from the aftereffects of a very, very bad day.

Faye couldn't get Dauphine to talk about it, and she'd spent the day getting nowhere with feeble jokes like, "If Miranda cursed you, can't you curse her right back, only worse?"

In answer, Dauphine would finger the vial at her neck or the hidden talisman in her pocket, saying only, "Such spells are beyond me."

Faye wasn't ready to say she believed in voodoo. And she wasn't ready to say she didn't. She'd seen some strange things one dark night when the scent of Dauphine's herb magic had hung in the air and clouded her mind. Still, Faye was at heart a rational person, and she wished desperately that Dauphine would snap out of it...or that she would come up with a miraculous counter-hex. Either would do, and as Dauphine's employer, Faye didn't care which it was.

At least the fact that they had found the mound quickly put a positive spin on this day. It was a welcome change from days spent poking through mud for historical objects that had left no trace. Joe was sketching the site while Faye took pictures, when she heard a dull thud that just couldn't be good.

The good news was that Michael was fine. Dauphine, being who she was, had clung to him with both arms rather than extending an arm to break her fall. The bad news was that Dauphine had paid a price for protecting Faye's son.

Dauphine had been picking her way down the side of the old mound, wading through the shrubby vegetation that covered it. The mound's builders had made it from a pile of oyster shells, many centuries before, so it had taken no voodoo hex to make her lose her footing on the uneven ground. She was on the hefty side, so no curse had been necessary to break off an inch-thick sapling when she landed on it. The fact that its broken trunk had stabbed deep into her right hamstring when she fell was completely explainable by simple physics. Nevertheless, Faye did not intend to argue with a heavily bleeding voodoo mambo who believed that another mambo had given her the evil eye. She just let Dauphine rave about Miranda's evil act, when the poor old woman was in all likelihood completely innocent. Faye knew she needed to focus on getting Dauphine to a doctor before she bled to death.

With Michael in his car seat and Joe in the backseat using Dauphine's own shawl to apply pressure to the blood gushing out of her wound, Faye dialed 911 while she made tracks for the main highway. They were so far out in the woods that it seemed worthwhile to meet the ambulance halfway.

Faye's mind was on her driving. She needed to push her luck just far enough and no more. How fast could she cross those raggedy little causeways? How fast did she dare make each turn? If she missed a turn, how soft was that shoulder, anyway? A hair-raising moment spent waiting for her right front tire to stop spinning and grab the ground told her that the shoulder was way softer than she wanted it to be.

Dauphine's head scarf was coming unwrapped, and a dangling end must have dragged through the blood, because it was red and dripping. Michael had settled into a pattern of rhythmic screams, as he clutched at Dauphine and she inexplicably didn't hug him back. She just threw her head against the seat back and chanted something in a language Faye didn't understand.

Dauphine might be convinced that Miranda was the stronger mambo, but Faye wasn't. She didn't know what Dauphine was saying, but she didn't like the sound of it.

Chapter Seven

The paramedics were working diligently, but Faye stood close-by and monitored their work, nonetheless. One of them had opened his mouth to suggest that Faye might have overreacted in calling an ambulance for something short of a bullet wound. Faye had silenced him by pulling back Dauphine's bloody shawl to display an injury that looked an awful lot like the work of a gun. Embedded pieces of bark and exposed fatty tissue made Dauphine's wound even more visually dramatic.

"She's a diabetic," Faye announced. "She can't wait to get that wound cleaned, not if she wants to keep her leg." The doubtful paramedic saw her point and loaded Faye's friend on the ambulance.

Many stitches, several bandages, and one prescription for antibiotics later, they escaped the hospital.

They did this slowly, because Dauphine was on crutches. Her badly damaged muscle and tendon were going to need some time to heal, but they would heal. This news was good, but Faye was now embarking on a consulting contract that was far too big to accomplish with just two people...and she was suddenly without a babysitter. Dauphine's doctor had ordered her back home to New Orleans for the foreseeable future.

Faye wondered if maybe Miranda had hexed her, instead of Dauphine.

◇◇◇

The full moon was rising when Faye, Joe, and Michael reached the marina after taking Dauphine home to New Orleans. Amande was sitting alone at a picnic table outside the bar and grill, one idle hand toying with a curl of her hair.

Faye already knew enough about the girl to know that idleness was unusual. She took Michael by the hand so that Joe could unpack their gear in peace, and she walked over to talk to Amande.

"The detective was here again," the girl said, staring absently at the rising moon. "He says Uncle Hebert hadn't been dead long when…when I found him. He isn't saying much—and why would he be expected to say anything to a kid like me?—but the grapevine works pretty good around here. Everybody says that the cops haven't got any solid suspects, but they've been talking to a lot of people who were just as scummy as my uncle. If that's even possible. I've heard that Uncle Hebert had been in three bars between the time he got up yesterday morning and the time he was killed, and that he'd tried to pick a fight with somebody in every one of them. He wasn't a nice man."

"But he was your uncle," Faye said, "even if he wasn't a nice man."

"I didn't know him. Not at all. Grandmère never even told me he existed."

Well, that was a stinging indictment. When your own mother never mentioned your name, then you had officially hit rock-bottom. Faye was guessing there were no baby pictures of Hebert decorating the houseboat.

Faye settled herself on the bench beside Amande and dandled Michael on one scrawny knee. In about six months, he was going to be too big for this. "You don't look like somebody who doesn't care about the dead uncle she never knew."

Amande looked down at her. Goodness, the girl was tall, even sitting down. "I look that bad? Well, I don't get a good hard look at dead bodies every day, but that's not the worst part. It's my poor grandmother."

"I can't imagine losing a son." Faye's mouth went dry as she said it. She pulled Michael's shirt down over his round belly.

"She doesn't even look different. You've seen my grandmother. The woman doesn't know how to smile." A bitter smile of her own threatened to twist Amande's mouth out of shape. "I just *know* she's suffering, because she's family and we live in the same house. I mean…we live on the same boat. I can hear it in her footsteps when she walks through the kitchen. She breathes different. She stands all wrong. She spends a lot of time sitting at her altar, staring at her voodoo gods and just watching a candle burn. She's suffering."

"I can see her when you talk. And I can feel her, because you describe her so perfectly. Have you ever thought of being a writer, Amande? Come to think of it, have you ever considered being a shrink?"

That made Amande smile, which had been Faye's goal. She felt almost like a shrink herself.

"A social worker came to talk to me today. Maybe the detective sent her to help me deal with the shock of seeing a dead man floating outside my home. I think she's kind of a low-rent shrink. No, I don't want to do her job. I'd hate it. I'd want to tell all my clients to stop whining about their problems and do something to fix them. 'Suck it up, people!', I'd say."

Faye snickered. "Me too, actually."

"But a writer? Oh, yeah. I've been hearing stories and telling stories and writing stories all my life."

Michael had gone to sleep, so Faye shifted him on her lap, cradling his head under her chin. Boat sounds surrounded them, as moored vessels shifted with the moving water and a sailboat's lines clinked against a metal mast. If Faye ignored the music seeping out of the marina's bar, she could pretend she was at home on Joyeuse, sitting on her own dock and looking out at water that, at a far distance, touched this water.

Faye was glad she'd left a moment of silence between them, because Amande finally let go of the thing that was really bothering her.

"I heard Grandmère on the phone with her lawyer today. She was asking questions about inheritance laws...questions I didn't understand. What could she possibly inherit from Uncle Hebert? He wasn't the kind of man who owned anything that he couldn't carry around in his pockets to buy beer with."

Faye tended to agree with her, but she said, "Well, it wouldn't be the first time somebody living in poverty died and left a fortune under a mattress."

Amande raised an eyebrow so high that she didn't even have to complete the teenager's routine of rolling her eyes and sighing, "Yeah, right."

"Or not," Faye said. It had been a long time since she felt this lame, and the girl had accomplished it with a single eyebrow.

"Grandmère didn't sound like somebody who was going to inherit the fortune under her worthless son's mattress. She sounded scared. One thing she said scared me, too. It scared me bad."

Faye waited.

"She kept asking her lawyer, 'But can we keep the boat? Are you sure?'"

No wonder the girl's voice was shaking. Faye flashed back to the years when she had held on to Joyeuse by her fingernails. She knew precisely how it felt to fear losing her home, her history...everything. And she'd been a grown woman at the time.

When Faye had been as young as Amande, she'd felt utterly secure. Their suburban Tallahassee house hadn't been anything special, but her mother's salary and her grandmother's pension had never once faltered. When Faye went to school every day, she knew that her home would still be hers when the final bell rang.

"It never occurred to me that Grandmère didn't own the boat. She's lived in it since she married my grandfather, so that was before Didi was born. That's plenty long enough to pay off a boat, it seems to me."

Faye knew enough about second mortgages and loan sharks to wonder.

"I've been crawling around the Internet, trying to figure out why Grandmère was worried about inheritance laws. I didn't find anything to explain her questions. The houseboat was my grandfather's when they got married. I know that for a fact. Uncle Hebert wasn't any kin to my grandfather, so he shouldn't have any claim on it at all. I understood that much of what I read. After that, the details got fuzzy. I only figured out one thing for sure."

Faye decided to risk speaking and showing herself to be lame. "And what was that?"

"Louisiana inheritance law is the squirreliest thing I've ever seen. Our laws are different from everybody else's. After I spent last night reading about all that weirdness, if you walked up to me and said, 'Hi, I'm Faye. I just inherited your home, so you need to take a hike,' I'd probably believe you. Maybe Uncle Hebert's death has triggered something legal that I don't understand."

Faye felt like she needed to do something, even if it was wrong. She shifted Michael's head, so that he could drool on a different part of her chest, and she reached out a hand in Amande's direction. She just rested it on the girl's back, between her shoulder blades, and hoped that was right.

Amande didn't shrug it away. She just kept talking. "I've been working on a plan."

Faye suspected that Amande always had a plan. Faye knew this because she herself always had a plan.

"If Grandmère loses the boat, I think I can get a job working offshore. Around here, there's noplace else to earn enough money to support us both and still save money for school. Maybe I'll have to be eighteen first, though. Not sure. The oil patch was my fallback plan if I didn't save enough money to go to college by the time I turned eighteen, but that's almost two years away. So I also have a Plan B."

Faye noticed that the girl wasn't daunted by the danger out in the oil fields, despite the fact that eleven people had just lost their lives out there. And she wasn't much concerned about whether or not she could even land one of those sought-after jobs. Amande was used to making a plan and then carrying it out, with or without the cooperation of the world at large. Faye liked that.

"What's your Plan B?"

Faye was not prepared for Amande to fix a supplicant's gaze on her face and plead, "Will you take me out into the islands? Maybe we can find where I got the silver coins. Maybe finding that spot will help you in your work. And maybe I can find some more, enough to send me to school."

Surely Amande knew that this plan was as unlikely as a sixteen-year-old finding work offshore. She was an intensely reasonable girl. The fact that she was banking her future on an unattainable job or an unlikely treasure hunt showed that she'd rejected all reasonable alternatives. Amande was desperate.

Faye's hand was still on Amande's back and she patted it awkwardly. "I can't take you out without your grandmother's permission, but I'll ask her. And I'll help you apply for school money. You should have seen the pile of scholarships and grants that landed on Joe after I filled out his paperwork for him."

"You did? Lucky man."

"Generally, I'd tell any woman planning to do a man's dirty work for him that she was nuts. So don't do what I did…unless you meet a man like Joe someday. He does what he does very well. There will always be food on our table, because he can shoot, trap, fish, and cook. He's a way better archaeologist than he realizes—detail-oriented, thorough, patient, thoughtful. He can keep the company books perfectly well, as long as I handle any interaction with scary folks like the IRS. In return, I figure I can be the buffer between Joe and bureaucracy, if he needs me to be. In any relationship, you just have to work things out. Right now, I'd say it was your relationship with your grandmother that needed tending."

Amande just nodded.

Faye rose, hefting Michael onto her hip. Her hand was still on Amande's back, so the girl stood with her. "Even if she doesn't want to talk about losing her son, you should probably be there for her."

As they approached the houseboat, Faye smelled the odor of incense drifting through its open windows. Miranda was preparing to remember her son's life in the special ways only a mambo knows.

Episode 2 of "The Podcast I Never Intend to Broadcast," Part 1

by Amande Marie Landreneau

Gola George didn't get religion after he escaped slavery. He also didn't decide to do something nice for the world out of gratitude to God or his African gods or fate or luck.

No. According to my Grandmère, he put all the slavers' African prisoners ashore on a deserted island, except for a handpicked crew selected from men who were willing to turn pirate. Now, I'm not sure what his options were, since dropping the Africans off at a seaport would have meant they went into slavery. And taking them back to Africa wasn't gonna happen, not without food and supplies. Still, based on the things Grandmère told me about Gola George, I'm thinking he didn't really care what happened to all those women and their children, and he certainly didn't care what happened to the weakling men who weren't good pirate material.

People said Gola George was seven feet tall. Or maybe he was just one of those men who could make you believe he was seven feet tall. Either way, he was a most excellent pirate. He grew his hair long and dyed it red. He tied finger bones in his curls, like Christmas tree ornaments. They clanked when he shook his head, which happened a lot when he was slicing people open and running them through.

He always wore a flowing white silk shirt, and he kept a plain white silk scarf wrapped around his head, but they didn't stay white long. Gola George made sure there was always a spot of blood showing on the white silk, but just one. That single spot of horror distracted his victims. They couldn't look away from George and his trademark bloodspots.

It occurs to me that George had been stolen from Africa, so he'd probably never been on a sailing ship before being taken as a slave. How did he even know what a pirate was? That question is just one of the things that makes me think that Henry the Mutineer was no innocent pawn, trapped into helping George because his only other choice was death. Grandmère's judgment was always a little murky where Henry was concerned because, you see, she always said she was supposed to be descended from him.

Myself, I think Grandmère's people are descended from Gola George himself. There have been times when I looked at Grandmère, stomping around our little kitchen and chopping squash with a big sharp knife and mumbling to herself in French, and I thought, "Yes. A pirate."

But there have been other times when I was the one mumbling angry threats. I was the one looking out at the water and wondering whether the engine on this old houseboat could take us somewhere. Anywhere. And I'm not any kin to Grandmère and her ancestor Gola George.

Maybe there's a little bit of pirate in all of us.

Chapter Eight

Another marked car circled through the marina parking lot, and Joe wondered whether he should pack up his little family and move. So he asked Faye what she thought. "Do you think it's a good idea to stay here? With the murder and all? We're gonna need to move, sooner or later. This new scope of work is too big for us to handle it all from here without driving all day. We could go on down to Venice and get a place for a while. Then we could go to Grand Isle. It's gonna take us several days to do all that work over there."

She'd said pretty much what he'd expected.

"This place is cheap and clean. The food at the marina is great. And did I already say that it's cheap? I heard that prices have gone through the roof in Venice since the media people came down to cover the oil spill. I think we should just get cracking on the job and not waste time with a move we don't have to make. There's time enough to get down to Venice."

Joe glanced out the window of their cabin at a lonely girl perched once again atop a picnic table near the home she might soon lose. He elected not to point out the real reason Faye was willing to stay in a place where the police prowled day and night. He wasn't too keen on leaving Amande alone in a place where a killer was running loose, either, and he thought that leaving her with that loopy grandmother might be as bad as leaving her alone. Or worse.

He took his cell phone outside where the reception was better. Michael had slept late, so Faye was simultaneously working on her notes and wolfing down a bowl of cereal. It seemed like a good time for Joe to inhale his own cereal and make some calls.

The client's project manager was in the Eastern Time Zone, so he was at work by seven o'clock, Louisiana time. By playing the time zones, Joe and Faye could add another hour to their workdays, and it was way better to bill nine hours a day instead of eight. Multiply that extra hour by the two of them, and the accountant in him was even happier, especially since they were working seven days a week.

It occurred to Joe that they should just take a project managed by someone in Japan. They could do their fieldwork while the sun shone, write it up at dusk, talk to the client as the stars came out, then spend a couple of nighttime hours dealing with client-generated hassles. He figured this would let them bill twelve or fifteen hours a day, easy. They might work themselves into early graves, but at least the company would be solvent.

There wasn't a lot of noise around the marina. People just weren't in the mood to fish when they knew that the oil could arrive at any time. Once the patrol car turned out of the parking lot and onto the highway, there was no sound but the lapping water and no motion but boats moving with that water.

This silence meant that the angry voices disturbed the peace as thoroughly as an angry flock of crows would have. Joe was on his feet as soon as the barrage of croaking, unintelligible words hit his sensitive ears. Miranda could naturally make a lot of noise and, when angry, it seemed that she preferred to make that noise in French.

Somebody else was making noise in English, and his voice was getting louder with every word. "It's legal. Every word of it. See the signature? Don't you raise your hand to me, you crazy old bitch!"

More croaking. More French. Joe could see Miranda now, and she was hefting a cast-iron skillet. She could no doubt do some damage with it, but Joe didn't care to see her tangle with the stranger in front of her. Even from this distance, Joe could see that he was six feet or so and built like a bouncer. Frizzy blond hair to his shoulders didn't hide the thick neck nor the belligerent set to his jaw.

Faye stuck her head out the door to see what the fuss was about, but Joe put out a hand that said, "Stay." He knew she had good enough sense to call 911, so he started running without a word. No way was Joe going to let an old lady go toe-to-toe with this man, not even when that old lady was Miranda.

A noise behind him said that his charming bride did indeed have enough sense to call 911, but that she was stupid enough to do so while running toward the very danger that prompted the call. She was falling behind, because her legs were way shorter than his, but she was matching him step for step.

Joe bellowed the only two words he knew that would make her go back. "The baby!"

Her stride did falter. She looked at him, looked over her shoulder, then fastened her gaze on Amande. The girl had risen from her seat at the picnic table and paused, momentarily unsure, but she would regain her wits in seconds. When that happened, she'd be at her grandmother's side.

Joe did not want that girl in the same county as the man hollering at Miranda. He needed to get to Amande before she moved, then he needed to do something about the man harassing her grandmother.

The look on Faye's face said that she'd made a decision, and that decision was to keep going. She ran twenty more yards in the wrong direction, away from their baby, hooked an arm around Amande's waist, and started back to the cabin before the girl even knew what had happened.

It almost worked. Amande was going with Faye, but still looking over her shoulder for her grandmother. Suddenly, Joe saw her dig in her heels. The girl was a full foot taller than Faye, and more than fifty pounds heavier. When she decided to stop running, there was nothing little bitty Faye could do about it. The two of them jerked to a halt.

"My grandmother. I'm going back for her."

Joe stopped and turned, balanced on the balls of his feet. He was not constitutionally suited to deal with three women in jeopardy, let alone a baby left alone in an empty cabin. Who should he help?

Fortunately, Faye was dealing with only one person.

"No!" she said to Amande. "Just no."

Amande was still pulling her arm away from Faye's grasp. Faye kept talking. "Let Joe take care of your grandmother. Michael needs me, and I have to go back. You need to come with me."

Amande was listening, but still she pulled against Faye's firm grasp. Faye didn't tug any harder, she just spoke in a voice so low that Amande was forced to lean down if she hoped to hear. "Come with me."

The girl towered over Faye. There was nothing to keep her from ignoring this little woman she barely knew, nothing to keep her from running headlong into danger, but she backed down. And Joe was painfully grateful.

◇◇◇

Michael was standing up in his portable crib, probably awakened by the sound of his mother rushing out the door. Faye was glad she hadn't stayed away longer, because she didn't trust the portacrib to keep him penned up. The child had barely started crawling when he'd learned to walk, and she'd already found him clambering up an overloaded bookcase. He needed her around to protect him from himself.

Amande was standing in the open doorway, peering out at the houseboat. Reaching into her equipment bag, Faye pulled out her binoculars and looked over the girl's shoulder. She couldn't get a clear view of Joe, Miranda, and the dark-skinned blond stranger, but it didn't look like any punches had been thrown. She saw no sign that Miranda had taken a swing at anybody with her cast-iron skillet, either. This was an encouraging sign.

"This is about to get more interesting," Amande said.

Faye thought it was already pretty interesting, so she said, "How so?"

"Two more of my worthless relatives showed up late last night. They were still asleep when I came outside because, well, they're my relatives and that means they're worthless. But nobody could sleep through one of my grandmother's rants, and those two love drama. They'll be outside as soon as they crawl out of bed. Or off the couch, as the case may be."

"Men or women?"

"One of each. But if you're asking because you think they might be some help to Joe…hmm. Aunt Didi makes her way in the world with her pretty face. She's not going to risk a broken nose. Uncle Tebo? He might help Joe if he thinks the fight would be fun. And he might help Joe if he thinks there's something in it for him. But he won't lift a finger just because Joe's in trouble and needs help."

Trying to think of something to say that wouldn't damn one of Amande's closest relatives, Faye said, "Joe *is* a stranger to him—"

Amande interrupted her to say, "I wasn't clear. Uncle Tebo won't be lifting a finger to help his own *mother*, not unless he thinks the fight will be fun or unless he thinks there's something in it for him."

Faye pulled the girl inside the cabin, just in case the intruder had a gun he hadn't pulled yet. This thought made her wish that Joe was wearing full body armor. She decided she was willing to take a tiny risk of catching a bullet herself, because she really needed to know he was okay. If she took a few steps through the open door, the binocs gave her a perfect view down the hill between the cabin and the scene unfolding on the houseboat's deck.

If Faye hadn't been so worried about her husband, she'd have been fascinated by the body language on display. Joe had stepped into the stranger's personal space and was looking down at him, silently making the point that, though they were both very large men, Joe had the advantage of height and reach.

Miranda, taking advantage of Joe's presence, took a step forward as Faye watched. She was still brandishing the skillet.

Faye could see her shaking her head slowly back and forth, her lips moving constantly.

Faye gave the stranger credit for guts. He didn't back down, not even when faced with Joe at his scariest or Miranda at her craziest. He did finally flinch, but not until two more players joined the home team.

Amande's Aunt Didi didn't carry a single ounce of extra flesh, yet the sun behind her revealed a remarkably curvy silhouette. Her hair, as dark as Joe's, was cropped into a wispy gamine shape. As Amande had predicted, she lingered just outside the doorway, far out of reach of fists and frying pans. Somehow, she managed to look like Miranda and be beautiful at the same time.

A small, wiry man pushed past Didi and stepped outside. His profile, stance, bone structure…everything said that he was Miranda's son. He looked fortyish, but Didi looked much younger. Early twenties, maybe. Amande had said that she and Didi had shared a room until fairly recently.

Faye tried to do the math. "The man's just your uncle by marriage, like Hebert. Right? And what about the woman?"

"Yeah. Tebo and Hebert were my mother's older stepbrothers. Uncle Tebo is a lowlife, but not as much of a lowlife as his brother Hebert, since Grandmère still speaks to him now and then. I've met him maybe four times. Didi was the only child she and my grandfather had together—so that makes her and my mother half-sisters, because they had the same dad. Is there such a thing as a half-aunt?"

Faye shrugged her shoulders. "I think so. But I don't think you can go to the drugstore and buy cards that say, "Happy birthday to my favorite half-aunt!"

"My family is such a mess. Even Grandmère isn't really related to me. She's my step-grandmother. Anyway, I'm actually blood-kin to Didi, if that's what you were asking. Other than my mother, and I don't count her since I don't even remember when she left, Didi's the only blood-kin I've got. Well, there's my father, but if anybody knows who he is, they're not telling me."

Faye nodded, more concerned about Joe's safety than Amande's complicated family tree. She pulled her phone out of her pocket and stared at the screen. It had only been a few minutes since her 911 call.

Amande said, "I wish the sheriff would send somebody quick."

Faye was thinking the same thing.

◇◇◇

Joe was slowly figuring out the cast of characters surrounding Miranda, just by listening to them yell at each other. The skinny girl wearing short hair and shorter shorts was named Didi, because he'd just heard Miranda holler, "Shut up, Didi!" The seedy-looking middle-aged man had responded with, "Settle down, Mother," so he was apparently one of Miranda's older children. Miranda had then barked, "Shut up, Tebo!' so now Joe knew his name, too.

The dangerous-looking stranger was the wild card. As best Joe could tell, none of the others knew who he was.

"Justine left everything to me. All of it. Her share of the boat, her father's stock, money…whatever you've got that belonged to Justine is mine now." He stuck a sheaf of legal-sized paperwork in Miranda's face and shook it. "You take care of this boat. You may be living in it now, but it's mine when you croak."

"Hardly," Didi said, taking a step out the door.

She struck a pose, one bare knee bent so that her hip cocked alluringly. It was possible that she didn't even know she was doing it. Joe sensed that every movement, for Didi, consisted of shifting from one pose to the next.

"Half of this boat is mine, and I'll get it when Mother dies," she said, "not to mention half the oil stock Daddy bought while he worked in the oil patch. The other half will go to Justine."

"You weren't listening, baby girl," Tebo said. "This man's holding something that he says is Justine's will. A will ain't all that interesting when the woman that wrote it is still alive. Is she? Is Justine still alive? What have you done with her? Goddamn punk."

The so-called punk's head jerked back and he moved to take a step forward, but Joe was standing in front of him. Joe spread his hands in a "we're all friends here" kind of way, and asked blandly, "What's your name? And tell us again…what's your business here?"

"My name is Steve Daigle. I was Justine's husband until the cancer got her last week. I came to tell her family she was gone, and I came to put my name on what's rightfully coming to me. Half of this boat is mine. And everything else that was Justine's is mine, too." He waved the papers yet again.

Joe looked Steve up and down. Was he Amande's father?

Maybe. Amande's dark skin tone certainly stood out in her lily-white family. Joe couldn't tell exactly what Steve's ancestry was, but it clearly didn't all come from northern Europe. Other than his mid-dark skin, he didn't look much like Amande, but yeah. He could be her father.

Didi's pose had failed her. She'd pulled the cocked hip into a more normal position and was standing, hunchbacked with her arms hugged across her small breasts. The short-shorts revealed trembling legs. Just when Joe realized that those legs might fail her, they did. Tebo, who was standing right behind her, did nothing. Joe's hands shot out of their own accord and caught her under the arms. He lowered her gently to the deck.

The stranger could have taken this opportunity to slug Joe while his hands were full of woman, but he didn't. Joe took this as a good sign.

"Justine's dead?" Didi melted into tears. Miranda and Tebo stood by, curiously unmoved.

"Was there a funeral?" Didi demanded. "She died last week? You should've told us then."

"That's what I come to do."

"No. You come to wave those papers around." Tebo said, watching Justine's widower through squinted eyes. When he saw that Steve was sufficiently distracted by the weeping woman on the deck, Tebo took the opportunity to snatch the paperwork right out of his hand.

Tebo looked the first page over, then the second, then the third and last. "The will's just one page. You brought three copies."

"You know lawyers. Everything in triplicate."

"It don't say anything except that you get everything she owned." Tebo handed two of the sheets back to Steve, pointedly folding up one copy and sticking it in the pocket of his t-shirt.

"That's all it needs to say, dumbass...everything goes to me. She was my wife and she left me everything she had."

Didi, who was working herself into a state of hysteria and who was doing a good job of it, suddenly wailed, "Amande! We're going to have to tell Amande her mother's dead!"

Miranda looked down on her daughter with eyes that seemed to have retreated to another world. Tebo just looked uncomfortable.

"Mother?" Steve looked from face to uncommunicative face. "Who's Amande? And whattaya mean when you say 'her mother's dead'?"

Tebo pulled a pack of cigarettes out of his shirt pocket and lit one. "What do people usually mean when they say 'mother' where you come from? Idiot. Amande is Justine's daughter. How long did you say you two were married? She never mentioned her own daughter?"

"Eight years. And no. She didn't. She didn't mention anybody named Tebo or Didi, neither. Just somebody named Hebert that she said was a wonderful brother and a sweet man."

"She damn sure didn't talk to you much, then, did she? Not if she forgot to tell you about a sister, a brother, *and* a daughter. Anyway, you missed Hebert by about twenty-four hours. He's dead."

Steve just looked at Tebo as if he'd never seen anybody that he wanted to pound so bad.

Suddenly, Miranda stirred. If Joe hadn't been between her and Steve, he believed she would have gone for the intruder's throat. As it was, he was forced to take the woman by both shoulders to keep her a safe distance from Steve. Joe hated manhandling women, but he did it when necessary. Like now.

"You'll get this boat when you're man enough to throw me overboard."

Joe knew that Miranda was accustomed to being feared by people who believed in her voodoo-practicing mystique. Her hand went to her apron pocket and didn't come out. Perhaps she had a protective talisman like Dauphine's in there, but Joe thought this was just as likely to be an offensive move as a defensive one. People who believed that Miranda could curse them would cower at the possibility that her hand would come out of that pocket full of hexing powder or graveyard dirt. Nonbelievers couldn't care less what a woman half their size did with her hands.

Steve did stop short of throwing her overboard, but Joe doubted he was motivated by fear of a curse. He'd credit the arrival of two sheriff's deputies for the fact that Miranda remained safe and dry.

Chapter Nine

The responding deputies had handed Steve Daigle over to the detective investigating Hebert's murder as soon as he arrived. The detective then released Daigle so quickly that Joe figured he'd said nothing to the man beyond, "What were you doing yesterday while a man was being knifed? You were busy not killing anybody? Cool! You're free to go!"

The detective and deputies hung around for a few minutes to say nice things to Joe about the way he'd defused the situation.

"Thanks to you, Sir, nobody got hurt here today."

This had felt real good, until Joe realized that Steve was now walking around free, perfectly capable of showing up again and causing trouble for Amande and her family. Just thinking about Steve coming within fifty feet of Amande gave Joe the creeps. The scumbag seemed like the kind of guy who'd really get into pretty sixteen-year-old girls.

Joe was beginning to think that he should have egged Steve on. If he could've gotten the man to throw a punch, maybe the deputies would have charged Steve with assault and hauled him off in handcuffs. As long as Steve was punching Joe and not Miranda, it would've worked out fine.

But no. Joe'd just had to have a Gandhi moment. In this case, it was possible that peaceful resistance hadn't been the best way to go.

The good part of all this, though, was that Faye was proud of him. As soon as the deputies were gone, Joe's irrepressible wife had appeared in the dining room of the houseboat, where Joe sat with Miranda and her older children. His fierce little woman now stood framed in the doorway with Michael balanced on one hip and Amande at her side, and she looked just as confident and strong as she did when she was squatting in an excavation and doing the work she loved.

He wasn't at all surprised to see her. It must have been hard for her to stand aside during the crisis, and he was more than a little grateful that she'd let him handle this incident alone. Maybe she was mellowing in her old age. Hmm...bad choice of words. Any wise thirty-two-year-old man with a forty-one-year-old wife would do well to erase the word "old" from his vocabulary, and Joe thought he was pretty wise. Wise enough, anyway.

The sight of Amande troubled him. Just because she'd never known her mother didn't mean that the news of Justine's death was going to be easy for her. He wondered if he and Faye should stay, so that they could be there for Amande when she heard the news.

He decided it would be strange for them to intrude on that moment, being as how they'd only known the girl for three days. Turning to Miranda, he asked, "Will you be all right if I leave? Or would you like me to stick around, in case that creep ignores the deputies and comes back?"

Tebo butted in before Miranda could answer. "I hope he does come back. I've got two fists and a knife with his name on 'em. Nobody talks to my mother that way."

To the best of Joe's knowledge, Tebo hardly talked to his mother much at all. Also, Joe considered the sentence "I've got two fists and a knife with his name on 'em," to be in exceedingly poor taste when said in the company of a woman whose son had been knifed to death the day before. It was even worse when that woman was your mother.

Joe dealt Tebo the blow that blustering losers enjoyed least of all. He ignored him.

"Ma'am? Will you be okay if I leave? I'll just be up the hill in our cabin. If you holler, I'll hear you."

Miranda was as experienced in dealing with blustering losers as Joe was. She managed to insult her son with her reply, merely by leaving him out of it. "I'll be fine, but it's a comfort to know you're close by."

In other words, having Tebo close by was no comfort at all.

With that statement, she picked up a banana off the dining room table and walked out of the room without taking their leave. Joe could see the half-made dolls that hung from the ceiling of her bedroom on their swaying strings. They disturbed him in a way he couldn't describe. In his mind, he knew they were only woven straw, but their motion had a gallows swing that gave him an electric shock of revulsion.

As he gathered his family to leave, he could see Miranda bustling around her tiny bedchamber. She spread a fresh silk cloth on her altar and plunked the banana atop it. Squinting at the arrangement for a minute, she picked the banana up and pulled the peel back, so that a third of the fruit poked out invitingly. Then she poured a couple of fingers of rum in a glass and carefully set it down beside the banana. After lighting an array of votive candles and arranging them just so, she'd pulled a cell phone out of her pocket and dialed it.

Her crow's voice carried to where Joe was standing. As he turned to leave, he heard her rasp, "Bernie, I got a question for a lawyer. You ain't much of a lawyer, but you're what I got."

Amande had settled herself at the table between Didi and Tebo. She was with family, and that's where a girl should be when she got the kind of news Amande would be hearing tonight. Nevertheless, Joe didn't feel good about leaving her.

Episode 2 of "The Podcast I Never Intend to Broadcast," Part 2

by Amande Marie Landreneau

My mother is dead. It's taken me a while to get my brain around that one, since she was never really alive to me when she was alive.

I didn't know her, no more than I knew my dead Uncle Hebert. At least I remember seeing Uncle Hebert, even if I'll only ever remember him as a corpse floating in the water. My mother is...a ghost. I don't mean that she's a ghost because she's dead. She's always been a ghost to me, a being who was real but who just wasn't there.

Even the pictures I have of her are ghostly. She ran away from me and Grandmère when she was only seventeen, not enough older than I am now to even count. We don't have any pictures of her that were taken after that. Somehow, I don't think that Steve was the kind of lover who took pictures and saved them like treasures.

The woman who died of breast cancer at age thirty-three couldn't possibly have looked like the pictures Grandmère gave me, not anymore. I have photos of her with braces on her teeth and acne, and I think they're interesting, but when I look at them, I don't think, "Mother." Now, I guess I'll never say "Mother" at all. Sally the Social Worker wants to know how I feel about that.

I have no idea. So I think I'll change the subject and tell one of Grandmère's stories. We podcasters can do that, because we're in charge of what we say and how we record it and where we post it for listeners to find. Not that I intend to post this at all.

I think I'll go with Gola George's story, because George got carried off from his parents and from his family and from everything he ever knew. He got dumped here in the New World with nothing and nobody, but he didn't let that stop him from taking his world by storm. Nothing could stop Gola George.

Gola George was an incredibly successful pirate. I've read everything about him that I could find on the Internet, and George was the real thing. He captured the biggest ships. He slaughtered the most sailors. He kidnapped the prettiest wenches. Brave men trembled in their kneepants and stockings and buckled shoes when they heard Gola George's name.

Maybe Gola George landed in the pirates' hall of fame because he was good at murdering and maiming. Maybe he was just lucky, although being stolen away from home to be a slave doesn't seem like something that happens to a naturally lucky person. It even occurs to me that maybe he raked in a lot of that plunder simply because he was good at public relations. Pirating would be easy if people dropped their valuables and ran at the very sight of you. I mean, think about those finger bones tied in his dyed red hair and those bloody silk shirts. The man was a marketing genius.

It's also possible that George owed his rising fortunes to his less flamboyant partner. I picture Henry the Mutineer as being like a pirate accountant, sitting at a desk lit by a whale oil lamp and keeping the account books with a quill pen.

Can't you just hear him telling his partner that the pirate business had been a little slow lately? "Hey, George...I'm having a little trouble making payroll for the crew this month. You need to be doing a little less raping and a lot more pillaging."

George and Henry terrorized the Caribbean together for more than a decade. Criminal partnerships don't usually last that long. Throw two sociopaths together, then add money to the mix, and somebody's going to betray somebody, sooner or later. And just because a criminal partnership doesn't end with one party stabbing the other in the back, it doesn't mean that it will end well. Think of Bonnie and Clyde...Butch and Sundance...

It may be that a successful partnership even puts a criminal in danger. The urge to protect a partner you care about—or even love—is a dangerous thing when there are bullets flying.

But Gola George and Henry the Mutineer made it work for them for many years. They were made for each other. Brain and brawn. Careful planning and sheer audacity. If only one of them had been a woman...or if only they'd both been gay...

If I were telling you this story about Gola George and Henrietta the Mutineer, I do believe it would end with the two of them dying together of old age in bed, surrounded by their lying, thieving, stealing pirate grandchildren, but no.

The story of Gola George and Henry the Mutineer ends poorly because Gola George ignored the sailor's cardinal rule: Never bring a woman aboard a sailing ship.

Chapter Ten

Faye needed some warm bodies to help her finish this project on time, and she needed them immediately. Rural Louisiana wasn't teeming with experienced archaeologists, but New Orleans was right up the road. Even better, her cousin Bobby was right up the road, and Bobby knew everybody.

Bobby also knew who was kin to who, and he knew who everybody had slept with, and he knew who wasn't speaking to who, and he knew how to properly use "who" and "whom" when writing in standard English. More importantly, he had the social skills to know that it was possible to be too pedantic about such things as objective pronouns and split infinitives.

There was no such thing as a short conversation with her dear cousin, because every mention of a human being required him to revisit, yet again, the question of who was kin to who. It was a good thing that Faye's cell phone plan included unlimited long distance.

"You've already talked to Nina, I'm sure?" he said, pinning an unnecessary question mark to the end of his statement so that she'd have to say she did. And then she'd need to give him the details of the conversation, including whether their friend and colleague Nina was dating anybody and whether they were serious, because if Faye didn't volunteer the information, Bobby would ask.

"Yes, I did. Her new boyfriend is in grad school with her, so I sent the two of them over to Grand Isle to do some initial survey work." She forestalled Bobby's next question by saying,

"His name is Mark, but he's from Philadelphia, so you don't know him. I mean Philadelphia, Pennsylvania, not Philadelphia, Mississippi."

"Oh." Bobby's social curiosity was bounded on the north by Lake Pontchartrain and on the south by the Mississippi River, and it dimmed considerably with each successive mile east and west of Jackson Square.

"Have you seen Dauphine yet?" she asked. "I gave her some library research to do and told her to get you to help."

Bobby's connections at the Historic New Orleans Collection had been a godsend for Faye, more than once. Rare documents, old maps, historic photos—Bobby could find paper proof of just about anything that had ever happened in New Orleans or its vicinity.

"Yes, Dauphine hobbled in on her crutches. She'll be coming in every day, until you finish working her to death."

Bobby was, in theory, against the notion of gainful employment. In practice, he was a tenured history professor who spent as little time as possible on campus. He came from a family that had only needed to work for a living in recent years…which, in Bobby's world, meant that it had been more than a century since they were wealthy.

Bobby had not accepted this fate with good grace, but Faye was always impressed with the way Bobby managed to look like a rich man while living on a historian's budget. He might someday get used to drawing a paycheck, but she doubted he'd ever lose his vaguely imperious manner. And Faye hoped he never did. It suited his slim and well-groomed good looks. So did his scholarly-looking glasses and his slightly too-long crop of dark curls.

"Do you know anybody else who could help me with this project? Archaeologists, history grad students, warm bodies who can run errands and do grunt work…I can use them all."

"I'll put out some feelers. Would you like anything else, dear Cousin? Perhaps someone to fan you with palmettos and feed you peeled and seeded muscadine grapes while your minions do your work for you?"

This sounded pretty good to Faye right that minute.

"If you knew anybody like that, they'd be fanning and feeding *you*, Bobby."

"And how do you know that they're not?"

Faye had to love Bobby's style. He gave her no choice.

"Do you have any lawyers on your long, long list of very dear friends? Preferably some who owe you favors?"

"Lawyers? Why do you need a lawyer?" His voice dropped a conspiratorial half step. "You've been arrested, and you've just wasted your phone call talking about work. Am I right?"

"No. I haven't been arrested."

"Then *Joe's* been arrested. I always knew that man had a shifty look about him. My lady love disagrees with me, but just because she's a police detective doesn't mean she's not wrong. Joe has the kind of virile good looks that make me hate him on principle. I think his muscles cloud Jodi's perspective."

Oh, joy. Bobby was sallying forth for another conversational joust.

"Focus, Bobby. We're talking about my friend's legal needs, not your jealous heart. There's nothing shifty about Joe, and there's nothing wrong with Jodi's perspective, except for the fact that she's still planning to marry *you*. Joe has *not* been arrested. There are plenty of true scandalous tales in this world for you to spread. There's no need to make one up."

"Well, you do have a point there. People have been misbehaving for millennia. This is why I love the study of history so completely. Okay, you win. Tell me why you need a lawyer. I'll shut up and listen."

"Thank you." Faye tried to gather her thoughts. Why did every conversation with Bobby leave her flustered? "I have a young friend who recently lost her mother. The mother's husband showed up with a will, saying that her mother had died and left everything to him. The estate includes half of the houseboat my friend lives in with her grandmother, and the widower would just love to kick them out of it. And I don't think the rest of the

houseboat belongs to the grandmother, either. My friend—her
name is Amande—"

"Pretty name."

"Yes, isn't it? Well, Amande is terrified that she and her
grandmother are going to lose their home."

"How old is Amande?" Faye was surprised at how completely
Bobby's tone had changed from playful to businessman-crisp.
"Do you know who owns the other half of the houseboat?"

"She's sixteen. And I believe her mother's half-sister owns the
other half of it. I have no idea why the two sisters were letting
Amande's grandmother use the boat. The dead woman, Justine,
had been estranged from her stepmother for years, and her half-
sister, Didi, didn't impress Joe as the generous type."

"They were half-sisters? Which parent did they share? And
is he still alive?"

"Their father. He's been dead for quite some time."

"Look. I studied the history of the Louisiana legal system
for two whole semesters, and I still only learned enough to be
dangerous. The whole system is counterintuitive, but this situation sounds relatively straightforward…if you can call anything
about our inheritance laws straightforward."

He sighed. "I wish we were in the same room so I could sketch
out a family tree and draw you a picture. Let's see how well I
can do with words. It sounds like the houseboat was not community property, and the dead man left his wife a usufruct on it,
either because he drew up his will that way or probably because
he left no will at all. The actual ownership of the boat went to
his children, but his wife has the use of the houseboat until she
dies. I'm guessing that's true of any other non-community assets
that he left."

Faye made a mental note to check Florida law, not to mention the wording of Joe's will and her own. "Poor Miranda…
she lost her husband and everything, all at once."

"Yes. Here's the important thing: Do not, under any circum-
stances, let your friend's grandmother do anything stupid like
hand over the boat. Not until she talks to a lawyer who knows

Louisiana law. Just because the man has a will showing that part, or even all, of the houseboat belongs to him doesn't mean that he has the right to evict her."

"Amande will be so relieved."

"And another thing…make sure the lawyer is looking after Amande's interests, not just her grandmother's. Amande may not have all that much to fear from her mother's husband."

"Amande's grandmother is meeting with her lawyer this afternoon, and she's actually asked me to sit in on the meeting. She respects education, and she wanted someone she could trust to explain things to her. I'm flattered that she feels that way. Anyway, I understand that the will is pretty straightforward. Everything goes to him. How a woman could cut her own child out…"

Bobby's voice went past businessman-crisp, going straight to evangelist-intense. "She *can't*. Or rather, she couldn't, back when she was alive. That's what I'm trying to tell you. Louisiana inheritance law recognizes 'forced heirs.' Most of the time, you can't just cut your children out of your will. The law forces you to leave them *something*. My guess is that, when the dust settles, Amande will find out that she owns a quarter of her mother's property, with the rest going to her mother's widower. That's going to put her interests at odds with her grandmother's, especially if there is other property besides the houseboat. Even more important, her lawyer needs to find out what else her mother—Justine, was it?—owned at the time of her death. Justine's husband may be forced by law to share it with Amande, no matter what that will says."

"I understand that there's some oil company stock. Maybe other stuff, but these are not rich people."

"It doesn't matter. Rich people fight over thirty million dollars. Homeless people will fight with the same intensity over thirty dollars. Or three. I'm a historian and I'm here to tell you that devastating wars have been fought over truly trivial sums. You've told me that Amande's aunt is not a nice person, and neither is her mother's widower. I think it's likely that your sixteen-year-old friend is now co-owner, along with those two, of a houseboat and some stock. This is not an insignificant pile of property. Any sixteen-year-old in that situation needs an advocate. If she's your friend, you need to help her find one."

◇◇◇

Bobby hung up the phone with a smile that was unseemly for a man who cultivated the illusion that he was way too sophisticated to be amused by much. Faye was fun. There was no other word for her. If she and Joe lived in New Orleans, he and Jodi would force them to be their best friends, whether they liked it or not.

Though Bobby's family had lost their old money sometime in the early nineteenth century, he still possessed their blue blood, so he was a member of the right Mardi Gras krewe and he got invitations to all the best parties. Faye, Joe, and Jodi would ordinarily have been frozen out of that society forever, because the partygoers would have been at a loss for anything to say to someone whose family wasn't traceable back to eighteenth-century France. Or, in some cases, seventeenth-century France. Actually, Faye's bloodlines intersected with his own slightly, but her family lost their high social standing in this part of the world at about the time they started pronouncing their name "LAWNG-champ," instead of "LAWN-shaw."

However, if the four of them sailed into a high-society soirée on the strength of Bobby's bloodlines, they would set the party on its ear. Joe would be fetchingly dressed in a white tie version of the buckskin clothes he made himself, with a feather poked into his long, thick ponytail. Jodi would regale staid partygoers with nausea-inducing police tales involving bodily fluids, and the crowd would love it the way they loved those CSI shows on TV.

And Faye would look like a tiny queen, swathed in a silk gown she'd sewn herself. She would behave herself until some boor called her "Little Lady" and made conversation by asking what her husband did for a living while she was lounging around getting her nails done. Then, with a single short sentence, she'd flatten him with the sheer force of her intellect, and all hell would break loose.

It would be a hoot. He wondered what it would take to get Faye and Joe to leave Joyeuse.

There was the rub. Faye was about as likely to leave her island home as Bobby was to leave New Orleans. Damn. Nevertheless, Mardi Gras was only ten months away, give or take. If he started now, he could wangle a pile of invitations to events so exclusive that even Faye wouldn't be able to say no.

The woman had better start sewing silk dresses. She was going to need a lot of them.

Bobby looked around him. He loved old maps, and he loved New Orleans. The historic collection housed in this place was as close to heaven as he cared to get without dying. How fortunate that he could hang out here, carefully fingering the merchandise, and call it work.

At a computer in the corner, he spotted a familiar face, a sunburned and freckled man in his mid-twenties with sunbleached hair. Bobby had seen him several times lately. He didn't look old enough to hold a PhD, but maybe he was a grad student. People who hung out at the Historic New Orleans Collection tended to be academics, and they tended to specialize in fields like history and geography, so they didn't often get sunburned. Like Bobby, they generally had the complexions of bookworms.

Archaeologists were an exception. If they weren't smart enough to wear hats and long sleeves and sunscreen, they always looked sunbaked. Maybe he should introduce himself to the man, in case he was someone who could help his cousin Faye. Bobby, like most people of his social standing, knew the importance of networking. Success in life was generally tied to who you knew and who knew you.

He walked over and extended a well-manicured hand. "I'm Bobby Longchamp. I've seen you here before. I know my way around these maps as well as anybody. If you're not finding what you need, maybe I can help."

The young man extended a hand. His fingernails were way too clean for an archaeologist. Bobby knew what Faye's hands looked like in the evenings, despite her protective gloves. He also knew the vigorous scrubbing and soaking she used to keep her hands in a ladylike condition. It almost worked, but her cuticles stayed red and rough as a result. This man had the delicate skin of a natural blond. If he played in the dirt on a daily basis, Bobby would be able to tell.

"My name's Dane. I think I've found what I'm looking for, but thanks."

Bobby looked over his shoulder at the list of maps Dane was planning to request. They all centered on a shallow portion of Barataria Bay that was dotted with small islands. Dane wanted to see bathymetric maps and fishing maps and satellite imagery of the area, and he didn't just ask for current maps. He'd asked for historic ones. Bobby noticed that he'd requested no topographic maps of the islands. So he was interested in the water, not the land.

If the man had only wanted to fish, current fishing maps would have been sufficient. He could have bought those at any marina, while he was buying bait and beer. Considering the rate the land changed down near the mouth of the river, historic fishing maps were fairly useless. Nevertheless, Dane wanted to see them. Bobby wondered why.

The bathymetric maps were something yet again. They would have been total overkill for fishing, when depth finders could be bought so cheaply. The man wanted to know the shape of the land beneath the water, and his desire for old bathymetric maps said that he wanted to know how the land under the water *used* to be shaped. Curious.

His request for a series of aerial photographs of the bay through time wasn't surprising, given the other requests.

Bobby took a stab in the dark. "Are you an oceanographer?"

Dane gave him a dark look, then hunched over his work as if to dismiss Bobby from his presence. That moment of non-collegiality made Bobby think, *Not an academic.* By process of elimination, Bobby knew what the man was studying. More precisely, he knew what the man was up to.

He was interested in the seafloor of that bay. He couldn't care less about the islands dotting it. And he wasn't an academic.

Bobby totted up the evidence and checked Dane over one more time. Yep, the hair was so short as to be barely there. Combined with a sunburn and soaked-clean fingernails, a haircut that would be no trouble underwater and would dry quickly made him look an awful lot like a diver. Secretiveness made him look an awful lot like a diver who had found something underwater that he didn't want to share.

The man's attitude had pissed Bobby off, so he took revenge in his trademark style, through a few well-chosen words delivered in a tone that sounded oh-so-friendly.

He clapped his hand on the young man's shoulder, as if he were giving a little brotherly advice. Then he put him in his place. "Many people wiser than you have wasted their lives looking for treasure in those waters. It's not there. Or, if it is, the Mississippi has buried it in mud. And even if it *is* possible for you to find it…I think you should let it rest with the bones of the people who went down with the ship."

Dane gave him a sharp look that told Bobby he'd guessed right.

Bobby released Dane's shoulder and watched the man pull away. He pretended not to notice, and he kept talking. "I can't stop you from looking for treasure. Even if you find it, it's up to the authorities to decide whether you broke any laws doing it. But I *can* do one thing. I will be watching the way you handle those maps. Some of them are priceless. Break one rule, and I'll have you kicked out of this place for good."

It was good to be a tenured professor, because it meant that Bobby punched no time clock and nobody cared if he sat at the Historic New Orleans Collection day and night, as long as his classes got taught. He had no classes today, so Dane would need to get used to having a spectator.

After about thirty minutes of spectating, Bobby noticed that Dane's short hair was damp with sweat. The man was not cool under fire.

The sound of heavy and uneven footfalls entered the room ahead of the woman who made them. Bobby knew that Dauphine had returned before he saw her face.

Dauphine had always been the kind of person who caught one's attention, even before she got hurt. Now her eccentric clothing and voodoo-priestess demeanor were ramped up a notch by her injury. The crutch under her arm looked like it had been whittled out of snakewood by an evil leprechaun, and her usually benign expression was twisted into a scowl by the sheer pain of walking. It took her several minutes to gather her research materials and settle her significant bulk into a chair. Bobby could see that Dane was watching her.

Good. It never paid to turn one's back on a voodoo mambo.

Bobby walked over to pass a little conversation with Dauphine, as he would have in any case, just because he liked her. After laughing at her description of little Michael's adorable naughtiness, he leaned down to whisper in her ear.

"See that blond man in the corner? Whenever you see him in here, make him feel unwelcome."

"You want I should hex him?"

"No. Well, probably not. If I change my mind about hexing him, I'll let you know. I just want you to keep him on his toes."

Thus commenced a very entertaining interval for Bobby. This was good because Bobby loved being entertained.

Every now and then, Dauphine looked up from her work and fixed her gaze on Dane. She left it there until he noticed, and no longer. After she'd seen him sneak a glance her way, she would shift her attention back to the book in front of her, but her hands continued in their intimidation campaign. They crept into her pockets or they stroked the amulet at her throat or they softly caressed a curl at her temple. She doodled spirals on her notepad, first with her right hand and then with her left. Even Bobby wondered what in the hell she was doing.

Within an hour, the pressure was too much for Dane. He was gone, and Dauphine walked out right behind him, taking her terror campaign into the streets.

Bobby was alone again, free to enjoy the leisure to research that came with the coveted title of tenured professor.

Chapter Eleven

Miranda fastened a beady eye on Faye. As usual, her glare made Faye want to take two steps back. This was impossible, because she was sitting down.

Miranda might respect education, and she might have asked Faye to help her interact with her lawyer, but that didn't make her responsive to every last suggestion Faye might make. She was out-and-out confrontational over the notion that Amande might need her own legal representation.

"My granddaughter already has a lawyer. He's my lawyer. Bernard Reuss took care of things for me when my husband died. He can take care of this…nuisance."

Miranda flapped a disgusted hand wave in the direction of the copy of Justine's will lying on her dining table. Tebo had donned reading glasses and was studying it, word by word.

"Bernard will be here any minute. You see how good he treats me? He comes to *me* when I need him."

Faye saw Didi perk up when she heard that a lawyer was on his way. The woman had been huddled on a low stool in the corner, silent and morose. Faye thought her sisterly grief exuded a look-at-me smell. Now that a man who probably had money was on his way, Didi had somehow managed to shove her grief aside. She was instantly on her feet, checking herself out in the mirror.

When the esteemed lawyer Bernard Reuss arrived, he wore a short-sleeved shirt with a wrinkled tie. His briefcase was tucked under his arm, because the handle was broken. Shaking Miranda's hand with a nasal "Afternoon, Ma'am. So sorry for the loss of your son," he then gave an obsequious nod to everyone else in the room, one at a time. A ski-slope nose and slickly combed-back black hair gave Reuss the look of an opossum. His habit of shyly ducking his head after each sentence enhanced the effect.

Faye wasn't big on judging people by their appearance, but the practice of law involves a certain amount of showbiz. Crackerjack attorneys manipulate their images to influence judges and sway juries. Success breeds success. Reuss' appearance was so far from awe-inspiring that Faye had to wonder whether he made house calls because he didn't have an office. Or because Miranda was his only client.

Faye had been fascinated to watch Didi turn on her sex appeal in advance of the lawyer's arrival. Her eyes had softened. Her lips had dampened. Her hands had slowly run down her torso, smoothing her tank top over a slim waist and full hips. At the sight of Bernard Reuss, that sex appeal had flipped off like a switch. A slump now hid the graceful body, and sullenness clouded the eyes. Faye could have sworn she saw the woman's lips dry up on the spot. She wondered if Didi did these things consciously, or if some women just had the knack of alluring men without really having to think about it.

If this was Miranda's idea of a perfectly good lawyer, then she was welcome to him, but Faye wouldn't have chosen him for Amande. She locked eyes with Joe and raised her brows, but he was playing things cool.

Reuss pulled out a pair of drugstore reading glasses and looked over the will, then told Miranda essentially the same tale that Bobby had told Faye: her dead husband's property wasn't hers, but she could use it till she died. Then it would be divided up between her husband's children—Didi and Justine. Since Justine was dead, her part of the estate would be divided between *her* heirs—Amande and Steve. As much as Justine might have wished to disinherit the daughter she'd abandoned, Louisiana wouldn't let her do it. Amande was a forced heir. The state said that she got a quarter of her mother's worldly goods and there was nothing anybody could do about it.

Hooray for Louisiana! Faye thought.

Didi watched Reuss' mouth the entire time he spoke, as if that were the best way to calculate exactly what she'd be getting on the day her mother died. Tebo just kept fingering the will, as if it might magically reveal a way that he could also get a windfall that day. After all, she was *his* mother, too.

Faye was pretty sure he was out of luck. *Hooray for Louisiana!*, again.

All Amande had to say was, "So you mean we don't have to move?"

The wormy little man smiled, revealing teeth that were far whiter and more even than Faye would have predicted. "No, Darlin', you don't have to move. Nothing has to change for you at all."

He reached into his briefcase and pulled out a legal-sized file folder. "I'm compiling an inventory of Justine's estate. I don't think there's going to be much. When people die of cancer, there's usually a long period of unemployment prior to death. Even if her scumbag husband—"

"Scumbag. 'Zat a fancy legal word?" Tebo asked.

Reuss squared up the stack of papers in his hand. "Based on my client's description of Steve Daigle, and based on the police report on his visit to this boat, 'scumbag' seems plenty accurate."

Tebo leaned back in his chair and laughed.

The lawyer's whiny voice resumed. "As I was saying, the scumbag may have cleaned out their joint account, or he might have truly been forced to spend everything to take care of Justine in her final months. I'm also of the opinion that Mr. Daigle is the kind of person who spends everything that comes in, regardless, and his income is always erratic. I get the impression that he's a day laborer who works construction when he needs money and lays on his butt when he doesn't. I doubt that we're going to find that her estate has much in the way of cash. There's a car and a boat in Daigle's name, purchased before the marriage, so my client has no claim on them. There is no vehicle in Justine's name."

"Shit," Tebo said, though Faye couldn't figure out why. He was not one of Justine's heirs, and he couldn't have been very emotionally invested in the idea of Amande having a car to drive when she got her license. She figured he was just enjoying the "something for nothing" aspect of the inheritance process, even though he wasn't the beneficiary.

"We can force an inventory of her personal property, provided Mr. Daigle hasn't already had a great big garage sale. I think it's worth doing. The little lady is entitled to a quarter of it, and she deserves to have some things that belonged to her mother, even if they're only of sentimental value."

Amande didn't respond. Faye couldn't imagine how the girl would feel about having something her mother had treasured—a necklace, say, or a picture or a jewelry box. Amande had to feel like she herself should have been her mother's treasure.

"I went through my files from the settlement of your late husband's estate, Mrs. Landreneau, looking for a record of the property that went directly to Justine upon his death."

Didi sat up straight and proved that she'd been listening. "*I* didn't get anything directly when Daddy died. How come Justine did?"

He peered at Didi over the rims of his reading glasses. "You're no relation to Justine's natural mother. Why should you get any portion of the property that came to Justine from her mother through your father? Once upon a time, Justine's mama died without leaving a will, and Justine was an only child, so any property that had been her mother's at the time of the marriage went to her, while her daddy got just a usufruct. When he died, she got control of what was rightfully hers."

Reuss made this pronouncement crisply, then turned his attention back to the matter at hand. Didi was dismissed. Faye thought that maybe Didi shouldn't have turned off the sex appeal.

"Justine's inheritance from her mother wasn't anything to write home about. A set of sterling silverware. Some nice china. Crystal goblets. I hope that husband of Justine's didn't sell it all on eBay, because someday the little lady here will have a place of her own. It would be nice for her to be able to set a table with heirlooms from her family. That's about it, except for one piece of real estate." He took his glasses off to look Amande directly in the eyes. "It's worthless, dear. I'm sorry about that. Still, a quarter of it is yours. Too bad you have to share it with the scumbag."

"Real estate? Do you mean land? I own a piece of land?"

Didi turned jealous eyes on the excited girl.

"Yes, you do, part of it, but don't get too worked up," the lawyer said with an indulgent smile. Faye suspected that he was the father of a daughter himself. "Your island's small, and probably growing smaller by the year, what with saltwater intrusion and all. It's a little bitty island out in Barataria Bay, in the direction of Grand Terre. Here's the location." He handed her a photocopy of a map. "It's sinking, like everything else around here. There's a fishing shack that was filthy and bug-ridden when Justine inherited it, even before Katrina came through. It's probably still filthy and bug-ridden, and I doubt it has a roof anymore. The china and the crystal goblets and the silver service are worth more money than your island, Dear. Trust me."

Didi got up and flounced to the room she was sharing with Amande. Miranda went after her. It was the first maternal act Faye had seen from the woman, beyond an occasional harsh nag in Amande's direction.

Faye and Joe looked at each other and stood. They'd done their best for Amande. She had a lawyer. The girl's lawyer was also working for her grandmother, which wasn't optimal, and he looked like a marsupial, but he didn't appear to be completely ignorant of how to handle the situation. It was time to go. They had work to do.

Amande hopped up and followed them outside, brandishing her map, with the look of a teenager preparing to convince an adult to grant a wish. Faye hoped the wish wasn't too outlandish, because she didn't think she'd be good at telling a determined adolescent no. She should have known what that wish would be.

"Will you take me out to my island? Oh, please. I want to see it so bad!"

"You remember that Mr. Reuss said it was just a worthless spot of land? Even the shack on it is falling down. If we go out there, we'll be an hour in the boat, each way. There will be nothing to see when we get there. Then we'll have to turn around and come back."

Amande shrugged away those petty concerns. "I've got it all figured out. I know you two have a lot of work to do—"

Faye was impressed that any teenager was mature enough to factor other people's needs into an attempt to nag them to do something.

"—but I think this trip to my island will help you out."

Uh-oh. Amande was unreeling a plan that would make it worth their while to do her bidding. Faye smelled trouble. She was learning that dealing with an intelligent and shrewd adolescent could be a minefield. Michael was already showing an ability to manipulate that made Faye quake in her workboots when she looked ahead thirteen years.

"I've spent hours and hours looking at maps of Barataria Bay. I've studied new maps and historical maps and aerial photographs and fishing maps, trying to find the island where I found those silver coins. I know that area better than I know my backyard. Well, I don't have a backyard, but you know what I mean. Anyway…I think this is it! I think it's my island! Look!" She unrolled the photocopied map to show them.

Faye thought she just might have found someone who loved old maps as much as she and her cousin Bobby did. Hating herself for indulging the adult's urge to burst an enthusiastic young person's bubble, she went ahead and did it. "What are the odds that your island, out of the thousands of islands between here and the gulf, is the one where you found that coin all those years ago?"

"I think I've figured that out. Maybe my mother remembered the island from when her mother took her there when she was a little girl. When she was older, maybe my age, maybe she took Grandmère out there. Then, later, Grandmère took me. It was the perfect place for a picnic. Some trees big enough to give shade. Really good fishing. And the shack didn't seem like a shack, really. It was old, with interesting woodwork and peeling wallpaper and a cute little kitchen. It was like a dollhouse. That's what it was, a dollhouse. I loved it."

She rolled the map up into a tube and gave it a tender little pat. "A few years ago, Grandmère stopped hoping my mother would come back. I think she never wanted to go back to the island, because it reminded her of my mother when she was a girl. There were too many memories there."

She unrolled the map again and looked it over, as if she couldn't bear being separated from her very own piece of the world. "My grandmother doesn't forget much. I've never believed she didn't remember that picnic we took."

Faye found that she was talking like an adult again, and she hated herself for it yet again. "If your grandmother doesn't want you to go out there, we just can't take you, Amande."

The girl grabbed for one of Faye's hands with both of hers. "Please. You can't possibly understand this, but I've never had a piece of ground that was mine. Not even a rented piece of ground. Look at my home." The houseboat rocked slightly beneath their feet. "I can't go out in my backyard when I'm mad at Grandmère, 'cause I don't have one. I have to go sit at that picnic table that belongs to the marina, and I can only do that if nobody's using it. And then I have to hope that none of the drunks from the bar decide to come blow their tobacco-y beer breath in my direction. That island's mine….partly mine…and I want to see it. I've just got to have a boat of my own again, so I can go there when I need to be away from people."

That last sentence rattled around in Faye's head. There were many reasons why she kept her impractical island home, and the need to escape from human weirdness was one of them.

"Here's the deal," Amande said. "I know you need to work. If I understand your project right, maybe you need to go check out this island where I found some very old Spanish silver. Maybe there was a pirate lair there. Maybe there was a shipwreck nearby. Maybe it used to be a big island and there was a trading post there or a plantation or even a little town. You won't know if you don't go check." The golden brown eyes narrowed. "And you can't go check without the property owner's permission. You need to see my island. And you *want* to see my island. To get my permission, you have to take me along."

Faye questioned whether Amande had the clout she thought she did. Most of the island actually belonged to Steve, but Faye was willing to overlook that little detail. She actually did need to go to Grand Terre, which was in its general direction. Grand Terre was the site of Jean Lafitte's pirate lair and it was right in the path of the coming slick, so she needed to get there fast before the oil did.

Amande's island might take the brunt of that slick as well, but Faye didn't feel like being the one to tell her. She was starting to warm up to the idea of taking the girl out there. If she and Joe were lucky enough to find evidence of human activity as old as that coin, then it would be nice to have someone with them who had seen the island before it was reconfigured by Katrina.

"All right," she said. "I'll talk to your grandmother. If she gives her permission, you can go."

Amande's eyes positively glittered as she placed her final chip on the table. "Tell her you need a babysitter, or you won't be able to finish your work. I'll work for free if you take me to my island, but don't tell my grandmother that. If she thinks I'm pulling in a paycheck, she'll let you take me to Cuba, as long as you get me home by dinner."

Flushed with victory, she said good-bye and turned to go back into the houseboat. Tebo's voice floated out an open window. He was making his opening move on his mother's estate, despite the fact that she wasn't even dead yet.

Faye heard him say to Reuss, in a man-to-man kind of voice, "Surely my mother owned something when she married Landreneau. It's not like she was a deadbeat welfare queen. Won't all of that pass to me when she dies, now that my brother Hebert's dead?"

Faye was so interested in Reuss' response that she put a hand on Amande's arm to keep her from opening the door and interrupting Tebo's gambit.

Reuss was silent for an instant longer than necessary, which gave Tebo time to correct his insensitivity toward his dead brother by adding, "Hebert...God rest his soul."

Reuss showed how well he knew his client Miranda by asking Tebo a few rapid-fire questions.

"Your father died when you and your brother were both still living at home?"

"Correct."

"Did you work and contribute to the household when you were a strapping sixteen-year-old and your little mother was supporting two boys who ate a whole lot?"

"Um...no."

"Did your brother?"

"Oh, hell, no. He never worked a steady job in his life."

"I didn't think so. Did your mother ever bail you out of jail? Or did she ever help you pay restitution on any of the several occasions you were on probation?"

"Well...hmmm...yes. I believe so."

"Your brother?"

"If his probation got paid for, it must have been Mother that done it. I don't know how else it would've happened."

"Then why on earth would you think that your poor mother had one red cent when she married Mr. Landreneau, or that she ever accumulated any money afterward when she was continually bailing out her worthless sons? If you disagree with me, then I suggest you get your own attorney. I work for Mrs. Landreneau and her granddaughter."

Reuss squared up the stack of papers in his hand yet again, then threw out a bit of advice that wasn't strictly legal. "As my client's advocate, I also suggest that you learn to show a little grief over your dead brother, even if you don't feel any. My client has lost a son. If her surviving son was much of a man, he'd be looking for the man that killed his brother, instead of looking for a way to get hold of some money or property that he didn't earn and that isn't his."

Faye was trying hard not to laugh, but she thought she might just choke. She waited until Amande went inside, then she caught Joe's eye. He'd obviously heard everything she had.

"Until this minute, I thought that man was the poorest excuse for a lawyer I ever saw," she said. "It's entirely possible I was wrong."

Joe threw Michael over one shoulder and the boy squealed. "It finally happened," he said. "Faye was wrong. When we're old and I tell our grandchildren the story of this moment, it'll start with, 'We were in Louisiana and it was a Thursday.'"

Faye punched him on the arm.

Joe leaned down and kissed the top of her head. "Don't make me drop the baby."

Chapter Twelve

The island was one of dozens. Hundreds. Thousands. It all depended on how you counted them, and on whether you had a healthy imagination. At what point did a tiny patch of marsh grass achieve the stature necessary to deem it an "island?"

When Faye spread a map out beside her, she could see the vast Mississippi delta, speckled by land and splashed by water. It was a good thing she had a GPS and the coordinates of Amande's island, or they'd be picking their way through this watery maze forever.

"There it is! I see it! There it is!"

Out in open water, well away from the grassy marshland, a spot of land poked up. It was far more deserving of the word "island" than the blobs of mud they'd seen so far, but it didn't remotely resemble Faye's own island. Joyeuse had supported plantation agriculture and a hundred inhabitants in its heyday. This island sported a thicket of scrubby trees and a shack covered with peeling paint.

If Faye had turned her back on the island and looked only at Amande's face, she would have thought the boat was headed for Shangri-La.

"It's just like I remember," the girl said, hopping overboard to help Joe as he raised the motor and dragged the boat onto the sand. "See! There's even a beach."

And there *were* a few square yards of exposed sand in front of the house. Even Faye wasn't scrooge-ish enough to criticize

Amande's sand for being less sugary-white than Pensacola's. Faye's own beach wasn't big and it wasn't tourist-worthy, but she'd spent many pleasant hours there.

Amande stood in the open front door of the fishing shack. "The roof's still on!" she cried, like a realtor pointing out the finer selling points of a suburban ranch home. "It's not leaking in the kitchen much at all. Come see!"

But Faye didn't budge. She'd found an eroded spot of soil near the copse of trees at the center of the island. The trees' roots held the sand around them in place, but rainwater and wind was carrying other soil to sea quickly. Faye's experienced eyes saw bits of weathered wood protruding from the newly exposed soil.

"Joe!"

A two-headed beast appeared. The top head, Michael's, looked completely ecstatic to be seated in a backpack that made him even taller than his daddy.

Faye pointed at the splintered wood in the sand. Joe squatted, keeping Michael carefully balanced.

"Don't you think I need some gloves and a little aluminum foil?" she asked.

"And some tweezers. I'll get them."

Fortunately, Joe kept such necessities around whenever they were working. There was no knowing when they'd need to collect a sample for carbon dating. She'd have the supplies she needed in the time it took Joe to lope to the boat and back.

If this wood turned out to be old, and if the site turned out to be significant enough to be included in her report, then Amande would never let her hear the end of it.

Amande poked her head around a tree. "I see you found the spot where I uncovered one of the coins. You found something else interesting, too, didn't you? *Didn't* you???"

Faye couldn't hide her grin.

Amande crossed her arms and leaned her head, capped with a fuchsia hat, back against the tree's trunk. "I told you so."

◇◇◇

Faye had bagged the side trip to Grand Terre. She'd spent too much time canvassing Amande's pitiful little island for more old stuff. She hadn't found much—mostly soda and beer cans from the past three decades—but the wood fragments that she'd collected had the look of age.

All the way back to the marina, Amande had fed Michael crackers and jostled him on her lap and lifted up his hat to rumple his hair and just generally distracted him from the fact that his life jacket made him sweaty and miserable. She also reapplied his sunscreen at least three times. The girl was certainly earning the salary Faye wasn't paying her.

"God, I miss my boat," she was saying for the tenth time.

Like Faye, Amande had piddled around in boats for as long as she could remember. Looking at Michael in his teensy life jacket, Faye knew that she planned for him to have that same freedom to explore the watery world. She was also pretty sure she was never going to be able to let the child out of her sight. Not even when he was forty. She had no idea how she was going to reconcile those two things.

"Grandmère used to keep me supplied with fuel and bait, as long as I kept the freezer full of fish. That wasn't so easy, back when I had to go to school every day. Now that I can do my schoolwork when I damn well please—"

She checked to see whether Joe or Faye was going to bark at her for cursing. Neither did.

"—now that I'm homeschooling, I could go out at dawn every day of the week. That's when you're *supposed* to fish. I don't know why Grandmère got so weird on me all of a sudden. I mean... she took my *boat*. And she *sold* it."

Amande sank into a funk for a moment, but Michael kept poking his fingers in her mouth until she gave up pouting.

"I guess I *was* spending a lot on gas, but she should've said something. I could've gotten a job. Or I could've saved gas by going out a little less. I really think she just didn't want me to go anywhere. Her kids are all gone, and they don't pay her any attention, none of them. When I leave, she'll be really lonely. But I have to go. I can't live on that houseboat and make dolls for the rest of my life. Can I?"

Amande had been boatless now for three months, with no end in sight. Faye foresaw an adolescent rebellion on the horizon. More than that. An adolescent explosion. Maybe getting her off the houseboat for the day had delayed that explosion for a while.

Once at the marina, Amande helped Faye and Joe unload the boat. Faye enjoyed watching the way Amande kept casting sidewise glances at the handsome young blond expertly piloting a boat loaded with scuba gear into its slip for the night. Further away, Faye saw Steve Daigle fueling the strangest looking boat she'd ever laid eyes on. Actually, the boat itself was nothing more than a johnboat painted in the dappled tans and greens of a duck hunter's camouflage, but the motor wasn't like anything she'd ever seen. A shaft as long as Faye extended diagonally from it, meaning that the propeller was several feet behind the boat's stern.

Joe saw where she was looking. "It's made for shallow water— really shallow water with a muddy bottom. That means it has to be air-cooled. If it was water-cooled like other motors, it'd be sucking mud all the time, which ain't good for moving metal parts. You can run it in an inch of water, if the bottom's soft, but it'll tear that bottom right up. I don't think that's good for the fish, personally. They hang out down there, and they gotta lay their eggs someplace."

Faye took this to mean that Joe wasn't going to be wanting to trade the perfectly serviceable motor on his johnboat for a fish-egg-destroying beast like Steve's. She was glad, because she thought it was ugly, and she was enough of a girl to want her boats to be sleek and pretty.

Michael toddled along between Faye and Amande all the way back to the cabin, while Joe stayed at the marina to talk to Manny about renewing the rental for another week.

"I'd better check in with Grandmère. It's almost dark. Thank you *so* much for taking me out to my island."

Faye's hands were full and Michael was on the cabin floor in full tantrum mode, so Faye just nodded and said, "Go. I'll talk to you tomorrow."

◇◇◇

Later, Faye would try not to beat herself up for being slow to respond to Amande's call. At the time, she'd been crooning tunelessly to Michael, who had finally gotten tired of screaming for no reason. Her ears were ringing from those screams. Those ears had been bombarded all day by boat noise and wind noise and water noise. And those ears were forty-one years old.

She would never know how many times Amande cried, "Faye! Faye, please come!" When she finally heard it, she snatched Michael off the floor and ran. Joe had been further away, but his ears were abnormally good. He was also a lot younger. He reached Amande on the deck of the houseboat a second before Faye did

"Grandmère wasn't here when I got home. She's always here. I checked the marina store, even though she hardly ever even goes that far. If I were old enough to buy her rum, she'd never have any reason to leave the boat at all. I'm the only one that ever goes over there. I shop for the groceries and everything else we need. She just doesn't ever *go* anywhere." As if to emphasize her grandmother's ever-presence, she repeated herself. "She's always here."

Faye moved toward the door and Amande said, "I told you, she's not there."

A faint shake in her young voice, as lovely in its way as a trilling bird's song, told Faye everything. The girl had marched, chin-up, through a childhood that would have leveled most kids. She had only recently looked a corpse in the face with more composure than most adults could muster. And her mother was freshly dead. Amande was an extraordinary young woman. Her grandmother had to share some of the credit for that victory.

Miranda was remote. Truth told, Miranda was strange. Nevertheless, she had provided Amande with a home, when she wasn't even the girl's natural grandmother. She had scraped together the money to raise a child who didn't appear to have ever gone hungry or been without shoes that fit. She had filled that most basic of parental roles: she was always there.

Until now.

Chapter Thirteen

It doesn't take long to search a houseboat, and it doesn't take two people. Three people and a toddler would have just tripped over each other, so Faye had left Joe on deck with Amande and Michael. She knew first-person how comforting Joe's brand of silent caring could be.

Built for economy of space, rooms on a houseboat are small. Furniture is swapped out for built-in drawers that lock, so that their contents don't spill out when seas are rough. Beds are bolted down, and the space underneath is filled with more drawers. There is no place to hide.

Faye took longer to search the boat than she needed, because she wanted so badly to find something that would reassure Amande. Maybe, somewhere, there was a note saying, "We needed tea and the marina was out. I'm walking to the grocery store." Or maybe even, "Walking to the liquor store because the voodoo gods and I need some rum."

Even if the note said something awful like, "Having chest pains. Called 911," it would be better than this emptiness.

Few things were out of place. The drawers in Miranda's room had been pushed closed yet not locked, which wasn't expected behavior for someone who had lived aboard a boat for many years. Faye didn't like their look.

What if she *was* looking at evidence of a thief? Had that thief simply left after stealing from a widow and a child? What if the intruder had been interrupted at work? Faye swallowed hard when she thought about what this might mean for an elderly woman caught unaware.

Faye's heart sank when she entered Amande's room. Several of her artifact drawers also stood open and unlocked, and Faye just didn't think Amande would leave her treasures vulnerable to dust. She was afraid to touch anything, lest she destroy fingerprints, but she knew that any thief would have had the brains to walk away with Amande's silver American money. That part of the girl's treasure was surely gone. She prayed that this thief was too unsophisticated to recognize the old Spanish coins for what they were, but she didn't check to see if they were still there, for fear of disturbing a crime scene.

Other than the open drawers, Faye saw no disarray in Amande's room, other than discarded girl clothes, just as Faye would have expected of a teenager who'd been ecstatic that morning over the day's trip to her island. When Faye was sixteen, she would probably have tried on four pairs of shorts before deciding which ones to wear, too.

Delayed reactions are not uncommon when a person is caught unaware. When Faye remembered the scene later, she wasn't surprised that it had taken her a few moments to realize that she should call the police. The mind naturally takes some time to shift gears from, "I wonder where Miranda is. I'll look for her," to, "Something is wrong here, and I'm afraid for Miranda. I'll call the police." It wasn't surprising that archaeology-obsessed Faye's mind first registered that she needed to report a crime when she saw that Amande's artifacts had been disturbed.

She pulled her phone out of her pocket and backed out of the room, but it made no sense to close her eyes. She could continue looking around her, cataloging details that could help in any crime investigation that might be forthcoming. As her fingers felt for the 911 buttons, she heard her own thoughts.

Eyes...

She could continue looking around...

Of course, she could continue looking around. Because she had eyes in her pocket.

Before dialing 911, Faye took a few seconds to snap photos of Amande's and Miranda's rooms with her phone. Backing out of the houseboat's front door, she snapped the kitchen and living quarters, as well as the bathroom, where she noticed a pile of male clothes and an ashtray full of cigarettes.

Faye stopped short. Where were Didi and Tebo? On second thought, maybe the clothes piled in Amande's normally neat room weren't hers at all. Didi seemed like the kind of woman who left a trail of discarded things behind her, never looking back.

Faye was drawn back to Miranda's room, as if its neat contents could tell her something about its mistress' whereabouts. The doll's heads still swung undisturbed from their ceiling hooks. Miranda's workbench in the corner was still festooned with straw for weaving and laden with tools to shape that straw. Her altar was still spread with pretty silk cloths, though the liquor had been drunk and the candles had been snuffed. Crumpled sheets of paper tossed onto the silk tablecloth caught Faye's eye. Some of them bore handwriting.

Faye was so curious that she reached out a finger and touched one of the pieces of paper, but she drew it back as if she'd touched a firebrand. Evidence. She needed to preserve this evidence. It was time to get out of there before she really screwed up, but Faye thumbed 911 into her phone *after* she took a photo of those slips of paper.

"I need to report a missing person and a burglary."

The operator asked her the right questions and she answered them, all the while uncrumpling those papers with her eyes and wishing she could touch them. Perhaps it was just as well that she couldn't, since she was probably risking a serious hex by disturbing a mambo's sacred space.

"I'm at the Lafitte Marina. I don't know the slip number, but it's Miranda Landreneau's houseboat. Somebody in the marina store can get you here."

The operator's tone said that she herself knew exactly where Miranda Landreneau lived, because everybody knew Miranda, but she was too professional and well-trained to let it show. Nevertheless, there was a note of concern in her voice when she said, "I'll have someone out there to you right away."

The papers on Miranda's altar bothered Faye. They hadn't been there before. Faye was certain of it. She remembered the altar as…pretty. Yes, pretty. It had been designed to look pleasing to the gods, yet now there was trash piled atop the silk. At least a dozen torn scraps of paper had been crumpled up and scattered over the altar.

Faye realized that she was risking a hexing, but she squatted down to get a good angle on one of those wadded-up scraps. In an old woman's spidery handwriting, it bore a single name, with a line drawn through it:

$$\text{Steve Daigle}$$

She took a picture while squatting, to document Steve Daigle's hexing. Now that she'd read the name in its entirety, she could read bits of Steve's name on each of the others. Faye was certain that they were all the same.

One of the candlesticks adorning the altar attracted her attention. Its base was a pewter skull so small and understated that she hadn't noticed it until this minute. Under it was another scrap of paper. Faye could read the last four letters of a name, written in the same spidery script:

$$\text{igle}$$

Steve Daigle, again. Justine's widower. In the short span of time since Faye was last in this room, Steve had been the focus of Miranda's voodoo-soaked brain.

Remembering Steve's behavior when he first met his step-mother-in-law, Faye would say that Miranda had possessed several good reasons to hex the man. As she looked over the altar again quickly, before going outside to wait for help, she brushed at her eye, which was prickling strangely. Big mistake.

Touching the rim of her right eyelid with her right forefinger made that eye stop prickling and commence burning. She rushing to the kitchen sink to wash out her eye, but remembered at the last minute that she shouldn't even touch the sink. Damn. Instead, she squinched the eye shut and pressed her left palm into it, while she studied her right hand with her good eye. A red powder smudged the pads of its fingers.

Its familiar look, coupled with the burning in her eye, prompted her to lick her index finger, which in retrospect seemed rather foolish. That hand could've been covered with graveyard dust or ground-up cadaver bones or something else awful out of the voodoo priestess' apothecary, but not this time. The red powder was nothing more than cayenne pepper.

Writing down somebody's name, crossing it out, sprinkling cayenne pepper on it, then tossing the crumpled paper onto a skull-adorned altar…it seemed to Faye that these things meant something. And they probably did not mean that the man in question was the voodoo practitioner's best friend.

Rubbing her eye with the back of her hand in case she hadn't gotten all the cayenne off her fingertips, Faye found her blurry vision focusing on the refrigerator. Another scrap of paper was fastened to its door with a magnet shaped like the state of Louisiana. Faye quickly snapped a photo of it.

The same spidery handwriting was scrawled on it, although the letters and numbers weren't crossed through. It was a simple note written from Miranda to herself:

Sechrist, Friday, 2:00

It *was* Friday. Or was it?

Faye's internal calendar was so scrambled by her seven-day work weeks that she had to think for a moment to be sure. Yes. It was Friday.

Had Miranda met with someone named Sechrist that very day? Or were they planning to meet in a week? Or maybe they'd met the week before, and Miranda was careless with taking down her notes to herself. Or perhaps the note didn't refer to an individual. Maybe Miranda had a business meeting or a doctor's appointment or...something else unexpected.

Faye looked at her watch. It was barely six thirty. Miranda might still be at the Sechrist meeting, but four and a half hours was a very long time. Too bad the note didn't say where the meeting was supposed to happen. Faye suspected that Miranda would have preferred to meet at her own home, given the choice. But maybe he hadn't given her a choice. Maybe Miranda had gone to a perfectly innocent meeting and she was on her way back, only to find that her home had been invaded in her absence. Might this mean that she'd been lured away to clear a path for the burglar?

This was the best possible scenario that she could muster, because it meant that Miranda would be walking in the door any minute, so it was the one she would present to Amande.

There was nothing left to discover in the houseboat. Faye decided to stop stalling and go talk to Amande, but her questions never got asked. She stepped onto the open deck, just in time to hear sirens and to see marked cars approach, just as they had three short days before when Amande discovered her uncle's dead body in the water. The sirens made Michael clap his hands over his ears and scream, but Amande stood absolutely still and silent.

Was it possible that the 911 response had come so quickly? Faye didn't think it had been a minute since she hung up the phone. Something felt very wrong.

Not knowing what else to do, Faye moved close to the girl. Joe, with the squalling baby in his arms, hovered close on her other side. There was nothing to do now but wait to see what the sirens would bring.

Chapter Fourteen

Faye was glad that Amande didn't have to hear anything the sheriff said beyond the fact that her grandmother was dead. She'd pulled the weeping girl aside and let Joe handle the rest, but not before she'd had the presence of mind to tell the sheriff that she and Joe were "visiting relatives." Something inside her couldn't bear the thought of Tebo or Didi being the go-between for Amande with the law.

By the time a woman with salt-and-pepper hair and a sober business suit approached, Amande had dissolved into the tears that she'd probably needed to cry all week. First, she'd lost her mother, which had cost her the fantasy reunion anyone in her position would have harbored. Now Amande knew, beyond all doubt, that Justine wasn't going to miraculously appear and explain herself, then take her daughter out for a girls-only lunch and shoe-shopping trip. She would never have her dream mother.

And now she had lost the woman who had not been a dream grandmother. She had been a real grandmother to Amande, in every way but blood.

Perhaps Miranda's devotion to this homeless child of her ungrateful stepdaughter was in Faye's mind when she ramped up the lie she'd told the detective. When a business-suited woman introduced herself as Sally Smythe, telling them she was a representative of the Department of Children and Family Services, a vision of Amande being handed over to foster care had congealed in Faye's mind.

Perhaps the foster parents would be perfectly nice people, but would they live where a boat-dwelling girl could see the water? Would they be able to handle a child who was brilliant and quirky and strong without crushing those things out of her?

And what if they weren't perfectly nice people? Faye had heard stories about beatings and neglect and molestation...no. These things were not going to happen, not if she could help it.

Faye's only motivation for the lie was to stall the inevitable. She thought that, by keeping Amande out of the insatiable maw of the foster care system, even momentarily, she might be able to steer the girl into a living situation that she could...well... live with.

The woman had looked at Joe as he smoothed the hair back from the crying girl's face, then asked Faye, "Do I understand that the two of you were relatives of the victim?"

Faye gave her a quick yes, then asked the question that was at the front of her brain and, coincidentally, would have been an important question for a real relative, as well. "Does anybody know where her Aunt Didi and Uncle Tebo are?"

Ms. Smythe pursed her lips and said, "I'm told that they were easy to find. There aren't that many bars around here. When Mrs. Landreneau's daughter was found, she was winning a drinking contest against three large men. Vodka shots are her weapon of choice. Or so I'm told."

"Tebo?"

"He's in custody for public drunkenness."

"Do they really arrest people for that in Louisiana?" Faye asked. "It's the home of the drive-thru daiquiri bar."

"If they're drunk enough, and if they piss the arresting officer off badly enough, then yes. They do. Tebo succeeded on both those counts. He's a charming man."

Ms. Smythe studied Joe and Amande again. Joe had lifted Michael by the armpits and was making him fly around Amande's head in an obvious attempt to get her to laugh. It wasn't working much.

Ms. Smythe looked Faye in the eyes and said, "Please tell me that Tebo and his drunken sister are not the only relatives who might be able to take this girl. She doesn't look like she's had any instruction from them in the fine art of being a barfly. I'd rather not place her with someone who will expose her to that. Foster care might be preferable."

Trying to minimize the number of times she uttered an out-and-out lie, Faye said, "Well, they're certainly her closest relatives."

She wondered if the fact that she, Joe, and Michael were some of the few people in the county with skintones approaching Amande's would give just enough credence to her lies. Other than Amande, Faye's family, and Steve Daigle, Manny the marina manager was the only person of color in sight. This was a very white part of the world. Faye's family *looked* like Amande's relatives; therefore, they *were* Amande's relatives. How far could she push her luck with this bureaucrat?

Sally jerked her head in Amande's direction and started walking. Faye followed her.

Sticking out her hand, she shook Amande's and said, "Sally Smythe. We met after your Uncle Hebert passed. Remember? It's my job to make sure you're okay, and I'm going to do that."

Amande looked terrified. No, she looked like a lonely little girl. She'd lost her grandmother and her mother, and she was smart enough to have already figured out that Miranda's death changed everything when it came to the houseboat. She, Didi, and Steve would be splitting ownership of it, and her share would be by far the smallest. There was every likelihood that she'd be forced to leave her home. What did any of that matter, anyway, while she was too young to handle her own affairs?

All those things paled, now that the foster care system beckoned.

Faye was capable of pulling facts out of the air and making a decision so fast that she almost felt careless later, as if she should have agonized more over the problem and its solution. She didn't consciously weigh the risks that Amande's family presented against the burden an extra child would put on her own family. She just heard herself asking the social worker a question she hadn't planned to ask: "Will a distant cousin do for a temporary guardian, until you can decide on the best placement for Amande?"

"How distant?"

"I'm her…"

Not being a practiced liar, Faye hesitated a moment too long. She saw a change in Amande, as composure settled on her and she, too, decided what to do without taking the time to sweat over the details. In that instant Faye knew that Amande, though impossibly young, was unmistakably the kind of person any woman would want on her side in a crisis. The girl knew how to do what needed to be done.

"Fifth cousin," Amande stated coolly. "We're fifth cousins."

Joe, wanting to help, popped in with, "Once removed."

Faye was pretty sure that Joe didn't even know what "once removed" meant, in terms of cousins. She regained control of the conversation with a feeble, "But we're very close. Amande's our… very favorite cousin. We're staying in the area for a few weeks. Why don't you let us take charge of Amande while we're here? Can we do that without her formally entering foster care? Later, the family can meet with you and decide what's best for her."

Faye was frankly amazed that this feeble seat-of-the-pants ploy got her as far as it did, but Ms. Smythe could only do so much. When she heard Faye say, "We're staying in the area for a few weeks," she'd started shaking her head.

After Faye had stopped telling bald-faced lies long enough to take a breath, Sally had explained the way things were. "I can release her to family, or even close friends, if they have an acceptable place to stay, and if they pass the background check, and if they agree to come get fingerprinted tomorrow. For starters. It's the government we're talking about, and we're talking about the safety of a child. But you tell me you're not from around here. Where *are* you from?"

Faye said, "Florida," in the same tone of voice she might have said, "The third circle of Hell," because she had a feeling that either answer would have carried as much weight with the state of Louisiana.

Sally shook her head some more. "There are ways to put her in your custody, but we would have to work with our sister agency in Florida. We'd have to find out for certain that you had room in your home for her and that you were suitable parents, even temporarily."

"But tonight…" Amande quavered.

"No. I can't send you with these people tonight. They seem very nice, but no."

A taxi pulled up and Didi flung herself out. "My mother! What's happened to my mother?"

A uniformed officer stepped forward. "I'm sorry, Miss. We found her in the water, stabbed. She's dead."

"Like my half-brother." Didi's hands flew to her face in a gesture that looked sincere to Faye, who figured that even the most self-centered person in the world could possibly harbor feelings for her own mother.

"Yes, Miss." The officer gave her a look that said he was susceptible to the tears of manipulative women, if they were pretty. "I'm very sorry."

Didi backed away from him, blindly stumbling into the bench of Amande's favorite picnic table. She dropped onto the bench. In one fluid motion, she lifted both feet off the ground, swung them over the bench and under the picnic table, then dropped her face onto her folded arms. Her narrow shoulders shook, and Faye actually felt sorry for Didi when she realized that there was no one to put a comforting hand on those shoulders. It certainly wasn't her place to do it. Maybe when Tebo was released from jail, he might be able to muster up a morsel of sympathy for his half-sister.

Faye saw Sally studying Didi. The social worker paused, but she must have decided to leave the young woman alone with her grief. Instead of going to Didi, she took Amande by the elbow. Faye watched as Sally led Amande away from the crowd and spoke with her for a half hour or so. By this time, Didi had raised her head and wiped her eyes, so Sally sat down beside her, spending almost as much time with Didi as she had with Amande.

Faye and Joe had nearly decided to leave when Sally walked their way again, saying, "Well, Didi doesn't seem all *that* drunk. Not anymore. Of course, I've just stalled for an hour. I was trying to give Didi's liver a chance to catch up with her."

Faye had the sick feeling that Sally spent a lot of time deciding which unsuitable adult was going to be put in charge of which needy child.

"There's no law against drinking," Sally said, "and Didi didn't drive herself home from her afternoon in the bars, so she didn't break any laws tonight, not that I know of." She gestured toward Didi, whose head was once again resting on her crossed arms. Amande was sitting silently next to her, staring at nothing in particular. "That's no condition to be in when you're responsible for a child, but Didi had no way to know she'd be coming home to find herself in charge. If I leave Amande with her aunt, for the time being, the child will be able to stay here on this houseboat in her own home. She'll be with family. And will she have you two around to keep an eye on things?"

"For another week, at least," Faye said.

"Probably longer," Joe added helpfully.

"Well, foster care may be the best place for her, but I'm going to let Didi try. We can revisit the situation in a few days, sometime before you have to go home. Didi says she can be responsible for her niece."

"Half-niece." Faye didn't know why she'd felt compelled to correct the social worker. It had just popped out.

Sally waved Amande's and Didi's fragmentary kinship away with one weary hand. "You cannot imagine the snarled family webs I have to untangle in my line of work. This one isn't really all that bad."

From a distance, Faye watched Amande sit silently beside Didi. Not a word passed between them.

Sally was arranging several folders full of paperwork in her briefcase, but she saw where Faye was looking. "The girl is going to need therapy, after all she's been through. If you have any influence with Didi, please ask her not to neglect counseling for Amande after I move on to the next abandoned child." Then, mercifully, she left.

Faye watched the pale gray of the woman's suit fade into the early evening as she walked back to her car.

Faye wanted to rush after her and ask whether she had any information on Amande's father. There just had to be someone better than Didi who could take her...someone like Faye.

Stop it, she told herself. *You cannot assume permanent care of this child, and the state of Louisiana won't let you do that, anyway. You* have *a child. But it would be really great if you could find someone to take Amande for good...preferably someone who has never been in jail and who isn't an alcoholic and who won't take her just to get hold of her very small inheritance.*

Where on earth were she and Joe going to find that person? Sally Smythe clearly didn't think such a person existed, or she never would have left a vulnerable young woman in the care of someone like Didi.

Chapter Fifteen

Sally Smythe didn't generally ask for proof of the relationship when an adoring Great-aunt Bertha arrived to scoop up an orphaned child. It could be impossible to dredge up a complete chain of birth certificates and marriage licenses linking a child to a distant relative. This was one reason that social workers did interviews and adoption case studies, in addition to bare records searches.

Pedophiles did still slip through cracks in the system, but they were usually related to the kids anyway. Sally couldn't remember a case where a pedophile masqueraded as a relative and fooled the department into handing over an unrelated child. It was true there had been days, many days, when Sally had been forced to send a child home with an adult she didn't trust, but those people hadn't been strangers to the child. On those days, she hated her job a whole lot.

Faye Longchamp-Mantooth was no pedophile, and neither was her handsome husband. Sally had her doubts as to whether either of the two was Amande's fifth cousin once-removed, but neither of them seemed like the kind of habitual liars with whom she rubbed elbows every day. There was a reason Sally took a good long shower every night before she sat down to dinner with her family.

Her kids were grown now, and they understood why Sally's work made her feel dirty. They had told her that, when they were little, her post-work cleanup ritual had made them think that social workers worked in the mud. If they only knew the truth. Mud could be a clean kind of dirty.

If she'd only had to deal with the Longchamp-Mantooth family, Sally might have been able to skip the shower until bedtime. But no. She'd been forced to spend time with Didi. Judging by Tebo's reputation, she'd have probably needed to pick up a fresh bottle of shower gel, if she'd been forced to speak with him. She would have been running up the water bill, trying to wash off his utter ickiness.

Finding a living situation for Amande that satisfied both Sally and Faye Longchamp-Mantooth was going to be tough.

Miranda Landreneau had been well-known in the community. In particular, she had known everybody's grandparents, so Faye could see that Detective Geoffrey Benoit was hell-bent on doing this investigation right. In fact, he had said as much to her.

"If I screw this one up, I'm going to have to answer to my own grandmother."

Faye had a feeling that the red-headed detective's complexion was always ruddy, but the thought of facing up to his grand-mother seemed to make him flush even more. He was a solemn man with an expression that Faye would almost call "hang-dog," but he was capable of flashes of deadpan humor that caught her by surprise. Then, while she was laughing, he followed up with a question she wasn't expecting. He looked way too young to be a detective, but maybe this poker-faced approach had worked well enough to propel him up the ladder quickly.

He'd questioned her at length about the boat trip she and Joe had taken that afternoon to Amande's island. In fact, he'd questioned her at such length and with such monotony that she wondered if he was hoping sleep deprivation would loosen her tongue. Faye had lost track of time, but it was very late and her body was screaming for her to close her eyes and rest. The detective's grandma would be proud.

"So you don't have an alibi for most of the day today? And neither does that big husband of yours, the one who looks like he belongs on the cover of one of those bodice-rippers you women read?"

"I *don't* read bodice-rippers, and I *do* have an alibi. Not unless you consider the dead woman's granddaughter's word to be suspect, simply because she's underage. If Joe or I had been missing long enough to find Miranda and kill her, don't you think Amande would've noticed? And don't you think that she'd have been interested enough in helping you find her grandmother's killer to tell you about it?"

"Settle down, Ma'am. Does that big husband have a temper to match yours?" His shock of orange hair, as stick-straight as Faye's, fell in his eyes. He shoved it back impatiently, waiting for her answer.

So this was how it was going to be. Joe was a big man, and he was a stranger to this tiny community of people who had known each other since childhood. That made him a suspect, even when it made no sense for him to be the murderer. "No," Faye said. "Joe has no temper to speak of. Sometimes I pick on him, just to see if I can get him to lose his cool. It never works."

"He never gets angry? Not ever?"

"Oh, he gets angry. Sure he does. He gets angry when old ladies get killed and when young girls are left without anybody to take care of them. But little things? Like when I forget to tell him that the checking account is running low before he takes the debit card to the grocery store? No. He never gets angry over stuff like that."

"What about when some doofus like Hebert Demeray gets up in his face, stinking like cheap whiskey?"

Did this man not remember that Joe's alibi for the afternoon of Hebert's death included both Amande *and* her dead grandmother? Unless he thought Hebert had been dead a lot longer than Faye had assumed, based on the good condition of the body.

Faye made an effort to keep her voice calm and patient. "Not too many people are tall enough or brave enough to get up in my husband's face. But when they do? He laughs at them."

"What about Steve Daigle? He got up in your husband's face, for sure, and his own face is certainly not fit for a book cover, so I imagine your husband didn't enjoy this. What do you know about him?"

"Well, I know that my husband had all kinds of excuses for beating the living hell out of him just a few days ago, but he didn't. Your deputies said as much. I saw Steve yelling at Miranda and her family, and I saw Joe stop him. I didn't hear a lot of what he said firsthand, because I was in our cabin, making sure that Amande and my little son didn't have to listen to him, but Joe told me everything. If you're looking for a big man with anger issues, I'd be checking Steve Daigle's alibi. Wait. I misspoke. I'd be checking both of Steve Daigle's alibis. We've got two dead people, and both of them were members of that family Steve was threatening."

"Tell me everything Joe told you about Daigle and his threats."

And now Faye saw that she was dealing with a man shrewd enough to cover his tracks, even during a routine interrogation. By any logic, he should have begun this interview with questions about Steve Daigle. The man had, after all, been seen publicly threatening the dead woman. Instead, he'd shoved Faye off-balance by firing off a series of sharp questions designed to rattle her. Detective Geoffrey Benoit rose a notch in Faye's estimation, but she felt compelled to push back with her own series of sharp questions.

Why? No reason, really, other than to keep him on his toes.

"Joe and I have both already told your department everything we know about Steve Daigle. What did you think about those slips of paper in Miranda's room with Daigle's name on them?"

"You saw those? What were you doing in Miranda's room?"

"I was looking for her. A frantic sixteen-year-old asked me to help find her grandmother, so I searched the boat. Miranda obviously wasn't there, so I dialed 911."

The freckled skin on his forehead wrinkled. Detective Benoit was not happy with her answer. "Did you touch anything?"

"No. I mean…yes. I did touch one of those slips of paper, because I thought they were so interesting, and I just wasn't thinking. But I didn't even touch it hard enough to move it, and I was sorry later."

"Sorry?" The word clearly surprised him, and he jumped on it. "How so?"

"I touched my eye with that finger, and I thought I just might go blind. Miranda had sprinkled something on those papers that I'm pretty sure was cayenne pepper. You might want to ask a voodoo practitioner what kind of hex she was trying to cast with that pepper. My guess is that she wasn't harboring any goodwill toward Steve Daigle. And why should she? You've heard how he behaved on the one occasion they met. Don't you think any self-respecting voodoo mambo would hex a man who wished she would die, just so he could have her home?"

Detective Benoit was tapping quickly on the keyboard of his smart phone, which destroyed the calculated rhythm of his series of pointed questions. Faye took this as a sign that she'd surprised the man.

"Did you disturb anything else on the houseboat?"

Anybody else would have just said "No," but Faye couldn't make the scientist in her shut up. "I didn't touch anything else, no. But just being there means that I probably left footprints on the carpet, and probably hairs and skin flakes, too. I didn't know Miranda had been murdered at the time. I was just in there looking for her."

"Fair enough." He kept tapping on his phone, using both thumbs with the agility of a man young enough to have played video games since shortly after birth.

"I did see something else that could be important. An appointment time that Miranda had written down and stuck on her refrigerator."

He looked at her through narrowed eyes.

Sensing disapproval, she plunged ahead. "I'm sure your people have already seen it," she said, gesturing at the boat where some evidence technicians were doing their thing. "But you might not have had a chance to look at it yet." She pulled her phone out of her pocket and used her forefinger to bring up her pictures, because it was quicker and because her thumbs were older than his. "There. See?"

He didn't look at the photo right away, because he was busy studying her. "You took a picture of it. Before or after you dialed 911?"

"I'm not sure. I did the two things at about the same time."

He took the phone and, without permission, scrolled back and forth, glancing at the series of photos Faye had taken while on the houseboat.

Afraid he was about to confiscate the phone, which would drive the last nail in the coffin of Faye's ability to finish her consulting project, she said, "I can email those to you right now."

He handed the phone back and said, "Please do. Here's my address. And, just for fun, why don't you tell me what that note on the refrigerator said? I can't read it on that little phone screen, not even with these expensive contact lenses stuck to my eyeballs."

Faye's glasses were on her nose, and she had the advantage of having already seen the name. "She had an appointment with somebody or something named—" She scrolled through the photos, looking for the man's name. "Sechrist. It said the meeting was on Friday at two, but it doesn't say which Friday. It might have been today. It might have been next Friday. Maybe she met with him last Friday, before Hebert died. Before Joe and I even got here. Only Miranda knew for sure."

"The little girl might know." His blue eyes rested on Amande, whose head was resting on her arms in a mirror image of the young aunt sitting next to her. His voice dropped a note and softened. "I'm making a list of questions for Miss Landreneau, so that I can bother her as little as possible."

"That's very kind of you." Faye heard her own voice grow quieter and softer.

"I have a little sister," he said. Then he brought his palm down firmly on the table, as if to say, "This is no time for sentiment. We're talking business here."

"Tell me whether you did anything else while you were onboard that houseboat that I need to know about. Even if you think I'll wish you didn't. Then I'll let you go about your business and you won't have to think about this stuff anymore."

"Nothing, really. I saw that somebody had searched the drawers in both Miranda's and Amande's bedrooms, which is one reason I took these pictures." She held up the hand clutching the phone.

Did she remember seeing anything else? Any minute now, he'd be moving on to the next witness, and any tiny bit of input she had into the investigation of Amande's grandmother's death would be ended. This bothered her more than it should.

"Could you tell whether the intruders had taken anything?" he asked.

"You're going to have to put that on your list of questions to bother the little girl with. I will say that it didn't look like someone tore up the place, willy-nilly. All the drawers in Miranda's room were slightly open. See? A few of Amande's drawers were still latched shut. Maybe the intruder was looking for something in particular, quitting as soon as it turned up."

Faye scrolled through the photos and her finger slowed when she reached the ones she'd taken in Amande's room. "Be sure you ask her to inventory her artifacts. She had a collection of old money minted while the US was still using silver. I'm not sure which drawer it was in." She held the phone out for him. "If it was in one of those open drawers, I'd bet money that those coins are gone. It took her years to find them all. Poor kid."

"Were any of her other artifacts valuable?"

"Yeah, but not everybody would have recognized it. She had a piece of a brass sextant. If it's as old as I think it is, it belongs in a museum. And she had two old Spanish coins. Both silver. And hefty. They didn't look like much, but if the thief knew what they were...yeah. They're gone."

She felt an idea coming on. It was one of those ideas that prompted Joe to ask questions like, "Couldn't you just once mind your own business now and then? You know...the business that pays both of our salaries and puts a roof over our heads and puts food on Michael's plate?"

Apparently, she could not.

"I've done law enforcement consulting before, Detective. I'm called in to answer questions about how valuable a stolen artifact might be on the black market, or to advise investigators on who might be interested in that artifact. I've helped on murder cases, more than once."

"I'll bear that in mind."

Faye couldn't keep herself from trying one more time. "If the thief is the same person who killed Miranda, and if that thief was savvy enough to recognize the value of those two corroded old coins—or any of Amande's artifacts, really, except for obvious things like the silver money, then I can tell you a lot about him. Or her. I think you should consider using my services."

"I said I'd bear it in mind. Would you mind fetching your cover-model husband? I don't think I have any more questions for you, and it's been a long night."

Faye nodded and headed for the cabin. Joe was sleeping on the couch with Michael balanced on his chest. She gently cradled Michael's head in the crook of her elbow as she shifted him into the portable crib, then she shook Joe awake. Like the hunter he was, he was capable of coming fully conscious in seconds.

"Detective Benoit wants to talk to you." She sat down next to him on the couch while he pulled on his moccasins.

"How's Amande doing?"

"She's still sitting at that damn picnic table. I think she's sleeping, or I would have brought her back here so she could be comfortable while the houseboat gets searched."

He nodded and said, "That would have been a good plan." Then he kissed the top of her head and left.

Michael stirred and mumbled in his sleep. Faye expected her frazzled mind to keep her from sleeping, but the long day caught up with her and she sank into a light doze.

In less than an hour, Joe was back, with Detective Benoit at his side.

"We took Amande through the houseboat, so that she could tell us whether anything was stolen," the detective said, instead of "Hello."

"What did she say?" Faye rubbed the back of her forearm over her eyes, trying to wake up. "What's missing?"

"Nothing. Nothing but those two old Spanish coins. Even the silver American money is still there. It was in one of the drawers that was still latched, so maybe the intruder didn't see it. The point is that the thief was clearly looking for those coins, quitting the search as soon as they turned up."

Faye was no hunter, but this news brought her awake as suddenly as the sound of a breaking twig could awaken Joe. "You need an archaeologist to help you with this case." It was a statement, not a question.

"Yes. But I don't have a budget for one."

"I don't care."

◇◇◇

Faye knew she shouldn't interfere in Amande's relationship with Didi. It was what it was. But she had stood motionless in the marina parking lot for the ten minutes since the sound of Detective Benoit's departing car had faded. If asked why she stood there, she would have said, "I'm waiting for something good to happen."

She was still waiting.

Didi was gone, and a light was on in Miranda's—now Didi's—room. She'd gone in there as soon as the technicians finished their work, probably because she needed to throw up and pass out. Amande lingered at her favorite picnic table, which seemed to be her second home and her only home on dry land.

Faye needed to say good night to her and go crawl in her own bed, but she couldn't bear for the child to be alone. Not on the first night after her grandmother's death. And so she'd stood here, with no notion of what to do.

Finally, she gave up resisting the urge. She walked over to Amande and simply put a hand on her shoulder. When the girl looked up and met her eyes, Faye saw the reflection of that day when she'd buried her own mother, three short months after she'd buried her grandmother. At least she'd been of legal age... barely...when fate threw her out into the world, alone.

There was nothing to say but, "I'm so very sorry. If you need anything, you know where Joe and I are. We're just a few steps away."

Tears ran into Amande's mouth when she opened it to speak. "Why are you being so good to me? Are you doing this just to get free babysitting?"

Faye was shaking her head when Amande's composure finished crumbling. The girl leaned her head on Faye's shoulder and just cried.

Episode 3 of "The Podcast I Never Intend to Broadcast," Part 1

by Amande Marie Landreneau

I've been recording these dumb little podcasts every day since my grandmother died. Sally recommended it on that first day, and I figure anything that gets Sally off my back takes me one step closer to getting my case closed. Also, there are only 672 days left before I turn eighteen, so anything that stalls the process of dumping me into foster care for even a single day can only be a good thing.

Faye and Joe are great, but they'll finish this project soon enough, then they'll be moving on. I feel bad about the time they spend on the phone with Sally and my wormy-looking lawyer. I feel bad about the time anybody spends with my half-aunt and step-uncle, but even Faye's not smart enough to avoid them all the time. Didi and Tebo are pretty good at avoiding Joe, since he looks at my half-dressed aunt like she's a bug and he looks at Tebo like the under-grown drunk that he is.

I pay Faye and Joe back for all their help in the best way I know how. I take care of little Michael while they work. The kid's so cute that I don't even mind changing his poopy diapers. I find this amazing.

Uncle Hebert's death has made me think about the simple...reality...of what happens when a body stops functioning...about the mechanics of it, if you will. I never knew him when he was a person, instead of just a dead...thing.

My mother's death just crops up in my mind as a puzzle to be solved, the way she herself did when she was alive. I used to think, She's not here. Why isn't she here? How am I supposed to feel about that?

Now, I find myself thinking, She's dead. I'm not sure how much different this is from when she was alive and she wasn't here. How am I supposed to feel about that?

Grandmère's death, though...it's like a hole. A hole in my life. A hole in the world. I look at our boat and I expect to see her on the deck. When I stay up past eleven o'clock, I expect to hear her scolding me in French. When I'm tempted to do something I know she wouldn't like, it doesn't do me any good to sneak around and do it. Somewhere up in heaven, Grand- mère knows what I'm doing.

Okay, now I'm crying. I should have left well enough alone, instead of thinking about my grand- mother up in heaven. That was stupid.

I think I'll drop this mopey stuff and tell some more of her stories, instead.

According to Grandmère, the legends of Gola George grew and grew. Was it really possible for one man to kill so many men, even when that man was plundering ship after ship after ship? (Geez, I seem to be on a death jag tonight. Just can't stop talking about it.)

He can't have killed every sailor on those ships he captured, because he made slaves of a bunch of them. I imagine they were mostly white. I don't know for sure, but I picture the sailors back in George's day as being white guys. Don't you imagine Gola George saw this as a little bit of revenge for being kidnapped out of Africa and chained up in the bottom of a slave ship?

On an island somewhere between here and the gulf, he built...well, I guess it was a little town. They say that Henry the Mutineer did the surveying and drew up the plans for the town and the buildings. He'd been George's navigator, or so they say, and there has to be a lot of overlap between surveying and operating a sextant and making scale drawings like an architect.

Henry and George built storehouses, lots of them, to store their treasure. I guess it was their treasure, and not just George's, even though Gola George was the big scary pirate captain. I think Henry was the brains of the outfit, and I think Gola George probably knew it. Without Henry the Mutineer, Gola George might not have lived to get rich and famous.

They built a big building for the harem of women that George's men kidnapped from every port in the Caribbean. And they built little huts for the mothers of the children that naturally result when women are kidnapped and raped and imprisoned. Harems and children just go together, don't they?

I asked Faye whether that little bit of wood she found on my island could have been Gola George's town.

She said, "Sweetie, an alien could've dropped it out of a flying saucer, for all I know. I need to get it dated, which is going to be hard to do, unless I can pry the money out of that pirate I call a client. I also need to do some digging to check out the context, but it's going to have to wait, because my pirate client ain't gonna want to pay for that, either. I can't see that your island was ever as big as, say, Grand Terre, which makes it hard for me to believe that a few hundred pirates and wenches and slaves and children ever lived there. But if it makes you happy to think so until we know otherwise, then you go right ahead."

I like Faye a lot.

Grandmère said that Gola George was notorious for leaving on pirating expeditions without getting somebody to take care of feeding the women. So if he didn't really kill hundreds and hundreds of people with his own sword, he probably starved that many. I've been thinking lately that some of the women must have found a way to feed themselves between visits from Gola George, because the stories all say that there were children in George's little town, and it takes nine months to make a baby and years for that baby to grow into a child.

That's a long time for a pirate to sit in port. It's also a long time to scrounge in the swamps for food. Grandmère said that, even after Gola George died, no one would come near the abandoned pirate town he left behind, because the cries of the children during those years had made them think the place was haunted.

And now I've moved from dead people to abandoned, hungry children. I really need to stop this now.

Chapter Sixteen

Faye had spent the last hours of the night staring at the dark ceiling above her face. There had been times when she knew Joe was awake beside her. She could tell by the way he brushed a reassuring hand on her leg as he shifted into a different uncomfortable position.

Insomnia gave her a chance to wonder why a cabin, intended to accommodate people on fishing vacations, who were frequently male and almost always large, had been equipped with two bedrooms with standard double beds and a small foldout couch. When he was stretched out to his full six-and-a-half foot length, it wasn't just Joe's feet hanging off the end. His legs dangled into space from the calves down. She didn't know how the man could sleep at all.

Right now, she thought he actually was sleeping. The arm next to hers was utterly relaxed. The breath sounds in his barrel chest came deep and easy. The sighs that wafted periodically out of Michael's portable crib were just as unfettered. By contrast, Faye's chest couldn't have felt more tight and constricted if she'd been corseted.

Faye had once tried to learn to meditate, and she'd had more than a little trouble controlling her hyperactive mind. Sitting still, to Faye, was an opportunity to plan her next onslaught on the world. The strategy brewing between her ears might be as simple as deciding to go get groceries after Michael napped, then using the rest of his naptime to make a shopping list while she waited. Or it could be as complicated as the development of the multiphase archaeological survey of a piece of land that had been inhabited since before the Europeans crawled out of their tall ships.

There was always a new and juicy tidbit for Faye's conscious mind to chew on. It was a wonder she ever slept.

Her meditation instructor had told her to just relax and watch the distracting thoughts flit in and out of her head. Eventually, the buzz between her ears would slow and stop.

Maybe it would…when Faye was dead.

She'd been trying to follow the instructor's advice for the past six hours. She'd watched passively as imagined images of Miranda Landreneau, bloody and dead, flitted through her mind. These mental pictures were followed by thoughts of Amande living with abusive strangers. Or, possibly worse, with Didi.

When she'd finally grown numb to tragedy, her brain had turned to her own worries. How on earth were she and Joe going to finish this humongous project?

Faye was a problem-solver at heart. She couldn't miraculously give Amande a happy home, and she couldn't bring Miranda back from the dead, but she'd never failed to deliver a project on time. Heck, she'd never even failed to deliver an elementary school homework assignment on time. There was no way on God's green earth that she was going to start failing now. Well, she was failing at meditation, but other than that.

Hours of failed meditation had solved at least one of her problems. She'd finally realized that she needed to hire people to do word processing and graphics. Not permanent staff. Temps would do. It simply made no sense for Faye and Joe to be dragging and dropping pictures and text all over their final report, not when they had so much other work to do.

Somewhere in heaven, her grandmother, who had worked for decades as a secretary, was glorying in the knowledge that her granddaughter was the boss. Or she was going to be, once she located a few temporary clerical workers.

A slender shaft of sunlight found a hole in the brown plaid bedroom curtains, shining brightly on the faux-wood paneling of the opposite wall. Faye took that as an excuse to get out of bed, despite the fact that it was hardly past six am Michael and Joe sounded like they were sleeping too deeply to hear her creep out of the cabin. It was worth the risk.

She slipped outside, notebook in one hand, cell phone in the other, and pen clenched between her teeth. The Internet connection on her phone would allow her to search for temporary employment agencies near her Florida headquarters on Joyeuse Island. The fact that those headquarters were in the Eastern Time Zone meant that she could have her clerical staffing problem solved in less than an hour. Score!

Maybe then she could stop doing management chores and start doing some archaeology, but she sort of doubted it.

Faye had finished researching clerical temp firms and had moved on to the day's next chore: downloading her client's template for preparing the final report. It still wasn't quite eight am in the Eastern Time Zone, so she didn't yet know *who* was going to be typing that report, but it wasn't going to be her.

Startled by a quick motion seen out of the corner of her eye, she set the phone down. The marina grounds were so quiet that she didn't even consider that a human might have been the thing in motion. Faye felt alone, so her first-blush assumption was that she'd seen some large variety of wildlife, probably a deer. The thing had been light-footed, so the possibility of a bear never crossed her mind, which was probably a good thing for her blood pressure.

She turned her head in the direction of the motion, only to be greeted by, "You need to hold this stuff for me, Faye. I can't keep it safe."

Did Amande remind her of a deer? Her coloring was a quiet brown and she moved as easily as a woodland creature. She was wearing none of her trademark Hawaiian shirts this morning, dressing instead in a t-shirt that was wild-animal brown.

Towering over Faye, she was certainly closer to the size of a deer than…say…a cottontail rabbit, and her eyes were as soft and vulnerable as a doe's.

"What stuff?" Faye mumbled intelligently. It was rather early in the day to be reading the erratic mind of a teenaged girl.

Amande held out something heavy and flat, and Faye recognized it as the folder full of coins minted back when the United States still used silver. Then the girl held out the jar of newer coins that she'd found with her metal detector. Amande was handing over her treasures.

"I heard Didi plundering through Grandmère's drawers all night long, looking for stuff, and she was so drunk that she was talking to herself about what she found. Mostly, she just said things like, 'Nice!', or 'That's a piece of shit!', but when I heard her say, "Gold-filled? What the hell can I get for something that'll turn somebody's neck green?', I just couldn't stand it any more. Faye. She's going to sell her own mother's jewelry before the body's even cold."

Amande thrust the box in Faye's direction. "Didi will be after my stuff tonight. She'd have already come for it, but she passed out in the middle of trashing Grandmère's room. She slept in her dead mother's bed *without changing the sheets*."

Faye wasn't sure why that image was so awful, but it was.

"She'll sell the silver money in a heartbeat, unless she's stupid enough to just spend it, and she *will* spend this jar full of new money." Amande held out the folder, waiting for Faye to take it. "That thief took my future. The rest of my stuff is worthless, compared to those Spanish coins, but the day may come when it's all I've got. Maybe that day's already here. Please keep these things for me? I know you've gotta go home soon, but will you keep them for now, until I think of someplace else that's safe?"

Hearing the girl's words, Faye knew that Amande had spent the night awake in bed, chasing thoughts that wouldn't go away. Just like Faye.

Amande had followed her fears to their logical end. If Didi was selling her mother's jewelry already, then nothing was safe.

If the child protection people named her Amande's permanent guardian, she'd be spending the next two years looking for ways to get her hands on the girl's small inheritance. Faye figured that, given two years to do it, Didi would find a way to spend everything the girl had, even if she had to reckon with a trustee to get it. Amande was smart enough to figure that out, too.

At first light, the girl had taken the only action she could to protect herself. She had come to Faye. How could Faye refuse to help her?

Faye nodded and took the folder and jar. Amande vanished as quickly as a doe when she hears a rifle's first shot.

Didi slipped on her favorite pair of shorts and a purple tank top that brought out the gold flecks in her brown eyes. The mirror said that she would need some extra effort to be pretty today. She didn't like the notion that vodka had put those baggy circles under her eyes, but something had done it. She was only twenty-three, so it couldn't have been time.

Didi considered switching to gin. There were herbs and stuff in gin, so maybe it was easier on the complexion. Nothing could have convinced her inner nicotine addict to look closely at the tiny lines forming around her lips.

There wasn't enough coffee in the house to meet Didi's current needs. She had to have a full pot of something black and strong and chicory-laden, and nothing less. There was no other way to face this day. Once she'd pumped herself full of caffeine, she'd be ready to question her mother's lawyer on the details of her inheritance. Didi slung her purse over her shoulder and left the houseboat, without announcing her intentions to the niece for whom she was responsible.

She drove past the two nearest bars and tried not to think about the men who'd been pawing her in both establishments, just the day before. None of them had been prizes, and the front-runner in the competition to take her home had been wearing the residue of thirty years of smoking on his teeth. By dying and forcing her to walk away from this man, her mother had been able to save her from at least one bad decision.

Now that the vodka had worn off, she needed to assume the role of bereaved daughter. And wife. She kept forgetting that Stan was supposed to be dead. Maybe he *was* dead.

There. She'd managed a few tears for her mother and husband. If she didn't wipe them away, maybe her coffee run could be parlayed into a little bit of sympathy for Didi and her plight.

And so Didi, a more accomplished method actress than most graduates of drama schools, sauntered into the local grocery store without taking note of a familiar gray pickup pulling into the parking lot behind her.

◇◇◇

Didi was not impressed with the store's selection, and she let the clerk and the manager know it.

"I've seen fresher lettuce," she sniffed.

"I can't sell it quick enough," the manager said, adjusting the lettuce display and wiping his hand on his apron. "I can't sell much of anything. There's talk of closing the gulf to fishing. There's talk of a moratorium on drilling. Nobody's sure they're gonna have a job next week. Everybody's cutting way back on their grocery shopping."

"I hear you," Didi said with a calculated quaver in her voice. "Stan works in the oil field, so who knows if he'll keep his job. Except—" The quaver modulated and deepened to a half-sob. "Except I'm pretty sure he was on the rig that blew up. He'd told me he had a new job with BP, and I don't always pay attention when he tells me where he's going to be. All I know it's some-where…out *there*." She gave an airy wave to the south. "I haven't heard from him since the day before the explosion."

"Really?" said the clerk, a graying woman wearing stretch pants.

Didi warmed to her audience. "Not a word. And I do so need to talk to him, since my mother died last night. I feel so… alone." The voice stopped shaking and dropped to a whisper.

"Now, Didi, you can't be alone here in Plaquemines Parish. Everybody here has known you all your life." These reassuring words came from the lips of an elderly lady that Didi thought she recognized as a lunchroom worker from her elementary school, though the woman's name escaped her.

Another woman and two men steered their shopping carts down the produce aisle, nodding their heads at the old woman's reassuring words. Again, Didi knew their faces but not their names. Now she remembered why she'd left home, even though she'd hardly gone a hundred miles. It could be hard to get away with anything when everybody in town knew your mother. Still, maybe she could work the situation to her advantage this time. Everybody knew that her mother was dead and maybe they wouldn't be so quick to judge her every little move.

"I heard you'd been asking last night at the bar whether any-body knew how to file for government assistance. Being as how you're a widow and all," the manager said, picking a feathery yellow leaf off an aging bunch of carrots.

Didi forgot to put a quaver in her voice as she quickly asked, "Do you know where I should go to do that? I didn't know whether to start with the government or BP or what. Or maybe I should just get a lawyer. Somebody should pay for what hap-pened to Stan."

"Dunno." The manager's gentle fingers explored the skin of a bright red tomato. Judging it to be too soft to sell, he dropped it into the basket hanging on his arm. "I imagine the govern-ment got in touch right away with the wives of the men who they *knew* was dead. Since nobody but you knows that Stan's dead…missing…whatever…I imagine you're going to have to go looking for someplace to file your claim. In the meantime—" He put the tired lettuce and aging carrots into the basket along with the tomato.

The clerk reached under her cash register and pulled out a phone book. "Maybe this'll help. Usually the government pages are blue. Let me see." She raked a well-chewed fingernail down the page. "Here's the emergency management department. I'd start there."

Didi reached out an uncertain hand and the clerk plunked the phone book firmly on her palm with an expectant look. The same look was on all the faces gathered around her. They all seemed to expect her to make the call then and there. Unsure why she was doing it, she pulled her phone out of her pocket and started to dial.

The person who answered the phone for the emergency management department listened as Didi stammered through her request. "I'm looking for help because my—my husband—I'm sure he's dead. He—he—just had to have been on the rig that exploded and...yes. I can hold."

Didi was surrounded by familiar faces of people whose names she didn't care enough to remember, and they were all looking expectantly in her direction.

"Did they put you on hold?" the manager asked.

She nodded.

"Damn government. If they can't help widows, then what good are they? " He held out the basket of not-quite-fresh veggies. "Here. Take this. Who knows how long it'll take you to get any help?"

Didi was looking at his offer of charity, without really reaching out her hand to take it, when she heard a familiar voice behind her.

"And here I thought my wife was cheating on me yesterday, rubbing herself all over anybody that would buy her a shot of anything. Naw. She wasn't cheating. Not even a little bit. She thought I was dead. I feel so much better now."

It took less than a second for a tall, brown-haired man to cross the space between the door and the spot near the cash register where Didi stood. He would have been good-looking if his jawline had been stronger.

Stan used a single finger to lift her chin, so that he could look directly into her eyes.

"How long've I been dead, Didi? A week? Two? If you're trying to get your hands on some government money or…I dunno… maybe trying to con some of these people out of their pocket change, you might want to try *acting* like a grieving widow."

He caught the eye of the manager, who gave him a slight smile. The other onlookers exchanged glances that told Didi the truth.

They knew. They'd known Stan was alive all along. They'd been stringing her along with their sympathetic murmurs and their urgings to get help from the government. And their charity. She took a step back from the manager and his basket of limp vegetables.

"Barry, over there," Stan said, pointing at the generous manager, "he called me yesterday when he saw you down to Helen's bar." Then he pointed to the elderly "lunchroom lady," who must have been Helen. She gave Didi an ugly smile and a wave.

Didi should have remembered where she'd seen that smirking face, but she'd been more focused on the vodka Helen had been pouring.

"Barry said it took two whole phone calls to find me. I've been staying down to Venice with Buster. You remember Buster? My best friend for my whole life? Dontcha think if my wife wanted to find me, maybe she might call my best friend, instead of making like I'm dead so's she can get some money from the government?"

He brought his face down to hers, nose to nose. "That's fraud, Didi. You wanna ask these people what they think of the cheats who collected big checks after the storm? Just how are you different from people that filed on property that wasn't fit to live in *before* that bitch Katrina rolled into town, then pretended they was homeless when they was really living in the same nice clean houses they'd lived in all along? What makes you better than people that went all over town from one Red Cross to the next, collecting one check after the other, because none of the people trying to help had time to check up on 'em?"

Didi still refused to answer him.

"Maybe you'll get something for nothing, now that your poor Mama's gone. Some of them stocks your old man left...a piece of that crappy houseboat...a set of silverware, maybe. But you ain't gonna get anything for nothing because of me, because *I ain't dead.*"

He took the basket of vegetables and handed it to Didi, then very deliberately leaned over and spit in it.

When he was sure that the automatic glass door had slid shut behind Didi's skinny ass, Barry-the-manager said, "Bitch," clearly and to no one in particular. Then, he dumped the old vegetables in the trash can, basket and all. To no one in particular, he said, "I feel for that little girl Miranda left behind. Can you imagine living on that boat with nobody for a mother but that skinny shrew?"

Didi wished she could wipe the contemptuous stares off her back. She could still feel the eyes boring into her. This was why she'd stayed away from home. Small-town people never forgot they didn't like you, and nobody around here had liked Didi since...

Nobody had liked Didi since ever.

They didn't like her when she was a pigtailed girl who taunted the fat kids until they threw up their chocolate milk when they saw her coming. They didn't like her in her teens when she wore her miniskirts too tight and her mascara too thick. Actually, in those years, it was just the women who didn't like her. The men had liked her just fine.

She'd gone through a lot of those men before Stan came along, so the men she'd loved and left didn't like her anymore. Neither did the losers she'd rejected. Stan had seemed to be a cut above all the other men she'd known. Marrying him had felt like a fresh start. It had been good to move away, even if she hadn't gone all that far.

Now, she had the feeling that she might have burned a bridge she hadn't intended to burn. She felt sure that Stan was finished with paying her bills. It was a good thing she had a houseboat—well, a piece of a houseboat—that would keep a roof over her head while she regrouped.

She needed to talk to the social worker about whether she'd get money from the child welfare people if she took charge of Amande permanently. And she needed to get clear on how much control she had over the child's inheritance. Part of the oil company stock that had helped her mother keep food on the table now belonged to Didi, and part of it now belonged to Amande. Some fraction of it that Didi couldn't cipher out belonged to Justine's widower, so she wouldn't be getting even as much income as Miranda had received. Still, if Didi played her cards right, she could spend Amande's money to run their little two-woman household and keep her own money for herself.

Didi liked this plan so well that working out the details kept her awake and alert until she was able to find someplace to buy coffee where nobody knew her.

Chapter Seventeen

Detective Benoit was back, and so was Sally the social worker. Amande knew that Didi was nowhere to be found, because she'd heard her slip out an hour ago. She wondered why the woman bothered to sneak out. Why should Amande care where Didi went or what she did at breakfast time on a Saturday morning?

Maybe Didi was just in the habit of sneaking off the houseboat, since she'd done it so many times when she was a teenager living there. Amande remembered. She'd been a little kid, maybe six or seven, but Didi had made sneaking out at night look like so much fun that Amande had tried it once.

She remembered standing on the shore, alone under the bright moon, looking around and wondering what to do next. She'd never been outdoors alone so late at night, but the novelty wore thin quickly, so she'd tried to think of something to do that had the extra cachet of being forbidden. The only really bad thing she could imagine was throwing trash in the water.

It had taken some doing for the little girl to hoist herself into the marina's dumpster and throw a big pile of beer bottles and cigarette butts out onto the ground. Amande remembered that she'd cut her foot while she was in there. Had she really done that while barefoot? It was a wonder that she hadn't gotten lockjaw.

Even at that age, Amande had possessed the presence of mind to pitch a grocery bag out of the dumpster along with the trash. Loading her trash into the sack, she'd hauled it to the water's edge, pitching the forbidden garbage into the water, one naughty piece at a time.

The beer bottles had sunk down into the murk, invisible even in the bright moonlight. That was no fun. But the nasty cigarettes butts had floated, bobbing on gentle waves. Amande had enjoyed watching them so much, leaning down ever closer to watch them dance, that it was no wonder that the sleepy child eventually fell in. Had she been brought up anywhere but on the water, Amande might have drowned that night, but she'd floundered among the marina's moored boats for a timeless time, until she reached a dock and, from there, a ladder.

Amande never knew how long it took her grandmother to find the moldy clothes stuffed in the back of a drawer, and she never knew if her grandmother figured out how they got that way. Miranda had never mentioned it. But the child was always pretty sure that Didi was having more fun when she left the house at night than Amande had enjoyed on her only night-time excursion, because Didi always walked away smiling, and Amande's adventure hadn't been any fun at all.

Amande was remembering that long-ago adventure as she squatted on the deck of the houseboat, watching Detective Benoit as he watched a diver work. The diver was plying the water in the precise spot where Amande had fallen in all those years before. Sally, who seemed to be some kind of kin to the detective, was standing beside him. They were murmuring, but Amande could hear them.

"I thought you already found the murder weapon," Sally said.

"One of them. We found the knife that killed Hebert. It was sunk in the water over there. No fingerprints, dammit, and nothing left behind on the shore that we could link to the killer." He gestured toward a seawall some distance away. "It wasn't a knife that killed the old lady. It was something shaped like this." He held up an index finger crooked into the shape of a number seven. "The forensics people could tell because it cut into her throat like—"

Only then did they notice Amande watching them and eavesdropping. Gangling, awkward Benoit had the good grace to look embarrassed. Amande found herself wondering how old he was. He didn't seem like he'd been doing this job for long.

Sally had looked at him hard. "You don't know what killed her? Have you asked the girl if she's seen anything shaped like that?"

"I asked her half-sister. I didn't want to upset her even more by talking about the way her grandmother died."

"Well, that train has left the station, hasn't it?" Sally jerked her head in the direction of the silent girl. She motioned to Amande to join them. "Besides, the half-sister is a half-wit. This is the person who may be able to help you. If you have questions, you should start with Amande."

Amande saw Sally beckon. Sally was a nice lady and Amande didn't like to disobey but, for once in her life, she didn't do as she was told. She backed away from Sally and the policemen and the diver who was looking for God only knew what. Scuttling sideways like a crab so that she could keep all those strangers in her sights, Amande hurried into the houseboat and into her grandmother's room.

Didi's things were everywhere, shoving Miranda's orderly belongings aside. Amande knew already, without looking, that all her grandmother's jewelry was gone, either taken to a pawn shop or on its way there now. Even Miranda's clothes would be gone soon, if Didi could find a consignment store that would take an old lady's unfashionable things.

The half-finished straw dolls had been cut down from their hooks and piled in a heap near the voodoo altar, but the basket of unwoven straw beside Miranda's worktable was untouched. Her tools still lay spread across that worktable. They were specialized implements, of value only to people interested in making straw voodoo dolls—which is to say almost no one—so Didi had very little interest in them. Until this moment, Amande had thought that she might want to keep those tools as a memento of the grandmother who had already begun teaching her to use them.

Amande picked the tools up, one by one, hoping they would all be there. But they weren't. One was missing, a cutting implement with a blade curved into a shape that could be called a seven. Miranda had kept its inner edge honed to razor sharpness, so that it would make clean cuts in the tough straw. What had that tool and its razor edge done?

Amande backed away, straight into Sally, who had come looking for her.

"What's wrong?" Sally asked, grabbing her by the elbows. "Amande, what's wrong?"

Amande wouldn't tell her. She couldn't tell her. All she could say was, "Get Faye. I want to talk to Faye. Please. Get Faye."

Joe enjoyed haunting pawn shops. He liked sorting through tools that had been used until they were worn and burnished. He always visited the guitars—and there were always guitars in pawn shops, because guitars were portable, easily sold, and non-essential—but he never bought one, because he'd never learned to play. Faye had once clasped one of his big hands between her two little ones and said, "I'd love to play the guitar, but my little wimpy hands just aren't made for it. Your hands are big, and your fingers are long and strong. You should make some music with these." Maybe someday.

He generally steered clear of the jewelry cases, because pawned wedding rings made him sad. Today, though, he headed straight for those glass display cases, because that's where small collectible items were stored. Faye had sent him out to look for some very specific objects.

"Got any old coins?" he asked the owner of the second hock shop of the day. Just as he had at the first shop, he'd watched the man as his hands had gone first to Lucite-encased sets of uncirculated proofs that had never been anything but collectibles. When Joe had shaken his head, saying just one word, "Older," the man had reached for a black velveteen display stand of silver American money, accented with just a few gold pieces.

Joe found it interesting that the man didn't bat an eye when he said again, "Older." Instead, the pawn shop proprietor had just spread his hands and said, "I wish I had what you people were looking for."

So somebody else was looking for something old and spendable. Joe wanted to know more, but he was too much of a fisherman to snatch his bait out of the water while the fish was still sniffing at it. He'd said, "I work for somebody who'd pay through the nose for really old coins. Gold bars would be good. Pieces-of-eight. Emeralds from the old Colombian mines. You know…pirate treasure."

Joe reached out a hand and gently lifted one of the gold American coins, safe in its protective case, after first making eye contact and getting a nod that said it was okay for him to pick it up. "Myself, I like these. They look like they're worth something, but my boss likes the really old stuff. To me, a chunk of silver that's spent a lot of time on the bottom of the ocean looks pretty much like a rock."

"You can restore it."

"If you trust the restorer." Joe held the coin case lightly between his thumb and forefinger and spun it, so that he could look at the coin's reverse. "Know any good restorers?"

The man wrote down a few names and phone numbers. Joe pocketed the list. He knew the first name, but the others were new to him. This ploy had gotten him some more people whose brains he could pick. He was glad he'd stalled and let this fish play with his bait.

He kept his focus on the gold piece, hoping that the prospect of an immediate sale would loosen the man's lips on the subject that was actually important—who else had been sniffing around for very old silver coins?

Joe laid the coin on the counter, closer to him than to the salesman, signaling that he was still thinking of buying it. Then, speaking off-handedly, as if he were trying to hide his interest in the gold piece by making idle conversation, he said, "I know a man named Leon who's looking for unrestored silver pieces, too. Not sure who he's working for. Leon is always a step ahead of me. Everywhere I go, he's picked over the merchandise. He been here yet?"

"Last name Sechrist?"

Joe recognized the name from the note on Miranda's refrigerator, but he didn't answer right away, so the man kept talking. "A man name of Sechrist was here more than a week ago. Looking for the same stuff as you. Don't remember his first name. Only reason I remember his name is that he gave me his card and the name of Christ just jumped out at me." He crossed himself. "No, wait. I do remember his first name. It was Dane. I remember because I used to have a Great Dane. Sweet dog, but dumb as a bag of hammers."

"Still got the card?"

"Naw. I th'ew it away. I ain't had the kind of coins he wants, not ever. I can't keep track of who wants what, for years on end. If people want what I got, they need to come back and look."

This lack of salesman-like drive explained the distinctly non-prosperous look of this particular store. The last store, up Plaquemines Highway nearer New Orleans, had been much bigger, so big that there were two people working when Joe arrived. Neither of them remembered anybody looking for Spanish silver, but there were surely others on the sales staff of a place that size. Joe knew he'd need to go back when they were on duty. This guy was a one-man shop, so Joe had been able to ask the right question of the right man on the first try. Sometimes a man gets lucky.

Behind him, he heard the sound of an opening door, followed by two heavy boots being scraped on the welcome mat. The pawn shop's proprietor nodded at the slouching newcomer, saying just, "Good to see ya, Stan. Got something for me?"

"Not today. Haven't been home lately, but I'm thinking my wife might've already hocked everything I got. She been in here?"

"Didi?"

"Only wife I got."

Joe got real interested in the gold piece again, stooping down to scrutinize it and letting his hair fall down around his face. He hadn't come here to get any dirt on Didi, but it was hard to maintain his poker face when that dirt presented itself.

"She was here this morning, but I doubt any of the stuff she left was yours. A woman's wedding band. A locket, gold-filled. A pretty little white-gold crucifix. I figure it was her mama's stuff."

"Did she manage to squeeze out a tear or two while she was snatching the money outta your hand?" Stan crossed the room, bellying up to the same counter as Joe. He nodded and Joe nodded back.

The store owner handed Stan a plastic grocery bag, saying, "Yep. Said it tore her up to part with her mama's things, and that she'd be paying off the loan as soon as she could, so she could come back and take her heirlooms home with her."

Stan pulled three little boxes out of the bag. They did indeed contain a wedding band, a locket, and a crucifix. "That what she called 'em? 'Heirlooms?'"

"She did."

"Don't hold your breath for her to come back."

"Not many folks ever do."

Joe stepped away from the counter and picked up a guitar. He didn't know how to play it, but he hugged it to his chest and plucked all six strings, one at a time. Cocking his head as if he could actually tell whether the guitar was in tune and whether it had a good sound, he plucked them again, very slowly. Then he checked out each guitar in the store, looking over the body and neck like he knew what he was doing. He studied those damn guitars one square inch at a time, so that he could eavesdrop on the other men's conversation without being obvious about it.

Stan lingered for five minutes or so, but he didn't say anything else interesting. He allowed as how he'd known his wife was a tramp when he met her, but he had a weak spot for tramps. The two men swapped information on where the fish were biting. They reminisced about a few times when they'd been memorably drunk together. And then Stan left.

Joe, still running his hands over a guitar he didn't know how to play, had been thinking during their monotonous conversation. He'd only come up with one notion that would interest Faye and the detective who had asked them to look into Amande's missing coins, and it was this. It was possible that there had been no thief and no burglary. Just because those drawers were hanging open and the coins were missing at the very time Miranda was killed, it didn't mean that there was a connection. Didi might have been searching her own house for things to hock. She could even have done it after her mother was killed or after Miranda left for her appointment with Dane Sechrist—Joe was pleased with himself to be able to give the man a first name—and before anyone else even realized that the old lady was missing.

Still, if Didi had stolen those Spanish coins, then wouldn't they have been in the plastic bag with her dead mother's jewelry? Joe doubted she had the initiative to look for a dealer who would give her a better price. No, this seemed to be her family's pawn shop of choice, since her estranged husband had also shown up in the same spot. According to the owner, the coins weren't here, and they hadn't ever been. Therefore, Didi probably hadn't taken them, but he'd be bouncing his logic off Benoit to see whether the officer agreed with it.

Joe couldn't say whether Dane Sechrist had taken Amande's Spanish coins or not, but he might have had an appointment with Miranda on the afternoon of her death. Joe now knew that someone by that same name had been looking for coins like Amande's, days or weeks before they were stolen and well before two members of the family that had owned them were murdered.

Joe still had more pawn shops to visit, and now he had a list of restorers to check out, but he already thought Faye would be pleased with the information he'd uncovered. And the sun was still crawling upward toward noon.

◇◇◇

Michael's afternoon nap was coming to an end. He was stirring in his portable crib. Faye saved the spreadsheet she was using to track the known archaeological sites in the path of the oil slick, because in thirty seconds she was going to be listening to a cranky baby.

She could really use another couple of hours to fiddle with the data. Maybe Amande would be willing to babysit. She had never intended to let the girl work for free, and Miranda's death meant that Amande needed the income even more. Faye was glad to have the opportunity to help her out. Even better, Michael seemed to think the girl was a great big toy.

Hoisting a newly diapered child on her hip, Faye trudged down the hill to the houseboat, only to find it empty. No Amande. No Didi. No Tebo.

Amande's well-used picnic table was empty. Didi's car was in the parking lot, but Tebo's wasn't. Faye couldn't picture the three of them in a car, cruising around like an all-American family. When she tried to imagine it, her brain kept putting Amande in the driver's seat, despite the fact that the girl lacked even a learner's permit. Faye couldn't even let herself imagine Didi or Tebo in a position to hurt Amande, and they were both often in no condition to drive.

Faye looked at her phone. It was about five o'clock, a little early for dinner, but maybe Didi had taken Amande to the marina's restaurant to get something to eat.

Michael was getting heavy and Faye's lower back ached, so she lowered his feet to the ground and grabbed his hand.

"Let's go find Amande."

"A-mah!" he said clearly. Faye's ears, tuned to his babyish diction, heard the word as entirely distinct from the "Ma-mah!" that he used to call her. She couldn't wait to tell Amande that he could say her name.

Michael's tiny shoes tapped on the wooden walkway that led to the restaurant. Faye's boots clattered in counterpoint to his rhythm. Faye couldn't get over how much the marina grill looked like Liz's place back home. She could have sworn she was looking at the same fishermen, sunburned and sweaty, wearing the same soiled t-shirts and telling the same fish tales. For Manny's sake, she wished there were more of those fishermen leaning their elbows on those tables, but greasy fried fish filets were not a necessity of life, so fewer people were buying them. She'd heard tell that Venice and Grand Isle were chockful of reporters with dollars to spend, but none of them were here.

The linoleum floor was as worn and as clean as the floor at Liz's place back home. The clattering racket from the kitchen was as loud. Someone with a voice as loud as Liz's was hollering, "Three eggs, scrambled!"

Reminded of the joys of eating breakfast at suppertime, Faye hoped that fried eggs and grits were on the menu. She wouldn't mind grabbing a quick bite before she handed Michael off to Amande and got back to work. Slipping a hand into her purse, she found a couple of jars of toddler food rolling around. Score! Eggs for her, chunky bits of mushy squash for Michael. Dinner was served.

She pulled her phone out of her pocket and texted Joe to tell him to find his own dinner, because she wasn't cooking any.

Remembering that she'd come there to look for Amande, not to get some grits, Faye looked around and spotted her at a table in the back. She was surrounded by some familiar faces, and Faye was struck by how few of the familiar faces in this community were attached to people that she liked very much.

There sat Didi, completely ignoring Amande while she had an animated conversation with Steve Daigle. Faye, having taken more sociology and anthropology courses than was good for her, saw that Didi was a textbook example of seductive body language. Her hands went frequently to her hair, smoothing it back and tucking it behind one ear. She bent forward from the hips at an angle designed to accentuate breasts that were small but perky. The chicken wings she was eating gave her frequent excuses to run a single index finger over her wet lips before gently sucking off the grease.

Steve seemed to be enjoying the show, leaning down to make eye contact and running the fingertips of his right hand up and down Didi's slender back.

Was Steve worth all that effort? Faye supposed he was attractive, if you liked a longhaired man shaped like a fireplug who had the face of a Pekingese puppy. Was Didi really attracted to him? Or did she just instinctively do these things the instant she smelled the pheromones of a human male...any human male? Had it crossed Didi's mind that this man had been her sister's husband until a week before? And had it crossed her mind that there was some possibility, however slight, that this man had killed her mother, just yesterday? In fact, anyone in the room could have done it. Maybe this would have been a good day for Didi to have a quiet dinner at home with her bereaved niece.

Instead, she was downing a shot and listening to inspired pickup lines like, "It's been a long time since I saw a body like yours."

Speaking of the bereaved niece, Amande did not appear to have absorbed Didi's teachings on how to handle men. Her chair was backed as far into the corner as it would go, and her hands were folded in her lap. She offered no encouragement to the man sitting next to her, other than the look of adolescent infatuation on her sweet face. Faye's maternal instincts rose up and demanded to know who the hell this man was, because he was clearly hitting on Amande and he was just as clearly too old for her.

Amande's dinner companion was the scuba diver she'd been eying just the night before. He was a lot better looking than Steve, with a deep tan, close-cropped white-blond hair, and intelligent brown eyes. Faye might have approved, if he'd been ten years younger. As she approached, he was talking with his hands, saying, "I've seen sharks this big—big enough to eat me, but I must look like I taste bad."

He wasn't touching Amande, but he was deep into her personal space, which was probably why she'd retreated so far into the corner. She was giggling at his story, but she retained her nervous pose.

Then, because there weren't enough sketchy men hanging around this underaged girl, Manny appeared at Amande's side, dreadlocks swinging and earrings dangling. When he grasped the girl by the shoulder, Faye snatched Michael off his feet and crossed the remaining space between them in three steps.

Before she got there, the situation exploded. Manny used his other hand to pick up the full glass in front of Amande. He took a swig, then slammed it on the table in front of Didi so hard that half its contents sloshed into the young woman's lap.

"Are you insane? What did you do, dump a full shot in the girl's Sprite? Two?" He slapped a long-fingered hand on the wet table. "Get out! Get out now. All of you. And you, Didi? Don't come back."

"Don't tell me you didn't drink when you were her age, Manny. I thought it was time she learned to hold her liquor, and I thought it would be better if she was with me, so I could look out for her."

Didi made her behavior sound so very reasonable.

Manny just shook his head and said, "There's no need for us to be having this conversation. I already told you to get out of my establishment."

Amande grabbed his arm in both her hands. "I wasn't drinking it. I saw her pour the shot in there, and I knew better. Really, Manny. Don't kick me out. I'm having a good time."

He didn't say anything. Faye's judgment was that he was too angry to speak.

Amande pulled Manny's arm hard, bringing his thin and dusky face down even closer to hers. "Are you saying I can't come over here any more, just to hang out? Even without Didi? Where else am I going to go? I don't have a boat. I don't have a car. I don't go to school. I don't even have a backyard. Are you telling me I'm trapped on that houseboat, day and night?"

He leaned down closer to her than Faye liked. Dammit, this man was too old for Amande by *fifteen* years. "It was one thing when you were a little girl and I let you hang out here in the afternoons, before the drunks really got rolling. You're too old for that now, Amande. You're also too pretty. And you're too young for...*this*."

He made an impatient gesture, first in the direction of the half-empty drink in front of Didi and then toward the blond would-be suitor sitting next to Amande. Then he looked the suitor in the eye and said, "She's underage, okay? Get out. All of you. And Amande, you go straight home. Don't let anybody in the door but your idiot aunt."

Joe appeared at Faye's side, as the tanned man was leaning back in his chair, saying, "Hey, I didn't know!" for the second time.

Amande looked at both Faye and Joe and said, "I didn't drink any of it. Truly. I'm not stupid."

"We know that," Faye said. "I came over here to see if you'd like to babysit for a couple of hours."

Amande cast a regretful eye in the direction of the handsome man who now seemed afraid to look at her, but she rose and said, "I'd love to spend some time with Michael."

"Hold up," Didi said. "What are you paying her to babysit?"

Faye wanted to say, "Are you her agent?" but she held her tongue. Instead she said, "Minimum wage."

"Good," Didi said. She looked at Amande and said, "I don't know when I'll be getting any income from the oil company stock. I guess I'll get social security for you, but it'll be a while coming. In the meantime, we can sure use some money, even if it's just a couple hours of minimum-wage work."

With that, she sauntered toward the door, with Steve two steps behind. Faye had no doubt that he would be following Didi home. Faye decided instantly that she would need Amande to babysit overnight.

Amande rose and made her way awkwardly out of the corner. She paused to say shyly, "I enjoyed talking to you, Dane." The embarrassed man ducked his head and said, "Same here."

Faye couldn't miss the meaningful grip that Joe put on her elbow. Who was Dane and why did Joe know more about him than she did?

Joe pulled her aside and whispered in her ear, "A man at a pawn shop today told me that a man named Dane Sechrist had been in there looking for really old Spanish coins."

"Sechrist?" Faye hissed, and a man sitting nearby turned to look at her, but Dane was still saying good-bye to Amande with the stiff body language of someone trying not to look like a pervert. Didi and Steve seemed not to notice the sound of Faye's voice in their rush for the door. Amande was hanging her head too low to notice anything but her own misery.

Detective Benoit would need to know that they'd found someone whose name matched the note on Miranda's refrigerator. According to the gossip Joe got at the pawn shop, he was known to be interested in the only thing stolen from the dead woman's home—really old Spanish coins. He also seemed to have a possibly unhealthy interest in Miranda's granddaughter.

Joe kept his lips next to Faye's ear as he jerked his head in the direction of Didi's departing backside.

"That woman's planning to take every cent we pay Amande. Whatever minimum wage is, I think you should double it, and tell the girl to hide half from her aunt."

She kissed his cheek as it brushed past her face. "That was my plan. And I do like the way you think."

Stan Channing watched his wife saunter out into the darkness with another man. Didi never seemed to need him, unless there was nobody else around to pay for her drinks.

The big frizzy-haired man who was rubbing his hand over the small of his wife's back wasn't familiar to Stan, but he fit the description of a man who'd been asking nosy questions around town a couple of days before he showed up on his late mother-in-law's doorstep. Stan had heard tell that this man had been looking for Miranda, probably since the day poor Justine passed. Stan's guess was that he'd been looking for all the people who might have a competing claim on the stuff he'd inherited from Justine.

Stan knew scummy men like Steve Daigle very well, since he had a scummy streak himself. He'd guess that when Steve had laid eyes on his dead wife's very attractive sister, he had decided that it would be far more pleasant to use romance than the law to wangle a rent-free houseboat.

Once Steve found out Amande existed, he might have thought she was going to be an obstacle to his plan to stop paying rent. That was because Steve didn't know Didi. If the law put her in charge of her niece, then she'd find a way right quick to spend Amande's money as if it were her own. If Steve had a gram of sense, and Stan wasn't sure that he did, then he'd do whatever it took to keep Didi interested. Living on a paid-for boat and sleeping with the very talented Didi would not be a bad life.

In fact, Stan would have preferred that life to the one he was living. Damn that woman for her pretty face and her distracting curves.

◇◇◇

Faye balanced two takeout boxes on one hip while she counted out the cash to pay Manny. If she ran to the cabin at top speed, her eggs would still be hot when she sliced open their yolks and stirred them into her creamy grits, and Joe's omelet would still be tender and light. If she moved any slower than a full-out run, their eggs would be rubbery and their grits would turn into glue. Joe had gone ahead to feed Michael and make a pot of coffee, so there should be nothing to keep supper from hitting the table about ten seconds after she arrived.

It was too bad that Manny's place offered a nightly floor show that began whenever his patrons got drunk enough to be entertaining. Tonight, Didi and Stan had moved the floor show out into the parking lot, so Faye nearly got herself ensnared in their drama by the simple act of walking out the door. Three misbehaving adults stood between Faye and her quiet supper with Joe. Not anxious to be drawn into the confrontation, she stepped into the shadows, fully aware that her grits were coagulating as she waited.

"How d'you think you're gonna come out in the divorce, Didi?" Stan's voice was quavery and his words were slurred. He didn't hold his liquor nearly so well as his wife did.

She rested a fist on her cocked hip. "You make a good salary, when you don't gamble it away. I imagine I'll see some alimony out of you."

"Not if I can prove adultery. Which won't be hard."

He swayed on his feet, which Steve took as an aggressive movement toward Didi. He stepped into the gap between man and wife, then showed that he was drunker than he looked by swinging at Stan and missing. Faye was glad for Stan's sake that Steve's fist had passed his jaw by. Steve might have been drunk, but he carried some weight, and he'd put every ounce of it behind that punch. He was still regaining his balance when Manny hustled himself out the door.

Manny grabbed Stan by both shoulders and steered him away from Steve and his fists. "What are you doing, man? You know she ain't worth it. Don't let your pride put you in jail. Or get you killed."

Stan didn't acknowledge him, hollering over his shoulder at Didi instead. "Maybe *I'll* get alimony. If they don't stop that damn oil from dumping in the gulf, *I'll* be the one out of work, and you're fixing to inherit Miranda's stuff. How will it feel to write *me* a check every month, bitch?"

Manny kept shoving Stan toward the door to the bar and grill, saying, "Don't make me call the police. I want you to come in here and drink some coffee and eat a piece of pie. Leave the whore alone. Do you really want her back? No. You don't. I'm telling you, pride can cost a man all he's got."

The doors closed behind them as Manny successfully steered Stan back inside. Steve and Didi resumed their walk to the houseboat, interrupted periodically to give Didi a chance to rub herself all over Steve, in case he'd somehow forgotten what it had felt like when she'd done that thirty seconds before.

Faye hurried to the cabin, because she was ready to stop breathing the same air as these people.

Chapter Eighteen

Faye wondered if she should put a revolving door on the rental cabin. Amande had earned her pay by getting Michael to go to bed without much intervention from Faye or Joe, then she'd stepped outside into the night. Wondering if the girl remembered that one or two killers were prowling around, Faye moved her computer to the chair closest to the window. Now she could work and keep one eye on Amande. Funny. She wouldn't have thought that a teenager would require the same kind of attention as a toddler.

At first, Faye thought the girl was talking on a cell phone, but then she remembered that Amande didn't have one. Her sigh of relief that Amande wasn't whispering midnight endearances to Dane Sechrist made her feel like a middle-aged thwarter of young love. It was hell to get old.

Squinting out the window at Amande, while trying not to look like a spying old woman, Faye determined that the device in her hand was a voice recorder. So this was what adolescents used for diaries these days. Amande talked to her hand for almost an hour, during which Faye wrapped up her work, then the girl came in and said good night.

The sound of rustling sheets had escaped their bedroom periodically during that hour, so Faye had known that, though Joe was lying in bed, he wasn't sleeping. She wasn't surprised to see him shuffle out of the bedroom, clad in his usual khaki shorts and wearing a t-shirt that Faye knew was for Amande's benefit. Modest Joe would eat dirt before he'd run around shirtless in front of a girl her age. She also wasn't surprised to see the pack of cigarettes in his hand.

Joe was no chain-smoker, but he believed in the old Creek ways, and those ways included occasional tobacco use as a spiritual practice. Faye hoped that it wasn't possible to give oneself lung cancer in really slow motion, by smoking every month or two. Sometimes, Joe just needed some time with that noxious weed and a campfire and the night sky and the old spirits that Faye couldn't see. She'd stopped nagging him about it long ago. That wasn't exactly true, but she *had* slowed down with the nagging, since it didn't work anyway.

She watched him gather firewood and arrange it in the fire ring provided by the campground, then she went to bed instead of standing guard, because Joe could take care of himself.

Hours later, he crawled under the covers beside her. She rolled onto her side and slung an arm across a broad chest, cool-skinned and damp with dew.

"You awake?" he asked.

Of course she was. When Joe's peaceful mind couldn't rest, then nothing was right with Faye's world.

"Yeah."

"I can smell it. The oil. I can smell it."

Faye sniffed. She smelled nothing but the night air and Joe's shampoo, but she didn't doubt his word. Joe's senses were honed by years as a hunter, and he had surely been a fearsome hunter to begin with, because he'd been born with the ability to sense things that others never noticed. Sometimes he knew things that couldn't possibly be detected with the five garden-variety senses that everybody else had. Faye firmly believed that Joe had at least seven of them. If Joe said he smelled oil, then Faye knew that it was spreading over the Gulf faster than even her imagination could grasp.

"My nose just isn't any match for yours," she said.

"But you can feel it. I know you that well."

And when he said it, she knew that she did. The tremble in the air. The prickle on her neck. The bone-deep sense that even the wind blew wrong.

Maybe it was because she watched the news compulsively over breakfast and at bedtime, hoping the engineers would shut off the gushing flow. Maybe it was because she brushed elbows with people whose offshore jobs were on hold, and with other people whose deep-sea fishing businesses were going without customers, and with still more people trying to run stores when everyone around them was afraid to spend money. There was something in the air. Maybe she couldn't smell it, but it was there.

"I've been all over the Internet," he said, "trying to figure out where the currents are going to take all that oil."

Faye knew this. She'd rarely seen him sit indoors for so long, with his face lit by a computer screen instead of the sun.

"Faye. What are we going to do?"

Even now, he couldn't say it. He couldn't say, *What are we going to do if the oil gets to Joyeuse Island? How are we going to protect our home?* They'd lain here, night after night, unable to say such a thing to each other, but Faye knew she wasn't the only one troubled by dreams of blackened sea grass and tarred beach sand.

And neither could she say, *What are we going to do if we can't meet the terms of this contract?*

If their company failed to complete a project of this importance, what client would ever trust them again?

"We'll have to split up," Faye said. "I've been talking to Sheriff Mike back home. He thinks he can get us some oil-absorbent booms. You'll be better at getting those deployed, so you should be the one who goes. I'll be better at hiring people to help us finish this project, and if we default on it, we won't be able to afford that money pit we call a house, anyway. So I'll stay here with Michael."

Faye had spent her entire adult life restoring her family's ancestral plantation house, and she'd spent nearly that long chasing her PhD and building this business. If she lost everything all at once, how would she face it without Joe here by her side?

"I don't have to go yet. We'll watch what the oil does. When I have to go, I will."

Episode 3 of "The Podcast I Never Intend to Broadcast," Part 2

by Amande Marie Landreneau

They say that Gola George liked having women around, but that he didn't actually like women. He thought they would make him weak, if he'd let them, and a weak pirate is a dead pirate. This would explain his habit of kidnapping whole harems full of women. It's certainly one strategy to avoid getting attached to any single one of them. It would also explain his habit of leaving those women alone with no food and no help for months at a time. Any of them who survived probably didn't like him much when he returned, but they were also probably in no shape to do anything about it.

I'm guessing that Henry the Mutineer, on the other hand, was the subject of much speculation in his younger years. He didn't seem to have any use for women at all. His sumptuous cabin aboard Gola George's ship was strewn with more than navigational tools and the piles of paperwork accounting for George's riches. He purchased books in every port. He knew where to find the finest wine, and he paid whatever it cost. He taught himself to play the violin and to paint in oils. He bought fine sable brushes and paints in every shade of blue, so that he could capture the colors of the sea and the sky, whether they were at rest or torn by storms.

Grandmère's descriptions of Henry always stopped here. If women her age are aware that homosexuality exists and that some people actually practice it, they live by an unwritten code that says, "You must not mention such things. Ever."

But really. I may have only lived sixteen years, but I still wasn't born yesterday. I don't think Henry the Mutineer wanted women at all. I think he wanted Gola George.

How could he not have wanted Gola George? George was the tallest, broadest, strongest, swash-bucklingest man in the New World. His skin was as smooth and dark as coal. His eyes glittered like coal set afire. His teeth were whiter than the ivory he stole from Asian trading ships. He dressed in flowing silk blouses and tight pants and tighter hose and silver-buckled shoes. Even when he didn't have finger bones tied in his dreadlocks, no one could look away from Gola George. Anyone, man or woman, who was born to want men, wanted George. Nothing in the stories, however, suggests that Gola George wanted Henry the Mutineer. So Henry poured his love into music and into painting and into managing the financial interests of the most fearsome pirate who ever sailed.

The stories are very clear that Henry was only a paper pirate. He plotted the courses for voyages that were destined to kill whole shiploads of men. He kept track, through newspaper reports and the gossip of loose-tongued sailors, of where the richest treasure ships would be. He invested George's bloodstained gold in land and molasses and rum and slaves, and he traded those commodities shrewdly.

Henry the Mutineer shared the guilt for George's murders, because he made them possible, but he never participated in the ugliness of boarding a ship and killing its crew. He carried no cutlass and no pistol, no weapon at all, other than a stylishly jeweled dagger tucked into one expensive boot. They say he only raised a hand against one man in his whole life.

You can imagine what the other men had to say about all that. Such speculations could have been deadly for Henry, if some murderous pirate had decided that he didn't like the way Henry was looking at him, but Gola George owed his life to Henry the Mutineer. Anyone who struck out at Henry was taking on Gola George, and this was not something a man did casually. Gola George was the biggest, the strongest, and his blood was the coldest. No man sailing the vast waters between Mexico and Spain was going to take on Gola George, so Henry the Mutineer was safe from their contempt.

Then the day came when Marisol boarded Gola George's ship, and George never put her ashore with the others. They say that anyone could tell by looking at her that she would not have survived George's usual rough treatment. She was impossibly slender, with tiny white hands and feet that bore not a single callous. Marisol had been a lady, and a rich one, but the stories don't tell us how she came to be in the kind of place where George found his women—wretched port cities, infamous for thievery and prostitution and free-flowing rum. The stories say that Marisol drew the eye, even when she stood in a crowd, simply because the light on her pale oval face shone like the moon. The woman couldn't hide. She was too beautiful.

This was her downfall, because the day came when Gola George's eye lighted on that beautiful face.

Chapter Nineteen

Faye rose early, hoping to drive a stake into the heart of that infernal spreadsheet before anyone else got up. She'd just stepped into her pants when the phone in the hip pocket buzzed. She stepped outside to take the call, since the cabin was full of sleeping people. Michael was snoring quietly in his crib. Amande was in Dauphine's old room, sleeping off her late night. And Joe was sleeping as only Joe could, as motionless and massive as a felled longleaf pine.

Detective Benoit was on the phone. After apologizing for the early hour, he said, "I interviewed Dane Sechrist at Manny's place after I talked to you last night. It might have taken us a good long while to find him, without your help. I wish he'd had more to say, but I do appreciate your tip that he was eating in the marina bar and grill."

"Well, I didn't figure he was going to confess to both murders, though it sure would have been convenient. What *did* he say?"

"He said that he was a scuba diver and that he was thinking of buying a boat he could live on. I get the impression he's one of those divers who's so into it that he doesn't want to do anything else. Living on his boat and eating a whole lot of fish might cut his expenses to the point where he wouldn't have to work much. If he's been saving for a while or he's got a nice little lump sum from an inheritance or something, maybe he wouldn't have to work at all. Anyway, he said he'd seen Miranda's boat and liked it, so he found Manny in his office at the marina and asked him for her phone number. He used the number and made an appointment with her."

"Did Manny back up his story?"

"Quite the amateur investigator, aren't you? I'd tell you to stick to archaeology, but your instincts are too good. Yes, I've already, at this early hour, talked to Manny. He remembers Dane buying Miranda a piece of apple pie."

"Why didn't he tell you that already?"

"I have quite a long list of people to interview, and it's only been a day. I hadn't gotten to Manny yet."

"I wasn't questioning your skills, Detective. I just wondered."

"Yeah, I know. *I'm* the one questioning me. Anyway, Manny checked his receipts and found a cash purchase at 2:07 p.m. that was probably the selfsame slice of pie, so everything checks out. According to both Dane and Manny, she was perfectly healthy when Dane left. Manny did not, however, remember giving Miranda's phone number to Dane or to anyone else. Dane was insistent that he did, so it was one man's word against another. Not sure how much it matters, since even Manny agrees that Dane met with her in broad daylight."

Faye who had once, long ago, lived on a boat, said, "Miranda's houseboat isn't meant for the kind of use Dane has in mind. It's too big, for one thing. It's meant to spend its useful life moored in one place, just like it is."

"Exactly. And that's what Dane said she told him."

Thinking as much about Amande's infatuation with Dane as she was about the murder investigation, Faye asked, "What do you know about Sechrist?"

"I asked everyone I've talked to since Miranda died if they knew the name, since it was on her refrigerator door. Nope. He's been hanging around here for awhile, but he keeps to himself. Whatever else I know about Sechrist I got from him, though now that I have his first name, I'll be digging around plenty, starting today. He didn't tell me anything especially exciting when I questioned him last night. He grew up on the Mississippi Gulf

Coast, in Biloxi, which explains his attachment to boats and the water. Everything about the man says his upbringing was middle class or better, and that makes him stand out in Manny's usual crowd of customers. He says he spent a couple of years in college in Hattiesburg, but that's just sixty-nine miles too far from the Gulf to suit him."

Faye had felt the same way while she was a college student in Tallahassee.

"Hey, this might interest you," Benoit said. "He spent the first summer after he dropped out of school on an archaeological research vessel. If we stumble over some more archaeology stuff, it might make some sense that we hired an amateur like you to help with this investigation."

"You can hardly use the word 'hired' when you don't pay a person. Did Sechrist's archaeological research crew work in the Gulf of Mexico?"

"Yup. Our boy just doesn't seem to be happy anyplace else."

Faye didn't hear anything that remotely linked Dane Sechrist to Miranda's death. Nor to Hebert's, so she cut to the chase. "Do you think he did either of the murders?"

"I see no motive. Compared to the other scumbags I've interviewed, he's a Boy Scout. Until somebody tells me some compelling reason he'd want those two people dead, I just can't imagine him committing any violent crime. But I've been wrong before."

Faye agreed with the detective, mostly, but until she was definitively able to mentally move Dane Sechrist from the category of Boy-Scouts-who-might-have-committed-murder to the kinder and gentler category of Boy-Scouts-who-were-way-too-old-for-her-friend-Amande, she was not going to be happy.

Chapter Twenty

Amande had gone back to the houseboat to shower and change clothes, before starting another day as Michael's paid playmate. Faye wasn't surprised to see her back, but she was a little startled by her appearance. Amande had plaited the hair around her face into tiny braids, but she seemed to be having trouble with the back of her head. When Faye opened the door, the girl was standing on her doorstep, holding a clump of hair skyward so that it wouldn't unbraid itself. With her other hand, she held out a bunch of elastic bands, saying, "Would you help me? I'm trying to cornrow it, but it's not as easy as it looks."

Having cornrowed a girlfriend's hair in high school, Faye knew that it wasn't easy at all. She also knew that doing a whole head of hair would take her all day. Fortunately, Amande had figured that out.

"I think I should have started from the bottom and worked up, but maybe we could just finish the hair on the crown of my head. Then I can do a little more every day. I was thinking of doing dreads like Manny's, but I'm not actually sure how to make those. Cornrows aren't hard to do, but I need so *many* of them to cover my whole head!"

Faye was going to ask her why she'd tackled this self-improvement project now, when she'd promised to be back in half an hour, but then she remembered high school girl impulsiveness. The answer to Faye's question was probably "Why *not* now?" Instead, she sat the girl down and started plaiting. And, once they were no longer face-to-face, she got the real answer to her "Why now?" question.

"Grandmère would've had a stroke if I did this to my hair when she was alive. If I'd done dreads, she'd have killed me first and then had a stroke."

"My grandmother pestered me about my hair hanging in my face until I finally cut it all off. I've worn it like this ever since." Faye ran her fingers through her close-cropped hair. "It works great on hot, sweaty days in the field."

"That's one reason I want cornrows. I think it'll keep my hair off my neck. And the other reason is that there's nobody left who'll tell me not to do it."

Then she fell into silence while Faye made braids, and Michael ran around the room with his arms outstretched like airplane wings.

Finally, Amande spoke again. "That first night after Grandmère died, I couldn't sleep. I was so angry that I wanted to punch out a window, but I didn't want to hurt my hand and windows are expensive. Instead, I picked up the doll she made, the one that looks like me. My guardian. I decided she was doing a piss-poor job of guarding me, so I started bashing her against the window. After I'd been bashing a while, the poor thing's head fell off. And I thought, "Who's going to put her head back on for me? My grandmother's not here to do it." It's almost enough to make me want to learn to use those basket-weaving tools, but not quite. And now that one of them is missing because…well, I just can't. My guardian doll's going to have to stay headless."

Amande didn't have much more to say, not even when Faye finished braiding and sent her outside to watch Michael run until he needed a nap.

◇◇◇

Faye had been working steadily at her computer for so long that she was glad to hear a knock at the cabin door. She really didn't care who was on the other side of that door. She was just grateful for the excuse to stop juggling budget dollars. Trying to estimate the cost of all the contract employees she'd hired was making her want to eat a pound of chocolate and take a month-long nap. She would have welcomed a drop-in visit from Attila the Hun.

Instead, she got Dane Sechrist. He stuck his hand out and introduced himself, which felt weird, since she knew exactly who he was, but she'd been too busy snatching Amande away from him to formally make his acquaintance the night before.

She wasn't sure she had anything to say to the man, but she fell back on the manners her mother had drilled into her and responded to him simply. "It's nice to meet you, Dane. I'm Faye Longchamp-Mantooth."

"Amande said that you're an archaeologist, and that you're looking for contract workers."

"I am, but this is such a fast-burn project that I can only take people with experience. Do you have a résumé?"

He reached into the beige canvas briefcase slung over his shoulder and drew out a single sheet of good-quality paper. It listed the brief work history of a man in his twenties, but his work experience was well-presented and some of it was slightly pertinent to her project. She saw the summer job with an underwater archaeology team that Detective Benoit had described, as well as a few shorter-term diving projects. All the projects were in the general vicinity of the mouth of the Mississippi, which was Faye's study area. Applying for a job with her company wasn't a bad idea for Dane, actually. Except for the fact that she didn't like him.

"I don't need a diver."

"I thought you were doing a comprehensive study of this area. I don't see how you can do that and stay on top of the water. There's so much history underneath it."

The man was right. He just didn't understand the limited scope of her project.

"Our contract is for an initial survey to document the condition of archaeological sites in the area likely to be affected by the oil spill, so that—"

"So that we'll know what we've lost when a thick layer of oily gunk spreads itself all over them."

Interrupting a potential employer was poor job hunting strategy, but Dane was right again.

He pressed his luck. "So why not send some divers out? I'm guessing the underwater sites are most endangered. Shouldn't you be documenting them?"

"I'm no environmental scientist, so I don't actually know which sites are more endangered. Will the oil settle to the bottom and gunk up shipwreck sites? Or will it float on in to shore and gunk up old forts and lighthouses and settlements? Hell if I know. But it'll be here in weeks or days. We don't have time to go looking for new sites, nor to do any serious exploration of the sites that are out there. I've got people researching everything that's known about archaeological remains in the study area, and I've got people doing quick site visits to document current conditions, but that's all the client wants. And it's all the client will pay us to do."

Dane was undaunted. "I've done plenty of library research. It's on there," he gestured at the résumé, "but it's buried in the write-ups for each job, because I wanted to feature my diving. I do a lot of it online, obviously, but sometimes you have to go to the source. Maps, for instance. Trying to read a scanned copy of an old map on a computer screen just doesn't work."

Faye knew that this was true.

"Besides," he continued, "I just like the smell of old maps. I'm on a first-name basis with the research librarians at the state archives."

Now Faye knew why Amande liked Dane so well. He was cute *and* geeky, just like she was.

She glanced at his résumé, looking for an excuse not to hire him.

He kept pressing his luck. "You don't like me much, do you?" Clearly, this man had never taken one of those courses on how to ace a job interview. "Dr. Longchamp-Mantooth, I swear I didn't know she was so young."

Faye raised a skeptical eyebrow in his direction.

"How could I know? When I first saw her, she was wandering around at noon on a weekday, waving a metal detector around. Teenaged girls are supposed to be in school at that time of day. And look at her. She's as big as I am. She doesn't *look* like a kid. Am I supposed to ask for ID whenever I talk to a new woman?"

Faye wasn't feeling charitable, so she said, "Maybe."

"Well, when you decide, will you let me know? Because I guess you're going to have to decide whether I'm a pedophile before you know whether you can use my help with your project. For the record, I'm not. I'm not a pedophile, I mean, and I'll never speak to your young friend again, if it'll make you happy."

Faye couldn't say that it would make her happy, but she was pretty sure she'd be happier. Still, was it her place to choose Amande's friends?

"While you're deciding my status as an employee and a potential pervert, can I ask you some questions? I've got some maps and journal articles here," he patted the briefcase, "and I'd like a professional opinion on some things."

<><><>

By the time Dane left, Faye knew quite a bit about him. He'd been careful about how much of himself he'd exposed, but he was ignorant of a piece of vital information: Faye knew a lot of people, and she knew people who knew a lot of people.

He'd couched his questions about sunken ships carefully, saying things like, "When I was working with Professor Morgan, we detected some anomalies in areas where we'd have never expected shipwrecks. Have you read any recent research that puts more wrecked ships in this area? Or maybe have you heard about findings that haven't been published yet? I'd really like to do more of that kind of work, but I don't have the right contacts. I need to know who's out there working in the field."

Dane could talk about mundane things like "making contacts," all he liked. Faye recognized the treasure hunter's light in his eyes. Dane thought he was onto something big, probably a shipwreck, based on the questions he was asking, but he wanted to keep the details to himself.

He'd spread copies of maps across her kitchen table and laid published papers beside them, blathering nonsense about job-seeking as he did it. She noticed that he'd chosen maps that covered a broad area, and he'd made no notes on these copies. He was being oh-so-careful to avoid letting her pinpoint the spot that interested him, but there was no doubt that he was trying to pick her brain. Again, classic behavior for a man seeking lost treasure.

Faye so desperately wished she knew the world-famous Dr. Peter Morgan well enough to call him and ask for his impressions of Dane Sechrist, but she did not. She did, however, know her cousin Bobby Longchamp very well, and Dane couldn't possibly have known the consequences of showing her a handful of maps and journals that were clearly labeled as being from the Historic New Orleans Collection.

Dane, by his own admission, was on a first-name basis with staff at the state archives. Judging by the origin of his research materials, Faye would bet that he was also best-friends-forever with the staff of the Historic New Orleans Collection. Bobby wasn't on staff there, but he might as well be. He was also an accomplished people-watcher and an incurable gossip.

As with any conversation with Bobby Longchamp, this phone call was going to take a while. Still, by the time Dane Sechrist had piloted his boat back to the spot where he hoped to find endless riches, Faye would have gotten Bobby to spill his guts. After she'd explained what she wanted to know, she fully expected him to be able to sweet-talk the collection's staff into telling him every last detail of Dane's research interests.

With Bobby's research skills, he might even be able to ferret out the truth of whether the man was a pedophile or not. Then Faye could sleep better at night. Maybe.

◇◇◇

"One child isn't enough for you, Cousin dear? Tell me again why you've acquired a teenaged appendage. Doesn't she have actual relatives to take responsibility for her?"

For a man whose etiquette was acquired at the knee of a blue-blooded mother who thought the Queen of England's bloodlines were a bit suspect, Bobby certainly didn't mince words.

"Amande isn't an 'appendage.' She's—she's my friend. And, oh, Bobby, if you could meet her aunt and uncle and stepfather. To call them worthless drunks would be to insult drunks everywhere."

The sarcasm left Bobby's voice, but he still made his position clear. "There are children all over the world who are in the custody of worthless drunks, my dear. Jodi comes home from the police station crying over them, sometimes. She can't save them all, and neither can you. I know the situation breaks your heart, but what makes you think you can save this one?"

"That's why Amande is different. She doesn't need saving. She could take care of herself right now, if she was of legal age and if she could be someplace where there weren't a bunch of scumbags running around. Hell. A place where *fewer* scumbags were running around would be an improvement."

"And you think I might know one of those scumbags?"

"About six feet tall, dark tan, really short blond hair. Broad shoulders. Muscles. Mid-twenties. His name is Dane Sechrist."

Bobby gave a gossip's short and gleeful chuckle. "I *do* know him. The man's on the hunt for sunken treasure, unless I miss my guess."

"I think so, too. What do you know about him?"

"Not much more than that. He's in the collection's map room so much that he can't possibly be burdened with a job. I didn't like his looks, so I spent an afternoon hovering around and trying to make him nervous."

"It worked, no doubt."

"So it appeared. I also sicked Dauphine on him."

"You didn't."

"I did."

"Bobby, that's cruel."

A laugh emanated from her cell phone that did, in fact, sound vaguely cruel. "I know. But Dauphine's so bored with this library work you've got her doing. She wants to be digging up things, and she wants to be chasing your little rug rat around. Giving Dane Sechrist the evil eye will keep her so distracted and happy that her leg will heal quicker. I wouldn't be surprised if her blood sugar comes down, too."

"Okay. You have my permission to keep torturing the man. What can you tell me about his research interests?"

"I do not think Dane wanted me to get a good look at what he was working on. Fortunately, these maps and photos are like my children. I know precisely where Mr. Sechrist is diving for treasure. I can tell you the very USGS quadrangle. From that, you can get latitude and longitude and any GPS will take you straight there. Hang on a second. I stepped outside to talk to you, but I can go back in there and pull the coordinates right quick."

Bobby was back in the time it took Faye to conduct a fruitless web search for Dane Sechrist. It took less time than that for Faye to poke the coordinates he gave her into a mapping program and pull up a photographic image of the area. Why wasn't she surprised to see that Amande's island was just west of the center of that photo?

Chapter Twenty-one

Joe eased his big frame back into the rented boat and shoved away from the muddy shore. This was the good part of archaeology. He was outdoors. The sun was shining hard enough for him to break a slight sweat. The air was dead still, but not when the boat was skimming atop the dark water. The wind rushing past dried the sweat off his face, and it blew away his cares.

Faye should be here.

He'd spent the morning ground-truthing the work done by Faye's hired data-gatherers. He'd found the foundations of an old fort right where they'd said it would be, although rising water levels made it look more like a little-bitty island than a relic of an old war. He'd walked the site and taken some pictures, then checked the list for his next destination.

Joe's job today wasn't to explore or excavate. He was just supposed to confirm whether the archaeological remnant was there or not. This one was. So he moved on.

His next stop was at a shell mound, as close to the water as the fort's foundations had been, according to his maps. The bayous and ditches and ever-shifting land had forced him to navigate by GPS and depth-finder today, and he wasn't happy about it. Joe could usually look at a map once, then get himself where he was going. He was pretty sure he could have done that today, but these bayous and ditches and mudflats were a special case. He needed the depth-finder to keep from running aground in water that was a different depth than it had been yesterday, or even five minutes ago. And he needed the GPS to keep him on-track after he'd made twelve detours around shallow spots that his depth-finder had warned him to avoid.

This mound was easily found, and it was actually on dry land, putting the lie to the maps that had said otherwise. He hadn't been expecting much, so he wasn't disappointed. Faye's researchers had said that it was small, and only a couple of feet tall, if that. They'd been correct. What they couldn't have known was that it had suffered the punishment dealt to any accessible piece of high ground in this flat place. It was covered with ruts made by dirt bikes and four-wheelers. It was also pocked with holes dug by people looking for cool and potentially valuable stuff.

Joe wasn't sure there was any point in documenting this mess, but he took some pictures, anyway. As he picked his way through the mudholes left behind by tires that belonged to cretins, he spotted a tiny beige bead trampled in the mud. He squatted down and took a picture, considering whether he should take it to Faye. This one little bead might tell her a whole book full of stuff about this site.

He thought about it a minute, then came up with a better plan. He wouldn't take the bead to Faye. He would take Faye to the bead.

His wife did not become an archaeologist so that she could manage employees and watch budgets. If she didn't get her hands in the dirt soon, she was going to make herself sick. Joe had been meditating on this issue for days, and he expected to solve it soon, even if the answer required another night spent smoking tobacco and looking at the stars.

The contract researchers were working out. Faye also had contract archaeologists out ground-truthing sites too far away for Joe to visit, and that setup was working fine, too. If…when… they eventually had a report written, she had people ready to do the typing and graphics. How hard would it be to hire an assistant project manager to help Faye shuffle those spreadsheets?

Joe knew the hardest part would be getting Faye to agree to this plan. Fortunately, he also knew his wife. If he got her out in the field, she'd be so happy that she'd agree to anything that would keep her there.

Joe wasn't a manipulative sort, but sometimes wife management required a man to resort to underhanded tactics.

◇◇◇

Faye's handsome husband filled the doorframe, broad shoulders stretching from doorjamb to doorjamb. She was always happy to see him, but today he was carrying a paper bucket full of fried chicken and a bag of potato chips.

"Let's take the boat out."

Faye took a look at the work piled on the table in front of her, then she took a look at the sunshine that streamed through the door and cast a big black shadow of Joe on the carpet.

"This morning's fieldwork went fine," he said, "but I think I need a PhD to look at this one site."

It was nice of Joe to give Faye an excuse to drop her paperwork like a bad habit, but he'd had her at "Let's take the boat out." She closed her laptop and threw some diapers and an already-prepared bottle in the diaper bag.

She peeked in the diaper bag again and saw bathing suits, a bottle of sunscreen, and hats for her and for Michael. If they were going to pretend to work, they should probably take some gear.

"What kind of equipment do we need?"

"The boat's loaded. Let's go."

Joe was indeed the best husband and business partner in the whole wide world.

With every step away from her paperwork and into the sunshine, Faye felt lighter and freer…until her eyes rested on the houseboat where Amande was trapped with Didi and Tebo. That poor girl.

Faye was never clear on how it was that Joe could read her mind. Maybe he heard a slight catch in her breath. Maybe he saw a miniscule hesitation in her step. Maybe he was conscious of her tiniest eye movements.

Whatever arcane psychic methods Joe used, they worked. He put a hand between her shoulder blades and guided her toward the dock. "She's waiting for us in the boat."

Seconds later, Faye got to see Amande grin as she heard Michael crow, "A-mah!" for herself.

◇◇◇

Joe had done an amazing thing when he spotted that barely visible bead. Faye was a better photographer than he was, so she'd spent a pleasant quarter hour searching for the perfect angle to show off its ancient patina. This required her to wallow in the mud atop the mound, adding an extra dimension to Joe's observation that she looked happier than a pig in slop.

While she was doing this, Joe crawled over the mound until he spotted a potsherd half the size of his pinkie nail, which gave her the happy chance to do some more muddy camera work. Amande and Michael whiled away the time by chatting with three preteen kids who'd gathered to see what was going on. Faye thoroughly enjoyed overhearing scraps of their conversation. Amande was in fine form as a community educator.

"You guys need to find another place to ride your bikes. You're messing up important stuff."

"Yeah!" Michael added helpfully.

"It's just a pile o' dirt, but it's a good place to ride," said the obvious leader, shoving her overlong bangs out of her eyes. "Franky catches air nearly every time. Sometimes Ginny does, too."

Franky jutted out his prepubescent jaw in pride. Ginny chewed on her pigtail.

"It's *not* just a pile of dirt! Indians built it…oh…hundreds of years ago. Maybe thousands. See these oyster shells? That's what they ate." Amande brushed a little sand off a shell protruding from the mound's chewed-up side. "And come see what Michael's daddy found."

"Dah!" shouted her tiny assistant.

Franky and Ginny and their talkative friend gathered around Faye and her camera.

"It ain't much of a bead. It looks like something that fell out of a bean bag. You know—those little white spongy balls. I've got a thousand of 'em on the floor of my closet."

"What's your name?"

"Lena."

"It's not spongy, Lena," Amande said confidently. "Spongy things don't last this long. What's it made out of, Faye?"

"Clay, I think. And you're right. It's really old. Get Joe to tell them about this other cool thing he just found."

Faye resumed focusing her camera, this time on the potsherd, but she heard Joe do a creditable job of explaining its importance in words of two syllables or less.

Amande was warming up for her lecture's big finish. "So you see, you have to leave this stuff alone. No riding bikes or four-wheelers on the mound. And no digging, because when Faye and Joe come back to study this spot, they won't be able to tell anything about it, not if you've messed it up. Maybe y'all are part Indian and your ancestors built this. Do you want to ruin it?"

Lena and Franky and Ginny decided that being part Indian was an excellent idea. Franky was pretty sure he had a bow and some arrows at home, so the little tribe departed. Faye figured the odds were damn slim that they'd leave this mound alone from now on, forever, because children were curious beasts. Nevertheless, she was proud of Amande for trying.

After another quarter hour, she stood and surveyed the muck coating her chest, elbows, and knees. Joe reached out a hand and took the camera. She ran across the strip of land separating her from the water as happily as a ten-year-old, and she kept going till she fell face-first in the water. Three splashes and a gurgly cry of "Maaaah!" told her that the rest of her field team had joined her.

It was almost like being on the beach at Joyeuse, except there was a lot more mud.

It hadn't taken much begging for Amande to convince Faye that they should take a field trip to her island. No. That wasn't true.

It hadn't taken any begging whatsoever. The conversation had gone like this:

"If we go to my island now, you'll have your tools. You can do a better job of checking things out, and I bet you'll find something important enough to put in your report."

Faye, enjoying the sun as it dried her wet clothes, had grunted and nodded.

"While you're doing that, Michael and I can check things out with my metal detector. I brought it."

An object the size of a metal detector was impossible to miss in a boat the size of the one she was sitting in, so Faye had already known that. Still too mellow to talk, she'd nodded sagely.

Joe signaled his willingness by saying, "You got your camera this time. You could take pictures of the place where you found that wood."

Faye leaned back and got comfortable. She could get used to having a fancy boat like this one, with cushy chairs that swiveled and reclined. Her oyster skiff and Joe's johnboat had their advantages, but this was a much better place to nap.

"I'm just along for the ride. Take me...wherever," she said as her eyes drooped shut. But what she really meant was, "Take me someplace as far from spreadsheets and project management software as I can possibly get."

Chapter Twenty-two

Amande's island was bigger this trip because the tide was lower. It was a lot bigger. There must be almost no slope to the land as it entered the water. Faye wondered how far it took for the land surface to drop even an inch.

Amande was ecstatic, because the extra land gave her great scope for her metal detecting adventures. She'd buckled Michael into the baby leash that he refused to wear for Faye and he was trotting beside her, looking over one shoulder to watch his footprints fill with water. With the leash looped around her left wrist and her headset on her head, Amande was leading her prisoner across the mudflats while she waved her metal detector around, and she was doing it with style. Today's baseball cap, lime green, contrasted sharply with her chocolate-brown hair and the flamingos on the shirt billowing around her in the breeze.

Faye could see no obvious way that this arrangement could result in a child lost at sea, so she followed Joe to the spot where they'd found weathered bits of wood on their last trip.

"Point that camera down here," Joe said, as he began removing silty sand, one layer at a time.

His work was swiftly rewarded. Amande was the proud owner...part-owner...of yet another old splinter. She would be so proud.

As Joe bagged the wood sample, Faye snapped a series of photos of a clearly demarcated area of discolored soil that had surrounded it. They might have uncovered something as mundane as a scrap of wood discarded when the cabin was built, but this was *something* manmade, and it wasn't left here yesterday, either.

"Maybe we should give Amande's metal detector a try," Joe said.

"Yeah. Maybe we'll get lucky and she'll find a penny. Reading the date off its face would be a lot cheaper way to date this stuff than sending it off for carbon dating."

Joe stood up and hollered, "Can you bring that thing over here?"

The wind was kicking up, and the sound nearly drowned Amande's smart-ass answer. "That's not a nice way to talk about your son."

Within a minute, she was beside them, headset in hand, still being a smart-ass. "So you two highly trained professionals can't find anything without my help?"

Faye silently held up the splinter in its sample bag. Amande squealed, then she obediently started scanning the area for signs of metal objects. Nothing turned up immediately, and Michael was fussing to get in the water.

Joe held out his hands. "Here. Give me that thing. Faye and I can figure out how to run it. You take Michael swimming."

Amande thrust the metal detector and headphones in his direction, saying, "It's old and quirky. You gotta keep it moving and listen good. But you can't move it too fast, either. Every time you sweep, count to three."

Amande was busy talking, so Faye didn't have to come out and say to Joe, "You're going to let a sixteen-year-old girl be the only thing between your son and death-by-drowning?" All she had to do was deliver her husband a look that said, "You just screwed up. Bad. Do something about it."

Joe rectified his error by saying, "Let me use the metal detector while the *three* of you go swimming."

Faye put her camera back in its bag and said, "I just now got my clothes dry. Let's go in the shack and put on our bathing suits."

Amande scooped up Michael and said, "We'll get there first!"

Since Faye was not sixteen and she did not have the long legs of a six-footer, Amande and Michael did get there first. This meant that there was a long and miserable space of time after she heard Amande's wail and before she could haul her forty-one-year-old self to the cabin door.

Chapter Twenty-three

Joe had adjusted the metal detector's headphones to fit his ears. He still needed to twiddle with the operating frequency, but the thing was working. He liked to learn by doing, so instead of fooling with the controls, he went straight to waving it back and forth, three seconds to a sweep. Amande had already swept the cleared area where he'd been working with Faye, so he thought he'd branch out a little by checking out the underbrush surrounding the clearing.

The chirping was so immediate and so loud that Joe's sensitive ears rebelled. The cache of metal that had set the machine off was nothing more than a couple of old soda cans, but the metal detector was as excited as it would have been if it had uncovered the lost treasure of the Aztecs. Joe ripped the headphones off and tried to shake the noise out of his ears.

That's when he heard Faye calling for him.

Joe wasn't even close to forty yet and he was way bigger than even a sixteen-year-old six-footer. He reached the shack in seconds.

He found a sixteen-year-old in the throes of righteous indignation.

"This is *my* island and *my* cabin," she was saying, blissfully ignoring Steve Daigle's claim on three-quarters of it. "It is *not* okay to slosh beer on the floor and throw the cans in the corner. It's *not* okay to leave a bowl of sugar and a bottle of whiskey on

the counter to attract ants, or a jar of instant coffee to attract...
whatever eats that stuff. It is also *not* okay to leave chicken bones
in my sink to rot."

So that was the source of the smell. It had been hours since
Joe's family and Amande had emptied their bucket of chicken,
which was probably a good thing. After getting a noseful of the
decaying flesh in the kitchen sink, Joe thought it would be a
while before he wanted to eat chicken again.

"None of this stuff was here before," Faye said, which was
code for, "Somebody's been here very recently." With murders
happening every couple of days, it paid to be cautious when
people were places they weren't supposed to be.

"Why don't y'all take Michael for a quick swim?" Joe asked.

Faye was looking at Joe as if to say, "I don't want to stay here
on this island anymore, not even another minute," so he added,
"But make it a quick swim. We need to leave in...oh...fifteen
minutes, if we want to get back before dark. I'll step outside
while you change."

He didn't add, "And I'm going to give this island a good
looking-over while you're doing that."

It hadn't taken Joe long to walk around the perimeter of the
fishing shack, and he'd been almost as quick about checking
out the pathetic little thicket of trees at the center of the island.
There was no place else to hide anything without burying it,
and the only things he'd seen above-ground were the soda cans
in the trees' weedy shadows.

Though the tide had come in a bit, there was still a broad
expanse of muddy sand between the shack and the water in
front of the shack, and an equally broad expanse of shrubby
undergrowth and marsh grass on the other three sides. When
Joe reached the far side of the mudflats, barely in sight of the
water where Faye and Amande and Michael were swimming,
he finally found more evidence of the person who had trashed
Amande's dream house—footprints across the mudflats in the
treasure hunter's telltale pattern. Somebody besides Amande

had been using a metal detector on this island, and they'd done it sometime since the last high tide.

Since their last visit to the island.

Since Miranda died.

If Faye hadn't decided that they all needed to go swimming in their clothes after they finished working at that shell mound, they might have seen the treasure hunter face-to-face.

Judging by the quantity of beer cans that had been discarded in the shack in the two days since Joe and Faye had last visited the island, there could be more than one treasure hunter. Or, if only one person had put away all that beer, the treasure hunter was a seriously hard drinker. This was a hard-drinking part of the world, so it was possible.

Joe didn't relish the company of a crowd of people who left beer and refuse all over a floor that didn't belong to them. Or even one that did. If all those empties were generated by one person, Joe was pretty sure he'd cross the street to avoid that person. He needed to get his family off this island, just as soon as he'd checked out the scuba gear piled in the only one of the shack's corners that wasn't full of garbage.

Joe idled the motor so that he could maneuver the boat into its slip. Amande took advantage of the lower noise level to broach a subject that had clearly been bothering her for a while.

"I heard you talking on the phone with Detective Benoit. About Dane."

"Detective Benoit talked to Dane after we left, because he thought Dane might know something about your grandmother's murder. And yes, Benoit called me the next morning at an unholy hour because he knew I'd want to know what he said."

"Did he think Dane killed my grandmother and my uncle? Because I don't think so. I *know* he didn't."

Choking back the questions she wanted to ask, like, "Did that man touch you?", Faye opted for saying something safe and obvious. "You like him."

"He's just so smart! The first time we met, we talked and talked about archaeology and pirate ships and sunken treasure. I showed him all the things I'd found, and he was interested in all of it, from the old coins to the little tiny pottery chips! Most people's eyes just glaze over. He—"

"You took him on the houseboat, alone—and into your room? Miranda couldn't possibly have been home, because she'd never have allowed it. And what do you mean when you say, 'The first time we met...'"

Amande ignored the final query and went with the first question. "She was taking a nap. So I wasn't really alone with him."

Faye would have grounded the girl on the spot, if she'd had any plausible status as a disciplinarian. Without that status, she could take no action other than to sputter. Most demoralizing of all...Amande's teenaged agony meant that she didn't even notice that Faye was on the verge of having a stroke over her behavior. She just kept babbling revelations that measurably increased Faye's risk of cerebral hemorrhage.

Joe, in the meantime, was displaying the timeless wisdom of a man who knew when to keep his mouth shut.

"When we were talking at Manny's place, just before you came, Dane asked to take another look at my Spanish coins, and I had to tell him they got stolen."

So the man had been wangling a second invitation into a sixteen-year-old's bedroom. Faye's resolution to stick with safe, obvious topics left her, but there were so many unsafe and obvious topics that she hardly knew where to begin. She decided to ask them in chronological order, from the moment of the quite adult Dane's hitherto unknown meeting with this underaged girl.

"You knew Dane Sechrist before the coins were stolen?" Faye's sharp tone scared even her, and her resolution to take the questions one at a time crashed and burned. "When did you meet him? He knew you had those coins before they were taken? How many times have you seen him, anyway?"

Amande's eyes went to the ground. "Just the two times. I met him at the marina a few days before you and Joe got here. He saw me outside with my metal detector and we started talking about archaeology. He asked for my phone number, but he never used it. All we did was talk…"

"Then why do you look like you just got caught robbing a bank?" A worse thought occurred to her. "Benoit said that he didn't talk to anybody who recognized the name 'Sechrist,' but he talked to you. Amande…did you lie as part of a *murder investigation?*"

"I could never have told Grandmère I'd been talking to a man Dane's age, and I think I panicked when Benoit asked me about him. Somehow, it felt like she wasn't really dead and that she'd *know* I'd been sneaking around. I felt…ashamed, I guess, and I didn't want anybody to know about…about Dane and me. He's got to be at least twenty."

There was no "Dane and me," as far as Faye was concerned. Also, Dane was looking at twenty-five in his rearview mirror, if Faye was any judge, but she kept her mouth shut on that subject.

"Well, this man that you've been sneaking around with, but know nothing about, *did* use your phone number. He used it to call your grandmother," Faye said.

"He did what?"

"He called your grandmother and made an appointment for the afternoon she was killed, which she kept. She had a piece of pie with Dane in Manny's restaurant, in fact. He and Manny may have been the last people she saw. Obviously, Dane said she was alive when he last saw her, but nobody knows if he's telling the truth. You need to be careful, Amande."

"I am careful. And I don't believe Dane killed my grand-mother. He just couldn't."

Faye knew that Amande was basing that judgment on Dane's friendly brown eyes and general good looks, and she knew she would have made the same judgment when she was sixteen.

It was a wonder anyone survived adolescence.

◇◇◇

"Would you mind taking Michael to the cabin to get a fresh diaper, Amande?" Faye asked, as soon as Joe had eased the boat into its slip outside the marina store, and before he'd even had time to cut the motor.

She watched the girl walk away before peppering Joe with the questions that couldn't be asked in front of her. "Did you hear what she said about meeting Dane before her grandmother died? And did you hear the part where she said he knew she had the Spanish coins in her room?"

"I did."

"Benoit's gonna blow a gasket when he finds out she lied to him."

"She's not the only one. Now we know that Manny was the one telling the truth. Sechrist never asked him for Miranda's number. He already had it, because Amande gave it to him. Sechrist lied."

Faye leaned down to gather Michael's toys from the bottom of the boat. "Why?"

"Maybe he didn't want anybody to know he knew about Amande's coins, which would have made Benoit suspect that he stole them and maybe even that he killed Miranda. Or maybe he just didn't want anybody to know he was talking to an underage girl. I think it was that, actually."

Feeling that she was getting a rare glimpse into the convoluted workings of the male mind, Faye said again, "Why?"

"Because he couldn't have gotten away with the lie unless he knew that Amande wouldn't tell people she gave him her phone number. They must have agreed to keep their relationship—"

"They only met twice!"

"Relationship. Friendship. Whatever. They must have agreed not to tell anybody. Maybe because he really did know that she was underage, or maybe because she didn't want her grandmother to find out she was interested in somebody, or maybe because he was up to no good. Hard to say. But I think they'd agreed to keep that first meeting secret, and Dane was sure enough that she'd do it that he was willing to lie to the detective."

Faye thought it seemed extraordinarily cocky for Dane to presume that a woman would unswervingly follow his wishes.

As she thought about it, though, she realized what Dane's experience with women had probably been like, so far. The women in his life would have had to be young, and they'd probably been willing to do pretty much anything he asked. When he got older, and when he started focusing on women his own age, he might encounter a rude surprise.

Of course, *she* was always willing to do whatever Joe asked.

Usually.

Sometimes.

When he was lucky.

Maybe it was time to change the subject.

"I know you walked all over that island while I was swimming with Amande and Michael. What did you see? And I know you noticed that scuba gear in the fishing shack, didn't you?"

"I did. Besides a few soda cans, I didn't see nothing but a bunch of footprints, far from where you were. But I do mean a *bunch* of footprints. Somebody was looking for something. It looked like they might've been doing it with a metal detector, because the footprints were…you know…back and forth, back and forth."

"Do you remember what brand of beer came in all those cans? I do remember that they were all the same. I'm also wondering what kind of beer Dane Sechrist drinks. If he's hunting for treasure out here, it only makes sense that he might use the shack as a base camp. I haven't had a chance to tell you what happened this morning. He came to visit me."

"He what?"

"He said he was looking for a job, and maybe he was. But he also spent a good amount of time picking my brain about local archaeology. He played it cool, but he mentioned shipwrecks a little too often."

"You think he's onto something? Maybe he's diving on a ship and he wants to know if it carried treasure?"

"I don't know. I think maybe *he* thinks he's onto something. But Dane's not nearly as smart as he thinks he is."

"Maybe he is, but he ain't as smart as you."

Faye liked it when Joe called her smart. For him, it was the same thing as calling her sexy.

"Be that as it may. Some of the documents he showed me were copied at the Historic New Orleans Collection. You know that place should just give up and hire Bobby, because he spends so much time there. He sees everything. He knows everything. He knows everybody."

"Bobby knows Dane?"

"Of course he does. Better than that, he knows Dane's research interests…and they center on Amande's island."

"So you think Dane is the slob that's been throwing Busch cans around Amande's shack?"

"Yeah, maybe Dane's our Busch drinker, but something feels wrong. First of all, he doesn't come off as a slob. He looks a little finicky to me. Every last little short blond hair is always in place. I got a look in his briefcase this morning. All the paperwork is neatly filed and in perfect order. I don't remember what he was drinking when we caught him hitting on Amande, but it wasn't Busch."

"It was Abita. I remember, because I like Abita. You don't remember, because you like the cheap stuff."

"Which makes me the perfect date, now, doesn't it?"

"It does," said Joe, leaning down for a kiss. "Even when you've got sand all over your butt. I mean, *especially* when you've got sand all over your butt."

Faye twisted in her seat to get a look at the back of her teensy bikini bottom, secretly glad that bathing suit manufacturers did not make mom suits in size 2.

"No need to twist yourself in a knot. There's sand back there. I already checked."

"Glad to hear it." She brushed at the sand coating her bare belly, but it wasn't going anywhere. Joe looked like he wanted to help. "Now I've lost my train of thought."

"You were gonna tell me you thought the scuba gear might belong to Dane, and I was gonna say that he seems real serious about his diving. He wouldn't be risking his life with gear that looks like somebody unloaded it cheap on Craigslist."

Amande appeared in the distance, with Michael on her hip. It was time to wrap up this conversation. Faye could see that her time to speak privately with her husband was going to dwindle month by month as Michael grew, and she felt a pang.

"There are a lot of people running around here who seem to have time on their hands," she said. "Take Tebo, for instance. I don't see him around much. Where does he go? And Steve… where does he go in the daytime? Didi's husband Stan turns up now and then. Where does he spend his time? Maybe he's been going out to the island to check out the part of Justine's estate that his wife *didn't* inherit, but that's a reach. He's probably more interested in whether he can get part of Didi's chunk of the houseboat and stock, since he's surely getting ready to file for divorce."

Joe grunted, managing to communicate his opinion of Didi's worth as a wife with that single inarticulate sound.

"It occurs to me that the person sloshing Busch on the floor of that shack may have a right to be there," Faye went on. "Amande isn't the only owner, you know. Do you remember what kind of beer Steve was drinking last night?"

"Nope, but he and Didi looked like an instant couple when we saw them at Manny's place. Maybe we need to visit Amande at home, so we can check the trash cans and see what they drank when they got home last night."

"Can we do it soon?" Faye asked. "Because I really need a bath right now, and if I go mucking around in Didi's garbage after I've had it, I know I'm gonna want another one."

"I think we should wait until tomorrow morning, while she's sleeping off tonight." Joe nodded at the deck of the houseboat, where Didi and Steve sat in folding chairs, giggling and fawning over each other. "See? Instant couple."

Faye tried not to gag.

"I think we're gonna need an overnight babysitter again. Don't you, Mrs. Doctor Longchamp-Mantooth?"

"Yeah, but first I've got to call Benoit and tell him that Miranda's sweet little granddaughter lied to him about knowing Dane before her grandmother was killed."

Benoit was not disturbed enough to suit Faye.

"You never did anything sneaky when you were sixteen?"

Faye was starting to wonder how long it had been since Benoit himself had been a teenager. Fifteen years, tops, probably less. That wasn't long enough.

"To the best of my knowledge," she said, "I wasn't spending time with possible murderers when I was sixteen."

"You were just riding around with boys who had brand-new driver's licenses, hoping to get hold of a fake ID that looked enough like you to fool bar bouncers. Maybe you might have been better off with possible murderers."

"Exactly how is that observation supposed to help me sleep better at night?"

Benoit emitted a sharp noise that might have been a laugh, but sounded more like, "Heh." Then he did it again, as if he were trying to convince himself that the situation was funny. "I told you that I have a baby sister about Amande's age. I don't sleep at night, no. Maybe one day I'll get used to it."

"You think you'll get used to watching your sister grow up and start hanging around with men?"

"No. I'm thinking I might get used to not sleeping at night. But we were talking about Dane Sechrist. What do we know about him? We know that everything in his story is something we can check out. By the end of the day, we'll know if he really did grow up in a nice home on the Mississippi Gulf Coast, and we'll know whether he did all that other stuff he told me. As I said before, Mr. Sechrist is the Boy Scout on our suspect list."

"But now we also know that he talked to Amande a week or more ago, before Hebert died and before you or I even knew she was alive. And he didn't tell you about that, now did he?" Her next thought was a new one, tying two pieces of information neatly together. "And we know for sure that he knew about the

Spanish coins. Amande said she showed them to him, and she said that he was sorry to hear that they'd been stolen."

"Praise God. My highly paid consultant has finally stopped trying to do my job for me, and she's started talking about the archaeology stuff, which is what I hired her for. So Dane knew about the coins. That means what, exactly? He talked to a pretty girl who's interested in the same things he is. He saw her in Manny's bar, sitting with a couple of lowlifes, and he talked to her again. I'll admit that it bothers me that she showed him the coins and now they're gone, but maybe she tells a lot of people about those coins. She showed them to *you*, almost as soon as she met you."

This time it was Faye's turn to belch out a "Heh," because she didn't have a ready answer for him. Time to change the subject again. "So you think it's a good idea for Amande to spend time with Dane Sechrist?"

"Did I say that? Hell, no, it's not okay for a teenaged girl to spend time with a man that age. But I don't say that because I think he's more likely to be our killer than any of the other characters hanging around that marina. I just say that because he's too old."

On this point, Faye agreed with him.

"Have you gotten any more information on the time of death for either Hebert or Miranda?"

"In both cases, eyewitnesses are giving us better information than we can get from a forensics lab. Hebert was seen alive at a bar near the marina just a few hours before you found him."

"I didn't find him. Amande did. Poor kid."

"Yeah, you're right on all counts. You didn't find him and she did. And that makes me want to say, 'Poor kid,' too. Anyway, other than Dane Sechrist and Manny, the poor kid was also the last person to see Miranda alive that we know about. The fact that both bodies were found in the water is a complicating factor."

"Because it changes the rate at which they lose body heat?"

"You got it," Benoit said. "You think like a scientist. The water temperature is way up in the seventies right now, so a dead body that started at ninety-eight-point-six doesn't have far to go. A body immersed in seventy-five-degree water is going to get to seventy-five degrees fast, just because of convective heat transfer, and then it's gonna stay there. We know that much. Also, we know that both victims were dead when they went in the water."

"No water in the lungs?"

"Not much. So there's no way to know whether Hebert's body cooled off in a bar's parking lot for hours, then got dumped in the gulf, or whether he went straight in the water and cooled off quickly there. The same thing's true for Miranda. She could've died right after she left Manny's place, or she could've died hours later, shortly before we found her. There are just too many variables, and the time frame is just too short."

"What was Steve Daigle's alibi?"

"It's the same for the days of both murders. He's staying in a motel a few miles from the marina. Steve claims he slept late both days—"

"Plausible. That's what drunks do."

"True. Then he says he ate an early lunch at the marina both days—which checks out with Manny—then spent both after-noons at some nearby bars."

"Any witnesses at the bars?"

"Yeah, but they're not real upstanding citizens. And the fact that he moved from one bar to another by himself shoots a big hole in his alibi. It gave him time alone to do both killings, easy."

Faye tried to picture Steve as he started getting drunk at one establishment, then moved to another, and then another. "Why do you think he was moving around like that?"

"Looking for someone, I expect. Maybe Didi or somebody we don't know about yet. Or maybe he just kept looking for bars with prettier women. We know he was with Didi when the sheriff finally found her and told her about her mother."

"He let her come home alone, after news like that? What a gentleman."

Who was she forgetting? There must have been others who might have killed Miranda, but who would want an old lady dead?

"What about Tebo?"

"Tebo is the least likely suspect among our three drunks. No, make that four drunks—Tebo, Steve, Didi, and Didi's husband, Stan. On the day of Miranda's death, he started making a spectacle of himself at a bar several miles from here about lunchtime. When the bartender had enjoyed quite enough of that, he had Tebo arrested—along with Didi's husband Stan, who you don't know enough about to wonder where he was. The two of them were within eyeshot of dozens of bleary eyes all afternoon, then they were in jail. I can't account for their whereabouts all morning, but if somebody killed Miranda that morning, then both Dane and Manny are lying, which makes them better suspects than Tebo and Stan. I think it's pretty unlikely either Tebo or Stan killed Miranda, but I'm still checking out their alibis for the day of Hebert's death."

Faye nodded abstractedly, because she was still trying to think of more suspects. As if she thought that the list of disagreeable people in her immediate vicinity was somehow too short.

Manny worked just a few steps away, so the fact that he was on the job from dawn till bedtime that day meant absolutely nothing. He could have walked away, killed Miranda or Hebert, as the case may be, then gone back to work. People would have just assumed he'd taken a bathroom break. But why would Manny have killed a woman who'd been renting a slip from him for years? And what did he—or anybody—have to gain from killing Hebert at all?

"Help me think through the people who would benefit from Miranda's death," she said.

"I can't think of any motive other than her possessions. She may have been a voodoo mambo, but she didn't seem to be active outside her own home, so I don't think she was out in the world making enemies through her magic. People tend to be a little skittish about killing folks skilled in the dark arts, anyway. And I don't think she was out there stealing somebody's boyfriend or breaking some poor man's heart, either. I think this is about greed. Either somebody wanted to steal her stuff—and they sure didn't get much, if they did—or they wanted to inherit her stuff."

"This is probably a question for a lawyer, but it's my understanding that the only heirs are Steve, Didi, and Amande. You and Joe are Amande's alibi."

"Like she's really a suspect?"

"I was just trying to be complete. Didi's giving the same alcoholic alibi as Steve: She says she slept late on the day her mother was killed, and then she got up and went drinking, winding up with Steve at the end of the day. She claims to have been alone at the apartment she shared with Stan on the day Hebert died, and nobody has admitted to seeing her around these parts until a day later, so her story tracks. I don't think that skinny girl stabbed her big ol' stepbrother to death, nor that she slashed her mother's throat. Something tells me that Miranda, even pushing seventy, could have taken on Didi, just out of sheer strength of will. But I absolutely believe that Didi could charm a man into doing murder for her."

"So it's possible that Steve and Didi are in cahoots?"

"Between the two of them, they will control way more than half of both the houseboat and the stock. As Amande's guardian, Didi could also tap into Amande's assets a lot easier than we'd hope, so she's probably looking pretty good to Steve right now. If you were an uneducated alcoholic that didn't like to work, wouldn't a free place to live and a small monthly income sound really good to you? Especially if there was a good-looking woman living there who liked scumbags such as yourself?"

Truth be told, a free place to live and a small monthly income sounded pretty good to Faye right that minute, and she was a highly educated professional who was capable of getting tipsy on a beer and a half.

Benoit kept dissecting Didi's and Steve's motives. "I'm not surprised to see them strike up a romance—"

"Romance is such a…pretty…word for anything Steve and Didi might do."

"Granted. Let's say instead that I'm not surprised to see them hooking up, and that doesn't bode well for Amande's future. But I don't see how they could have conspired to kill Hebert, if Didi truly wasn't in town yet and hadn't met Steve. Her mother? I devoutly hope Didi didn't conspire with him to kill Miranda. That would be just too terrible."

Faye agreed, but she wasn't sure she'd put it past Didi.

"Absolutely nothing we've said about possible motives applies to Hebert," she pointed out. "His killing didn't affect the inheritance of Miranda's boat and stock one bit. He was never an heir to anything, other than maybe a few of her fairly worthless personal possessions. He had nothing of his own, so nobody killed him for his stuff, either. He seems to have had no contact with any of his family members for years prior to his death. If he has any relationship to Dane or Steve or Manny or Stan, we don't know about it. So why is the man dead? Is it possible that the deaths were unrelated? Was he really killed in a random bar brawl just three days before his mother was murdered? Or is it possible that we don't understand the reasons for either killing?"

"Oh, we don't understand the reasons, I know that for sure. But I don't believe that their deaths were unrelated."

"Because it's just too unlikely that the murders happened so close together?"

"No. It's not too unlikely, not at all. Stranger things have happened here in these swamps, believe it. No, ma'am, I say I think the murders are related, because I saw both bodies. The murder weapons were different, but they were both sharp implements, and violent people have clear preferences in the way they do their violence."

Faye thought that made sense, in a twisted kind of way.

"The marks on the bodies weren't exactly the same, but my gut tells me that it was the same person, using the motions that felt the most comfortable. Someone struck Hebert a death blow or three from behind, while he was still standing, which is about the only way to kill a man that size easily, when you're using a knife. There were abrasions on his throat, from where the killer grabbed him for leverage, and there were marks on his side where somebody kicked him damn hard. But the first deep stab wound was the thing that immobilized him. By the time the third one struck, he was paralyzed and bleeding from his aorta. Dying didn't take long."

Faye really didn't want to hear the answer, but she asked the next obvious question. "And Miranda?"

"Killing an old lady the size of a pelican ain't hard. She had some broken fingers, probably because she'd hidden that basket tool in her pocket, then tried to use it to defend herself. We haven't found it, and we don't know where the killing happened, but there's no blood in the house or anywhere around. We found the spot by the water where Hebert was stabbed, and there wasn't a whole helluva lot of blood there, either. The killer was strong and fast. Hebert's body was in the water before his heart stopped beating."

"I laid awake last night wondering if Miranda suffered."

"She did." Benoit's voice struck just the right note of solemnity. He wasn't calloused to the death he dealt with every day, but his tone wasn't cheesy and funereal, either. Faye realized that she liked him.

After a respectful pause, he continued describing Miranda's murder. "Since there was no blood or evidence of a struggle, I think she was lured away or kidnapped, then killed elsewhere. Either way—lured or kidnapped—she knew something wasn't right, because she took that cutting tool with her. When the time came to defend herself, he—and I think it was a man just because he was big enough to kill Hebert—took her weapon and broke three of her fingers doing it. There were some minor cuts on her hands and arms, like she was trying to get it back. There were bruises all the way around her body, like somebody big wrapped his left arm around her, trapping both her arms. And then there were the stab wounds. Three of them, made by a right-hander with a lot of upper-body power. Just like Hebert. Only they were made with the blade her killer had just taken from her. Then he slashed her across the throat, just for laughs."

"The same guy."

"Yeah, I think it had to be a guy. He had an easier time of it, stabbing the life out of an old lady, but yes. My judgment is that the same man killed both victims. And he is not someone who needs to be walking the same earth as you or your little boy or Miranda's granddaughter or…well…anybody. I'm going to find him, ma'am. And I do appreciate your help. You're the best unpaid consultant a man could want."

Episode 4 of "The Podcast I Never Intend to Broadcast," Part 1

by Amande Marie Landreneau

A woman aboard a sailing ship brings bad luck. Men have been saying so for many, many years, but that doesn't make it true.

Yes, I'm sure that having a woman aboard—or even a few—will bring about jealousy aboard a ship full of men so lonely that they will fight for a woman, any woman. When pirates are involved, then fighting is the same as killing, I'd guess. So unless there's a woman for every man, I expect there would be trouble, but I wouldn't say it was the woman's fault. The bad luck comes when men misbehave, so I'd say it was their fault, wouldn't you? Regardless of where the fault lies, the "no-woman" rule wasn't a bad one, when it came to keeping the peace aboard ship.

Every man who sailed with Gola George knew the rules. No one without a Y-chromosome boards a pirate ship. Actually, come to think of it, George was already violating that rule. He was stealing women, or buying them, at every port in the Caribbean, but they didn't stay on his ship long enough to cause trouble. That was the point of his island harem—to keep his ships free of women.

I'm sure he intended to dump Marisol in the hell-hole where all the other women lived, and I'm sure you think I'm about to tell you that Gola George was so taken with her beauty that he couldn't bear to see her go.

No.

It was Henry the Mutineer who couldn't bear to see something so beautiful crushed into the mud. Henry was the one who flouted the pirate code for Marisol.

Surprised? Maybe you're wondering what use a gay man would have for the companionship of a pretty woman? If so, then you're on the right track. The word "companionship" is the key to the story of Henry the Mutineer and Marisol and Gola George.

Probably, Gola George wanted Marisol, just for her beauty, but what could a gentleman's daughter have to say to an illiterate man who rose to riches because he was able to kill people well? George was no companion for her.

I think Henry the Mutineer wanted George for the same reason George wanted Marisol—for his beauty. That is why he stayed on the pirate ship where he so obviously didn't belong. But what, really, could they have had to say to each other, once the loot from their last voyage had been duly entered into Henry's account books? Henry was forced to seek companionship with his books and his paints and his music.

Marisol's arrival changed all that. She changed everything.

Marisol was thrilled by the breadth of topics covered by Henry's library. She shared his tastes in art and music, especially music. Grandmère's stories all say that Marisol played the lute and that Henry bought her one, so that they could play music in his chamber at all hours. He had a berth built in his cabin, just for her, probably because leaving her alone while she slept on a ship full of lonely, barbaric men would have been just stupid. He bought her silk dresses in every color, which sounds exactly like something an artist would do with a beautiful woman when he didn't want to sleep with her.

The descriptions of Marisol that survive sound like they come straight from an artist's lips: Her hair was golden and red, like sunrise over Barataria Bay, and her deep green eyes were the color of the Bay's shadowed depths. *I don't know how many times I heard my grandmother say those words, and I still believe that they have come down to us from Henry's lips.*

Henry taught her to play chess. Marisol taught him to play her lute. He bought her bonnets to shade her fair skin and—this is important—he bought her an intricately carved ivory fan, for those times when a lady must fend off prying eyes.

Surely George was jealous, but of whom? Was he jealous that Henry's devotion made Marisol sexually unavailable to him? Many other women were available, but George was the kind of man who wanted what he couldn't have. So maybe he just wanted Marisol to himself.

Or was he jealous at having lost Henry's single-minded attention? None of George's words have slipped down through the years, so we will never know, but the stories all agree on one thing: George did eventually snap.

On the day that he grabbed Marisol's slender body with both meaty hands, she fended off his kiss with a swiftly lifted ivory fan, the way a lady would deter an impulsive gentleman. George was only deterred for the split-second it took for him to shatter the fan against the bulkhead behind him. Marisol's fate should have been sealed, but Henry the Mutineer was capable of things that George could never have imagined.

Chapter Twenty-four

As it turned out, neither Faye nor Joe had to concoct a reason to go check Didi's trash cans. When Amande left after breakfast, she asked Faye to meet her at the houseboat later.

"I called my lawyer and told him that a client who had lost three family members in a week deserved more attention than I'm getting. Especially since I'm being forced to live with a woman who's planning to take everything I have."

Faye swallowed, trying to decide how enthusiastically to agree with Amande's assessment of Didi's plans. She thought the situation was about as dire as Amande said, but what would be the point of rubbing the girl's face in it?

"I also told him that I'd come to him, because I don't want Didi to be part of the conversation. He offered to pick me up, since he knows I can't drive, but I don't even want her to know I'm talking to him. So could you pick me up, pretending like we're going out to check some more historic sites?"

Faye had agreed.

"I wanted to make the appointment early, so that Didi would still be in bed and we wouldn't have to deal with her, but Reuss couldn't do anything earlier than eleven. I guess he *does* have some other clients. Still, even though Didi will probably be awake, she won't be real sharp. I'll take any advantage I can get."

And then Amande was gone, leaving behind two adults shaking their heads at what the girl had accomplished for herself after they were awake, but before they were real sharp.

◇◇◇

Dane Sechrist cut his boat's motor, listening to the shush and grind as its hull slid over the sand ringing the little island where he'd been mooring for weeks now. Now that the motor was silent, he could hear the radio better. The newscaster was saying the same thing he'd said yesterday and the day before. That busted well was still pumping crude into the Gulf, and there seemed to be no way to make it stop. At least, that's what the oil company responsible for the whole fiasco was saying.

He was trying to wrap his brain around the idea that a big thick layer of oil could come ashore hundreds of miles from the gushing well, spoiling beaches and marsh grasses and wide-open bays. There was almost no hope that it would fail to reach the secluded coves where he'd learned to fish, nor the bayou where he now sat.

Fish glinted in the clear water surrounding his boat. Pelicans plunged from high in the sky, scooping breakfast into the sagging pouches behind their bills. In just a few days, everything was going to change.

What would the oil do to the shipwreck he was hunting? Every instinct told him he'd nearly found it. The Spanish coins— one gold one and two nearly identical silver ones—mocked him. He'd found one of the silver coins here on this island, with a metal detector way more sensitive and expensive than the one he'd seen that sweet little girl waving around.

He could have thrown a rock into the water and hit the very spot where he'd found the other silver coin and its gold brother. And near *that* spot had been the great pile of ballast stones that mocked him still. At low tide, he could almost walk to it. The water was so shallow here that the island swelled and dwindled with the tide. An island was a landlubberish thing for a diver to crave, but Dane wanted this one badly.

Why? It wasn't just because the logistics of recovering a shipload of gold and silver would be easier and cheaper if he could set up a base camp on a handy piece of solid ground. Although it would.

Dane had spent some time in legal libraries, and he'd developed an opinion on salvage law and the law of finds. His first opinion was that the United States and her various sovereign states had not been consistent in applying those laws, so there had to be loopholes to be exploited, if he should ever need to defend his right to salvage this shipwreck he believed he had found. Mel Fisher had certainly parlayed the *Atocha* into a nice pile of money, so it could be done, but Dane thought he'd found a workaround that would keep him out of court altogether.

As he understood the law, the Abandoned Shipwreck Act of 1987 vested ownership of abandoned shipwrecks beneath state waters in the federal government. This, in Dane's opinion was bad, very bad. Congress had then transferred those property rights to the states. Dane wanted the property rights for himself, so he didn't see this as an improvement...if this wreck was beneath state waters. But was it?

The navigable waters of the state of Louisiana extended three miles offshore, but Dane wasn't sure he'd ever want to be a judge who defined precisely where the Louisiana shore was. It varied with the tide and the wind. It changed as the river deposited silt here and there, and it changed some more as the land sank beneath the encroaching Gulf of Mexico. Unfortunately for Dane, this island and its probable wreck were in Barataria Bay, well within anyone's definition of "three miles offshore."

However, state waters had to be navigable, and he wasn't all that sure most people would put these waters in that category. Most of the time, they looked more like mudflats than navigable water, and this played right into Dane's hands, because there was another quirk in the case law. He'd found more than one instance of a wreck being awarded to a landowner, because it was embedded in soil on land owned by that landowner.

There was a solid chance that there was a shipwreck embedded in soils that could be reasonably claimed to be part of this island. The coin he'd found on dry land had been found in a place that was unequivocally part of it. Amande's description of the spots where she'd found her own coins had been vague, but they'd matched what he'd seen during his own work, and one of her coins had been found on land that was always dry, as well. Therefore, Dane needed this dry land badly.

As long as he could plausibly claim that he believed the wreck to be on his island, and therefore that he believed it belonged to him, he figured he had a reasonable defense against accusations that he should have notified authorities as soon as he found it. He could work alone in this remote spot for a long time, possibly forever, without attracting attention. Why should fishermen care what he was doing?

And in the meantime, who was going to know where he found any riches he uncovered? Whether he found his treasure buried on the island or in the mudflats or far out in open water, Dane's notes would say it was dug up on the island. Case closed.

He would get the island, no matter what he had to do, but the oil worried him. Just a little more time, just a few more dives, just a bit more patience, and he was confident that he'd find the important part of the wreck where the gold and silver waited. But if the oil came, would he be able to dive that wreck? Would the government let him pilot his boat into polluted water? Would all of the oil float, or would some portion of it sink to the bottom, settling over the wreck so thickly that he might never find it?

Damn the oil. Damn BP. Damn that little girl for not being able to describe to him exactly where she found those old Spanish coins. Damn the screwy title on this island. Damn Justine Landreneau Daigle for dying before he could buy it from her while the place was still owned by one single, solitary human being who probably would have been happy to sell. Who owned it now, anyway? Dane sure as hell wasn't handing any money over to Steve Daigle until the man could prove that the land was his to sell.

Dane stepped out of the boat and started unloading his gear. The cool, wet sand molded to his bare feet. It was time to get out there and dive. He needed to find that wreck while he still could. But first he needed a cup of coffee.

Dane was just enough of a caffeine addict to have set up a camp stove in the abandoned shack, so he could have his hot coffee when he needed it. And his sugar. He liked his coffee sweet, so he'd brought plenty of sugar out here, stored in a sealable plastic sugar bowl to keep out the bugs and vermin. He made do without cream, because carrying a cooler back and forth was a whole lot of trouble. Besides, there was no caffeine in cream, so it wasn't necessary to Dane's happiness.

Dane walked to the cabin with a gallon of bottled water in each hand, purchased at the gas station because the water at his rented place was so vile. As he passed through the half-open door, he heard a clank as his foot hit an empty can lying on the floor.

As his eyes adjusted to the dim light, he saw cans lying everywhere, all of them that familiar Busch blue. Because beer didn't have enough kick to keep a true alcoholic happy, there was a bottle of Jack Daniels on the counter next to Dane's camp stove and sugar. He had a pretty damn good idea of who'd left these things.

In the corner was some of the junkiest diving gear he'd ever laid eyes on. That lying bastard was moving in on the wreck, and he didn't care if Dane knew about it.

He stalked back out to the boat without even setting down the water jugs. The man had overstepped some important boundaries, and Dane needed to establish, once and for all, where those boundaries were.

◇◇◇

As the morning passed and their minds grew sharper, Faye and Joe had concocted a reconnaissance plan that involved a banana and a can of Coca-Cola, then Joe had headed out for some field work. As she walked to the houseboat, Faye was sipping on the Coke and enjoying the opportunity to consume empty calories for the good of mankind.

This was a very pleasant way to recover from a morning spent firing a researcher who thought it was okay to make things up, so long as the lies were meticulously footnoted. Faye wasn't sure she was cut out to be a business owner.

As she sipped, she walked to the houseboat with Michael, hand-in-hand. The little boy chewed slowly on his banana. As they approached the door, he finished it on cue, and handed her the slimy banana skin. This event set up the next part of her plan: to ask Didi politely where the trash can was, giving Faye the opportunity to check its contents while getting rid of the peel.

This plan would fail if Didi took the nasty banana peel and threw it away herself, but Faye couldn't imagine that she was that good a hostess. It would also fail if Didi and Steve recycled their beer cans. This would be an unlikely display of good citizenship, but it wasn't out of the realm of possibility.

Proving her resourcefulness, she had developed Plan B, the Coca-Cola. If Faye didn't get access to the kitchen trash because Didi threw Michael's banana peel away for him, she would at least have located the trash can. At that point, she would suck down the last of her Coke, walk over to the can where Didi had just dumped the banana peel, and toss it in for herself.

If she *did* get access to the trash but saw no beer cans, all was not lost, because the Coke can served a dual purpose. The absence of cans in the trash would be a clear sign that there was a recycling bin full of cans somewhere, because Faye had seen beers in their hands as they sat on the boat's deck just the night before. And she knew in her heart of hearts that both Didi and Steve had both been too hungover that morning to have taken out the trash already. To get access to the recycling bin, all she'd need to do was brandish the empty Coke can and ask where she should throw it. Didi and Steve had to put their empty beer cans somewhere, and either the banana peel or the Coke would take Faye straight to them.

Faye was proud of the banana-Coke plan. Too bad it was unnecessary. When Amande opened the door and let them in, she saw that Steve and Didi couldn't even be bothered to throw away their empties. The kitchen counter was covered with Coors Light cans and Busch cans, in equal quantities. If forced to guess whether it was Didi or Steve drinking the light beer, Faye was going to go with Didi.

She wished Joe were there so she could give him a high five or a fist bump or something. Then Tebo rose from the couch. Damn. How could she have forgotten that a third person of drinking age was hanging around the houseboat? Maybe because he didn't seem to be there too awful much.

Maybe Tebo was the Busch drinker. Maybe Steve and Tebo *both* drank Busch. Or maybe the person hanging around Amande's island was some other Busch drinker entirely. It wasn't like they were looking for someone who only drank a private-label microbrew. Still, Faye noticed that, despite the open door into the room where Didi was sleeping, Steve was nowhere to be seen. Was he already out of bed and in his boat, heading toward an island that didn't completely belong to him? Maybe. Steve wasn't around much in the daytime, either.

Didi and Tebo waved good-bye as Faye took Amande off their hands once again. It was only a five-minute drive to Bernard Reuss' office, located in an unrestored Victorian house that was, like most homes and businesses in the area, just a stone's throw from Plaquemines Highway. Faye could see the levee from Reuss' front yard. His house must be sturdily built to have stood through more than a century of hurricanes.

Reuss' office, in his old home's parlor, was nicer than Faye would have expected. Maybe the man *did* have other clients who had actual money. The upholstered guest chair was worn but comfortable, and the aged wood floor had been recently waxed. Reuss waved Amande into it while he moved a second chair from the dining room for Faye. Then he found a box of brightly colored toys to keep Michael happy.

"I've been thinking about you, Amande. It's way past time for us to have this conversation. It's good that you called."

Faye was glad he'd admitted that a sixteen-year-old had been forced to light a fire under her lawyer to get him to do his job.

"Your case has stayed front-and-center on my schedule, though. I've had four visitors come here separately to talk to me about you—Steve, Didi, Stan, and Tebo."

Steve and Didi were Miranda's other two heirs, and Stan had a plausible interest in the property of the woman to whom he was still technically married, so Faye had no doubt why they'd been to visit Reuss. But Tebo?

Maybe he just couldn't make himself believe that he had no claim on anything Miranda had left behind. Faye had been wondering why he'd lingered in the area after he and Didi had decided not to waste money on funerals for their dead loved ones. By all rights, he should have gone back wherever he came from by now. Maybe he stayed because of a vain hope that Louisiana's weird inheritance laws might still cough up something for him.

"What did they want?" Faye asked.

"Money," Reuss answered in a "you idiot" tone of voice. Something about his tone made Michael look up from his toys and giggle. Faye realized that she could imagine this unprepossessing man dealing successfully with a jury and a judge, after all.

Then Reuss said, "I take that back. I'm not a hundred percent sure they were all sniffing around for money. Didi and Steve certainly were. Stan wasn't quite so straightforward, but his intent was obvious. They all wanted information that would help them get their hands on Miranda's estate. I reminded each of them that I was Amande's attorney, not theirs."

The words, "And I'm not yours, either," hung unspoken in the air.

"I talked to Tebo a little longer than the others, because he has a bit of stealth about him. He just wanted to talk about whether Didi was really going to get custody of Amande. I don't think he believed the legal system could be that stupid. Maybe he was hoping to get her and her inheritance for himself, but he didn't say so and he was faking concern for my client pretty well, so I talked to him for quite a while. I wouldn't trust him with a gerbil I liked, but I did talk to him."

Then he turned away from Faye toward his client. "Amande, it is very likely that the state of Louisiana will leave you in Didi's care until you're eighteen."

"She's really going to be my guardian?"

"Actually we use the word 'tutor' instead of 'guardian' here in Louisiana, but I don't like the term. It confuses people. And since she's the easy and obvious candidate, yes, I do think the state will put you in her care. You're old enough that they'll listen to your opinion, but the only other realistic option I see is foster care. You'll have to decide how you feel about that option."

Faye couldn't help herself. "Didi? A tutor?"

"I know," Reuss said. "She's not likely to teach my client much, other than how to drink beer, but—"

"Vodka shots, actually," Faye observed.

Reuss cringed. Faye couldn't help noticing that there were seven photos scattered around the office, featuring girls whose ages ranged from preschool to early adolescence. This tracked with the oversized play structure dominating the front yard. Maybe Amande's case hit a little close to home for this man.

"Didi's planning to teach me how to watch my bank account drop to zero. My aunt just cannot be put in charge of my money." Amande reached out a hand and tapped on his desk to emphasize her words. "She cannot. I'll be on the street by the time I'm eighteen. And the houseboat—how can that possibly work? It looks like Steve thinks it would be real cozy for us three owners to live there together, and I think Tebo's planning to sleep on the couch forever. I don't want to live this way, and I don't see how things can possibly be different. None of us is ever going to have enough money to buy the other two out."

Reuss pulled Amande's folder out of his desk drawer and slid a pair of reading glasses onto his face. "Hold on. Let's take one thing at a time. I can put your share of the oil stock in trust for you. I could be the trustee. Didi wouldn't control it."

"No, but she'll be in here once a week with a new story about how she's got to have some money because I need medicine or flute lessons or something. She'll keep coming up with stories until you give her the money. The result will be the same. I'll be broke when I'm eighteen."

"Maybe you underestimate my ability to play hardball with your trampy aunt."

Amande crossed her arms and leaned back in the chair. "Now you're starting to sound like an attorney-at-law."

"Why, thank you, ma'am. So glad that you approve. Now let's talk about the houseboat. No, Didi is never going to have enough cash at one time to buy you out, and neither is Steve. If you try to set up a payment plan, you'll just be back in court every time one of them defaults. Even if I cut my fees to the bone, you can't afford to keep coming back to me and, much as I'd like to, I can't afford to work for you for free. But there are other options. Maybe you three can rent the boat to somebody else and split the income. Or maybe you could sell it and split the money. Both of those options make the roof over your head go away, so I'd wait to do either of those things until you're of age."

"Both of those options also leave me homeless at eighteen."

"Or you could sell the oil stock and use the money to buy out Didi and Steve. Again, I'd wait until you were of age."

"That option leaves me broke at eighteen and living in a place with no college within driving distance. And no car to drive, anyway. Nothing you've suggested gets me free of Didi before then. I came here to get legal advice I could live with."

Judging from the uncomfortable look Reuss was wearing, he was completely aware of how little help his legal advice was going to be to Amande, and so was everyone in the room, except for Michael. None of her options were attractive.

Amande let out a short breath that a poker player would have recognized. The girl was ready to put all her chips in the pot. "I want you to get me emancipated. Then we can decide what to do about the boat before Didi has a chance to drain my stock brokerage account dry."

Faye knew she should have seen this coming. She probably *had* seen this coming, but she hadn't wanted to entertain the idea of a young girl taking on the world alone.

Amande was still talking. "Won't I get Social Security payments, now that my mother's dead? And can you find out how much I'll get every month from the stock dividends? It may not be much, but it'll be something, and I can flip hamburgers, too, if I have to."

Reuss put up his hands as if to tell her to settle down. "First of all, I'm not entirely sure you'd keep getting survivor's benefits from Social Security if you got yourself emancipated. I've never had need to find out, so I'll have to check. Second, in case you haven't noticed, there was already a recession on, even before that oil spill out there knocked a bunch more people out of work. There are grown men flipping burgers out there, these days. Look up and down Plaquemines Highway. How many burger joints do you see? How many businesses of any kind have Help Wanted signs hanging out front? Just because you want to be able to take care of yourself doesn't mean that you can, Sweetheart."

It was as if she hadn't heard him. "How long does it take to get emancipated?"

"You know what the court system is like. Slow. I think you'd be better off to hunker down and survive the next year or two with Didi. Truly, I do."

"If I tracked down my father, he could sign paperwork to get me emancipated."

"Nobody knows who he was. Your mother took his name to the grave. My guess is that he's sorry enough to go after a piece of your inheritance, as the price for his signature."

Realizing what he'd just said, he hurriedly added, "I'm sorry, Sweetie, I didn't mean to say bad things about your father."

"It's okay. If my mother thought he was a nice person, she would have left me with him, instead of her stepmother. Anyway, there's another way to get emancipated."

She fixed a level gaze on him, as if she were daring him to say it first. Faye had the feeling that she wasn't going to like the sound of this.

She was right. When Reuss lost the game of chicken he was playing with a teenager, he revealed Amande's final playing card and, no, Faye didn't like the sound of it at all.

Faye actually snorted out loud when Reuss said, "Amande Marie Landreneau, I want you to forget any notion of emancipating yourself by getting married."

"Married?" Faye squawked.

"I do give you credit for doing your homework," Reuss went on, "but if you were mine, I'd ground you from the Internet for the foreseeable future to keep you from coming up with more lame-brained schemes like this one. Besides, your guardian—meaning Didi, probably—would have to sign for you to get married."

Amande rolled her eyes and said, "It is so frickin' inconvenient to be a minor. I'll get Didi to sign, one way or another. Maybe I'll convince her that I'm marrying somebody rich. Or maybe I'll just get her drunk. She's easily influenced and she's predictable. I can do it."

Reuss twisted the arm of his reading glasses until it fell off, then he studied it for a few seconds. "Yes. You probably can. And I'm reasonably sure that you'll lose your Social Security benefits just as soon as you do, so factor that into your little scheme. Who were you planning on marrying, anyway?"

"Never mind that. I see the way men look at me. If you can't find a better way to get me out of Didi's clutches, I'll find somebody to marry. If you don't want me to do that, then you find me another answer to my problems."

Reuss spoke slowly, maybe hoping that his brain would catch up with his mouth. "Give me some time before you run out and ruin your young life, okay? If we can't get you emancipated, we'll need to work with the legal situation as it is. You're going to need another tutor besides Didi, someone who has your best interests at heart or, at the least, someone who is easier to handle."

"What's to keep *you* from being my guardian? Tutor. Whatever."

"Nothing, really. It's not out of the question."

Amande continued, inexorably laying out her plan. "You could help me cash in the oil stock and buy out Steve and Didi—"

"If the stock's worth enough to do that. I don't imagine that the current situation is doing anything good for oil companies and their stockholders."

"Presume it is, for the moment. You could help me buy them out and get my Social Security checks flowing. I think Manny would let me work in the marina grill. That should give me enough to live on, if I own the boat outright. Eventually, I'll finish high school and I'll need to rent the boat out and move away, but I'll deal with that when the time comes. I don't mean to be rude, but I don't want to live here with you, even if you're my guardian. I'd feel stupid trying to jam myself into somebody else's family. I'm too old for that. I would live on the boat, and you'd help me handle my money, and you'd come check on me now and then. That's all you'd need to do."

"I'll have to think about it, Amande. I'm not convinced it's your best option."

Amande rose. Faye was still too flummoxed to join her, so she stood alone, while Michael played on the floor as if nothing had happened. "Well, you'd better think fast. This nice lady and her husband have helped me a lot, but they're gonna finish their work and go home to Florida. If you can't show me a better plan by then, I'm going to start looking for a husband. Don't think I won't do it."

Chapter Twenty-five

Faye didn't say much on the drive home. Part of her wanted to shake Amande and holler, "Get married??? Are you insane???" Part of her was seriously considering handcuffs and shackles for the girl. And yet another part of her remembered what it had been like to be alone at twenty. Amande was in a far worse position than Faye ever had been.

She hated to be suspicious of the entire world, but sometimes the world seemed to deserve it, and she was more than a little disturbed by the last turn Amande's interview with Reuss had taken. It had seemed that the idea for the lawyer to take over as her guardian had come from Amande. But had it? Or had she been cleverly guided in that direction by a man who was remarkably good at looking dumber than he was?

For a big-city attorney, raiding Amande's little inheritance would have been hardly worth the risk of an ethics complaint. Here in bayou country, where the only real money came off the gulf in fishing boats or drove up Plaquemines Highway in the pockets of offshore oil workers, the economy had tightened overnight when the oil spill affected all those jobs. When people don't have money, they can't hire lawyers. Reuss was as affected by the crisis as anybody. Was he maneuvering Amande into giving him access to her money?

Michael had gone to sleep as soon as the car started to roll, so Faye wouldn't have had much to say to Amande, regardless.

New parents rarely risked doing things that might wake a sleeping child, like talking. Still, it felt like she was giving the girl the silent treatment, and she felt bad about it. She wasn't Amande's mother. It wasn't her place to dole out disapproval. Still, she kept her silence, because she couldn't think of anything constructive to say.

Her cell beeped and she dug it out of her pocket, forgetting that she was setting a bad example by doing that while she drove. It was Benoit.

"I had to come out to the marina to talk to Manny, and I thought I should touch base with my favorite cut-rate consultant. But you're not here."

"I'm just turning off Plaquemines Highway now. Look up and you'll see my car. Why did you want to talk to Manny?"

"He called me because he'd remembered some stuff. I noticed from the very start that Manny sees everything that goes on around here, so I came right out as soon as he called."

"What did you learn?"

"I learned how long Dane Sechrist has been hanging out in Manny's bar. It's been months, although it's only been the past couple weeks that he turned into a regular. And I learned that Manny's seen Dane having private conversations with Steve."

Faye parked the car. "I see you standing over there. Let me hang up the phone and come talk to you in person."

Amande followed Faye to where Benoit stood. Without waiting for the adults to speak, she blurted out, "Why were you talking to Manny? He's not in trouble, is he?"

Benoit shook his head. "No, Sugar, I was just talking to him about the goings-on here at the marina. You know—people getting killed. Stuff like that. Manny's here all the time, and I thought he might have seen something helpful."

Amande was not to be dissuaded from defending her friend. "Manny wouldn't hurt my grandmother. He was good to her. He never raised the rent. If he didn't see her for a few days, he'd ask me how she was or come check for himself. When either of us came in for groceries, he'd look around and find out-of-date food, just so he could give it to us instead of throwing it away. Manny taught me everything I know about computers, and he let me do my schoolwork on his old one until I saved up enough money to buy it from him. You leave him alone."

Amande's tone made Faye wonder whether Manny would be the lucky guy if Amande decided she needed to propose to somebody.

"Amande, would you go...um..."

Faye wanted Amande out of this conversation with Benoit, and she was too poor a liar to come up with a diversion quickly. Michael's diaper was freshly changed, and it wasn't time for his lunch or nap. Maybe she could send the girl to the marina for ice cream...

"If you want to get rid of me, just say so." Amande's tone was matter-of-fact. No hurt feelings. No attitude. Just an offer to disappear. Maybe she was tired of listening to people try to figure out who killed her grandmother. "I have some homework to do, actually. I've been neglecting it lately."

Benoit smiled down at her, and the smile did nice things for his dour face. "I think you've had some pretty good excuses. Miss Faye and I are gonna walk you over there. Just to make sure there's no bad guys lurking. You lock yourself in, okay? You're doing that all the time now, aren't you? And keep a phone handy. We can practically see your bedroom window from here, but there's no sense in being stupid."

After Benoit and Faye were satisfied that the houseboat was empty, except for a napping Didi, and after they were sure that Amande was safely locked in, Faye asked, "Where were we? Oh, yeah. How come Manny's just now telling you this stuff?"

"Good question. If he's being straight with me, it's taken him a while to piece together that I'd want to know this. When I questioned him after Hebert's death, Steve hadn't showed up on Miranda's doorstep yet and you hadn't seen Dane's name on Miranda's refrigerator yet, so we didn't even have either of them in our sights. Since Miranda died, word has gotten around that I was looking for someone with the name Sechrist, but Manny didn't know Dane by name at the time. However, the sight of that man hitting on his little friend Amande put Manny over the edge. He spent some time yesterday finding out who he was, then he grilled the poor kid about just how well she knew Dane. He even went back through his orders to see when his Abita sales picked up."

"Are you sure you don't want to fire me and hire Manny to be your unpaid consultant?"

"Manny's too smart to work for free."

Faye waited for his deadpan expression to crack. It didn't.

He went on. "When Manny pieced together that this person flirting with his young friend was definitely the same Sechrist I was trying to find, he called me. He's sure that he saw Dane and Steve together at least a few days before Miranda died. Before even Hebert died. Manny says he distinctly remembered Amande sitting at the bar, like she always has, talking to him while he dealt with his credit card receipts. Dane and Steve and their beers were just a few feet away. That was the day he realized that a pretty sixteen-year-old shouldn't be in a room where somebody like Steve was drinking. Other than the one time you saw her, she hasn't been back in the bar since Hebert died, not even just to hang out, because Manny hasn't allowed it. He made an exception that night she came in with Didi, and he lived to regret it."

Manny's story hung together. If things had truly happened the way he described, then Faye liked him. Respected him, even.

"What does it mean that Steve and Dane knew each other before Steve even showed up on Miranda's doorstep?" she mused. "How likely is it that they could have randomly met?"

"I know that life is random, but I don't like it. I'm always going to look for a reason things happen."

Faye nodded her agreement and waited for Benoit to continue.

"So Manny says that Dane and Steve have some kind of history, even if it's only a week or two. Even better, Manny is the only person I've talked to who knew Hebert, outside his family. Lots of people knew who he was, but they were mostly bartenders and drunks. In a bar, you stand beside a stranger and drink, or you stand in front of a bartender and drink, but you don't really know those people. Manny actually knew Hebert as a person. He said that the man was a drunken jerk who had a soft spot for his little stepsister Justine, which meant that Manny had a soft spot for him. When Justine ran away from her baby and her stepmother, Hebert stopped coming around. I think Manny missed him a little."

"Maybe because Manny's got a soft spot for a teenaged girl, too. Does his interest in Amande seem unhealthy to you? Miranda would've gone head-to-head with any thirty-year-old man that she thought was after her granddaughter, don't you think?"

"Actually, I think she would have just hexed him, but I don't think she did. Manny seems to be the nice guy Amande thinks he is."

"If you say so. So forget Manny for now. I'm more interested in the fact that Dane has known Steve for a while. Did I tell you that I believed Dane was diving for treasure somewhere near Amande's island…the one she owns with Steve? And would you be interested to hear that he's been over here picking my brain about local archaeology? Or in the fact that somebody's been hanging out in the shack on that island, drinking beer and scuba diving?"

One of Benoit's orange eyebrows rose a millimeter. "Yes, on all counts. So do you think Dane has been squatting on Amande's island around-the-clock while he looks for the treasure? Because evidence says otherwise. He gave me an address for a rented fishing shack. I drove past it. It's rustic. Damn rustic. Latrine. Hot, plastic-tasting drinking water that comes from rain barrels. I could maybe see Hebert living in a place like that, but Dane grew up in a nice house. If he's been staying there for months, and it looks like he has, then he really wants to be here. Your suspicion that he's treasure hunting sounds about right."

Faye looked away for a second, checking that Michael was still within arm's reach. "That reminds me of something I've been wanting to ask you. Where is Steve staying? Because it didn't look to me like anybody was living in that leaky and bug-ridden island shack. I saw beer cans and diving gear, but I didn't see any clothes."

"Steve had a cheap motel room, but he gave it up two days ago when he took up with Didi. Not only is his car overnighting in the marina parking lot, but his boat is now being moored at the dock that services Amande's houseboat. Surely you've noticed."

Faye gave a quick nod. "I've seen it here, but I didn't know if it was moored in that spot all the time. So he's given up his hotel room and moved in with Didi full-time after what? Two dates?"

"If you can call them dates."

"Charming. I've been doing my best to keep Amande away from that man, but there's only so much I can do when he's living in her house."

"You know that there's absolutely nothing you can do about that. Unless you're willing to call child services and try to get her put in foster care."

"I just might get to that point. But never mind Steve. I'm starting to think Amande's island is the center of all things."

"It's Steve's island, too. Don't forget that he owns three-quarters of it. What makes you say that?"

"Dane obviously thinks there's treasure nearby, and there may be some unknown Busch-drinker out there poking around underwater, too. I'm thinking it's Steve. Now Manny has neatly tied the two guys together by telling us that they've known each other awhile."

Benoit was shaking his head. "I don't know, Faye. There's no link between the island and the two murders. It passed directly to Amande and Steve from Justine. Neither of the victims, Hebert nor Miranda, ever had any claim on it. The houseboat and stock *did* pass through Miranda, giving a motive to the people in line to inherit. That would be Didi and Steve, and maybe Stan. Also, technically, Amande."

"I sure wish we could link Hebert to the island. At least we know Miranda was out there at least once, because Amande remembers it," Faye said.

"Hebert didn't have a boat, and he didn't have the money to rent one. He didn't even have a car."

The word "boat" caught Faye's ear. "Who *does* have access to a boat?"

"You are really hung up on that island, aren't you?"

"Not just the island. Didn't you say that Miranda's body had gone right into the water, and that you hadn't found the place where she was killed? And hasn't it been bothering you that nobody saw Miranda and her killer leave the marina area? How hard would it be to bang an old lady in the head in her own kitchen, and load her unconscious body in a boat? It's moored on the far side of the houseboat, you know, out of sight of the whole world. The killer could take off from there across the water to a place where it was more convenient to murder her. And neater, too."

"Everybody knows Dane has a boat. Tebo's no more got the money to buy a boat than Hebert did, so not him. Manny? Of course he has access to a whole bunch of 'em. He manages a marina. Stan may have a boat—most people around here do—but I have no idea if he brought it with him when he came here to watch his wife cheat on him. Steve has one, of course. We've already been talking about it."

Faye scanned the parking lot. Steve's shabby green Ford was there, so she was guessing he'd taken his boat out. But where? To the island? Or somewhere else?

"Where do those people go in the daytime?" she mused. "Didi, Tebo, and Steve, I mean. We know they spend a lot of time in bars, but where else? I'm thinking Steve spends time drinking Busch and scuba diving without proper certification. Didi seems to have business around town. I've heard Amande mention her going to the grocery store or to government assistance offices. Tebo, though. Where does he go?"

"I'll ask around and see if I can find out. In the meantime, I hope you'll humor me and focus on the archaeological stuff I hired you to do. It's gotta be less dangerous than talking to lowlifes."

"So you're going to find out where those lowlifes go when they're not setting bad examples for a teenaged girl?"

"Yep, and you're gonna see if you can figure out how those missing Spanish coins fit into all this. You're also gonna try not to get crossways with a killer while you're doing it."

Faye sat idle in front of her computer, completely aware that she should be working. The cabin door protested as someone large pushed it open, and a long, tall shadow fell across the floor. There was no reason for Joe to leave his work and come home for lunch, so he had come for a reason and Faye knew what it was. They'd both been pretending this conversation wasn't coming.

"We need to talk," he said, taking her by the hand and sitting next to her at the dining table.

How many times had she heard the words, "We need to talk," from Joe's lips?

Not once. Joe was a doer, not a talker.

"I've been listening to the news," he began. "We've got to get home. The oil's been heading east for days."

"But it'll take a while for it to get there, yet. We can—"

"It's gonna take a day for us to get home. I've gotta get the booms from Sheriff Mike. I don't know how long it's gonna take to get 'em set up. Those booms might keep the worst of the oil away, but if they don't get set up in time, it could cover our beach and smother the plants in the salt marshes. I don't know what's gonna happen to the wading birds and the crabs and the fish, but we have to do what we can. We need to go now."

Faye took her hand from his and spread it atop the paperwork that was keeping her awake nights. "We can't default on this project, Joe. We've spent too much money getting it done. It'll bankrupt us, and we'll never get work again."

"There's nothing you can do on that computer in this cabin that you can't do at home. Yeah, I'm out there most days doing field work, but we can hire that out. You know we can. We've hired the rest of it out, and that's working fine."

Faye could feel it all slipping away. The project she'd worked so hard to land. The company she and Joe had struggled to build. The PhD that had taken half her life to get. And her home, lying defenseless in the path of an endless rush of crude oil.

She took her hand off the stack of paper, and gripped Joe's hand with it. "You win."

◇◇◇

How many times had Joe heard the words, "You win," pass Faye's lips?

Not once. Not until now.

She wasn't known for changing her mind, but he acted quickly, just in case.

"How long will it take you to pack? I'll gas up the car."

"I think you should pack enough of your own things for today and tomorrow, then go. It'll give you a fighting chance of getting home by midnight. There's a lot to do to get this place ready for checkout. Somebody needs to let Manny know we're leaving. The rental boat has to be returned. The refrigerator needs to be emptied. I'll stay here and shut things down."

Joe was beginning to suspect that Faye hadn't really meant it when she said, "You win."

"When you say, 'I'll stay,' do you mean a day or a month?" he asked.

"I mean two or three days. Some of our contract workers are a little lacking in their work ethic. I need to meet with them face-to-face before I go. I need to talk to our client liaison and make sure we're not freaking him out when we shut down our on-site headquarters and move to a whole nother state. I can do it, Joe. Just not today, and probably not tomorrow."

"If you don't come with me today, you'll be making a nine-hour car trip with a one-year-old. Alone."

"I find that jelly beans make good bribes." She looked out the window in the direction of the houseboat.

He squeezed the hand resting in his. It looked no different than it had the day he met her, small, brown, narrow-fingered, with close-clipped nails. The seven years that had passed were invisible, without leaving even an age spot to mark their passage, but the time had gone by. Years pass, and things change. Where would he be, if he hadn't found Faye?

He nodded his head toward the window. "You're gonna have to say good-bye to her, sooner or later."

"I just wish I knew she was going to be okay. I was hoping to leave her in a good place."

"I know, but there's no help for it. We have to go home."

Chapter Twenty-six

Faye had hardly kissed Joe good-bye when her cell phone rang and she saw that it was Reuss calling. After a perfunctory hello, he said, "Look. I didn't want to say this in front of the little girl this morning, but I think somebody needs to know. Calling you about it is irregular, ethically. I should be talking to my client or her guardian, but I think it'll be obvious why I can't take this to Didi. Amande doesn't have anybody else but you to look after her. And yes, I know she's only got you for another week or two, but I'm afraid she's going to have to take the next two years one week at a time."

Actually, Amande would be on her own far sooner than "another week or two," since Faye was packing even now, but Faye kept that to herself. "What's the problem?"

"I was being completely straight with her when I said that Steve, Didi, Stan, and Tebo had all been to see me. I left out the part where Steve asked me if it might be possible for him to get custody of Amande. Just this morning, in fact."

"*What?*"

"Yeah, I know. I couldn't come up with a less suitable guardian for a teenaged girl if I trolled maximum security prisons. He fed me some line about how he wanted to make sure his dead wife's little girl had a good future, but think about it for a minute. He's got even more to gain from getting control of Amande's inheritance than Didi does. Amande and Steve together will hold half of the houseboat and stock, but Steve didn't talk much about that. He was more interested in understanding how ownership of the island would be handled. This took me some time to explain, because the man is not overblessed with brains. Finally, he got the picture: Didi has no share in the island, because Justine owned it alone. If Steve gains custody of Amande, he'll control the island outright, presuming he can get a cooperative trustee for the girl's inheritance. If he *is* the trustee, she's in deep trouble."

"And you think he wants that island."

"Oh, there's no doubt. He wants it."

"No sane judge would give that girl to Steve Daigle. Am I right?"

"Probably, although not all our judges are sane in these parts. But think about this. Amande says she's looking to get married. What will happen if she marries Steve?"

"He gets control of the whole island." She struggled to untangle the legal details she'd discussed with Reuss just an hour before. "She can't get married unless Didi signs. Steve is *Didi's* new boyfriend, so she's not gonna be real excited about marrying him off to her niece…"

There was silence on the other end while Reuss waited for her to finish thinking.

"…but Didi's not real dedicated to the sanctity of marriage, is she? There would be no reason for her to stop seeing Steve, just because he married her niece. And she can be bought." When Faye sifted through Amande's possible custody arrangements, she saw that Didi might be a lowlife, but she wasn't stupid. "By taking up with Steve, Didi's put herself in a no-lose situation. It doesn't matter to her whether she is Amande's eventual guardian, or if Steve is, or even if the girl gets emancipated by marrying Steve. Under all those scenarios, she and Steve will control the boat, the stock, the worthless island that everybody seems to want—everything."

Faye wondered whether pillow talk, for Steve and Didi, involved brainstorming ways to cheat a young girl of what was rightfully hers.

"That settles it," she said. "I listened to Amande's social worker when she said that Louisiana wouldn't want to place her with someone who lived out-of-state, but there has to be a way to do it. I cannot believe that any sane judge—"

"I told you not to presume any judge is sane."

"Anyone with a beating heart, then. No one with a heart would put that child with those people. You're her lawyer. I'll pay you to find a better place for her to live than with Didi or Steve. Maybe it'll have to be foster care, but I hope it will be with me. In the meantime, she will not spend another minute aboard that boat with those people. I won't leave here until I've found someone to keep her until things are settled. If Didi tries to make trouble with the child services people, well then, it'll be time for Amande's lawyer to explain to them just how unfit she really is."

"Yes, ma'am. I'm sure there's an ethical loophole that'll let me do an end run around my client and her guardian. I'll get right on it."

◇◇◇

The phone was still in Reuss' hand when the knock on his door sounded. Dr. Longchamp-Mantooth's husband stood outside, looking confident and trustworthy and altogether suitable as a father for his favorite client. He also looked like someone who had just made a decision.

The man didn't seem to be a big talker, but he knew how to make his point. After shaking hands and saying hello, he said, "Faye and I have to go home to Florida. My wife will not rest if she thinks Amande isn't being taken care of. I want you to do whatever it takes to get the state of Louisiana to name us as her guardians. Or foster parents. Or adoptive parents, I don't care. It don't make a hill of beans to me what people call us. She'll be treated the same as our own. Bet on that."

"Have you talked to your wife about this?"

"I wanted to ask you whether it was even possible before I did. It ain't like I don't know what she's gonna say."

Reuss nodded to concede that obvious point. "It'll take time."

"I figured that. Will the girl have to stay with her no-good aunt until we get this thing worked out?"

"She may have to go into foster care, unless we can find friends or family willing to take her."

"I have some ideas about that. Let me do some talking around."

Reuss watched the man open the leather bag hanging at his waist. He saw a couple of hand-chipped stone tools, a roll of fishing line, a small plastic box of fishing hooks, and a plastic bag of nuts and dried fruit. This guy was a fisher and a hunter, and Reuss wagered that neither he nor his family would ever starve. Again, not a bad father for his favorite client.

The big man held out a business card as he left, saying nothing more than, "Keep me posted on what I need to do to help this thing along."

Reuss studied the name on the card. *Joe Wolf Mantooth.* It suited him.

It had taken the two archaeologists a while to jump into instant parenthood. It interested him that they'd done it without consulting one another, but with the calm confidence that the other spouse would back the decision. Reuss knew his wife would shoot him dead if he came to her and said, "Honey! I decided we needed eight kids, so I brought another one home to go with the seven we've already got! Here she is!" but he'd come close to doing that today, because Amande Landreneau deserved better than the things life had dealt her so far.

By taking Amande before he did, Faye Longchamp-Mantooth and her husband may just have saved his life.

Faye wasn't a list-maker, because she tended to lose the lists once she made them. Closing down their temporary business office in south Louisiana was a task complex enough to require a list, so she'd forced herself to make one.

The list depressed her. The oil encroaching on Joyeuse Island depressed her. The necessity of leaving Amande depressed her heavily. The thought of leaving the site work in the hands of contract employees who had not shown themselves to be self-starters—this thought was infuriating, but it was also the only one of her problems that she could attack directly. She needed to go find a couple of her sometimes-competent workers and put the fear of God into them.

"Guess what we're doing this afternoon!" she burbled to Michael. "We're going on a boat ride."

"Boat!" he said, showing off the third word he'd learned, after "Dah" and "Mah."

She had two sites to the southwest, and they were being surveyed by two of her weakest contract workers. She thought a surprise visit from corporate management was just the thing those two employees needed to gain a healthy respect for deadlines and quality work.

Faye also thought she needed a boat ride more than she needed air.

It was way quicker to get to those sites by boat than by car, so she had an excuse for that boat ride. Even better, the time would be billable to the client. If she spent the afternoon jerking a knot in her lazy staff, she could spend the next morning closing down the cabin and returning the boat and still be at home on Joyeuse by bedtime.

Sometime in the next twenty-four hours, she would need to say good-bye to Amande, but that thought made her want to eat a bag of jelly beans. This meant there'd be none left for bribing Michael, if she got desperate on the car trip. Maybe that was a good thing, because she might indeed go to Mother's Hell if she stooped that low.

◇◇◇

"A-mah!" Michael said, as they walked across the parking lot and veered left toward the rental boat without stopping at the houseboat.

Faye didn't think she could talk to Amande without crying. Maybe she'd be able to manage it after she'd spent an afternoon on a boat, skimming between the sky and the Gulf. Besides, she needed to talk to Joe before she committed to making Amande a part of their family. She knew he would agree, but the capriciousness of the law scared her. Some judge she'd never met was going to decide whether Amande came to live with them, and when. She had to trust that it would happen, all in good time.

"We'll see Amande when we get back," she said.

Michael expressed his feelings about leaving Amande behind by starting a quiet but continuous whining in the back of his throat. The noise had the potential to cost Faye what was left of her sanity. She walked even faster, hustling him along, because she knew that the boat motor would drown out the noise.

In minutes, he was in his life jacket and Faye was in one of the happiest places she knew, in command of a boat.

Amande had been putting off her statistics exam for a week. She wasn't dreading it because it was hard. She was dreading it because statistics was mindless and boring.

She'd also been putting it off because playing with Michael was fun, and the tests took so frickin' long. The school system was dead-set that all students experienced a full quotient of misery before earning their credits, so the test was timed. Even if you could finish it in twenty minutes, you had to sit at the computer until the two-hour clock ran out, occasionally poking a button that signaled to the computer that you were still sitting there, suffering.

Amande had long since finished the test and checked her work, so she was now in the button-poking-and-suffering stage. She'd passed the time so far by eating a sandwich and part of a big bag of barbecue-flavored potato chips, but a girl could only eat for so long.

Didi poked her head in the bedroom door. "I'm going to the Social Security office again to see what it'll take to get us some help. We need those checks to start coming in now, not next year."

Amande poked the button and told her statistics test that she was still alive. "Good luck with that," she said, without looking up.

Didi gave being maternal a shot. "You'll have the house to yourself while I'm gone. Try not to mess it up any worse than it already is. Even better, why don't you run the vacuum?"

"With Tebo on the couch and Steve in your bedroom, this place isn't ever going to be all neat and tidy. Somebody needs to take out the trash."

"Very funny. For your information, Tebo is nowhere in sight and Steve went fishing. It'd be nice if he caught something. There's no downside to eating supper for free."

Amande stifled the urge to point out that catching the fish would cost Steve something, in terms of boat fuel, and that cooking it would cost Didi something, in terms of propane for the stove. She just stared at her computer screen and waited Didi out. Soon enough, her aunt walked away and left her alone.

Faye's first stop had been so short that Michael had slept through it. She'd just needed to pilot the boat down a narrow bayou to a barely discernible shell midden, where she had politely asked her field tech why in the hell it was taking him two days to walk the site and take some pictures. Once she'd finished terrorizing the young man, she had eased the boat back down the bayou. Mission accomplished.

The next stop would actually be fun. There were two contract employees working at that site, and they weren't lazy. They were just young, inexperienced, and burdened with a site so interesting that it was freaking them out. Faye had sent one of them to check out the site of an old lighthouse that was probably long-gone, but a quick walkover of the surrounding land had uncovered potsherds from the time of European contact, a chunk of English pottery from the eighteenth century, and a piece of glass that just might be a rum bottle from the early nineteenth century. Faye figured a personal visit and a pep talk would keep them focused.

She also figured that there was no harm in taking Michael swimming at the conveniently located spit of light brown sand

just a few feet away. She was sure that thirty minutes in the
water was all that she needed to restore her sanity. Pretty sure.

As Faye puttered down the bayou that led away from the first
site, she checked her phone's connection periodically, waiting
for Joe to notice that she'd left him a message. The man was
hopeless with technology less than five hundred years old. His
phone was probably resting in his pocket, dead, and it would
remain that way until he wanted to use it. After they'd had a
chance to discuss things, she'd go talk to Amande.

Faye tried to remember whether she'd brought a dress on
this trip. And makeup. It felt wrong to say, "Would you join
our family?" while wearing shorts and flip-flops. But what if
Amande didn't recognize the heavily made-up woman asking
to be her mother?

What had Amande's real mother looked like, anyway? Faye
had never even seen a picture of her or of the grandfather who
had left behind the property causing all this trouble. Justine had
been no relation to Miranda. The faceless woman hadn't been
related to thin and homely Tebo or to fat and homely Hebert,
either. Didi and Amande were her only blood relatives that
Faye had ever met. They were both inordinately pretty, so Faye
pictured Justine as being fine-boned and elegantly built, like her
daughter and half-sister. But was she brunette like they were?
Was she tall like Amande or petite like Didi?

Following the branches of Amande's family required more
mental effort than Faye wanted to exert right this minute, not
while she was preparing to complicate her own family tree. She
wondered whether they themselves remembered how they were
related. Or how they weren't related. Miranda's death had drawn
lines in the family that might have been forgotten.

Before Miranda died, had it really mattered to any of them
that Didi was only Amande's half-aunt, or that Miranda's sons
had been her stepuncles and not her uncles? And Steve, who
had only known as much about these people as his dead wife
had told him—he must be dizzied by the effort of keeping

everything straight. The law was now making those distinctions very important, financially.

Joe had given her a priceless description of Steve, doing a doubletake at Tebo's casual revelation that Steve's wife Justine had left behind an abandoned child. Then she remembered the impact of that information in terms of cold, hard cash. Amande's very existence was going to cost Steve money when Miranda's estate was settled. So was Didi's.

As Faye neared the mouth of the bayou, she cut back on the throttle, hoping that quieting the engine would help her concentrate. Who *had* Steve known about? He'd known about Miranda, surely, and about her usufruct on the houseboat and stock. How else would he have known where to bring Justine's will? And how else would he have known that he'd have a stake in the boat and stock when she died?

Hebert. He'd known about Hebert, because he'd said that Justine had told him Hebert was a wonderful brother. This must sting for Tebo, since his dead stepsister seemed never to have mentioned his name to her husband. Justine seemed to have been a person who didn't just cut ties with a loved one. She amputated that loved one from her life. Thanks to Justine's habit of severing ties, Steve had known about Miranda and Hebert, and that was all.

Faye cut the motor and let the boat float in the motionless spot where the bayou opened its mouth into Barataria Bay. She knew why Hebert was dead.

Chapter Twenty-seven

The computer asked Amande, again, whether she was still there. Amande responded in the affirmative. Her body was trapped at this desk, but there was nothing to keep her eyes from wandering to the calm blue water outside her window.

Her hand moved toward the basket on her desk. She reached in and fingered the artifacts she'd spent her childhood collecting. Smooth, sharp-edged, chipped stone. Chunks of old pottery shaped by the fingers of long-dead men and women. Why did she love these things so? Her hand went to the empty space at the back of the drawer where the old Spanish coins had rested in their box. They were gone, like her grandmother, like her dream of meeting her mother. Like everything, soon enough.

She pulled the brass sextant out of its drawer and rested it on the palm of her hand, wondering why it didn't tell her which direction she should take. Oddly enough, it was pointing at the door when the knock came.

There were precious few people to whom Amande would have opened that door. Faye and Joe, surely. Manny, probably. Didi and Tebo, yes, but only because they were kin.

Dane Sechrist, with his well-scrubbed face and shy grin, was on that short list of people whom Amande instinctively trusted. She opened the door.

◇◇◇

It wasn't easy, holding onto her cell phone with one hand and hanging onto a child who had suddenly decided he needed to go swimming with the other. Sometimes, Faye missed regular old phones, with receivers that could be pinched between shoulder and ear, leaving both hands free.

Benoit was being obtuse.

She tried explaining her conclusions again. "What do you mean, you don't follow me? Don't try to disentangle all those family ties and all the inheritance laws. They're too confusing, and they've kept us distracted from a motive for murder that's not all that complicated. Greed."

"We've suspected that all along. The trouble is that *all* these people are greedy."

"Forget 'all these people.' Just concentrate on what Steve knew when he came to town. He knew that Justine's stepmother Miranda had the lifetime use of most of his wife's estate. He knew he'd be waiting to collect his inheritance until Miranda died but, when she did, he'd be set for life with monthly income and, if he played his cards right, a free place to live. He knew he was going to have to share that income and home with the other heirs, but it was still a sweet deal. Now tell me this. Who did he think those other heirs were?"

Benoit sat silent for a second. "He knew about Justine's 'wonderful brother' Hebert. It doesn't sound like Justine explained that he wasn't her brother by blood. He would have thought that Hebert was another heir, and the only one, because he didn't know about Amande, Didi, or Tebo. Are you saying that he came to town to kill Miranda, so that he'd inherit the boat and oil stock, but believing that Hebert also had a claim on it?"

Good. He'd understood her first major point. Onward.

"I am," she said. "But he couldn't kill *just* Miranda, unless he wanted the goods to be divided between him and Hebert. Hebert needed to go, as far as Steve was concerned. I think it's significant that Hebert went first, before Miranda, to keep his heirs from showing up and wanting a cut."

"I'm not sure that makes a difference. If Hebert had left heirs, they'd have been entitled to his claim on Miranda's stuff, anyway."

"I know, but that concept is a little sophisticated for Steve, don't you think?" Faye could see that getting this lawman to stop focusing on the letter of the law was going to be tough. "That's what I keep telling you. We've been thinking about this all wrong, worrying about the fussy details of inheritance. It's isn't important what the law says, or what the truth is. The important thing is what someone of Steve's limited intelligence believed at the time of the murders. I believe he thought that taking out Hebert left him as the lone person holding a claim on Miranda's stuff after she died...I mean, after he killed her."

"So you think he killed Hebert by mistake?"

Now Faye felt like she was getting somewhere. "*Yes.*"

"Then why'd he go ahead and kill Miranda, after he found out that he was going to have to share the houseboat and stock with Didi and Amande? Was he going to kill them, too?"

"Maybe. But by then he'd seen Didi. Steve is dumb and dangerous, the kind of person who puts other people into just two groups: opportunities and obstacles. A pretty woman who owns a big chunk of the property he'd like to control would be a fairly irresistible opportunity for someone like Steve. Romancing her, promising her money and a place to live and security... wouldn't that be a good way to control Didi? Even better, this pretty woman is the only likely candidate to get custody of the girl who owns the rest of her mother's estate. Together, Steve and Didi could live on easy street, partially funded by a sixteen-year-old girl."

"You think her judgment is that poor."

Faye thought he must be kidding, but she indulged him by answering the question. If she hadn't had unlimited minutes on her cell phone, she would have skipped the answer and just laughed at him.

"She cheats more openly than any married woman I've ever seen. She thinks that teaching a child to hold her liquor is one of the responsibilities of motherhood. According to the gossip that's rampaging through Plaquemines Parish. Didi is so unburdened by guilt that she was willing to pretend her husband was killed when the oil rig exploded, so she could weasel herself into some undeserved widow's compensation. Yes, I think her judgment is poor enough to allow her to take up with a man like Steve."

"I take it that you don't like Didi."

Even when she was holding a wriggling child with one hand and trying not to drop her phone overboard with the other, Benoit's understated style could make her laugh...

...until he turned around and made her stop laughing, just by making a logical point. "Steve and Didi have a problem though. Their plan only works until Amande is eighteen. Then she'll control her own property and her own money."

Why did Benoit have to point that out? Deep down, she knew that Amande was worth more dead than alive to Steve and that this would be even more true when she came of age, but she couldn't think about that now. Amande was vulnerable to Steve in yet another way, and she needed to make Benoit understand that.

"Follow me just a little further, Detective. Consider Amande's island. When Steve came to town, he probably knew about it, but he thought it was worthless compared to the houseboat and stock. Suddenly, it has become a very popular place. We have a treasure hunter, Dane Sechrist, sniffing around those waters, and Manny has told us that Steve was hanging out with Dane even before he showed up on Miranda's doorstep. Right?"

"So Manny says."

"We know from my cousin Bobby that Dane is interested enough in the island to drive to New Orleans and study old maps of it. We also know that somebody who is too sloppy to be Dane, somebody who is probably Steve, has been storing diving gear on the island. That island has become the center of the universe for some people, and I think it's obvious why. Whether there's treasure out there or not, people *think* there is, and treasure has been the motive for many a killing. Who owns that island?"

"Justine's heirs—Steve and Amande. That's all, I think. Not Didi, because she wasn't related to Justine's father."

"*Yes!*" Faye said again. "Now tell me…how can Steve get control of the island?"

"It's even easier than controlling the houseboat, because Didi has no ownership in her own right. He can control the island by controlling Amande's guardian—Didi—or he can get himself named Amande's guardian."

"Or he can get her to marry him." The very thought made Faye want to wash her brain with soap.

"Or he could kill her. That's all very complicated, Faye."

"Sure it is. Life is complicated."

"Let me uncomplicate it for you." There was pity in his voice. "Here's what I think, and you're not going to like it. Didi and Amande have no other known living relatives, correct? Other than Tebo and Amande's missing father?"

"Correct."

"In the absence of some guy with DNA that proves he's Amande's father, who would have the best chance of inheriting Justine's stuff if Didi and Amande died? I'd say that Justine's widower would have the best shot, wouldn't you?"

"Yes."

"You've told me that you think Steve is capable of committing murder twice, in such an out-front and straightforward way that it's sheer luck we haven't found witnesses or evidence yet who can help us nail him. He's been lucky. What's to keep him from believing he can get away with doing it twice more?"

Faye couldn't think of an answer she liked, so she said, "I need to go back to the marina and get that girl. I can be there in ten minutes."

"Was Steve around when you left?"

"No. I'd have noticed that stupid-looking boat."

"That's not to say he's not there now. I'm on my way, and I won't be alone. Call me when you get close to the marina."

Chapter Twenty-eight

Dane stayed a shy step further from the door than most people would have.

"Hey, there," he said to Amande.

If Amande had been more experienced with romance, she would have been amused at this grown man, tentative in the presence of a sixteen-year-old girl. She would also have been able to see that he liked her and that he didn't know what to do about it, because she was sixteen. "I have something to show you," he said, holding out a bag.

Still feeling awkward and tongue-tied, she took too long to speak and he blundered on. "Some artifacts, I mean. I've got some things that I know you'll want to see. Do you—" He looked around him and noticed two deck chairs and a low table nearby. "Do you want to sit out here and look at them?"

Amande, feeling that refusing to let him in her house would say she thought he was some kind of a criminal, said, "Oh, the sun's kinda brutal out here. Do you want to come in?"

She let Dane in and, knowing that Detective Benoit would be proud of her, she locked the door behind him. Amande had never entertained a guest of her own, not in the role of hostess, but she didn't want him to know that. She played it cool. "Would you like something to drink? Maybe a beer?"

"It's a little early for me. I just had lunch. Some water would be fine."

So much for her effort to be sophisticated. Now he thought she was as big a lush as the rest of her family. Amande wanted to drop through the boat's deck and never look at Dane again. She hurriedly stuck two glasses under the tap and filled them with water, then she dumped the rest of the barbecue chips into a bowl. How sophisticated.

Dane didn't even look up when she put his glass of water in front of him. He had reached into the bag and pulled out three broken pieces of pottery and a smaller bag.

"Look," he said, holding out the pottery and finally meeting her eyes. "I found these yesterday, and I've been all over the Internet, trying to date them. I think they're pieces of an olive jar, very old. This is probably a piece of the rim. And here... see? This piece is curved like the neck of a jar."

She picked up the curved piece and ran a finger over it. "They look like they came from the same jar. Wouldn't it be cool if you could put all the pieces together? How old do you think it is?"

"Maybe from the sixteen hundreds."

"Where'd you get these?"

"From the bottom of Barataria Bay, right where the pirates used to sail."

Amande held another potsherd up to the light and sighed. She was too distracted to notice the intent gaze that said Dane had never met a woman who cared about such things, except for the much older and very married Dr. Faye Longchamp-Mantooth.

"Do you think there's a shipwreck down there?" she asked.

"Yes. Of course there is. There's lots of shipwrecks down there that nobody will ever find. But have I found one of them? Yeah, I'd like to think so."

He opened the small bag and pulled out two boxes. "I didn't find all of these, but I thought you'd like to see them. Especially since yours got stolen." He handed her the first box.

Nestled on cushioning material at the bottom of one shallow box were two silver coins and a gold one. He gestured toward them and said, "I found those. But I bought the others."

The second box held two silver coins. Even if she hadn't recognized the box, Amande would have known them. She'd looked at them under magnification countless times. She'd held them in her hand until her fingertips knew their shape and texture. She knew them by their weight, to the very last gram.

She grabbed her coins, one in each hand, and rose to her feet. "Of course, you didn't find these. *I* found them." She started backing toward the door, reaching behind her to unlock it. "If you took my coins, you probably killed my grandmother. Why did you bring them back here? Did you think I was so young and stupid that I couldn't figure it out?"

"Wait!"

Oh, God, now he was coming after her.

"No, I didn't take your coins, and nobody could ever think you were stupid."

How far was it to the door?

She took a step backwards, then another. "Those coins were in my drawer when I left that morning with Faye and her family. When I got home, my grandmother was dead and my coins were gone. If you have the coins, then probability says that you killed her. It's simple statistics."

"I bought the coins, honestly. Steve told me they came from his island, the one he wants to sell me as soon as—"

"As soon as he figures out a way to steal my part from me. You bought these coins from Steve? Are you nuts? You're ignoring the obvious."

It was Dane's turn to look awkward and clueless.

"He stole my coins, you idiot. He killed my grandmother and stole my coins. I bet you even told him I had them, didn't you? Steve probably stole them because he knew you were looking for stuff from the sixteen hundreds and would buy them from him. And because he knew that telling you he found them on the island would make you want to buy it even more. Geez. How stupid can you be?"

Amande reached the door and fumbled behind her, only to feel the doorknob vibrate as someone on the other side turned a key in the lock. The door opened and she fell into Steve's arms.

Dane's eyes locked on Steve and, for a moment, Amande could see that he had forgotten her. "You stole her coins? When? Did you sneak over here while I was talking to Miranda about buying Amande's share of the island?" Dane said. "That was idiotic. I *asked* her if she knew where the coins came from, for God's sake. And you knew I was planning to ask her that. Surely, you knew she would suspect me…or maybe you knew she'd never get a chance to suspect me, since you were already planning to kill her when you came over here."

"You didn't need to be dealing with the old lady. I told you I could get control of the whole island, if you gave me time."

"I've got no time to waste, not with the oil coming."

Amande knew that she should probably let them forget she was there while she came up with an escape plan, but she had listened long enough to the two of them discussing ways to cheat her.

"You were trying to get Grandmère to sell you my island? And then you stole my coins? When is somebody in this god-damn world going to recognize that something…anything… belongs to *me?*"

Amande dropped into a squat and leaned hard to the left, hoping to use her body weight to throw Steve off-balance. It was worth a try, because she was sturdily built and no shorter than he was, but he still had a hundred pounds on her. He yanked the girl to her feet, and she could feel new bruises on her rib cage. She wasn't surprised when Steve pulled a knife from a hidden scabbard in his pants. She had felt the shape of it digging into her back when he first grabbed her.

The point of the knife was poking into her throat, just below the jaw. Dane's freckled face bore a sheen of perspiration. "What good is this going to do you, Steve? All you need to do is get control of the island for me, so I can solidify my claim on the wreck. When I find it, I'll buy the island from you at twice what it's worth. Tell you what. If you let the girl go, I'll raise my offer to three times the island's appraised value."

"When you find it...that's the problem, ain't it? How long you been diving for it, and you still don't know where it is? This little bitch knows where she found them coins, and I think it was on that island I own a piece of. Maybe there's more out there. More old silver can't be a bad thing, even if there's not a shipload of it. Maybe if I know where her coins come from, I won't need you to figure out where the treasure ship wrecked."

Steve was obviously proud of this feat of logic, so much so that he decided to parade his mental superiority in front of Dane and Amande. "If you're not smart enough to find that boat after all that diving, then I got no more use for you. I got diving equipment. When the island is all mine and I'm living rent-free in this houseboat, I can look for the treasure ship myself, any time I feel like it."

"What happens to us, now that we know you killed my grandmother?"

Steve ran the point of the knife along Amande's jaw, heading for her ear. "I never said I killed your grandmother. I think maybe you should probably stop saying it. We need to get in the boat now and go find that shipwreck."

"The wreck's mine," Dane said. Amande thought it was rather brave of him to talk back to an armed man, though his bravery was mitigated by the fact that it wasn't his throat being caressed by a humongous hunting knife. The romantic in her hoped that he was doing this to get Steve to rub the knife all over *his* throat, instead of hers.

No luck. Dane was still focused on the wreck. He was still negotiating a business deal.

"We agreed early on that I'd buy the island from you, then I found out that you didn't own it all. We have a deal when I can see a way to get full title to the island, not before. That's all the money I'll ever owe you. You've got no piece of the wreck."

Amande felt cool metal travel down to the hollow of her neck.

"The island belongs to me and this girl. Three fourths of it is mine. The rest is hers. If I kill her, it'll all be mine. Then we'll have a deal, won't we, Sechrist?"

Ignoring the fact that calling a knife-wielding man names was unwise, Amande said, "You really are stupid. If I die without a will, the state of Louisiana will decide who gets my property, and I bet it won't be you. I'm thinking it'll be Didi. But maybe I do have a will. You don't know, do you? If I do, I can guarantee that *you're* not on my list of heirs."

"Shut up."

She felt more bruises form under his cruel hands.

"The girl's smarter than you are, and she's right. I won't be buying that island until I know for sure that you have the title, and I won't be showing you where any of the artifacts were found, ever."

"Yes, you will. You'll take me there, if you want to keep this little bitch alive."

Chapter Twenty-nine

Amande tried to turn her head enough to look Steve in the face. "I'll show you the rest of my coins and I'll tell you where I got them, if you let me go. Some of them are silver, so they're worth something. They're in my room."

She eyed Dane. He knew that she didn't have any more artifacts that Steve would give a damn about, because she'd described her collection to him in excruciating detail, but he was keeping his mouth shut. Maybe he was on her side.

Steve twisted Amande's arm behind her back and shoved her toward her bedroom. Dane followed.

She pulled the folder of silver American money out of the drawer first and handed it to Steve. With luck, he'd be too intoxicated by the smell of a precious metal to notice what else she was doing.

While he was pawing through the twentieth-century coins, she reached in the drawer again and pulled out a tray of stone tools. A flint blade lay atop the other implements. Joe had praised its finely honed edge. She palmed it.

With her free hand, she retrieved a tray of European import goods—buttons, a pipe, a green glass jar. After she handed it to Steve, who was starting to need more than one free hand to deal with everything she was throwing at him, she surreptitiously swiped the sextant from her desktop and crumpled a carefully chosen map around it in a loose wad. Those import goods were all far newer than the seventeenth-century shipwreck Dane and Steve were hoping to find, but Steve didn't know that. It would take him a few moments to rifle through them and find that they bored him. Maybe in those few moments Amande would think of something to save her life.

Or maybe in those few moments someone would come to help her. Faye would be at her side in an instant if she knew Amande was in trouble, despite the fact that she was just a brand-new acquaintance who would be going away soon. Amande had known the same kind of loyalty in her grandmother. She wondered if she would ever have that in her life again.

Steve thrust the trays back at her. "Nothing's in here that's any good. We're going out to the island, and you're gonna show me where you found them Spanish coins."

He twisted her right arm behind her again. It hurt, but if one of her arms had to be yanked half-off, this was the one she wanted yanked. The stone blade was wrapped tight in that hand where he couldn't see it, biting into her palm, and she didn't need it right now. She did need her left hand free, and she let it dangle beside her leg, keeping her body between Steve and that hand.

There were more things than a sextant and a crumpled map in that left hand. As he dragged her to his boat, she dropped tiny potsherds that she'd grabbed from the basket on her desk. One by one, they marked her trail. Dane followed them silently. Once, she saw him nudge a sherd with his toe, moving it into a position that would be more obvious to anyone searching the boat. It felt good to have an ally, although she would have been more grateful for an ally with a gun.

At the door, she let the sextant drop. The map wrapping it cushioned its impact with the wooden deck, so it fell silently. Dane nudged it with his toe until the paper opened slightly, revealing old brass. She could see that it had fallen so that it pointed toward the spot where Steve's boat was moored, the very boat he would be using to take her from her home. Could her meaning possibly be more clear?

Come and get me. Come this way...

Amande hoped it was Faye who found the trail she'd left behind. Some people wouldn't understand the meaning of those cast-off pieces of old trash, but Faye would know to look for her on the island, the only place Amande had ever found anything of value.

Faye would come get her. Amande hoped she had enough sense to bring Joe.

◇◇◇

Joe was still far enough away from New Orleans and its urban amenities to enjoy crappy cell phone coverage. He figured he must have driven through a tiny zone where his phone worked, because Faye's messages and texts had all come through at once. He wasn't as much of a talker as Faye, so he'd just sent her one text that read, in its entirety:

I think we should adopt the girl. Reuss is working on it.

Going by the length and number of her messages, some of which rambled on about how awful it would be if Amande married somebody to get herself free of Didi, he inferred that he had underestimated the amount of communication an event like adoption required. What else was new?

He also inferred that she hadn't received the one succinct message he *had* sent. Joe had been married long enough to know that he probably needed to talk to her in person, before her emotions got away from her. Faye might be a doctor and a scientist and probably the smartest person he would ever know, but she was also a woman. When it came to emotional stuff, life worked better when they did things her way.

He'd spent a fair amount of time talking to Reuss, then he'd stopped for gas and a cup of coffee, so he really hadn't gotten very far down the road. It only made sense to turn around and go talk to Faye.

◇◇◇

Faye wasn't at the rental cabin. Joe thought maybe Amande might know where she was, so he went down to the houseboat. No one answered his knock there.

Standing at the front door, he dialed Faye and actually reached her. "She's not here. Nobody is," he told Faye. "Didi's car and

Steve's boat are gone. Maybe Tebo is keeping one of them company. Maybe Amande is, too."

Faye's tart response was, "Please God, don't let her be off marrying someone awful."

When he didn't laugh, she followed up with, "Is something wrong?"

"Naw," he said, "I just saw something weird."

At his feet, he noticed the sun glinting off something metallic and a dull red-gold. He bent easily to pick it up. "It's the old sextant fragment Amande found, wrapped in paper and lying just outside the doorframe. I coulda stepped on it."

"Amande wouldn't be so careless with something that old. Since her coins were stolen, that's the choicest artifact she has."

"I bet somebody came back to steal the rest of her stuff, and they dropped this."

"I'm out in the rental boat, but I'm on my way back. I can be there in ten minutes. Less."

He reached for the doorknob and it turned in his hands. "The door's unlocked. Wouldn't she have locked it when she left?"

"If she left. She could still be in there, tied up by the thief or…you've got to go in, Joe."

"I'm already in. Call Benoit and tell him to send somebody over here. Then get your butt home."

"He's already on his way. So am I. I bet I can get there first."

Benoit's voice blasted out of the phone at Faye's ear, cursing her in real time while Joe was getting killed by entering the houseboat alone and unarmed. Or so Benoit presumed, as he described in excruciating detail what he thought Steve was doing to her husband, even as he spoke.

She chose not to tell him that Joe was never unarmed. He hated guns, and he didn't understand the point of metal knives when there was flint in the world, but he was never unarmed.

"Give me his number," Benoit said. "At least I can be talking to him while he's getting stabbed."

◇◇◇

Faye revved the motor. It was time to quit lurking in this bayou while she talked on the phone. It was time to get back to where the action was. Carrying on a phone conversation would be impossible while she was underway, with the wind and the boat noise in her ears, so she was going to have to maintain contact with Joe and Benoit by text. It hardly mattered. She was only a few minutes from the marina.

Then she heard a boat louder than hers whoosh past her secluded spot in the bayou. It was painted in a dappled green-and-tan camouflage, and it had an odd-looking motor protruding from the stern.

Faye idled the motor and snatched up her binoculars. She could make out two blond heads and a brunette one. Steve was a long-haired blond and it was his boat, so identifying him was a no-brainer. Dane was the only other blond she'd seen lately, and the second man had a close-to-the-head haircut very like his. But who was the brunette?

She could have gone through an elimination process—the boat's occupant was too big to be Didi and too dainty to be Manny and the hair was too long to be Tebo and the brightly colored shirt was a dead giveaway—but she had no need. She knew without thinking that the person sitting way too close to Steve was Amande. Mothers know these things.

She tapped out a text, addressed to both Joe and Benoit.

> *Steve has Amande on his boat. Don't know where he's taking her. Probably her island. Will text you if I'm wrong. I'll follow so we don't lose sight of her. Come help me.*

Joe entered the houseboat cautiously, but there was no one inside. No burglar, no slutty aunt, no worthless uncle, no sleazy step-father, and no sixteen-year-old girl. Amande's room looked no different than usual. Benoit had called his cell and was even then yelling at him for going in alone, but Joe was only half-listening.

The only noteworthy things in the room were Amande's computer, showing nothing on the monitor but the screen saver, and her open artifact drawers.

Joe peered into the drawers without touching the handles or their contents. There was a lot of stuff still in there, and it didn't look like some ignorant thief had been plundering through it. The basket of potsherds still sat atop Amande's desk, holding down her school papers. If anything that had been in this room was missing—other than Amande—it had been carefully selected and removed without disturbing the remaining items.

He'd let the phone drop from her ear, but Benoit was yelling loud enough that he could hear him anyway. "Are you okay? What's happening? I've got some people coming your way, and I really hope we don't find you dead. Stupid and dead, that's what you'll be. Say something to me, Joe."

"I'm fine. There's nobody here, but keep those officers coming. I feel like something's wrong."

"They're already in the car, and so am I."

Joe took the phone away from his ear again and used it to nudge the computer's mouse. The screen saver went away and Amande's statistics test appeared. At the bottom of the page was a series of messages that said:

Test will time out in 10 minutes. There will be a 10-point penalty for failing to pause properly.

Test will time out in five minutes. Click "pause" or you will need to begin again.

Test will time out in one minute. Click "pause" or you will lose your work.

Test is timing out in thirty seconds. Click "pause" now…

Timed out.

Joe checked the time stamps on these messages, then he looked at the time on the face of his phone. Those messages told him that Amande had been gone ten minutes, tops.

They also told him something else. Living with Faye had taught him something important about good students. They were predictable. They jumped every hurdle set by their teachers, no matter how nonsensical, if that was what it took to make good grades.

Amande had lost ten points on her statistics test by failing to make a simple mouse-click. Something was wrong.

"I'm still okay, but hang on a minute," he said to Benoit, using a pencil eraser to scroll through Amande's statistics test, but no other clues waited there.

Squinting at his phone and trying to remember how to work it, he successfully navigated away from his conversation with Benoit and opened up a text to Faye.

She's not at home. Something isn't right. Need you here.

Switching back to his call with Benoit, he said, "Amande walked away from a timed test and she left the door unlocked behind her. Her artifact drawers are open, but I can't tell that they've been disturbed. There's no sign of a struggle."

"You've determined that the girl's not there. Now get out into the parking lot where my people and I can see that you're safe when we get there."

"Just one more minute."

"Now, Joe!"

Joe turned silently, scanning the room's floor and walls and ceiling. The pieces of Amande's guardian doll still lay piled beside her full clothes hamper. Her bed was made. Everything looked normal.

He took a step back to get a better look at one of the posters on her bedroom wall, and something crunched under his heel. Joe knelt down and gathered bits of crushed pottery, hundreds of years old, in his fingers. It wasn't like Amande to leave her treasures in harm's way.

Still kneeling, he saw Amande's version of the bread crumbs that trailed behind Hansel and Gretel. There was a potsherd lying on the floor near the door that opened between Amande's room and the room that had been Miranda's, and another one just inside the door that led from her grandmother's room out into the main cabin of the houseboat. Joe would lay odds that he'd stepped over another potsherd as he entered the boat, and that more were outside, waiting to lead him to a girl needing rescue.

He followed the sherds, leaving each one where it lay, in case he got more data and needed to follow the trail again and reinterpret Amande's message. When he reached the spot at the door where the sextant had served as his first signpost, he pulled it from his pocket. Unwrapping it, he saw that he'd missed another clue. The sextant was wrapped in a crumpled map—not a copy, but an original. Amande wouldn't mess up an original.

Opening the map, he saw that her island was dead in its center. It was as if the girl had left him a note that said, "Come get me." If she'd had a chance, Joe believed she would have taken a pen and labeled the map with an X that marked the spot. He replaced the sextant and map where he'd found them, as best he remembered. Then he stepped back and studied Amande's trail of clues.

A moment later, he was distracted by the pounding sound of a pair of dress shoes worn by a man unaccustomed to running. Benoit came into view, followed by two uniformed officers. Joe put up a hand, palm out, so that they wouldn't stomp onto the dock and crush Amande's plea for help.

The trail of potsherds pointed Joe out of the living quarters and onto the houseboat's floating dock. The last two potsherds lay on that dock. Like all the scattered sherds, they were tiny, barely visible to anyone who hadn't spent the last few years searching for such things. He wasn't sure Benoit and his technicians would have been able to tell them from miniscule gobs of dried dirt.

In aggregate, all the clues pointed to the spot where Steve's boat had been moored.

Joe ran around the boat and scanned the parking lot. Steve's car was there. Logic said that he'd left in his boat. Joe's intuition and Amande's map said that Steve was headed for the island. The potsherds, sextant, and map all said that Amande was with him.

But where were his wife and son? Faye had said she was so close to the marina that she would beat Benoit and his guys. Well, she hadn't. Every second that ticked past made Joe antsier.

He tried to call her, and her phone went straight to voice mail. This did not make him feel any better.

Impatiently, he showed Benoit the sherds and the sextant and the map, and started explaining what he thought they meant. The clock kept ticking. Still no Faye.

Faye was finding her boat chase to be remarkably tame. Steve didn't know anyone was on his tail, so he wasn't traveling particularly fast. Well, yes, he was, but Faye was known for her speed. Right this minute, she felt like she was just puttering along.

There was another reason for her lack of speed. She was making good use of the only advantage she had—her binoculars—and they enabled her to hang back. She didn't know whether he had a pair, too, but he had no reason to be looking for a tail. She presumed he was operating with his naked eyes, which meant that she could lurk just inside her binoculars' limits and he'd never know she was there. Judging by his heading, she grew more sure with every minute that Steve was indeed taking the girl out to the island they shared.

She wished Joe or Benoit had answered her text. She wasn't sure how much time had passed. Fifteen minutes? Twenty? She wasn't moving at top speed, but she'd been traveling inexorably away from them for every one of those minutes. Faye pulled the phone out of her pocket, hoping the wind had drowned the sound of a return text.

No. It hadn't, and the truth was so much worse. The wind had drowned the familiar sound of a dying phone. Her battery hadn't survived the hard work she'd put it through that morning. All those calls and texts to Benoit and Reuss and Joe had taken their toll. Thank God she'd had a chance to get that last text out before she went incommunicado. She'd guess that Benoit's people had boats that would move like bats out of hell, so they'd be showing up soon.

She trained her binoculars behind her, hoping to see the cavalry riding to her rescue. Not yet. What would she do if they didn't show?

Another, worse, question bubbled into her brain. What would she do if that text hadn't gone through? Was her phone already dying when she sent it? Had she been momentarily out of range? If so, she would have gotten an error message, or maybe a message that the text would go through once she was back in range. And maybe one of those things had happened, but now the screen was dark and blank, so she couldn't check.

Should she turn back? If her rescuers were *en route*, they'd probably be in binocular range very soon. If they weren't coming, then she needed to go all the way back to the marina to get help, then turn around and head back out. This would give Steve nearly an hour to take Amande…anywhere. She couldn't bring herself to leave the girl without a protector, even such a feeble protector as herself.

She tried hard to think of other reasons than murder for Steve to take Amande.

To bond with her as a potential adoptive father? Doubtful.

To get her to help him with his search for island treasure? Maybe.

Miranda's fate nagged at her. Faye thought she'd probably been murdered on a boat, then dropped into the water. Is that what Steve had in mind for Amande, opening the way for him to jockey for ownership of everything—the island, the houseboat, and the stock? Faye could think of no reason why it wasn't.

And Dane. He was on the boat, so Faye figured he and Steve were working together. It made sense. They both wanted the island, and Amande kept them from controlling it.

She wondered why Dane had never just come out and asked how much Amande wanted for her share. Certainly he wasn't rich, but the girl needed money. More to the point, Didi needed money, and she would have cut Dane a deal, even if Amande didn't want her to sell. Then Faye remembered that she was dealing with a treasure hunter. He wouldn't want to give away the secret of what he'd found and where he'd found it. No, cutting a shady deal with Steve made a lot more sense than going for a straightforward purchase.

Faye kept worrying over her text to Joe and Benoit. Even if they didn't get it, they had known she was out on the boat, and they were smart men. When she didn't show up, surely they'd be able to figure out where in this vast expanse of water to look for her.

Her common sense asked her how much difference her presence made to Amande. What could Faye do to save the girl from a large and dangerous man?

Not much, without a weapon more fearsome than an archaeologist's trowel. But if the worst happened...if Steve wasn't taking Amande to the island to hunt for treasure...if he was planning to do to the girl what he'd done to her uncle and grandmother...

If someone had come along right after Hebert and Miranda had been stabbed and thrown into the water, maybe they could have been saved. If Amande went into the water bleeding, then Faye, with her binoculars, would know. She could be there instantly. The slender chance that this was true drove Faye forward, not back.

Nobody had to tell Faye that desperate mothers placed their bets on slender chances every single day. She stroked Michael's cheek and adjusted his hat to better shade his face, glad that he'd drifted off to sleep again. And she kept the boat moving.

Chapter Thirty

Amande had caught the first whiff of oil when they were barely out of sight of the marina. The further they traveled, the more its mineral odor invaded her awareness. Now, after nearly an hour on the water, her eyes burned and her mouth tasted like she'd been sipping turpentine.

Yet another gleaming streak passed beneath the boat as the oil slick reached its fingers inland. Barataria Bay spread out around her, and she couldn't remember when they'd last seen another boat. Of course all the fishing boats had gone home. Why would they be out here now? Who would want to eat fish taken from these waters?

What was her island going to look like when they finally got there?

Joe squatted beside the sextant and the wrinkled map wrapping it. There was no question that it depicted the area surrounding Amande's island. In his mind, he knew that Steve had a claim on it, too. In his heart, though, it belonged to Amande.

Catching Benoit's eye, Joe jerked his chin in the direction of a tiny ceramic chip that looked pretty much like a fleck of dirt, since pottery is nothing more than petrified dirt. It lay a few feet from another, similar chip. Then he turned and jerked his chin at two more potsherds lying on the floor of the houseboat's main cabin.

"It ain't much different from tracking deer. The girl left us a trail from the houseboat to where Steve Daigle has been mooring his boat. There's a few drops of water on the deck over there, probably splashed up when he shoved off. It only makes sense that she was on the boat when it left."

"You hunt?" Benoit might as well have asked Joe if he breathed. "You see anything else my investigators might've missed?"

"Fifty feet that way," Joe said, waving in the direction of the marina, "is a low spot where water collects on the dock. Next to it is a footprint, nearly dry, where my little boy stomped in the water. I hope that means he wasn't on Daigle's boat. If he wasn't, then my wife wasn't. I can guarantee you that. Thirty feet past that little footprint is the slip where we keep the boat Faye rented for the project. My guess is that Michael stomped in the water while my wife was on her way to that boat. There's no sign that the boat ever came back, even though she told me she'd be here by now. I think she figured out where Steve was taking Amande. If so, then I know where she's going."

Benoit nodded, but Joe wasn't finished. "I'm going to go rent a boat from Manny, then I'm getting on the water and going out to this island here." He pointed at the map. "You police people can do what you please. You can come with me or not, but I'm going."

◇◇◇

Amande could tell that the tide was high, because her island was far smaller than it had been during her last visit. It was hardly bigger than the low rise beneath the cabin and its adjacent copse of trees. Iridescent brown smears marked the sliver of sand that remained, and the hot sun made the stink of oil even more pronounced. Steve had cut the motor when the island came in sight, but he still had one arm around her like a crawdad's pincer. The knife had stayed at her throat for the entire ride while he operated the tiller with his other hand.

"Where is it? Tell me where it is."

Steve didn't sound rational. He'd never sounded rational.

"Where's what?" She hated the sound of her voice, squeaky and shrill. If he planned to kill her, she didn't want to die sounding like a scared little girl.

"I'm not talking to you. Where's the wreck, Sechrist?"

Dane had been silent and still since they left the houseboat. It wasn't obvious to Amande whether he considered himself Steve's partner or his prisoner. "I told you. I don't know."

"I've never believed that. You say it all the time, but I don't believe it. You been looking too long, you been spending too much money, you been offering me a big pile of money for an island that ain't worth nothing. Where is it?"

"I never found anything but a pile of ballast stones. Honestly. The pile was big enough to be a ship. For a while, I thought it was. I've been burning time and money ever since, because I'm just so close. When I found the underwater coins, I thought I was in the debris trail. Then nothing. Then I found another coin of the right age, and some worthless things like nails and hinges were with it, but they were on the island, on the far side from the sunken stones. Now I'm thinking the crew dumped the stones during a storm to keep from running aground and maybe the wreck isn't as close to them as I thought."

He scanned the horizon like a man looking for something precious that he lost just yesterday, something that he could find if he looked a little longer and a little harder.

Steve's mouth was so close to Amande's ear that she could feel the spit when he talked. But he still wasn't talking to her. She was only a tool to control Dane, and she was useful as a source of information that could lead to a boundless treasure. From the way he moved when he held her body against his, she'd begun to fear that he intended to use her for other things far worse.

One thing was clear. Her worth began and ended with her usefulness to Steve. How could her mother have lived with this man?

She hated the sound of his voice in her ear as he taunted Dane. "Maybe it worked. Dumping the stones, I mean. Maybe there ain't no treasure ship here at all. If they dumped the stones to save the ship, then you gotta take into consideration that maybe they saved the ship. Don't tell me you been wasting my time."

Amande thought this was a remarkably astute observation from someone as stupid as Steve.

Even in crisis, Dane couldn't be made to imagine that his treasure ship wasn't there. He rose to its defense. "Then why did Amande and I both find gold and silver? You don't throw the treasure overboard unless you're on the verge of going down. It's human nature. If a crew gets desperate enough to throw away gold, the ship is already lost, ninety-nine times out of a hundred. There's a treasure ship here waiting for me. It's a sure thing."

Amande knew enough about statistics to know that "ninety-nine times out of a hundred" was not at all the same as a sure thing.

"Then show me the big pile of rocks and show me where you found the coins, asshole. I'll take it from there."

Dane sat for a moment, looking from the water to the knife to Steve's face. For a moment, Amande thought he was going to defy a man with a deadly weapon, just to protect a treasure ship that might not actually exist. Then she saw the dreamer's light in Dane's eyes fade as he made his choice.

"It's back there. We came right over it a minute ago," he said, gesturing behind Steve.

The big man turned to look over his shoulder. "Where?"

Behind them was nothing but open water, dotted by grasses.

"I use my GPS nowadays, but I didn't have one when I first started diving, so I learned to use landmarks. See how some of these islands are big enough to have a few trees? I picked four of them. Draw a line in your head from this one to that one, and from that one to that other one over there. X marks the spot."

Dane gestured with both hands at faraway trees clinging to tiny specks of dry land, and Steve turned further in his seat as he tried to spot the imaginary crosshairs marking an old pile of submerged stones. Then Amande found herself facedown in the bottom of the boat as Dane grabbed with his right hand at the hilt of the knife Steve was holding to her throat, using his left hand to throw her clear.

If Dane hadn't been such a gentleman, things might have turned out differently. As a slender but well-built six-footer, he was no physical match for a man who was his equal in height, but weighed half-again as much. And he was no match in ruthlessness for a man who had killed at least twice.

However, Amande, too, was a slender but well-built six-footer. If Dane hadn't tried so hard to get her out of reach of the knife, they might have been able together to overpower Steve. Failing that, she might have been able to go for the tiller and gain control of the boat, although heaven only knew what good that would have done.

Instead, Dane's mutiny was over in seconds, and it ended with a blade in his throat.

Amande was astonished by how quickly Steve heaved Dane's bleeding body overboard and held his head underwater until there was no doubt he was dead. This explained a lot about the investigators' failure to find physical evidence of her grandmother's and uncle's murders. There was hardly any mess to be seen aboard the boat after Dane's murder, beyond a few blood spatters on Steve's face and shoulders. Steve had been able to prepare for the other killings, choosing his time and method of attack, so there likely would have been even less telltale gore. Amande supposed this was how it would be when he eventually killed her.

Why couldn't she stop thinking about Gola George and his bloodstained white silk shirts?

Faye was still shaking. This would be a poor time to break down completely, body and soul, but what really is the appropriate response to watching a young and vital man be knifed to death? For a timeless time, she'd thought it was Amande's limp body being thrown into the bay, and she'd heedlessly gunned her motor and rushed toward the scene of a murder. Steve had been busy being a killer, so she'd had no sign that he'd heard or seen her before hurrying from the scene.

She knew long before she got near the body that it belonged to Dane and not to Amande. Once again, the binoculars came in very handy. They showed her the sun glinting on his golden hair. They also told her that he was floating facedown with no sign of a struggle, so she knew he was beyond help. They did not tell her the right thing to do.

Every instinct told her to go fish the poor man's body out of the water. It seemed so disrespectful to leave him there. But she didn't think she was strong enough to do it alone, and all the while she was trying, Steve would be taking Amande further away.

When the binoculars showed her fins—many fins and big ones—gathering around Dane's body, she knew what she had to do. She couldn't take this boat into a group of sharks and fight them for a bleeding body. When she made the decision to leave Dane's corpse defenseless, that's when the shaking started. There were no tears yet, but they would come. Right now, Faye needed to get control of her rebellious body. She had no time to go into shock, or even to just sit and weep.

Why couldn't she look away from Dane? In a totally inadequate way, training her binoculars on him felt like a way to be his companion on this last journey. As she drew closer, she could see streams of his blood weaving through floating bands of oil.

She imagined that she could smell the blood, but the truth was that its iron odor was swamped by the unnatural stench of petroleum. She forced herself to point the binoculars at Steve's boat, because she needed to focus on maintaining the right distance and on formulating a plan. Every passing minute that didn't involve Amande's corpse being thrown overboard into the water and oil and blood was a good one.

She busied herself by making a mental list of her advantages in a contest with Steve for Amande's life. She didn't have a weapon, and he surely did. It would be reasonable to assume he had a knife. It would also be reasonable to pray that he did not have a gun, so she did.

While she was at it, she prayed that Joe had gotten her message and that he was coming to her rescue at top speed.

In the meantime, Faye's binoculars were her only inarguable advantage. She'd combed through the equipment stored on the boat for something that resembled a weapon, but her pointy and sharp-edged trowel was the best she could do. She wasn't actually sure it was a better weapon than the small pocketknife she carried everywhere, but it was bigger and heavier. That must count for something.

Michael stirred in the bottom of the boat, and Faye's denial cracked. What did she think she was going to do? She couldn't walk into a confrontation while holding him by the hand, but her mind wouldn't stop cataloging the things that Steve might be planning to do to Amande. Why did parents ever choose to have more than one child? There was no way to put each of them first, always.

Her pale and weak plan traded heavily on the binoculars. After Steve's boat reached the island, Faye would lurk in her boat, far from shore, and watch for a chance to…um…do something heroic. Her grasp of the details was still a little vague.

◇◇◇

Steve dropped the anchor and stood, wrapping both arms around Amande and dragging her with him as he climbed over the side and into the water. She went down on her knees, drenching her clothes from the neck down, then he hoisted her to her feet. "The coins, bitch. Where did you find them?"

Amande considered what she should tell him. One of her coins had come from a spot currently submerged in three feet of water. The other one, though, had been in the place where Faye had uncovered bits of very old wood. This suited her purpose better. Steve would spend more time poking around in a spot where it was easy to dig and where he stood a chance of finding something soon enough to keep him distracted. And distracted was good.

He nodded when she pointed to the trees, saying, "Yeah, Justine used to tell me about digging up stuff on this island. Maybe that was the spot. That goddamn Dane was obsessed with finding a shipwreck. He just wanted the island to use as a base. Said it would be a lot easier to salvage a big load thataway.

And there was some fancy legal reason that having the island would help him claim the treasure, but none of that makes any nevermind now that he's dead. Justine knew a lot more about this island than he did, and she always thought there was a chest of gold buried here. We come to look for it a few times, before she got sick. I'm going with her story."

Getting there was a slow experience, since Steve insisted on dragging her. He seemed to think it was too risky just to let her walk. As they walked, Amande thought of her mother as a child, running free over this very same patch of sand.

Steve kept her body clamped against his, her back to his chest and his knife to her throat. When they reached the spot, the disturbed soil from Faye's digging was still visible. The tremble in Steve's body said that he wanted to drop everything and shovel dirt until he got to a pile of treasure. But he couldn't do that with his arms wrapped around a prisoner.

Amande felt a tremble seize her own body. This was a moment when he might decide to kill her. Seconds passed and she was still alive, so he either thought she still possessed valuable information, or else he had other plans for her before she died. She felt a chill at her core that only made the trembling worse.

Then Steve spoke, but his words didn't reveal the full scope of his plans for her. They only gave a glimpse into the next phase of her torture.

"I got a shovel in the cabin. And some rope."

◇◇◇

Faye had found a handy patch of marsh grass big enough to hide her boat. She'd anchored, then slid overboard with her trowel in one hand, her pocketknife in the other, and the binoculars hanging around her neck. Standing in waist-deep water, she'd maneuvered herself into a spot where she could see the entire near side of the island without much risk of being seen.

Michael had been inconsolable when he saw that she was "swimming" and he wasn't, so she'd put him in Joe's backpack and strapped it on herself. He wanted to be fully submerged, but his little legs were dragging in the water, so he was happy enough for the moment.

Faye had watched Steve drag Amande into the cabin and come out alone.

It made little sense to pass up the opportunity for a neat and tidy murder aboard the boat, like Dane's, opting instead for messing up the interior of a house. Granted, it wasn't much of a house, but what kind of nut would leave a young girl on its floor in a puddle of blood?

The same kind of nut who had been committing low-stakes murders all week, that's who. Was a treasure that might not even exist worth doing murder? If you were a person who would kill for a ratty old houseboat, Faye figured it was.

She had to get into that cabin.

If she came ashore on the far side of the island, Steve's view would be blocked by the trees and by the tallest part of the island and by the cabin itself. By making her way from one clump of grass to another, she could maintain some degree of cover for most of the journey.

It wasn't going to be easy to do this while carrying a one-year-old on her back and a trowel in one hand. Even the binoculars were starting to look heavy to Faye. There was no help for it, so she took the first step. Michael splashed his feet into the water and laughed out of the sheer joy of being alive in such a beautiful place.

At least her passenger was happy.

Amande lay spread-eagled on the floor of the cabin, one arm and leg tied to a post in the middle of the room that had apparently been installed to hold the sagging roof up. Her other arm and leg were tied to a tremendous old brass bed that was topped with a soiled and rotting mattress.

Her brain didn't seem to be working well. She'd always been able to count on her sharp mind but now, when she most needed it, she found her thoughts to be as slippery as wet swamp muck.

She should be thinking of a way to escape, instead of lying here in this most vulnerable of positions, wondering what Steve had planned for her when he got tired of digging for treasure. Efforts to free herself had accomplished nothing, other than to show just how tightly Steve had tied her bonds. There seemed to be no way to cut those bonds, when she couldn't reach the stone blade hidden in her pocket.

Instead of plotting her escape, she found her mind wandering in the direction of Henry the Mutineer. Henry had been kidnapped and forced to serve on a pirate ship, then lived to rule a pirate ship himself, at Gola George's side. If only she had a seven-foot-tall pirate coming to rescue her...

But that pirate had turned on Henry the Mutineer. No, wait. Her frantic brain was scrambling the story, and that just wasn't like her. Gola George had indeed turned on Henry the Mutineer, but Henry had betrayed him first. On the day that George put his hands on Marisol, and she defied him by splaying her ivory fan in his face, George had shattered the fan with one big hand and prepared to take her by force.

How could he have possibly predicted that the foppish Henry would pull his jeweled dagger from the decorative scabbard strapped to his leg, burying its blade in the thick shoulder muscles attached to George's sword-wielding arm?

And then Henry and Marisol had run for their lives. They ran from George and from his crew of pirates, who would have turned on Henry the instant they heard what he'd done. They ran from Henry's paintings and Marisol's lute and their silk clothes. They fled down the gangplank, straight through the shabby settlement where George housed his women, and right out the other side. They hid deep in the swamp, so deep that Marisol had to shed the heavy skirts that dragged in the mud and caught in the thick grasses. She stripped to her linen chemise and drawers, and it was a long time before she owned clothes other than those.

Just before dawn, after the pirates had given up their hunt and gone to sleep, Henry and Marisol stole every last rowboat and dinghy in the settlement. Why did two people need all those boats? And how did they steal them, with only the two of them to row?

They needed all those boats for Henry's final mutiny, because they took every last one of George's women with them, and all of George's children. Amande had heard it said that George hunted Henry till the end of his days, but she doubted it. According to the stories, Henry had hidden in plain sight, with the river pilots who lived near the great river's mouth at Head-of-Waters. If Gola George had wanted to find Henry and kill him, he could have done it. But that would have meant looking straight in the face of his betrayer and his lifelong friend, and he would have had to do it while knowing full well that, by attacking Marisol, he had betrayed Henry, too.

It was no coincidence that Amande was thinking of Henry's spectacular escape and of the rescue of Gola George's women and children, and she knew it. She was a self-sufficient person, and she liked to think that she could take care of herself, but at that moment, right then, she knew that she just couldn't. Sometimes a person needs rescue. Amande wondered if a rescuer would ever come for her.

Perhaps she had been hallucinating, but she could have sworn she saw something at the moment of Dane's death. It was nothing metaphysical. She'd seen no spectral spirit rising heavenward, but at the moment she rose from the bottom of the boat where Dane had thrown her to save her life, she'd seen…something. It had been nothing more than a speck on the horizon that was too hard-edged to be natural, but it had been something.

Amande's dreams of rescue had been dashed with Justine's death. Her mother was never going to sweep into her world and fix it, but maybe there was somebody out there who would.

Something about that speck on the horizon had brought Amande comfort and hope.

Something about it made her think of Faye.

Chapter Thirty-one

Faye's goal was in sight. She had a clear view of the path Steve would take when he returned to the cabin, so she knew that Amande was still in there alone. The only door was on the far side of the cabin, which wasn't as bad as it seemed. There was no need for her to walk around and go through that door, risking being seen by Steve. The glass had been gone from both windows on her side for years, from the looks of things.

It wouldn't be easy to shove Michael through one of them and then crawl through herself, but it wouldn't be the hardest thing she would do before bedtime, either. The land between her and the cabin was covered with shrubby underbrush and marsh grass where she wouldn't leave obvious footprints. For once, nature was on her side.

Faye had lingered in the water until she'd almost worked out a way to get Amande out of there and to get all three of them off the island, but Michael's presence complicated every plan she tried to make. She was going to have to improvise. She'd never seen an old movie that climaxed with the cavalry topping the hill, coming to the rescue with bugles blaring, while the soldiers cared for the toddlers astride their saddles in front of them. This did not mean that it couldn't be done.

Sticking a pacifier in Michael's mouth and clipping its handle firmly to his shirt, she crept up to the window and manhandled him and herself through it. Her little pocketknife was sufficient to cut through the ropes binding Amande, but it took some time. Finally, the girl was free. It was time to get out of the cabin.

Faye struggled back through the window, then took Michael from Amande and helped her crawl through. Bowed down by the weight of Michael in a heavy backpack designed for Joe, she could barely stand, but it made more sense to crawl anyway. Only the waving of the underbrush and marsh grasses would give away their position as they made their way back to the boat.

It would have made sense to shift Michael from her scrawny back to Amande's broad, strong one, but Faye knew that her last nerve would snap into two ragged pieces if she lost the ability to protect Michael with her own body. Also, Amande looked like she was one adrenaline jolt away from complete collapse.

They had no choice but to move slowly. Michael was so heavy that Faye regretted every spoonful of baby food that she'd ever shoveled into him. He was enjoying their adventure, burbling constantly, and Faye was grateful that the wind had kicked up. She could barely hear him over its noise. If Steve were to find them, it would be by sight, because he wouldn't be able to hear them and he damn sure wouldn't be able to smell them over the pervasive stench of oil.

Faye found a spot sheltered from view by a low sand dune on the bay side and by vegetation in the other directions. It was a good place to pause and get a bearing on Steve's location, after having spent a few minutes with her vision blocked. Still on all-fours, she raised herself up enough to peer over the dune. The sight of Steve standing in the water beside her boat was nearly enough to make her lie down and quit.

The words, "He knows I'm here," escaped her lips and she wished them back with the adult's instinct to protect a child from bad news. It was a ridiculous feeling, since there was no way to hide the situation from Amande for long, but she felt it anyway.

Faye's world grew even darker when she saw Steve remove the hose that carried fuel from her boat's tank to its engine. His boat, on the opposite side of the island, was now their only exit.

Hose in hand, he stormed toward the cabin, passing uncomfortably close to their hiding place. He leaned his entire upper body into one of the open windows, then emerged, stomping and gesturing and, presuming Faye's lip-reading was accurate, cursing. Now he knew that Amande was gone.

The wooded area was the only obvious hiding place on the island, so he must be headed past the spot where he'd been digging, deeper into the copse of trees, on the theory that they'd somehow sneaked past him and hidden there. It would take only a few minutes to search that area. If she could get Amande and Michael to Steve's boat in that amount of time, and if he'd left the keys in the boat, then they were saved.

Unfortunately, she didn't think it was possible. The distance was too far. Michael was too heavy. There was no cover on that side of the island, so they would be visible as soon as they got past the cabin. It was entirely possible that Steve would be able to see them from that very moment, and he looked capable of outrunning Faye, even when she wasn't burdened by a backpack full of her cherished son. She couldn't know where Steve was or what he could see until she committed herself to making a run for it, and she simply couldn't take that gamble with the children's lives.

Faye needed to make her decision, and she needed to move. She did so.

"Follow me," she hissed. "I'm going to hide you two in plain sight. Since he's already checked the shack, it probably won't occur to him to search it again."

Once through the window, she lifted Michael from her back and handed him to Amande. Shedding the backpack, she took her pocketknife and cut off her own shirttail. Amande followed her, wearing a question mark on her face, as Faye fashioned the scrap of fabric into a tight roll. Moving to the kitchen counter, she opened Steve's bottle of Jack Daniels. Amande's expression said she was shocked to see Faye suddenly starting to behave like her drunken relatives.

Faye doused the roll of fabric with copious quantities of Jack, soaking it through, then she stuck it deeply into the plastic container of sugar sitting beside the liquor bottle. Handing Amande a sugar tit that would have made Miranda proud, she said, "Here. If Steve comes back, Michael cannot make a sound. Not a single solitary sound. He needs to be unconscious. Keep this in his mouth the whole time I'm gone. Put some more whiskey on it, if you need to. Now give me your shirt."

As Faye stripped off her own shirt and handed it to her, Amande stood there with the baby on her hip and her mouth agape.

"I'm going out this window," Faye said, "and I'm going to get Steve as far from his boat as humanly possible. And I do mean far…way out there in the water." Faye gestured out the back windows, far into the bay. "When that happens, you take Michael and you go out that door. Get in Steve's boat and go home."

"That would leave you here alone with—" Amande stopped and tried again. "He messed up our boat. If I take that one, you'll have no way to get off this island."

"Yes, I will. You'll tell Joe and Benoit where I am, and they'll bring me some help."

"That's too long for you to be out here alone with Steve. He'll…Faye, he killed Dane. And my grandmother and my uncle, too."

"I know."

"I won't leave you here with him."

Faye reached up and grabbed Amande by the shoulders, bringing the girl's face all the way down to hers. "Yes. You will."

She let go of Amande with one hand and used it to cradle Michael's round cheek. "Look at this child. *Look* at him. He cannot take care of himself. I can, but I have to know that you and Michael are safe first. This is what it means to be a grown-up."

Amande was shaking her head and pulling away. Faye gripped her shoulder and brought the panicked girl back down to her level. "You have to help me by getting the two of you off this island. Believe me when I say this: when the turmoil is all over,

I'll still be standing. Now give me that shirt. And give me that purple hat, while you're at it."

Amande pulled off the shirt and hat and her dark curls streamed over the tender skin of her bare shoulders. "Here," she said, handing them over, tears streaming down her face. "Take this, too." She reached in her pocket and pulled out a stone blade that Faye recognized from Amande's collection.

Faye handed Amande her own shirt in trade, then grasped the wrist of the hand holding the blade and pushed it back toward her. "No, you might need that. And keep this trowel, too. It won't help me where I'm going. Don't worry. I'm armed and I have a plan." She brandished her pocketknife. "When Steve is completely focused on me—you'll know when—make a run for his boat. If something goes wrong and he comes here instead of chasing me, take Michael and get in the broom closet. If he doesn't look for you in there, then you'll have another chance to escape when he leaves."

Faye pulled Amande's shirt on and drew her hat down low on her forehead, then she kicked off her shoes. She reached out her arms and drew Amande and Michael close, saying nothing but, "I love you both." Then she went out the window before she had a chance to change her mind.

◇◇◇

Amande stood at the window and watched Faye run. Wearing Amande's brightly colored hat and shirt, she'd lingered at the corner of the shack, fully visible in three directions, until Steve came into view. When Faye knew for a fact that he'd seen her, she'd run for the water. Steve had taken off at a run, as Faye had known he would.

Amande had watched Faye run toward the boat Steve had disabled and past it. He'd followed. She'd kept a hand on her head as if to hold the purple hat on, but Amande could see that her real motive had been to obscure her face. From a distance, it wasn't completely obvious that she was far smaller than Amande. Were the distinctive hat and shirt enough to convince him that this was the girl he needed to silence? Maybe. They had certainly provoked the desired response. When Steve saw her, he took the bait.

As she watched, Amande poured more whiskey on the sugar tit and stuck it in Michael's mouth again. Faye had told her to get in the broom closet with him the instant that Steve headed their direction. It hadn't happened yet, and maybe it wouldn't, but she wanted to be ready. If the opposite happened, if he continued chasing Faye in her guise as an Amande decoy, then she was to pick the right time and run for Steve's boat, keeping the shack between her and Steve. This plan seemed quite workable as a way to get Amande and Michael off the island, but Amande saw no way that it could turn out well for Faye.

As Faye reached the edge of the water, she kept running. It seemed to take forever for the water to reach her hips, but when it did, she threw off the hat and struck out swimming. Steve lumbered into the water, clumsy but strong, and soon enough he was swimming, too.

Faye was faster than he was, but what was she planning to do? Swim all day and all night, until she reached help?

Suddenly, she stopped swimming and Amande could see that she'd reached a spot that was deep enough to tread water. As she hung still in the water, waiting for Steve to catch up, she looked up at the shack as if to catch Amande's eye. It was her signal to go. But how could she turn and run when Faye was hardly an arm's-length from a killer?

Michael gave the sugar tit a weak lick, then laid his head against Amande's arm. His dark eyes were so trusting. She knew what she had to do.

Backing away from the window, she kept Faye in sight as long as she could. Then she turned and ran out the door.

There was no sound but the wind as she ran. No shouts or screams made their way over the slight rise of the island, so there was no way for her to know what was happening to Faye. There was nothing for her to do but save Michael.

He was so heavy, draped over her shoulder in a sleep so deep that it was one step short of death. She could hardly breathe when she reached the shore, but she had to go further, pushing through thigh-deep water until she reached the spot where Steve's boat was anchored. Panting, she lowered Michael over the side and climbed in.

Only then did she know for sure that they were saved. Steve's keys lay waiting in the captain's seat. Now Amande knew what utter joy felt like.

No, that wasn't true. Utter joy came for Amande when her eyes lighted on the boat's radio. It would have taken her an hour to go get help and another hour to bring them back. Being able to call for help would cut that time in half. Faye was facing down a killer *now*, so this radio didn't solve their problems, but it certainly didn't hurt. How fortunate it was that Amande knew how to operate both a boat and a radio.

"Mayday, mayday, mayday, mayday! Who's out there? Mayday!"

◇◇◇

Faye assessed her opponent. Steve could handle himself in the water, but he didn't have the streamlined speed of a slender woman who had spent her adult life living on an island and swimming in open water. Out here, where there was nothing solid to use for leverage, his weight and strength were not the advantage they were on land. There was nothing she could do about his superior reach, but counterbalancing that superior reach was her superior intellect. Steve had been so dead-set on catching her and killing her that he hadn't even had sense enough to take off his shoes before he ran into the water.

She kept herself just out of his grasp. As expected, he pulled a big knife and she backed away another few inches to account for its extension of his reach. She held up the fist holding her own pocketknife, and he actually laughed at its inadequacy. Then his knife arced for her throat and she dove for the bottom. She heard the bubbling whoosh of his arm slicing through the water, and she knew that he'd missed her by an inch at most.

Hovering near the bottom, obscured by the sand Steve had kicked up, she had time to consider her best target before she struck. She buried her short blade in his calf muscle and watched both legs thrash with his pain. Then she made two slashes at his thighs and his buttocks, before propelling herself off the bottom, arching away from him as she came up for air. A thin smear of oil coated her skin, and it stank.

She saw a blind light in Steve's eyes. Hatred, murderous intent, madness—whatever it was called, it made a man dangerous, but it did not make him rational. He lunged at her, aiming the knife at her chest this time. He could not conceive of any attack other than a killing blow. She dodged him again, diving to strike at Steve's exposed skin—at his belly where the shirt had ridden up beneath his armpits and at his back and at the ankles above his shoes.

Surfacing once more, the oily, salty water dripped down her forehead and stung her eyes. Further out, a huge oil slick made the water shimmer in every color. And just beyond that, Dane's body was the source of a great plume of blood that was still drawing predators to feed. It was only a matter of time before they smelled Steve and saw the fascinating movements of his legs dangling in the water. Faye's primary goal now was to avoid letting her own blood be spilled. She was perfectly happy for Steve alone to serve as shark bait.

When she saw the fins approach, she dove once more and opened up a few more wounds for the sharks to smell, then she pushed hard off the bottom and swam for shore. She needed to get far from this place. The sharks were coming and Steve's blood was calling them in.

Chapter Thirty-two

When the boats appeared on the horizon, Amande didn't wait to find out whether they were captained by Joe or Benoit or some random boat-owning souls. She gunned the motor and headed around the island, motioning for them would follow.

She was horrified at the thick layer of oil being blown in from the open water. It was coming from the direction where she knew that Dane's body must still be floating. She tried not to look there.

Following the curve of the island, she caught sight of something awful. Idling the motor, she focused her young eyes on the things floating in the water. Was that Dane at the center of the circling fins? Or was it—

Oh, please don't let it be Faye.

Then she saw someone on the shore standing near the shack. That someone was wearing her shirt.

Giving the sharks a wide berth, she maneuvered closer in, close enough to hear Faye yelling at her. "I told you to go get help!"

Amande held the radio receiver high. "I did! I got through to the sheriff's office, and they got me through to Benoit. He and Joe left the marina just after we did. They're right behind me." She raised the motor and hopped out, dragging the boat onto the sand.

Looking out into the water where Steve's body bobbed, Amande asked, "Did you know that my grandmother had a special bond with *La Sirene*? The mambos say she's a voodoo goddess who lives in the water. My grandmother would say that *La Sirene* sent the sharks to you."

"Dauphine told me about *La Sirene* a long time ago. Maybe she did send me the sharks. Or maybe your grandmother did it."

Faye deliberately turned her back on the water and on the sharks and on Steve.

"I thought it would be hours before I saw you," she told Amande, "so I've started poking around in the artifacts Steve had already found and stored in the shack. Come see."

Faye led her into the shack and picked something up off the kitchen counter. She held out an open palm so Amande could see. Resting in it was a corroded iron shackle, half the expected size.

"It was used by slavers, probably while they were transporting children from Africa here to be sold," Faye said. "There's no other explanation. There could be a reasonable explanation for adult-sized shackles to confine prisoners or, in those days, the dangerously mentally ill. But what other reason is there to put shackles on a child?"

Amande took a step back and instinctively turned Michael's dozing face away from the tiny shackle.

"Steve didn't know what the hell he was doing," Faye continued, "but he'd brought some interesting stuff up off the bottom of the bay. A few ballast stones. Broken pieces of pottery that looked like it came from olive oil jars. Lots of glass."

"No treasure?"

"No treasure. I don't think Dane would have ever found his treasure. I'm not sure he would have ever even found his ship, because he was looking in the wrong place."

"You don't know where he was looking. I'm not even sure I know. He told Steve, but he might have been lying."

"I know he was looking underwater, but I'm sure there's no ship there. Sweetie. *This* is the ship." Faye spread out her arms, encompassing everything around them.

Amande was beginning to suspect that Steve had bonked Faye on the head. "This?" she asked, looking around at the dumpy shack.

"The island. I think the ship went down right here, in fairly shallow water, and that it was slowly buried by silt over the years. I think the wood remnants that Joe and I uncovered came from the old ship itself. And I don't think it was a treasure ship."

"That makes some sense," Amande said, thinking fast. "Dane said he found a pile of ballast stones nearby that would have been dumped while the crew was trying not to run aground."

"Exactly. But it didn't work, probably because they waited until the ship was too far gone before they lightened her load."

"Dane said that, too. But why do you say that it wasn't a treasure ship? We both found silver coins. And Dane found a gold one."

"Remember the little shackle. I think the ship beneath this island carried slaves, not treasure chests. A slaver's crew would have had money of their own, and there might have been money aboard that was collected from the sale of the slaves, if that happened before the ship went down. But there would've been hardly any gold and silver aboard a slave ship, compared to what would have been loaded on one of the old treasure ships that were built to carry the spoils of the New World back to the old one. Just think. Your island is one big artifact. Lucky you."

Amande looked at the floor under her feet. "Wow. I'm standing on a slave ship, hundreds of years old. Cool."

Faye put a hand on Amande's forearm. "Hey. Thanks for coming back for me, even if I did tell you to make tracks in the opposite direction."

"Any time. Want to hold a drunken baby?"

Faye held out her arms. "Come to me. Both of you. I thought we might all be dead by now."

"Now you tell me. You were talking real big right before you ran out and attacked a crazy man."

"I was bluffing."

Amande wrapped her arms around Faye for a moment, then she helped Faye get Michael draped comfortably over her shoulder. He never stirred as his mother took him. He just kept snoring.

Faye ruffled his hair. "Please do not tell my husband that I got our baby plastered."

"He stinks like Jack Daniels. I think you're busted."

Amande felt Faye take her hand and squeeze it, then she stood dumbfounded when Joe burst in the door and the toughest woman on earth began to cry.

Chapter Thirty-three

"We have to go home."

It was a simple statement, and everyone present knew that it was true, but it was the reason for calling them all together. When Joe spoke those five words, it was as if he'd called the meeting to order. In response, Didi's temper tantrum began, as expected.

"Well, you can't take my niece with you. She belongs with me."

Faye sat at Amande's favorite picnic table, because there were just too many people at this meeting to squeeze into the houseboat's main room. Joe sat on her right and Amande sat on her left. Didi, Tebo, and Sally the Social Worker sat on the other side of the table. Faye's cousin Bobby and his girlfriend Jodi had pulled up chairs. Benoit sat behind them, not because he had any business there, but because he was interested. Also, Reuss thought that Didi would behave better if the law showed its face, even informally.

Reuss himself sat at the head of the table, presiding over this potential zoo. "My client has an opinion on where she should live during the two years before she reaches her majority."

"Well, like I said, she should live with me," Didi said. "I'm her only blood kin. There's no reason for her to live anyplace else. You can't tell me that the state of Louisiana would take Amande away from a relative and give her to a stranger. It's just not right."

"There are a lot of things in this world that ain't right," Joe said, his cool and passionless hunter's eyes fastened on Didi's face. Faye was very glad he had never pointed that expression at her.

"I'll fight it. She's my niece. You can't take what's mine."

"The department makes its own decisions," Sally said. "You can appeal, but having a lawyer would help and they're very expensive."

Amande's own lawyer said, "Even if you are in fact made Amande's guardian, you'll still have a fight on your hands. She has instructed me to pursue emancipation if she is placed with you. With her obvious capabilities, and with the support of the people around this table, I think she has a good chance of getting it. But why should she? Why should she have to throw herself out into the world, alone, when Mr. Mantooth and Dr. Longchamp-Mantooth are willing to take her and she wants to go with them?"

Tebo raised his hand, as if he were a child in school. "I got a question. I been spending a lot of time over at the marina in Manny's office, looking at the Internet. Ain't the state of Louisiana going to have something to say about these two people taking her off to Florida?"

So that's where Tebo had been spending his time.

Reuss shot Tebo a glance that spoke of respect, but Sally answered his question.

"It will take time. Louisiana will have to be satisfied that Mr. Mantooth and Dr. Longchamp-Mantooth will be good parents and that they have an adequate place for Amande to live. Our sister agency in Florida will have to agree to take over this case. I've seen photos of their home, and I've spent time with the couple personally. I can't see that there will be any problem with placing Amande in their care, but we'll need to jump through some hoops—interviews and home studies and such. In the meantime, she'll have to stay in-state. That's where Mr. Longchamp and Ms. Bienvenu come in."

All heads turned to Bobby and Jodi.

"I'll eventually be the girl's adoptive cousin," Bobby said, "so I'd think the state should be okay with her living with Jodi and me temporarily. Sally's getting it all worked out."

He was too well-bred to mention that his family connections had gone a long way toward getting Amande's placement with him fast-tracked. Faye was hanging onto the hope Bobby's status as a man who knew people who knew people would make the adoption happen quickly, as well.

"We want kids pretty soon," Bobby added, "so it seems like a good idea to practice with one who can already walk and talk and eat without drooling."

"We're in an excellent school district," Jodi added. "And if the state's unhappy that we're living in sin, we could rush up the wedding."

"But it might kill our mothers." Bobby kept talking, despite Jodi's visible kick under the table. "They've been harassing florists and caterers for six months, at least."

Amande's triumphant expression was too much for Didi, who reached across the table, grabbed her by the hair, and raised a hand to slap her. Benoit and Reuss bounded to their feet barking orders, but Amande just looked her coolly in the eyes and said, "You won't do it. You're not woman enough."

Tebo was the one who yanked Didi off her feet and away from the girl. "Oh, she'll do it. I saw her slap her own father in the face."

"Yes, I did. And he deserved it, too. Let me go!"

Tebo gave his struggling half-sister a shake. "Funny thing. When I was looking at the Internet, I spent all kind of time ciphering through inheritance law. That 'usufruct' stuff that cheated our mother out of full-out inheriting our stepfather's stuff...you know it's a real old law, don't ya? That's why it's so weird."

"Oh, it's weird. Like you. Let me go right now!"

"I read online that there's ways children can lose their inheritance, automatic. And one way to do that is hitting their own father or mother? Am I right?"

Reuss nodded.

"'Zat mean that Didi lost her claim on everything just now when she admitted she slapped her own father?"

Reuss shook his head, but he looked like he was sorry about it. "You've done a beautiful job of Internet research, Tebo, and if life were completely just, then yes. Didi would be penniless right now. But the only way for her to be disinherited due to striking her father would have been for your stepfather to cut her off before he died, and he didn't. Didi does still own half of the boat and stock. On my client's behalf, I'd like to recommend to her eventual guardians that she liquidate as much of her stock as it will take to buy out her mother's half-sister. After that, we'll have to determine who Mr. Daigle's heirs are, so we can buy them out, as well. Manny says that he'll manage renting the boat out for Amande. It should yield her a nice income that she can save for college."

Didi sensed money coming her way, so she perked up. Reuss looked her in the face and said, "I have no doubt that your money will be gone in six months. Stan has already filed for divorce, and I don't think your kinfolks at this table ever want to see you again. If I were you, I'd start making a plan for being alone in the world."

"I'll use that money to fight for Amande. I can make some trouble with it."

Tebo put a warning hand on her shoulder. "I'm the man of this family, and I say it's time to settle this. Didi, the law ain't gonna give you squat. I can't make you stop fighting these people, but I can tell you that I think keeping it up would be a waste of money that you ain't got. Get your stuff and go. I'm going to do the same. And I think you'd better go far, because if you put a foot down wrong in this parish, that man is going to make you pay."

He nodded at Benoit, who gave Tebo a wolfish grin that scared Faye a little.

Tebo nodded at Joe and then at Faye, saying, "The little girl's always been worth more than the rest of us put together. You people take good care of her."

"We'll bring her to see you," Faye began, but he interrupted her.

"The reason for sending her off to live with you people is to give her a good influence, and I ain't one. I imagine she'll keep in touch with Manny, and he'll let me know how she's gettin' along." He turned a shy eye on Amande. "Ain't that right, honey?"

◇◇◇

After the meeting to decide Amande's fate dispersed, Jodi and Bobby lingered long enough to show Faye the humongous Longchamp family diamond that Bobby had put on Jodi's left ring finger.

"Do you people have any of those rocks lying around that a distant relative could wear now and then?"

"Maybe. I'll ask my father."

"She'd just get it all dirty, digging in the dirt," Joe pointed out.

This was true, so Faye gave up her piratelike lust for gem-stones and gold.

"I brought you something," Bobby said, holding out a rolled-up piece of parchment.

"A map?" Faye asked, reaching for it and spreading it across the table.

"See for yourself."

It was a detailed genealogy, hand-lettered in beautiful cal-ligraphy and reaching back many generations.

"You made this?"

Bobby inclined his head with a little modesty, but not much.

Faye spotted her name in one corner. Amande's name was lurking far across the page in the other corner. Unless she missed her guess, this piece of paper said that they were fifth cousins, once removed.

"Is this true?" she squeaked.

"Don't be ridiculous. Of course it's not true. When you told me that you were lying to the cops about being Amande's distant relative, I just…made it so. I like it when you're not in jail for perjury."

"Me too," Joe said, slipping an arm around her waist.

Bobby pointed to a name near the top of the page. "You and Amande both have ancestors named Taylor…here…and there are about a billion Taylors in the world, so I did some creative fact finding and…abracadabra! Your Taylors were magically related to her Taylors. If someone examines this document closely enough, and if they're anal-retentive enough to check every last item on it, then that person will find the little seam where I sewed your two families together. But can you imagine anybody looking that hard? Anyway, it doesn't look like you're going to need to prove that you and Amande are blood relatives after all, but I thought you might want this as a souvenir."

"You're at your best when you're not burdened by the truth, Bobby."

"I like to think so."

◇◇◇

Amande knew that Faye had sent her alone to the marina to return the rental boat for a reason. She had wanted her to have a private moment to say good-bye to Manny.

Handing him the keys, Amande took the receipt, folding it neatly and putting it in her pocket so that Faye could file it with her taxes. "Thank you, Manny. For letting me follow you around ever since I was a stupid little girl and for teaching me to use a computer and for keeping the drunks from bothering me and for…oh, for everything."

Oh, crap. She was going to cry.

"You were never stupid, not in your whole life."

Now she thought he was going to cry. That was way worse.

She held her hand next to his, and their golden-brown skin tones weren't so different. "I used to think maybe you were my father. Then I did the math, and I figured you weren't old enough."

"Well, I guess I could've been your father, but I'd have had to start really early and try really hard. It might've been fun."

That made her laugh, which helped with the tears. Then he added, "But I wish I'd been your father. He's not nearly good enough for you."

That did it. The tears were rolling. Probably it was the stupid tears that kept her from realizing what Manny had said for a full five seconds.

"You know my father?"

"Yes, I do, and no. I'm not telling you who he is. He's trouble, Amande."

"Of course he is. He's related to me. Do I know him?"

"No. He went west before you were born. Last time I heard, he was—" He stopped. "No, I'm not even telling you what state he lives in. I taught you how to use the Internet, so I know what you can do. With that much information, you'd be on the man's doorstep by dinnertime tomorrow."

He was right. She absolutely would.

"I have a right to know who my father is."

Manny studied her for a moment, then he said. "You're right. You do. But not until you're older. Then maybe you can deal with the shit he dishes out. Excuse my French." He stuck his hands in his pockets and eyeballed her some more. "When you're eighteen…no, that's too soon. Come back here when you're twenty-one. I'll pour you your first drink, and I'll tell you everything I know about your father."

She stuck out her hand and he shook it. "It's a deal."

Amande's clothes were packed in the new suitcase Joe had found at the Walmart down the road. Michael had decided that nothing in the world was more fun than pushing that suitcase around Amande's tiny bedroom. Faye could feel three new bruises on her shins, so far.

It was time for the last task before they hit the road. Faye and Amande were carefully boxing her artifacts so that they would travel safely. As each box was packed, Joe took it to the car, even though they were so small that he could have waited and carried all of them at once. Nervously padding around the room in his moccasins, then disappearing to the car every time they packed one little box—these were his ways to hurry them along.

If he'd been the kind of man who wore a wristwatch, Joe would have been tapping it. They needed to go. Every day, even every hour, of delay gave the oil slick more time to reach Joyeuse and wreak havoc on their home.

Amande's artifact collection was complete again. Her Spanish coins had returned home, left behind on the table by Dane when Steve had come to kidnap them. He'd left his own treasure coins, as well, which Faye had offered to his parents. They hadn't even wanted to look at them, and she couldn't blame them. They were stored safely with Amande's coins now.

As they finished, Amande stooped to pick up the broken pieces of the guardian doll that her grandmother had made for her. She stroked its raffia hair and said, "I guess she worked. I came through everything in one piece, even if she didn't. Maybe I learned enough about weaving straw from Grandmère to fix her."

The doll was too big to be easy to carry. Amande wrapped one arm around its body and hugged its head to her chest with the other. Looking down through the torn neck opening, she said, "Hey! There's something in there."

Faye helped her retrieve a folded piece of paper that had been placed in the doll's head while it was being made. Written in an uneven cursive hand was this message:

> To the spirits who guard young women and watch over children,
>
> The spirits my mother knows so well,
>
> I charge you this—
>
> Take care of my little Amande.

And it was signed *Justine Marie Landreneau*.

Faye was fumbling for her phone. This was going to delay their departure yet again. Her dear husband was going to be oh-so-happy.

Joe was not over her brush with death yet, although even he'd had no answer when she asked him, "What would you have had me do? Leave the child alone in the hands of a killer because I was afraid to go after her?"

He had no answer, because he knew she was right. This didn't mean that she didn't wake up every night to find that he'd hauled Michael into bed with them. And it didn't mean that she didn't wake up dreaming about being crushed by an anaconda, because Joe had one long musclebound arm wrapped securely around her, with the other wrapped around their little boy. It would take them both a long time to get over the terror of that day. And now, today, he was going to have to get over his impatience with her inability to leave this place and go home, because she had a call to make and an errand to run.

Reuss really needed to see this note, because the handwriting on it did not in any way match the signature on the will that Steve had come to town brandishing. If Steve had forged that will, then Justine had died without one, meaning that all her worldly goods went straight to her only heir. Amande. Even more important to a girl who'd been far more wounded by her mother's absence than she would ever confess…if the will was a fake, then Justine did not try to deprive Amande of her inheritance. She'd abandoned her, yes, and she hadn't even come back to make amends when she learned she was dying, but the coldblooded act of cutting Amande out of her will had simply never happened.

When they'd last spoken, Reuss had told Amande that buying Steve's relatives out of their interest in the houseboat and island would mean cashing in every last share of the oil company stock. If Justine's will was invalid, then Steve had inherited nothing. There was no one left to buy out. Not even Didi, since the paperwork was already in process for her to sell her share of the houseboat to Amande.

With no man to take care of her and no skills and no ability to drain Amande's inheritance, Didi was now living in a precarious situation she had built for herself. When Didi finished drinking her beauty away, her life would be grim indeed.

Amande, on the other hand, wasn't going to be a wealthy woman the day she turned eighteen and gained control of her affairs, but the inheritance passed down from her mother and grandfather would give her a solid start. Until then, she would have safe and loving homes, first with Bobby and Jodi, then at Joyeuse with Faye, Joe, and Michael. And she would have loving parents. Faye could guarantee that.

She stopped dialing Reuss long enough to watch the girl set Michael atop her new suitcase and wheel the giggling boy around her childhood bedroom. Joe came back from packing the car and decided that there wasn't enough turmoil in the little room. Michael needed to fly. So he picked up the other end of the suitcase, and he and Amande swooped out the door with Michael balanced between them like a little genie on a magic carpet.

Something told Faye that her life was about to get even more interesting.

*Episode 4 of "The Podcast I Never Intend
to Broadcast," Part 2*

by Amande Marie Landreneau

Grandmère always hinted that there was some connection between Gola George and Henry the Mutineer and our family. Knowing what I think I know
about Henry, I doubt that he had any descendants,
unless you count all those children he saved and
all their children and all their children, all the way
through the centuries. The stories say that they lived
and died right here in this area.

Henry taught them all to be the best navigators of
their time. He built a settlement near Head of Passes,
where the river forks and heads to sea in three directions. Few things are more valuable at Head of Passes
than navigation skills. Henry hired himself out as a
river pilot and, as the children came of age, they all
took up the trade. Lately, the old sextant has become
my favorite artifact, because it might have passed
through some of their hands.

So were my grandmother's stories true? Does my
family descend from the people in Grandmère's tales?
I just can't see any way to track back through all those
generations of people since then who couldn't read
or write, and who surely never had a birth certificate.

I don't even think Faye's Cousin Bobby could do it, so I'm not going to try. Probably.

If Henry the Navigator never had children, which seems likely, Grandmère's belief that we are his descendants is only wishful thinking. I guess there's a decent chance we're descended from one or more of those children he and Marisol saved. Our family has lived in these parts forever, and those genes had to go somewhere. That would make us descended from Gola George.

Something in my blood tells me this is true. Look at Didi and Ṭebo and Hebert. Wouldn't any of them have crawled on a pirate ship and gone pillaging, if they'd had the chance? Even my grandmother had a pirate streak in her. Anyone who met her could see it.

And maybe my mother did, too, though it's hard to know. Her handwriting looks sweet and girlish, not like a pirate's at all. That note is the only piece of her I'll ever have. I keep it under my pillow, and I always will. I don't think Faye will mind, even when I finally get home to Joyeuse.

Faye calls me every night, not because she has anything much to tell me, but because that's what mothers do. She makes Michael say, "A-mah!" into the phone every night, and it's cute every night. It's going to take me a while to get used to being mothered. And fathered, too. Joe gets on the phone when Michael toddles away, because he wants to tell me what kind of fish he caught for dinner.

The kids at school used to complain when their parents did the same boring things, day in and day out, but I think they're idiots. I'm pretty sure I'll be able to get used to this.

Guide to the Incurably Curious—

*A Personal Note for Teachers, Students,
and People Who Just Like to Read*

I've included a *Guide to the Incurably Curious* in each of my books since I learned that book groups and school classes were reading my work. Since I can't sit with every group and I can't visit every classroom, this is my way to be part of the conversation.

In other books, I've done things like distinguish actual historical fact from things that I just made up. (I'm a novelist, so I get to do that.) I've also pointed readers at books and websites that I used for research, in case Faye's adventures have set them on fire to learn more about Choctaw folktales or the conquistadors or the history of the Confederate States of America. Sometimes, I've suggested questions that a book group leader or classroom teacher might use to take a discussion deeper, then I've provided my own answers so that I could join in the discussion from a distance. I think readers like hearing about how books came to be.

When the *Deepwater Horizon* exploded and sank in 2010, I watched the news closely, because it was a horrifying event in both the real world and in my own imaginary world. If the coastline in the vicinity of my fictional Joyeuse eventually became inundated with oil, then I would need to deal with it in the next book. (Fortunately, this did not occur, so Faye's home is as it always was.)

Because I spent a summer working offshore south of Grand Isle, Louisiana, my real-world memories were triggered by the spill. I remembered driving down Plaquemines Highway from New Orleans to Venice, then climbing aboard a helicopter that flew me over the marshes and the blue waters of the gulf until the great metal skeleton of a natural gas production platform rose up in the distance. At some point, I realized that there was a book to be written about the archaeological remnants that the spreading oil would affect, and that this was my book to write.

Since I'm serious about my research, I felt that I couldn't make *Plunder* the book I wanted it to be if I didn't go take a look with my own eyes at the damage. I went in June 2010, while the oil was still flowing unimpeded into the Gulf of Mexico. Its effects were already being seen on-shore. Tar balls were washing ashore in Pensacola, and a huge area of wetlands near the mouth of the Mississippi had taken the brunt of the damage. I came home with the sense that there was a story to tell, and that it would be told in terms of the people affected by an environmental disaster that covered such a large area as to be almost incomprehensible to a little tiny human being.

Since then, engineers were successful in stanching the flow after many months. Doomsday scenarios bandied about by the press were avoided, and the media has taken its flea-sized attention span elsewhere. We can't *see* the bottom of the Gulf of Mexico, and we can't smell petroleum diluted in its water, therefore it isn't there. Despite the fact that I've worked as an environmental consultant, I wouldn't hazard a guess to the answer to the question of, "Just how much damage was really done?"

The more important thing, I think, is to take a moment to think about the immensity of a problem that erupted after a small-by-comparison piece of equipment failed. And then, I hope, we will take more moments to consider what it would take to prevent such failures in the future.

Here is a first-person account of what it felt like to look that failure in the face.

◇◇◇

A Matter of Perspective:
A Novel-Writing Engineer Takes A Look
at the BP Oil Spill

June 2010

When you work offshore, water is everywhere. The horizon is a great blue circle encompassing everlasting waves. This is not surprising, miles from land. The surprising thing is the water below. Your steel-toed boots rest on metal grating, and you can see through it to the next floor below you. It is also made of grating, revealing another floor below. And another. And another. Beneath it all is the blue water.

It has been nearly thirty years since I worked in the Gulf of Mexico. Still, when I heard about the disastrous end of the *Deepwater Horizon*, I could only think of the people trapped in that inferno, surrounded by endless blue.

In the intervening years, I've worked as an environmental engineer, doing occasional projects in the fragile and overworked Mississippi River delta. These days, I work as a novelist. When the *Deepwater Horizon* went down, leaving us with a volcano of underwater oil, I knew I was meant to write about it. For me, writing about something means that I need to see it first.

I live in north Florida. Driving west, I was never out of earshot of people terrified for their future. Radio stations in Pensacola and Mobile and Gulfport blared classic rock, except when they were reporting on the appearance of tar balls on sugar-white beaches. I drove all day, and not slowly. (My father said he never understood how a foot so skinny could be so heavy.) Yet I couldn't drive out of this thing. It was too big.

I reached New Orleans, crossed the river, and hung a left. Sunset lit the everpresent clouds as I settled into a borrowed house in Myrtle Grove. (Of course, clouds are everpresent. Water is everywhere, even underfoot. Why shouldn't water gather in the air above?)

Driving south the next morning, I stopped at Fort Jackson. The fort has been a military site since 1822, but it's a national monument now, so I didn't expect the constant thwap-thwap-thwap of helicopters taking off in quick succession. Something unidentifiable dangled from each chopper's belly.

When I asked two gentlemen in protective gear what they'd seen, they just said, "The oil's fifteen miles out." The twisting river makes local geography mind-bending, so I couldn't relate the fifteen-mile distance to any familiar place—Venice? Grand Isle?—but I did know that fifteen miles wasn't very far.

As helicopters lifted above the old fort, the men explained that the choppers were dropping sandbags into passes between barrier islands. Again, the enormity of their task staggered me. Sand is heavy. Each helicopter carried just a few sandbags. How many trips would it take to move enough sand to make any difference whatsoever? But we wouldn't be human if we didn't try.

In Venice, the highway ends. A command station there sent out throngs of workers and lots of boats and miles of boom. At Myrtle Grove, I saw yet another command station. More workers. More boats. More miles of boom.

Next day, a friend took me out in a borrowed boat, looking for oil. Again, we saw workers and equipment but, for a long while, we saw no oil. We didn't even smell it.

Eventually, we reached Barataria Bay. Still, the water looked clear. Then my friend said, "Look at the grass." That's when we noticed the stains at the base of the grasses extending along the shoreline, as far as we could see. Perhaps the tide had brought the oil in to foul the wetlands, then receded. Or perhaps the hard labor of all those workers had skimmed any oil from open waters. But you can't skim a swamp and you can't rip out several parishes worth of wetland grasses. Some mistakes just can't be fixed.

During the ride back, I finally got a good noseful of oil. Why was that odor so elusive when I was on Barataria Bay, surrounded by the stuff? The chemical engineer in me says that the most volatile compounds had evaporated as that oil made its way to me. And the oil I did smell? Perhaps that air blew in off the gulf, where fresh oil had bubbled to the surface. And it was, still.

I take research trips to add realism to my books and to find perspective. What perspective waited in the river delta?

I saw herculean efforts to set things right. I saw helicopters, people, boats, and equipment in quantities that would be staggering if they could be gathered in one place. Spread across such vastness, that effort is simply dwarfed. We're only human.

And I, for one, felt small.

To receive a free catalog of Poisoned Pen Press titles, please contact us in one of the following ways:

Phone: 1-800-421-3976
Facsimile: 1-480-949-1707
Email: info@poisonedpenpress.com
Website: www.poisonedpenpress.com

Poisoned Pen Press
6962 E. First Ave. Ste 103
Scottsdale, AZ 85251